W9-BLD-301

the
right
address

the right address

Carrie Karasyov

and Jill Kargman

Broadway Books / New York

BROADWAY

A hardcover edition of this book was published in 2004 by Broadway Books.

THE RIGHT ADDRESS. Copyright © 2004 by Caroline Karasyov and Jill
Kargman. All rights reserved. No part of this book may be reproduced or
transmitted in any form or by any means, electronic or mechanical, including
photocopying, recording, or by any information storage and retrieval system,
without written permission from the publisher. For information, address
Broadway Books, a division of Random House, Inc.

This book is a work of fiction. Names, characters, businesses, organizations,
places, events, and incidents either are the product of the authors' imagination
or are used fictitiously. Any resemblance to actual persons, living or dead,
events, or locales is entirely coincidental.

PRINTED IN THE UNITED STATES OF AMERICA

BROADWAY BOOKS and its logo, a letter B bisected on the diagonal, are
trademarks of Random House, Inc.

Visit our website at www.broadwaybooks.com

First trade paperback edition published 2005

Book design by Donna Sinisgalli

The Library of Congress has cataloged the hardcover as:

Karasyov, Carrie, 1972–
        The right address / Carrie Karasyov and Jill Kargman.
            p.   cm.
        1. Upper East Side (New York, N.Y.)—Fiction.   2. Park Avenue
(New York, N.Y.)—Fiction.   3. Apartment houses—Fiction.   4. Rich
people—Fiction.   5. Socialites—Fiction.   I. Kargman, Jill, 1974–
II. Title.

PS3611.A7775R54 2004
813'.6—dc22
2004041050

ISBN 0-7679-2126-7

10 9 8 7 6 5 4 3 2 1

To Our Families

Carrie & Jill thank . . .
First of all, we'd like to thank our amazing and brilliant editor, Stacy
Creamer, who made the book so much better, and without whom we'd
be Guffeyless. Thanks to Irene Webb for having early faith in the book
and selling it; and to our incredible agent, Debbie Deuble; our trusted
lawyer, Steven Beer; and our fantastic new dream team, Binky Urban
and Jennifer Joel. Also special thanks to Mary Stanford and Beth
Buschman-Kelly and to our early readers who provided countless in-
sightful notes: Lisa Wolfe Ravitch, Liz Carey, Laura Doyle Hammam,
Kathy Doyle, Harry Kargman, and Vasily Karasyov.

Carrie thanks . . .
A special thank-you to the early enthusiasts and cheerleaders whose
palpable excitement helped assuage any writer's block or anxiety: Julia
Van Nice and Kimm Uzielli. Lesbia and the entire Huitz family: I
couldn't have written this without your help, gracias! And thank you
Justin from Newstand #2 in Santa Monica for supplying me with *New
York Post*s so that I could keep up on all that important *Page Six* re-
search material.

And to the family:
Thank you Liz and Laura for worshipping me and so gracefully coming
to terms with the fact that I am the favorite daughter. (J.K.) But seriously, your contributions to this book were invaluable. I couldn't ask for
better sisters. Also thank you to Alex, Zayd, Finn, and Liam for acces-
sorizing the family so well. Dickie Ravitch: You got me down the aisle
and you got me an agent. Now all I need is another trip to Jamaica (and
please get your apartment in shipshape for when I move back and in).
Thanks for all the help, free meals, and the pepper grinder. Also thank
you to all the extended Ravitch family: Lisa, Joe, Michael, and Daniel.
Merci to my sis-in-law Nadia for her Mach 10–level excitement when-

ever I do something, no matter how minute. And to my in-laws, Dmitri and Tatiana. Thank you, Mama (Kathleen M. Doyle): You must have done something right to have such a superstar daughter! But we both know I couldn't ask for a better Little Woman. And to my late father, William Doyle, who I know would be busting with pride right now and convinced that this is what happens to a nice Catholic girl when she goes to Bah-nahd College.

And a special spasebo to my hubby, Vas, and my "most precious gift to the world," James. I'll save all the mushy stuff for a Post-it.

Jill thanks . . .

Unlike some of the characters in this book, I am so effing lucky to have the warmest, smartest, most supportive, nurturing family and friends in the galaxy. First, I want to thank my beloved Kopelclan—my mom, dad, and brother Will—for all their love, enthusiasm, and sage advice. You are the wind beneath my wings. Just kidding. Slash not. The three of you have made my sense of humor what it is and I worship you for always making me cackle for twenty-nine years. You are my most trusted advisors, teachers, and pals and I love you.

A massive merci to my wise, hilarious, and badass chère posse who are the sisters I never had: Vanessa Eastman, Jean Beinart, Dana Wallach, Lisa Pasquariello, and Lauren Duff. Plus special thank-yous and many **XOXO**'s to: Ruth Kopelman, Herzl Franco, Trip Cullman, Tara Lipton, Jacky Day, Teresa Heinz, Frances Stein, and to my in-laws, Marjie, Bob, Bess, and Sophie Kargman. And last but not least, a special all-caps THANK YOU SWEETIEKINS to my teammate and suit of armor: my lion cub and bestest friend, my husband, Harry, and to our precious little cub, Sadie.

chapter 1

"She has zero taste."

"Zilch."

"What's that outfit all about? One-way ticket on the Tacky Express."

"Like Roberto Cavalli threw up on her."

"And her apartment . . ."

"You've been?"

"No. But the Kincaids have."

"And?"

"Constance said it looks as if it was decorated by Charles and Wonder."

"Oh, right, the cheesy firm that just did that new *Architectural Digest* cover from Hades?"

"No. I'm talking Ray Charles and Stevie Wonder. Only a blind person could select those horrendous fabrics."

"Oh, Joan, you're too much!"

As Wendy Marshall and Joan Coddington reapplied their lipstick and skewered their fellow guests at the Bateses' cocktail party at the Union Club, Melanie Korn sat paralyzed, in earshot but out of view. She had been unlocking the door to her stall in the powder room when she heard her name in the same sentence as the words "cheap," "classless," and "fried hair." She froze. At first she thought they must have been speaking of someone else. But as the duo continued, sharpening their swords and tongues, rendering her a decimated Melanie-kebab before her very ears, the blood slowly crept to her face. With stealth moves, she relocked the door to the stall and crept back to the toilet, where she sat down on the lid and pulled her legs up to her chest so no one would know she was there. She felt like the little boy in *Witness*, only *she* was the murder victim.

"I mean, did you see those hideous metal cranes that she gave the Bates as an anniversary gift?" asked Wendy, incredulous. "Ugh! It was like Bangkok exploded in the foyer."

"Tell me about it," said Joan. "The worst."

"Admit it: they look shipped over from some Thai junk shop. You've got to be certifiably insane to buy those."

"Regina said they went right in the trash."

"I'm sure."

"She couldn't even give them to Goodwill. It would be *bad* will to rewrap those."

"Poor Arthur. He totally downgraded wives. I don't think he has a clue that Melanie is so déclassé and *malelevé*. Most men trade up with their second wives."

Trying to avoid Oksana Baiul–style waterfalls of Max Factor, Melanie lifted a quivering finger to her eye. She had thought those cranes were so chic. She'd seen something similar in the Powells' apartment in *House Beautiful*. And hell, they were expensive.

"Diandra Korn, she was another level entirely."

"A class act."

"I heard Arty was devastated when she bailed."

"Destroyed."

"I mean, she was the embodiment of refinement. This one will never have it."

"You wouldn't think it would be possible for one person to get everything so wrong. Her nails? The red is like *secretary red*. So much orange in it."

"Like I said, what do you expect from a pageant queen–turned–stewardess?"

As their laughter mixed with the sound of compacts snapping shut and Judith Lieber bags being reclasped, the two women exited to the dining room in a flurry of silks, gold, and perfume. As Melanie's knees were shaking both from squatting in a full-on Ashtanga yoga position and from sheer humiliation, she rose unsteadily to her feet. She listened again to make extra sure that her pummelers were gone, then walked out to look at herself in the mirror. What was wrong with her outfit? Roberto Cavalli was on Madison! Maybe it was a little tight, but hell, she had the figure for it, didn't she? Her jewelry seemed right—Catherine Zeta-Jones had worn this very necklace to the Oscars. Arthur had told her just minutes ago that her hair looked very pretty. No one could accuse her of having roots. Until her spill of tears, her makeup had been perfect. She didn't understand—what was so wrong with her? Why were people snickering behind her back?

As she rinsed her hands, she felt her sorrow morph into fury. That there had been no welcome mat put out when she married Arthur was enough to deal with. She had assumed it was because this social set preferred the status quo. But what had seemed at first to be a few idle comments about how wonderful Arthur's first wife was had cascaded into a tidal wave of glowing superlatives. Everyone—from the ladies who lunch down to the waiter at Payard and even her own butler, Mr. Guffey—seemed to belong to the Diandra Korn Fan Club. The stiletto shoes Melanie had to fill just kept getting bigger. How could she compete? Even Arthur had once said there was "no comparison" between the two.

Melanie finally pulled herself together enough to leave the bathroom with her head held high, but when she saw Joan and Wendy passing before her, she ducked behind a sweeping Brunchwig & Fils patterned curtain. They fluttered by with gale-force velocity, blind to their cowering, shattered eavesdropper. It seemed so harsh that they could be so happy-go-lucky after savaging her evening.

In the car home, Arthur Korn put a comforting hand on his wife's knee.

"Are you okay, sweetie? You've been pretty quiet. Which is not like you, my little chatterbox."

"I'm fine," she said. Somehow she just couldn't bring herself to confide in Arthur and tell him about the Melanie-in-Cuisinart remarks she had overheard.

"Boy, that party was like a casting call for *Night of the Living Dead*. Boring zombies at every turn. I was dying for an ejector seat. That snob Philip Coddington talking my ear off, with his family crest blazer. Doesn't let anyone else say a word. What was that crest, anyway? It's like Bambi and a tree or something."

"I'm not sure . . ." murmured Melanie.

"It's ridiculous, whatever it was. Looks like the stupid deer is taking a piss in the woods. What's so fancy about that? He's so proud of his moron ancestry."

Melanie was barely listening. She stared out the drizzle-splattered window, lost in her thoughts. She was motionless except for her right thumb furiously moving over her index finger, chipping away the "secretary red" nail polish. And as the Korns' Bentley glided up Park Avenue, piece after piece of fire-engine-colored lacquer fell to the floor.

chapter 2

SHIITAKE HAPPENS.

The phrase was emblazoned on the apron that Madge, the Vances' housekeeper, wore as she made the final preparations for dinner on a breezy Wednesday night in early September. Drew and John, the Vance boys, had given the apron to her last Christmas after being immediately attracted to the lopsided drawing of an almost psychedelic-looking mushroom.

Madge sprinkled sprigs of parsley on the pummeled veal, scooped some Uncle Ben's onto each plate, and added the buttered haricots verts before bringing the tray of food into the dining room.

"So there we are, in this house in Middle-of-Nowhere, Vermont, baked out of our minds," continued Drew, ripping off a piece of his dinner roll. He nodded thanks to Madge as she placed his meal before him.

His father, Morgan, frowned. "You know that marijuana is not only illegal but also very bad for you—kills the brain cells," he said sternly.

"Yeah, yeah, yeah. But, hey, it's nothing our last president didn't do. Anyway, don't be judgmental. It's a really great story," said Drew.

"So then what?" asked John, his younger brother.

"So we're, like, so out of it. The heater is blasting and no one can figure out how to turn it down, so Cynthia and Whitney just take off their shirts. They're just sitting there in their bras—"

"Who are these young ladies?" interrupted their mother, Cordelia.

"You know them—Cynthia Whitaker and Whitney Coddington," said Drew.

"I can't believe they'd be so promiscuous," said Cordelia disdainfully. Madge put a plate in front of Cordelia, who stared at it with surprise, as if astonished that she would be expected to actually consume something.

"Oh, you'd be amazed, Mom. Anyway, can I finish?" asked Drew.

"Yes, get to the end, for chrissakes," said John, shoving rice and string beans into his mouth. "We don't have all night."

"So, finally there's a knock on the door, and we're like, 'Who the hell is that?' and it's a *cop*! A female one. And she comes in and looks around, she sees all the bongs and empty beer cans and shit like that—"

"Drew!"

"Such language!"

"Sorry. And she's like, 'Mr. Lewis asked me to check in on you. He was worried about you guys being out here alone. What I see here is a disaster. It's all illegal, you guys are in big trouble, blah blah blah.' "

"Why didn't you tell us about this? You'll need an attorney!" said Morgan with concern. "I should call Sy Hammerman right now—"

"Wait—hold your horses before you spaz! So then some of the girls start crying. They're totally freaking out, we're so screwed. And Carl is, like, shitting, cause he's on probation for that open can of beer in Martha's Vineyard, and suddenly the cop flips on the stereo and starts taking off her clothes!"

"Heavens!" said Cordelia, raising a hand to her chest.

"She was a goddamn stripper!" Drew said, laughing.

"Awesome! Who hired her?" asked John.

"Well, that's the best part—Carl hired her. He wanted to scare the girls into thinking we'd be busted, but he was too stoned to even remember, so he was freaking out more than anyone at first!"

John and Drew burst out laughing. Morgan studied his boys with contempt mixed with envy. In his day, he would never have used profanity in front of his parents. There was such a lack of respect among the younger generation today. On the other hand, Morgan saw very little of his parents when he was growing up, having been shipped off to boarding school in England at the tender age of six, so he was proud and grateful to have an open relationship with his sons. He didn't want to be the severe disciplinarian that his father had been; he remembered that terrified feeling at the dinner table, when it was politics instead of antics. Morgan couldn't even remember his father very well, just that he read the newspaper a lot and was always away on business, amassing the multimillions that now earned enough interest for them to live, fairly comfortably. He was unable to recollect even one happy family dinner. Not one. He and his sisters were usually relegated to the children's dining room while their parents ate in a very far away parlor in their wing of the house. He had much warmer memories of his nanny, Ruth. She had been the one he missed the most when he was away at school. In retrospect, his parents' complete diffidence toward him seemed like a form of stealth cruelty.

"Mr. Vance? There's an urgent phone call for you," said Madge, standing at the threshold.

Morgan rose quickly. "Thank you—I'll take it in my study. If you'll excuse me, Cord."

Cordelia looked up from her untouched plate. "Of course, dear."

Morgan walked over to her and pecked her on the cheek. "Thank you for dinner. It was wonderful." He left the room.

"Mom, we're outie too," said John.

"Where are you off to?"

"We're going to head downtown to check out Chester's band at Luna Lounge."

"Is that Clark Winthrop's boy?"

"Yes, Mom, and he's twenty-three now. No longer a boy," said John.

"You children are growing up so quickly. Gosh, it seems like just yesterday when I caught you boys running through the apartment throwing water balloons out the window," said Cordelia with a sigh.

"Yeah, Mom, that *was* yesterday," said Drew.

"You scared the daylights out of poor Mrs. Cockpurse," admonished Cordelia.

"That was hilarious!"

"It cost your father a tidy sum to dry-clean her mink jacket. She had to send it to Maximillian's," she recalled.

"That's 'cause John put Gatorade in his water balloon."

"She shouldn't have been wearing a friggin' fur in September."

"When will you boys grow up?" asked Cordelia, secretly hoping that the answer was never.

"I don't know, Mom," said John, rising. "But thanks for dinner."

"When do you head back to Trinity, John?"

"Tuesday."

"Well, we'll have to have another family dinner before you go," said Cordelia.

"Sure. Come on, retard."

Drew got up and pecked his mother's cheek. " 'Bye, Mom, thanks."

The boys left the room and Cordelia stared at their vacant seats. The grand mahogany dining table could comfortably fit twelve, so it looked very empty with just one seated at the head. Cordelia glanced distractedly around the room. The walls had been painted the color of red licorice and featured old Dutch master paintings that had been in Morgan's family for generations. The sideboard was English, George II, as was most of the Vance furniture, which had been both inherited from Cordelia's family and bought at auction, with the occasional purchases from dealers in shows in Maastricht and New York. Silk taffeta curtains reminiscent of turn-of-the-century ball gowns adorned the windows, and an Oriental carpet lined the floor. Mario Buatta had decorated the apartment in the late eighties, and Jerome de Stingol, Cord's best friend in the world, had given it a little "refreshing" just before the millennium. It was a beautiful home, full of exquisite and valuable treasures, treasures that Cordelia and her family had long since ceased to notice.

In fact, Cordelia felt that she could not appreciate anything anymore and that there was nothing to look forward to. It was a strange time. The boys were growing up, Morgan's work was becoming more distracting, charity balls were less interesting: it seemed that life was winding down. She thought about how empty she felt as she distractedly played with her fork. She pushed all of her food to one side of the plate—she had eaten practically nothing at all—and looked down at the delicate rose pattern on the Tiffany china. It was her wedding china. She ran her finger along the gold rim. It had seemed so fancy and elegant when she had registered for it with her mother. Now it had become mere everyday dinner china, nothing special. Funny how things change. Suddenly—she didn't know why—she recalled the words from a song that one of the boys had played over and over again when he was in prep school: "I have become comfortably numb." That said it all.

————

Meanwhile, across the sixteen-room apartment, Morgan was anything but numb as he clutched the phone in his study. His blood pressure was boiling, and sweat was sliding down his forehead past his graying temples, settling in a pool in his glasses.

"Maria, Maria, just calm down," he whispered into the phone. He glanced nervously through the crack of the door to make sure no one was eavesdropping.

"You want me to fucking calm down?" yelled Maria in her thick Mexican accent. She was calling from the Central Park South apartment that Morgan had recently sublet for her. "Don't you tell me to calm down, mister. My water just broke and I'm here alone! YOU calm your own ass down."

"Maria, what do you expect me to do?"

"I just called the car. It is coming in fifteen minutes to take me to New York Hospital. You get your fucking ass down there as soon as possible or I cut off your balls!"

"I can't, Maria. It's not a good time."

"This baby is coming out of my vagina right now and she doesn't care if it's a *good time*. You get your fucking ass down there NOW!" screamed Maria, slamming down the phone.

Morgan was now turning pale, and his hand was aching from gripping the phone so tightly. *Okay, deep breaths,* he reminded himself. He walked down the long hall back into the dining room. Cordelia was staring at her china, a dazed look on her face.

"Everything okay, darling?" asked Morgan. He walked over to his seat and took a large swig from his tumbler of whiskey.

"Sure. Who was that?"

"It was work. Something's come up—our deal with Japan, you know, they're on a different time zone, they don't get it—so I, uh, have to go to the office for a bit," said Morgan, not looking his wife in the eye. He took another gulp of his drink.

"Okay."

"Don't wait up—it might be a late night. You know those Japanese. They work really hard," added Morgan. "Plus, it's tomorrow there, morning—"

"Okay."

Morgan stared at his wife of twenty-eight years and felt an enormous rush of guilt.

"What are your plans for tomorrow?" he asked.

"I'm leaving early to go shopping with Jerome."

"Fantastic!" said Morgan, with an overabundance of enthusiasm. "Buy yourself something special."

"Okay."

Morgan walked over to give his wife a kiss good-bye. "Oh, and it's Wednesday! Your favorite show is on!"

"*Law and Order,*" said Cordelia, nodding.

"So you won't miss me!" said Morgan, putting his hand on his wife's shoulder before walking out of the room. On his way to the elevator, he glanced back at her from the hallway. She was still sitting at the table, languidly staring into space. She looked almost sedated.

The scene was much different at the hospital, where Morgan would have given his eyeteeth to have had Maria tranquilized, as piercing shrieks could be heard from the elevator banks. Every movie, every prime-time season finale, every Learning Channel birthing video, was Little League next to Maria's over-the-top drama. Move over, Demi Moore and Jennifer Aniston: their birth scenes had nothing on this spawn expulsion. Maria Garcia was the new queen of scream.

"AAAAAAAAAAGH! This fucking thing is going to rip me in fucking half!" screamed Maria.

"Calm down," scolded Morgan.

"AAAAAAH! Don't tell me to calm down, you fucking asshole!" shouted Maria. She was clenching his hand so hard he thought it would fall off. *Six hours of this torture, and still no baby,* Morgan thought with misery. And why did he have to actually be in the room with her? Cordelia had allowed—insisted, even—that he sit in the waiting room and not see her or the babies until they had been demucused, bathed, and wrapped with a blue blankie. *It was correct that way,* thought Morgan. *I'm not a hippie—I'm a businessman. I don't need to see blood and shit being squeezed out of a woman who isn't even my wife.*

"FUCKING SON OF A BITCH!"

"Let's discuss names, that should distract you. How about Juanita?"

"Aaaaaaaaagh!"

"Lupe?"

"Aaaaaaaaaagh!"

"It's a lovely name. My aunt had a nurse named Lupe."

"Fuck, no!"

"Concepción?"

"AAAAH! Don't you give me those fucking names!"

"I thought you'd want names to reflect your heritage. Ones that go well with Garcia," said Morgan, trying to remain calm.

"You mean that goes with *Vance*. Fuck if she doesn't kill me first!"

What? Morgan was freaking out. And now the doctor's hands disappeared deeper into Maria's genital area. Morgan thought he was going to pass out right there.

"You're doing great, Maria. Just one more push," said the doctor.

"One more fucking push?"

The baby is going to be called Vance? Over my dead body, thought Morgan. He'd have to talk her into a Spanish name, one that would sound ridiculous with Vance. "How about Josefina?" he offered.

"I want a fancy name—Tiffany or Tristan or Schuyler!"

Suddenly there was a wail. "It's a beautiful baby girl!" boomed the doctor, holding up the blood-drenched child.

Maria collapsed back in her bed. "Schuyler. Schuyler Vance," she announced.

Morgan fainted.

chapter 3

Several floors below the Vances' apartment, another phone rang during another dinner. Mr. Guffey, the Korns' butler, raised his eyebrows at the kitchen staff. The cook, the maid, and the housekeeper all knew what he was thinking. *What ghastly human would call at this hour? Doesn't everyone know that civilized people eat at eight?* But what they knew best of all was that Mr. Guffey was furious to be interrupted during his *own* dinner, so before he threw down his napkin and huffed to the phone, Juanita the maid leapt to answer it. Minutes later, Juanita entered the dining room.

"What is it, Juanita?" asked Arthur.

"I'm sorry, Meeses Korn: they say it urgent," said Juanita sheepishly. She was not in the mood to endure her boss's reproaches, but the man on the phone had been insistent.

Melanie sighed deeply and scraped back her chair. "All right," she said. She knew that if Mr. Guffey had allowed Juanita to interrupt her, it must be serious. Mr. Guffey was very strict about those sorts of things, and no one would dare risk his ire. Even Melanie, despite the fact that she was his employer.

Melanie walked down the foyer to the closest phone, which was perched on a drop-leaf table in the den.

"Hello?"

"Melanie Sartomsky?"

"Yes . . ." sputtered Melanie, surprised. She'd dropped her maiden names years ago, even before she was married. "It's Melanie Korn, now."

"Are you Cal Sartomsky's daughter?"

Was this a prank? Was someone having a goof on her? "Maybe . . ." she said tentatively.

"Yes or no?" the gruff voice on the other end of the phone demanded.

"Yes," she said reluctantly. It wasn't her fault she was his daughter. He'd banged her mother thirty-five years ago, then would come back periodically for money to blow at the bar or casino. When a four-year-old Melanie had her arms outstretched for a hug, yelling, "Daddy!" he walked right by her to check what was in the fridge.

"Well, then, Melanie Sartomsky, I regret to inform you that your father, Cal Sartomsky, passed away last evening in his cell at Faudon State Prison. We send you and your family our deepest condolences at this difficult time. We do offer plots on the grounds free of charge, or you may send someone to pick up the body and make your own arrangements."

Melanie was in shock. Her father . . . dead. It had to happen, she hadn't spoken to him in years, and yet she felt a tsunami of sadness wash over her. She gulped down the rising lump in her throat to try to answer.

"M-m-my husband is in the life transition business," she stuttered. "We'll take care of it. We have our own caskets . . ." was all Melanie could think to utter before putting down the receiver and returning to the dining room.

"What is it?" asked Arthur, alarmed at his wife's face.

Melanie resumed her seat, put her napkin on her lap, and took a sip of water.

"My father died," she said finally.

"Oh, honey," Arthur said, reaching over and patting her head softly. "I'm so sorry. I'll take care of everything."

She looked at him with her wide blue eyes. She had a beautiful face, and though Botox had been able to conceal most of her expressions, her eyes reflected her grief. Not over his death, but over his life—which had never included her.

"We'll get him the nicest coffin, baby, top of the line: the DX5000, with the beautiful mahogany wood and the imported Chinese silk lining. We'll get the one with the CD player inside . . ." Arthur trailed off as Melanie remained motionless.

"Sounds good," she said vaguely.

Arthur watched his gorgeous blond wife as she folded and refolded her napkin on her lap. She was always so strong and assertive, and for the first time in a long while, she seemed confused. He waited before he spoke again, wanting to feel her out. Minutes passed, and he dared not eat.

"I'm okay, sweetie. Seriously, I'm fine," she said, wiping one errant tear.

Arthur leaned over and kissed her. Boy, was his wife a winner: so strong, so self-assured. This was a woman who was going places. He'd known that the second he met her.

"Are you sure? You're probably in shock."

"No, no," insisted Melanie, wiping a hair off her forehead. "I am no longer Melanie Sartomsky. I can't cry over the past; it's behind me. I am Mrs. Arthur Korn of Park Avenue. Next case," she said, cutting into her steak. And when Melanie said "next case," it always meant that the topic was done and never to be discussed again.

One thing you could say about Melanie was that she was resilient. And she had to be: her climb to Park Avenue had not been easy. She was born in a triple-wide motor home on the outskirts of Cashmere, Washington (the heart of apple country), but spent most of her teenage years near Tallahassee, Florida, after her mother's death in a drunk-driving accident when she was fourteen. It was the classic white trash–ascent story that makes America what it is. Mom dead, dad boozed up and drifting in and out of work, little snot-nosed siblings to look after. And like Shania Twain, nothing was going to hold her back. Even with her mullet and feathered bangs, acid-washed jeans, and varsity cheerleading jacket, it was obvious from the start that this gangly teen who developed early was destined for greener pastures. Her mom used to say, "Don't marry for money. But it don't hurt to hang around where it's at." Melanie had always been headstrong and determined, and her ambition to get out of her town fueled her sojourn into the world, and she never looked back. Maybe money didn't buy happiness. But it helped.

After stints as a hotel concierge at the MGM Grand in Las Vegas, a hostess in Palm Springs, and a personal assistant to the wife of the producer of *Hollywood Squares,* Melanie made what proved to be the most prudent decision of her life. She became a flight attendant. She excelled at her job and was lucky enough to work her way into serving United Airlines' first-class passengers. And after a bumpy flight from Miami one cold winter Sunday two years ago, the friendly skies got even friendlier when she met multimillionaire Arthur Korn, who was on his way to visit his eighty-two-year-old mother, whom he had recently installed in a beachfront condo with full-time help.

"Pretzels or peanuts?" Melanie asked in a seductive whisper. Arthur lowered his *Wall Street Journal* and came face first to Melanie's ample chest, which was bursting out of her blue uniform.

"Both," said Arthur, entranced by her breasts, without even thinking. Then he flushed, turned a deep crimson, and quickly tried to recover. Melanie smiled. There was something about this middle-aged man with a protruding paunch that seemed, well . . . *nice*. He also seemed a bit wounded in the same way she was, and the more they spent time together, the more they both seemed to heal. Arthur extended his trip first by days, then by months, and when Melanie was on layovers they danced the night away in Miami's nightclubs and dined at quirky restaurants off the beaten path. It was a whirlwind courtship.

And ultimately, although Arthur may have saved Melanie from removing foil from chipped beef, she saved him right back. When they met, he was extremely vulnerable as a result of his recent divorce. He had been married to Diandra Chrysler, the New York socialite, whom he'd met when both were vacationing at Canyon Ranch (she was there celebrating her second divorce—he should have seen the warning flags then). And although Arthur was born and raised in New York City, he had spent most of his life living in the outer boroughs—Queens and Brooklyn to be exact—so he was not really considered a native son by the current company he kept. It had been only through Diandra that he was able to gain entrée into this discriminating and prestigious world. She was a complete insider and had set them up in the glamorous life, full of Page Six parties and yachting jaunts with ambiguously gay fashion designers. When it was all over, after four short years, he was stripped of fifty million dollars, all of their antique furniture, and worst of all, his self-esteem.

Arthur had been very depressed, planning on hiding out at his mother's until the New York press was done with its field day with his personal life. He was so morose that everything seemed opaque, as if under water. That is, until Melanie came along. When she flew into his life it didn't matter that she was distributing honey-roasted peanuts at a cruising altitude of thirty thousand feet; it was if he had been reborn. She was funny, exciting, tenacious, and refreshing—someone who spoke frankly and honestly. And it all truly happened like a fairy tale. Just two months after their airborne meeting, Arthur and Melanie wed in Florida.

When Arthur carried Melanie over the threshold of his Park Avenue pad, she was slack-jawed. She knew Arthur had money, but she was completely in the dark about the depth and breadth of it. Their entire courtship had been a magical bubble in the sultry Florida heat, and arriving on the Upper East Side made Melanie feel as if a storm cloud had burst over her head. When she realized what she had married into, regardless of her enormous love for her Arty, she felt . . . nauseous. Her youth and beauty immediately inspired the wrath of the ladies who lunch, and Melanie knew she was in over her head. She wanted to grab Arthur and run for the hills, but he seemed happy in this world.

So Melanie settled in as the dutiful wife and tried to make her husband proud. It was a feat as daunting as Oprah's weight battle. Every time she seemed to make progress, she was thrust back into her outsider place. Arthur was always supportive, but there was one nagging fact of his life that haunted her: Diandra. Never had she heard a name uttered with more reverence than the first Mrs. Korn's. Everyone was always ready to hand out accolades to this mystery lady, who was incredibly present for someone who didn't even live in New York. She had become a thorn in Melanie's side. Worst of all, Arthur refused to discuss her, so great was his grief over their rumored catastrophic breakup.

chapter 4

"To die for."

"Tell that to the Himalayan mountain elks!"

In a kaleidoscope of vibrant colors—raspberries, fevered pinks, lemons, turquoise, mustards, scarlets, and lilacs—throngs of couture-clad ladies were nibbling tea sandwiches and throwing their heads back in orgasmic fits of shopper's delight.

It was the first semiclandestine shahtoosh party of the season, held in a glittering, cathedral-ceilinged suite at the Pierre Hotel. The upper ranks of Manhattan's wealthy Roman numeral set had gathered at this Tupperware party–like fete to buy highly coveted—and, incidentally, illegal—shawls. Shahtooshes are spun from a much softer form of cashmere, taken from the neck of what turned out to be an endangered species, not that anyone gave a shit. In the gilded suite, the plight of the Asian deer that had sacrificed themselves for fashion happily seemed light-years away to the platinum card–toting matrons whose abodes were candied penthouses west of Lexington. The $3,000 price tags were of no more concern to the women shopping that day than the dwindling number of deer. If anything, the contraband wraps had more appeal because of the difficulty procuring them, and the result was a champagne-kissed buzz of naughty flirting with the law.

Wendy Marshall's joined-at-the-hip cohort, Joan Coddington, had yet to arrive, and Wendy was increasingly concerned. Not because their standing lunch reservation at La Goulue on Madison was in twenty minutes—James the maître d' simply did not like to be kept waiting no matter *who* you were—but because the best hues were being snapped up by the multitudes of manicured hands.

Cordelia Vance, with whom Wendy had been making small talk, continued to peruse the rainbow-tinted, buttery offerings.

"These shahtooshes put pashminas to shame!" Wendy exclaimed, trying to make more conversation with the grande dame of Park Avenue and epitome of impeccable taste. Wendy carefully examined Cordelia's perfectly assembled outfit: the Oscar de la Renta suit, the Birkin bag slung casually over her arm, and the jewels, always magnificent. She was flawless. Cordelia was married to Morgan Vance, of the Hobe Sound and Locust Valley Vances. How could Wendy not be drawn to such a bona fide fixture of the crème de la crème? But Cordelia had an elusive quality about her, and while her body was dripping in the world's most glamorous labels and expensive jewelry, her head was often in the clouds.

Wendy, on the other hand, was always rooted firmly in the social moment, observing every last accessory on every woman in the room, rifling through her mental Rolodex to recall where each one lived, what her husband did, which clubs her grandmother belonged to. Although her own wardrobe was impeccable, she was still using last year's handbag, and the price of all of her jewelry combined wouldn't be as much as the simple emerald and diamond ring Cordelia wore on her right pinky.

"I am a little bit concerned about these being illegal," Cordelia said to Wendy. "Imagine going to jail for a wrap!"

Wendy laughed lightly. "It's ridiculous that the U.S. marshals have pronounced these contraband!" she said, marveling at the sheer insanity of it all. "I mean, don't they have bigger fish to fry, like, say, crack dealers? Plus, if federal agents could afford this level of softness, you know they'd be greasing palms at customs too!"

Cordelia looked torn between the different colors she had selected. She felt them all once more to try to decide, as if trying to decide if the seafoam green might be even softer than the apricot.

"I'm going to take the celadon and the cream," she pronounced. "Oh, and maybe the rose as well . . ."

Wendy, who wasn't even sure she wanted, let alone needed, one, saw Cordelia snatching up four and knew she had to acquire one as well. She settled on pale azure. "Aren't they fabulous? I mean, it's never been this easy for me to part with three grand!" Wendy said. Cordelia smiled. "Not to be gauche," Wendy added nervously.

Looking out the wall of windows facing the treetops of Central Park, Cordelia drifted over to the cashier's table with her loot.

Joan Coddington burst in and made a beeline for Wendy before embracing her dramatically and kissing both cheeks. "What a *nightmare!*" she exclaimed. Joan hugged Wendy with genuine relief as if she were a buoy and she herself was lost, bobbing and breathless, in the Indian Ocean. Meanwhile, they had seen each other as recently as yesterday. "Oh! I had a hell of a time getting here! Fifth was a *disaster*—the entire avenue is jammed because the doormen are all barricading the tree gardens for the Puerto Rican Day parade!" boomed Joan.

She fanned her face rapidly with her hand and exhaled, trying to compose herself. Everything about Joan commanded attention: her platinum beehive-ish hairdo that a forties film star might have worn, her bright red lipstick, her gravelly smoker's voice, and her Jackie O sunglasses. Right behind Joan was Melanie Korn, who had entered with her. Neither Joan nor Wendy acknowledged the dreadful parvenu.

"I know—it is utter chaos, but we shouldn't complain. I'd rather have a little bumper to bumper than beer cans and chicken bones in my mums. I mean, why pay sky-high co-op maintenance for landscape designers when these hooligans are going to muck it all up?"

"Wendy, you are too much!" Joan said, laughing.

Melanie got a flash of self-consciousness and took a deep breath.

She couldn't forget what she had overheard the other evening. To Joan and Wendy she was just a human piñata. But she refused to be cowed. Somehow, she'd win them over. She'd get them to accept her; she felt she owed it to Arthur. Maybe she wasn't born as high class as Arty's first wife, but she was determined to be viewed as an asset—not the embarrassment that this pair had decried.

"It's actually the Dominican Day parade," Melanie piped in. The two women turned to look at her. "The Puerto Rican Day parade is in June."

"Why, Melanie, I didn't know that you were Puerto Rican," said Wendy.

"Actually, I'm not!" said Melanie, turning bright red. She gulped and added, "But I have a housekeeper . . ."

"Well, whatever the ethnicity of those people, it's still an odious tradition. Why can't they have a parade in their neck of the woods?" asked Joan. "March on the Bronx or something. I mean, why stomp down Fifth?"

Melanie thought they probably deemed her just as much of an alien on their avenue. "Arty doesn't like to be in the city during parades," Melanie said, trying to side with them. "We're generally away on weekends anyway."

Wendy and Joan, without speaking, exchanged half-hidden glances that seemed to say in facial code, *We detest this bitch*. They clearly could not abide her presence. Meanwhile, Melanie reddened even more, realizing too late that she might have seemed like a show-off dropping the weekend house.

"Oh, yes," Joan replied sarcastically, "I pity the poor souls who are still languishing in Manhattan on the weekends."

Joan flashed Wendy an eye roll, and Melanie sensed she was not wanted. Why? What did she do wrong? And why was she obsessing about it so much? On the one hand, these two gossips each had twelve years and twenty pounds on her and dressed like shoulder-padded librarians, so why was she so nervous about their opinions? Because they were quick-witted vipers and she bristled at the thought of anyone hating her. She finally shrugged and walked off in her ass-enhancing size-two skirt and Jimmy Choo heels and decided to browse the goods. Wendy and Joan watched her thin calves as she crossed the room, and sighed.

"Tell me you didn't come here with Melanie Korn," said Wendy.

"I wasn't *with* her. She was in the elevator."

"She's garbaggio," said Wendy, shaking her head. "Well, on to far more important things. You must, must, *must* pop over here and claim a few of these shawls before they're all devoured. I was nervous you'd miss the best of the lot!"

Joan reached out to feel the shawls. "Oh my god," she squealed. "These shahtooshes make my pashminas feel like sandpaper. Thank the lord for crooked customs officials."

Cordelia, who was leaving with her new purchases wrapped in red tissue, stopped by Joan and Wendy on her way out.

"Should I be feeling guilty?" she asked them.

"Of course not," said Joan. "They're already dead."

"I meant about spending so much."

"Don't be crazy," said Wendy. "How else is one to keep warm this winter?"

"Morgan would absolutely insist," declared Joan firmly.

"You're right," said Cordelia, as if that sealed the deal. "And they are sheer divinity."

"I can't wait to curl up in mine tonight," said Wendy.

Cordelia waved and climbed into the burl-inlaid elevator and descended to her awaiting chauffeured car. She hadn't really been concerned about spending so much but did feel that it was somehow appropriate to feel a sense of *something* after dropping twelve thousand dollars on shawls. Just acknowledging it once made her feel comfortable enough not to think about the price and to stuff the bag of illicit goods in the back of her closet, where hundreds of unopened shopping bags lay forgotten.

"It's time for our favorite chopped salads with truffle vinaigrette," Wendy reminded Joan.

"I know," she said, confirming the hour on her Cartier watch. "Who are we going to steal a ride with?"

"Oh, it's only four blocks, Joan."

"In Manolo Blahniks, you have to multiply by three, so it's really twelve blocks."

Melanie, who was herself laden with shahtooshes in every color of the spectrum, couldn't help but overhear. Maybe they would like her if she gave them a lift? "Girls, do you want a ride? I have my Bentley downstairs . . ."

"That's okay," said Wendy.

"We'll take a taxi," said Joan.

"Okay," Melanie said. These two were going to be tough to win over. Wendy and Joan gave Melanie a head start.

"I'm not spending any more time with that terminally gauche woman than I have to," whispered Wendy.

Once they were sure Melanie had left the building, they took the elevator to the grand marble lobby and climbed into a taxi. After the epaulet-wearing white-gloved doorman closed the cab door, Joan and Wendy rolled down their windows as if their lives depended on it.

"This taxi-driver stench is just *unacceptable*," said Joan between lung-filling gasps for oxygen.

"Ugh—Chanel Number *Two*."

"Do these people have curry-flavor deodorant?"

"Joan, darling, I don't think they have any deodorant."

"Clearly."

Sitting in Madison Avenue traffic moving at a snail's pace, the two ladies reflected on their run-in with the tacky upstart.

"Who does that Melanie Korn think she is?" asked Wendy.

"It's the second-wife syndrome. She thinks she's entitled to just march in and name-drop the Bentley."

"What a climber," said Wendy.

"It makes me shudder," Joan replied.

"Get this," said Wendy, setting the stage for a story. "Last week I was stranded on the corner of Fifty-seventh and Park, trying desperately to hail a cab. Guess who pulls up?"

"Don't tell me—"

"Melanie Korn in her giant Bentley—not the gold one, the steel one. Anyway, I know it sounds irrational, but I needed a ride . . ."

"You didn't."

"The clouds were starting to look threatening and I had just had a blowout at Fekkai," Wendy said defensively.

"Oh, okay, then."

"So, I guiltily climb into her chariot. And she says, 'Oh, I'm just doing a little shopping, it's *sooo* great how AmEx Black has no limit. I just love it!' "

"No, she didn't—"

"Wait. *Then* she leans over to her driver and goes, 'Gunther, can you take this lady to 1002 Park Avenue, please?' "

"She knew your *address*?"

"Yes! Total stalkerazzi—I was shocked. She's so obsessed with who's who she must've memorized the Verizon phone book."

"Sad."

"It gets worse."

"How could it? That little climbing Panhandle slut."

"Then, as we're driving up Park, she asks, 'When you were married to Chip, you lived at 627, right?' Can you believe that? That ferret totally investigated my life!"

"How dare she?" Joan put her hand on her chest as if the news was giving her coronary palpitations. "And to bring up Chip—how odd!"

"Then, as we're pulling up to my awning, she has the audacity to say, 'Chip is remarried, right?' As *if* she knows my family!"

"I can't take this. I am *ill*."

"I want her dead," said Wendy, filling with venom. "I just coldly thanked her for the ride and slammed the door."

At their destination, Joan paid the cab fare and the two entered the posh bistro. Joan was still reeling from the tale of the recent incident, horrified by the trauma her dear friend had gone through at the hands of a reinvented trailer trollop.

To Joan and Wendy, Melanie was an interloper, a charlatan, a meretricious social climber with chronic verbal diarrhea. She had come on too strong too quickly. She wanted to be a social doyenne right away, and she threw her money around with such speed so that she wouldn't have to wait for committee offers and trusteeships. And she touched a nerve with Joan and Wendy particularly, because their position in society had become tenuous. Wendy's divorce had devastated her. She was completely unprepared when her husband walked out on her for another, younger, woman. The nanny, no less. And Melanie had everything Joan didn't: a svelte figure (she would die for those hips!) and an indulgent husband who footed the bill. Joan had been bankrolling Phillip since the day they met, and although he had a porcelain pedigree, she wished he would sometimes get off his ass.

"She enrages me!" said Joan, in the taxi home after La Goulue. Joan and Wendy had discussed many other topics at lunch—Fernanda Wingate's face-lift; the renowned plastic surgeon Dr. Simon Brooks and his affair with the Palmolive heiress; the Mastersons' divorce—but had always returned to Melanie, their shared bête noire.

"I know, I know," agreed Wendy.

Joan paused in disgust and looked out the window. They were stopped at a red light outside 741 Park Avenue, the most coveted building in all of New York City, where, not coincidentally, Melanie and Arthur Korn now resided.

"It's vile. She was a lowly mall rat who was offering chicken or beef on a 747 and now she's living the high life in 741 with the crème de la crème. The ascent of white trash," said Joan. Whenever she was irate, her vitriolic tongue reached new heights.

Wendy stared at the prewar, fifteen-story limestone building with the Irish green awning.

"It's the chicest building in New York," said Joan. "Arthur Korn never would have gotten past the board if it weren't for his first wife; it's only because Diandra was wired that he got accepted. He and Melanie would be laughed out if they applied now."

"Laughed out. It really is the best. Everyone lives there."

"Morgan and Cordelia Vance."

"Olivia Weston, the Fanny's Pharmacy heiress," added Wendy.

"Emma Cockpurse, that senile billionairess who wanders down to the lobby naked."

"Mademoiselle Oeuf, the canine who inherited the ten-million-dollar apartment from Mrs. Lloyd," added Wendy hastily.

"To think that old bag left her apartment to a dog!" cried Joan.

"It *is* a thoroughbred poodle from those exorbitant lesbian breeders in Minnesota," said Wendy.

"Still."

"Well, it's still not definite. The children are contesting the will."

They glanced again at the building. The doormen, in their crisp gray uniforms, were opening the door for a nanny with a stroller.

"The Wingates live there," said Joan, continuing the list.

"The Powells."

"The Rothmans."

"The Aldriches."

Joan and Wendy knew the list of residents by heart, and in fact recited their names every time they passed the building. They ran through every denizen and always ended up with the Korns.

"And Arthur Korn!" said Joan, with the lingering disbelief that this man and his wife could make it into such a bastion of exclusivity. Joan tried to be philosophical. "I mean, I pity him. He's not so bad. He did manage to work his way out of Queens."

"What a schlepper."

"Well, he is a billionaire."

"True, true," said Wendy, nodding.

"But he runs the most depressing business!" exclaimed Joan.

"He does."

"I mean, how genius was he to expand that casket business into funeral homes and now retirement homes?" asked Joan.

"Apparently he owns one out of every three funeral homes in the country," said Wendy, knowing full well that this fact was true.

"He really cornered the market on death," praised Joan.

"People generally like him; he's not really the Grim Reaper," said Wendy, looking at Joan out of the corner of her eye, making sure she agreed.

"His wife is the only bad egg in the building. It's a travesty," said Joan dramatically.

"She's a true bitch," agreed Wendy.

They continued the conversation uptown by calling Melanie Korn every pejorative adjective that they could think of until they reached

their final destinations. Then they got on the phone and continued their
tirade of insults until dinnertime.

chapter 5

Under the domed, hand-carved ceiling in the sweeping lobby of
741 Park Avenue, Eddie and Tom, the building's evening shift doormen,
stood by, attentively waiting for a tenant's car to pull up to the grand
double doors adorned with filigreed brass and swirling latticework. The
building was completed in 1904 by architects McKim, Meade & White
and was registered by the New York Landmarks and Preservation Society in 1946. The limestone facade was built from the best quarry in the
world, and every detail in the perfect lobby was approved by not only
the hawkeyed board of trustees but also Sister Parish herself, whose
firm was commissioned to renovate the public rooms in 1974.

The stunning splendor of the entrance was not lost on Eddie and
Tom; they knew they were not just opening doors for the elite. They
were the eyes and ears of the lobby, piecing together gleaned information about the roster of residents whose names appeared not only on
the building's shareholders list but also in *Fortune* magazine.

The sons and daughters of these families never had a request denied; everything their hearts desired was granted in a New York
nanosecond, often as a substitute for genuine affection. Drew Vance
was a preppy girl's Lilly Pulitzer–laced dream; from his confident stride
to his all-American lacrosse status to his sterling lineage, he was the
catch of young Manhattan. The country club Muffys he brought in
through the lobby were a revolving door of perfect blondes who would
kill to be a Vance, so their manicured talons were always in deep, making Drew an accidental serial heartbreaker.

And Eddie and Tom, the watchers of the hallowed halls, knew it all.
They were the star witnesses in everyone's personal trials: the comings
and goings, the friends, the enemies, the purchases, the decorations,
the lawsuits. They were the invisible presence in the elevator. Guests
would leave a dinner party and gossip about their hosts (*She really is in*

the dark about his extracurricular dalliances) or make commentary on their taste (*Awful new Rauschenberg, way too late a piece to collect*). The doormen were there to imbibe the dirt and were a repository of information, always cataloging the social snubs, the affairs, the triumphs.

"Did you see the tits on that chick that came home with Drew Vance last night?" asked Tom, the young, handsome Dubliner. "Sheesh."

"I wished I could bend her over that little bench in the elevator, mamma mia," replied Eddie, a second-generation Italian hailing from Palermo via Secaucus.

"Drew's probably way too much of a pansy to give it to her right—he subscribes to *GQ*. I bet he couldn't even get the job done, the faggot."

Arthur Korn had had a long day at work. He exited his car, finally home. As he got out and walked toward the building, Eddie raced out to close his car door for him and Tom stiffened attentively and rose to take his worn-in briefcase.

"Good evening, Mr. Korn," said Tom politely.

"Good evening, sir," added Eddie.

"Evening Tom, Eddie. Have my suits arrived from the tailor?"

"Not as of yet, sir, but we'll bring them up right away when they arrive."

Arthur thanked them and entered the elevator. His floor, eleven, was already lit up by Eddie, who controlled the security panel by his podium so that any tenant or visitor could go only to his or her appointed floor. (During parties and rush hour a third doorman was called on to act as elevator operator, as actually *pressing* the buttons might prove too tiresome to the denizens.)

"Lucky bastard," whispered Eddie under his breath. "I'd love to nail his wife."

"In the Bentley," Tom added, with a sly smile.

"But you just know she's been around the block," Eddie said. "And I ain't referring to rides in the car."

"She's got that Heather Locklear thing going on. So hot."

Suddenly both stood up straight again, and the guileful whispers were eclipsed by proper, well-mannered greetings.

"Miss Weston! Good evening. May I take your packages?"

The elevator door was about to close when Arthur heard her enter. He recognized her step even before Eddie had breathed a word.

"Miss Weston, we'll hold the elevator for you," said Tom, carrying her T. Anthony monogrammed weekend tote and groceries from E*A*T.

"Thank you," she replied quietly.

The drop-dead gorgeous heiress was twenty-eight and already worth at least a hundred million dollars. The daughter of Russell and Eleanor Weston of Greenwich, Connecticut, and Fisher's Island, and Prout's Neck, Maine, Olivia Weston was a true beauty, with glowing skin that looked painted by Whistler and all the trappings of a true lady to the manner born. She was exactly the sort of mysterious creature that Arthur had imagined when he thought about New York society.

She nodded hello to Arthur and then turned away to watch the elevator move up the floors. Arthur's palms began to sweat the moment she entered the lift, standing to his left, slightly in front of him. The smell of her perfume permeated the space, and he looked at her neck, the elegance and beauty of which rivaled Audrey Hepburn's.

Now that's class, Arthur thought to himself. He wondered how such a perfect creature could be so close to him—her shiny hair, her pearls, her skin: she was luminescence embodied. She seemed so pure, so untainted. He felt like such a fraud sharing an elevator with her.

Suddenly, to his horror, his stomach growled, breaking the silence of their slow ascent.

"Sorry," he said, mortified. "Skipped lunch."

Olivia turned to him and gave a curt half smile before facing forward again. Arthur felt like a raging idiot. He knew she thought he was a world-class gormph. An old, second-rate goof. *Skipped lunch. What the hell does she care?*

Olivia ran a perfect white hand through her hair. The small, casual gesture was enough to make Arthur swoon.

"Beautiful day, wasn't it?" he said, trying desperately to make up for the stomach noises and to camouflage any further gut grumblings.

"Autumn in New York is magical," she said.

"Oh yeah, fall is my favorite season," he said.

"Mine too."

How strange. Arthur could not believe they had so much in common! They both lived in the same building, they both thought fall was the best—there was a connection here . . . what else to talk about?

"So did you catch that Yankees—"

"I don't really follow sports," she said with a helpless smile. The door opened to her floor. "Good night." She smiled and exited into her hand-stenciled foyer.

"Have a great night!" Arthur said, with way too much eagerness. He felt like a complete zero. The Yankees. Damn. Why did he have to bring up stupid sports? *Of course she doesn't care about baseball.* It was knee-jerk panic. Why did he always do that? He knew he was lousy at small talk.

The elevator door opened to a small, elegant foyer with an art deco table and an elegant bouquet from Renny. (It was an exact copy of the Vances' foyer several floors above. When Melanie—desperate to please—had "accidentally" stopped on the Vances' floor and spied their decor, she'd had her decorator replicate it down to the umbrella stand.) Arthur turned his key and entered his nine-thousand-square-foot duplex. He shouted a hello and made his way through the apartment to find his bride. Arthur interrupted her downward glance at a book in the lamplight.

"Hi, honey," he said, kissing her forehead. "Reading the Torah?"

She smiled, putting down her *Zagat* guide.

"I was trying to calm my nerves by browsing *Zagat's*. I'm already at K and it's not working."

"Your dad?" asked Arthur, immediately sympathetic.

"I've been thinking about him, too, but it's other stuff . . ."

"What, someone steal your Amex card?"

"Ha-ha, very funny. No, I was having a perfectly nice day—or I thought I was having a great day. I beat out Gayfryd for the last size thirty-two at YSL—the one on the cover of *Town and Country*—and then I got home to find this."

Melanie thrust a copy of the new *10021* magazine in his face. The magazine, given gratis to top buildings, featured Olivia Weston on its cover, with the headline THE NEXT MIMI HALSEY. Bedecked in a sweeping Lacroix ball skirt, Ralph Lauren cashmere twinset, and her grandmother's jewels, she stared coolly off the page, pure elegance and unfet-tered grace. She even looked a little like a young Diandra.

"That's . . . Olivia Weston."

"They're calling her the next Mimi Halsey, who was the next Brooke Astor ten years ago."

"So?"

"So it bothers me. I feel like I can't ever compete with these women, like I'll always be swimming upstream. I mean, that little drug-store heiress was born with a silver thermometer up her butt. She hasn't worked a day in her life, let alone done a stitch of volunteer work. She doesn't know what real life is like, and she's *the next Mimi Halsey*, vaulted above everyone else."

"Why do you care? They just give silly titles like that to sell maga-zines," Arthur offered, patting Melanie's head.

"Arthur, they don't sell this magazine. It's free to everyone in our zip code. I just don't get it, Arty. It's like, I try and try and try: I raise money, I volunteer my time, I pull four million strings to get celebrities like Gary Coleman and Joan Lunden to chair our events, and no one ever seems to recognize my efforts."

"It will come, sweetie. And, besides, maybe Olivia has been doing this for longer."

"Doing what?" sighed Melanie. "I know for a fact that her work is done after the invitations go out. She just lets them use her name and doesn't even show up at half the meetings."

"Why is this upsetting you so much?"

"Because I want to know what I'm doing wrong," said Melanie, with palpable distress. "I just don't get it. I always thought I was a quick study, but I'm at a loss. I mean, we do so much more than people like Olivia, and I'm still an outsider and she's the crown jewel. We've given millions to Memorial Sloan-Kettering, to the New York City Ballet, to the Museum of the City of New York, the Henry Street Settlement—"

"Honey . . ."

"I've personally chaired countless benefits and gotten ads for all the programs. And she does nothing, but somehow she's the hero and I'm the chump. So she wrote a little ninety-seven-page 'autobiographical novel' about her summers in Fisher's Island, big deal."

"She did?"

"I've done everything, and I'm not even in a party picture this issue."

"Please explain why you care about those crappy party pictures. They're the size of a postage stamp, anyway."

Melanie paused. She knew damn well why she cared.

"Mr. Guffey said Diandra was in at least every other month."

Diandra. Is that what this was about? Arthur wished Melanie wouldn't think twice about her, but he knew that she kept some sort of internal scorecard. Arthur stroked her hair. "It's meaningless, kiddo. No one cares about this stuff."

He saw his wife's face fall in frustration. God, she wanted to be loved so badly. "Don't worry." Arthur tried to mollify her frazzled nerves with a hug and kiss. But when she was in a state she couldn't be stopped.

"Even Cordelia Vance, that snobby, giant Valium tablet with a face, is mentioned as being among the city's most charitable set," she continued. "She's never friendly to me and I'm always so nice! She's so frigid. No wonder I hear Morgan rolls in other beds."

"Melanie, calm down. You never know what goes on behind closed doors."

"Arthur, memo to you: where there's smoke, there's fire," said Melanie, violently sliding her Asscher-cut ten-carat diamond engagement ring up and down her finger. It had become a habit for Melanie to play with her ring when she was enraged, a habit she had cultivated, eager to draw as much attention as possible to her expensive bauble so that people would be impressed.

"Well, I can't be bothered with that," said Arthur, tossing down his briefcase. "What I want is dinner. I'm starving," he said, walking toward the dining room.

Melanie realized she had gone on too long, so she decided to drop the subject presently. She grabbed Arthur's arm and walked with him down the hall.

"I ordered your favorite!"

"Corned beef?" asked Arthur, surprised.

"No, silly, filet mignon," said Melanie. That was what she thought should be Arthur's favorite.

"Oh, great."

Just before they reached the dining room door, Melanie stopped dead in her tracks.

"Darling," she said seriously.

"Yes?" asked Arthur, concerned.

"I know now what I have to do."

"What?"

"I have to get on the board of the Metropolitan Museum."

"What are you talking about?"

Melanie put her hand to her chest. "Mr. Guffey explained that the only way people will realize what a powerhouse I am—we are—is if I get on that board."

"You think that will help?"

"Of course it will. Remember, sweetie, what I've told you a zillion times: in New York, money is the great democratizer, and as we both know, anyone possessing large amounts of it can buy themselves into the upper echelons of society. But to be truly accepted and revered, one needs to be on the board of an important philanthropic endeavor."

"Are you sure that's true in this day and age?"

"Poz. Unlike London, where it's all about land and titles, in New York, it's all about boards. And I have to get my ass on one—the most important. The Met."

"Here we go—more millions to another museum," groaned Arthur.

"Oh, really, sweetie. You sound like it's such a big hardship. People die every day. You just have to work harder at getting more bodies into a Korn Kasket."

"You're on a rampage tonight," Arthur said, amused.

"I know, I know. I'm being bitchy."

"You always fly off the handle when you feel challenged; it's your feisty fighter side rearing its little head."

"You said you loved the fighter in me!" said Melanie, teasing.

"Melanie, you're too much," said Arthur, with both pride and bewilderment. "Now come on—let's eat. I'm *starving*."

chapter 6

After a lazy morning flipping through the *New York Post*, *Women's Wear Daily*, the *National Enquirer*, and *Star*, Melanie finally got motivated to make it out of the house.

"Off to a dinner party?" asked Mr. Guffey.

Melanie stopped short in the front hall. "No . . ."

"Oh," said Mr. Guffey, in his clipped British tone. He raised his eyebrows and gave Melanie the once-over.

"Why do you ask? I mean, it's lunchtime . . ." said Melanie, faltering.

"No reason, madam," said Mr. Guffey, frowning at the water ring Melanie's Pellegrino glass had left on the ebony side table. He disapprovingly placed a coaster underneath the sweating glass, making sure that his employer saw exactly how he felt about the oversight.

Melanie was now totally conflicted. She had a lunch date with two society doyennes that had taken her weeks to finagle, but after one reproving comment from Mr. Guffey she knew immediately that she didn't look the part.

"You think this is too dressy?" asked Melanie, opening up her fur coat as wide as a flasher would his trench. She revealed a flowery Ungaro dress, with leafy colors that Melanie thought perfectly matched the crisp day, and her new ruby necklace from Verdura that she had been dying to debut.

"You know best, madam," said Mr. Guffey, realigning the art books and Jackie Collins novels strewn all over the coffee table into a giant fan.

Melanie took a deep breath. "Please, Mr. Guffey. It's a very important lunch, and I have to be perfect. It's with Pat and Blaine," added Melanie with pride. She knew this would impress Mr. Guffey. It was like saying she was off to lunch with Gwyneth and Uma, only better.

"I see," said Mr. Guffey.

Melanie waited while Mr. Guffey stared at her.

"I'd rethink the jewelry," he finally uttered.

Rethink the jewelry? She could do that. Sigourney Weaver told Melanie Griffith the same thing in *Working Girl,* and at the end of the movie, Sigourney was out of a job and Melanie had gotten not only a corner office but Harrison Ford as well.

"Phew! I can just take off the necklace—that's easy," said Melanie, quickly unclasping the precious stones. She placed them with a clank in the silver dish on the hall table and was about to turn and leave when Mr. Guffey continued.

"Of course, no one really wears evening gowns to lunch dates, but perhaps in Florida things are different."

Melanie stopped again. "You think this is an evening gown?" she asked, crestfallen. "The salesgirl said I could absolutely wear it to casual events," said Melanie defensively. "Day into night."

"Of course," said Mr. Guffey, neatly arranging the television re-motes. "If the salesgirl said it."

Melanie felt stupid. She was running out of time, and she needed help. Where was Emme and her *Fashion Emergency* team when she needed them?

"Please, Mr. Guffey. Help me pick something out. I don't have much time."

Minutes later they were in the sixteen-by-eighteen bedroom that housed Melanie's clothes. Melanie was standing impatiently, desperate to urge Mr. Guffey to hurry but scared that he would refuse to be of any help if she yelled. She silently bit her lip.

After tsk-ing through most of Melanie's wardrobe, Mr. Guffey fi-nally pulled out a sea-grass YSL suit, Sergio Rossi heels, and a delicate gold bracelet from Harry Winston.

"This is perfect, Mr. Guffey. Thank you," said Melanie, spinning around her room in front of the 180-degree mirror.

Mr. Guffey followed her out to the front hall, where she grabbed her fur coat and began to swaddle herself.

"Madam, you might want to rethink the fur."

"Oh, no, Mr. Guffey. Here's where I know you're wrong," said Melanie confidently, happy that she knew a thing or two after all. "You can never go wrong in fur. I learned that long ago when I was working in the hotel business. Someone sees a fur and they know that person is a force to be reckoned with. But thanks for all your help," said Melanie, fluffing her hair over her enormous coat and opening the front door.

Mr. Guffey handed Melanie her cream-colored quilted purse and closed the door after her. Then he returned to the kitchen, shaking his head. He couldn't believe a tart like that was his actual employer. Boy, would the old gang at his finishing school in Mayfair have a laugh. He had originally worked for the first Mrs. Korn, when she was Mrs. Notbridge of 951 Park Avenue and still married to her first husband, the investment banker from a reasonably good family. He had stayed with her when she moved to 772 Park Avenue with Mr. Paulson, her second husband, who worked in import-export and was from an okay family. And he was with her right through to Mr. Korn, who was from the type of family you'd want to flush down the toilet. Mr. Guffey had been prepared to continue on with Diandra and Mr. Diaz, her latest husband, until she informed him that she was moving to Florida. That was that. The balmy weather did not agree with Mr. Guffey's complexion or lifestyle, so he had agreed to stay on with Mr. Korn. And as it turned out, Mr. Guffey had actually been quite pleased with the arrangement. As the first Mrs. Korn had absconded with most of the furniture, there had been little housekeeping to oversee. Mr. Korn rarely entertained, and when he did, it was the corn nuts–and–Jack Daniels crowd from his past, who were easy to delight as long as hors d'oeuvres came in frozen-food packaging and the ratio of alcohol to soda in their drinks was four to one.

But then, one day, out of the blue, Melanie arrived. Mr. Guffey thought that Mr. Korn was taking the piss out of him (as the British say) by introducing her as the next Mrs. Korn. But when he realized that he was serious, that this slag drenched in Glow by J.Lo was there to stay, he immediately gave notice and started to look for another placement. He searched halfheartedly for several months while the Korns were on their European honeymoon. Upon their return, he increased his efforts. The woman drove him mad: the way she spritzed the rooms with CK One, the way she pronounced the s in hors d'oeuvres, her pathetic little attempts to build a social life. But Melanie, for some reason, was so dazzled by Mr. Guffey—perhaps because of the British accent, perhaps because he spoke the Queen's English, or perhaps because she knew he was the most pedigreed person she had ever met in the flesh—that she had Arthur beg him to stay. At first he refused. He had a reputation to maintain. But when they offered first to double, then triple his salary, he acquiesced.

And now it was actually quite amusing for him. Everything about Melanie was so obvious, so garish, so in-your-face, so *American*. Sometimes he felt that his life had become a sitcom. Just when he thought the wretched woman couldn't surpass her latest faux pas, she exceeded it. Mr. Guffey had trouble believing there wasn't some gag writer serving up material for her. And when he realized that Melanie both feared and revered him, and that her ignorance of anything tasteful and classy was becoming painfully obvious to her, he realized what a wonderful opportunity he had. A few snippets there, some supercilious glances there, and his favorite—the arched eyebrow—had Melanie begging him for advice at every turn. It was a frothy little game now for Mr. Guffey. Mrs. Melanie Korn was officially putty in his hands. How many butlers could boast that?

chapter 7

"He's a modern-day Michelangelo."

"Rodin."

Wendy and Joan were settled in their corner banquette in the back room at Swifty's, drinking in the tide of perfumed ladies who fluttered in for their liquid lunches. Every woman was dressed to the nines, and it was, in a sense, a kind of fashion show—designed not to impress their husbands but one another. The long, narrow restaurant was packed, as usual, and this day was a particular social jackpot, with Dominick Dunne and Nan Kempner in one corner, the society columnist from *W* in another, and the Miller sisters having a mini–family reunion in the front. Wendy and Joan's gaze happened to be on Cordelia, who was on her way out.

"But she just had a revamp two years ago," said Wendy. "Are you sure? I mean, she does look fabulous . . ."

"I just saw her in the restroom. Fluorescent lights," Joan testified solemnly, as if she were in the witness booth.

"Oh. Those never lie."

"No, they don't. She's definitely been to Sherrell Aston. I know his work a mile away."

"As I said, he's an artist," said Wendy.

"I know last time she had it all done: neck fat, eyes, tits, chin. The works."

Joan caught sight of herself in the blasted mirror over Wendy's head and pursed her lips, making her cheeks hollow to see her cheekbones and check the wrinkle status.

"I myself am due for a touch-up," she said.

"Yeah, me too."

"Here she comes."

Cordelia walked up to them, her new shahtoosh thrown casually over her arm. Beside her strolled Jerome de Stingol, the heavyset legendary *10021* walker slash decorator slash designer slash alleged S&M queen by night.

"Hello, Wendy, Joan," said Cordelia politely.

"Cord!" said Wendy, as if surprised to see her. "And Monsieur de Stingol!"

Jerome kissed Wendy's hand. Then Joan's.

"Darlings," he said, with the bursting drama of a *Hamlet* monologue. "Looking *rrrravishing*," he added, rolling the *r* Juan Perón–style.

"You're such a sweetie." Wendy blushed.

"Off for a little shop?" asked Joan.

"Of course!" Jerome leaned in conspiratorially and whispered, "The mint squab is nothing short of divine. Order it."

"Absolutely," said Joan. "We always trust your taste."

Jerome nodded, put his arm through Cordelia's, and walked out onto Lexington Avenue.

The women paused with held breath until the exiting pair was no longer in front of the window, and then uncorked.

"He's a vile man."

"A dirty bird."

"He is, isn't he?" said Wendy. "I've never been able to stand him. I'm surprised Cordelia can."

"He's her only real friend," said Joan sadly. "I bet she doesn't even knew that de Stingol is an anagram for Goldstein."

"Of course she doesn't. That gal is in the dark," said Wendy, shaking her head. "Although . . ." she added with a mischievous raised eyebrow (perfectly tweezed by Svetlana at Georgette Klinger), "I hear he is too, in a manner of a speaking. He's a naughty boy. Apparently he has some interesting extracurricular activities north of 125th Street."

"*Really.*"

"Oui."

The waiter approached. Joan and Wendy each placed their orders for mint squab.

"And Cordelia, she's a real shopaholic," said Joan, worried, as if it were heroin instead of size-four designer labels.

"If there was an Olympic sport for it, she'd medal."

"She's always clad in the latest."

"She's always showcasing her jewelry."

"Must be Morgan making up for his affairs."

Wendy thought about this for a second.

"No," she said. "I think she just likes to buy things."

"Well, of course—I'm just saying it's an emotional Band-Aid," added Joan. "I mean, at that auction last week her paddle was just permanently up! I thought her arm was having a muscle spasm or something."

"What a waste of a life."

Suddenly the two women heard screams coming from the front room. They nervously sat erect, clutching their Hermès Kelly bags and looking at each other, alarmed. The sounds of a man screaming something muted became louder, and into their room burst a greasy-haired, obese pig of a man carrying a giant FUR KILLS sign written in mock blood. He wore a T-shirt for TAG, Treat Animals Good, the organization that regularly harassed wearers of flesh-based fashion. He whipped his head around the room, his beady eyes searching for something or someone; then, spotting his prey, he marched over to Lady Beatrice Harvey's table. The British socialite had just taken the reins at *Harper's Bazaar*.

"Special delivery for you, Lady Hah-vee!"

Beatrice looked up just as the maniac threw a bloody raccoon carcass on her plate. It transpired as if in slow motion—the raccoon landed with a soggy plop on her salad plate, causing flecks of balsamic vinegar and oil to splash all over the tablecloth. Her dining partner recoiled while Beatrice appeared unmoved and expressionless. The crowd in the room gasped in horror as the raccoon slid off the plate and onto the floor. It was a bloody mess, although Beatrice's Calvin Klein suit was left mercifully unscathed.

"FUR KILLS! You're MURDERERS! MUR-DER-ERS!"

Three waiters managed to drag him out while two others removed the carcass.

Beatrice, unfazed, asked for a new steak. Extra rare.

Joan and Wendy were paralyzed. Not with a jolt of fear, but with the excitement that they were on the front line of what they knew would be legendary, citywide, wildfire gossip. And they would light the match.

"My goodness, what was that all about?" said Joan.

"Animal rights activists," Wendy said with a shrug. "Obviously they weren't cc'd on the memo that their cause is so late eighties."

"I'm so tired of them. When Binky's daughter worked at *Vogue*, they all had to have personal bodyguards when they did the 'Fur Is Back' issue."

Wendy was about to respond when she noticed Melanie Korn walk in wearing a giant white fur coat. It was a crisp September day, not cold enough to warrant fur.

Melanie saw the two ladies across the room and decided to approach and say hello. They were so superintimidating, but she just had to suck it up, because it would be worse to not acknowledge them. She took a breath and told herself to be breezy.

"What was all the commotion outside?" Melanie asked Wendy and Joan.

"Those anti-fur losers from Treat Animals Good," said Wendy, blowing it off.

"Harassing people who have real lives," said Joan.

"Time to get a job," added Wendy. They both tried to downplay the scenario so that no one would spread the news before they had a chance to.

"Oh, yeah, anti-fur is, like, so yesteryear," said Melanie, for lack of anything better to say.

Joan and Wendy just stared at her blankly. As soon as Melanie had spoken she felt idiotic, so she tried to recover by quickly bolting. "Well, I'm off to lunch with Pat and Blaine. See ya!"

Melanie waved and walked off. As she turned around, Wendy and Joan's eyes widened to the size of the china plates just placed at their table: there was a giant blob of red paint down the back of Mrs. Korn's coat. Joan and Wendy, unable to contain themselves, burst out laughing.

chapter **8**

Arthur was like a kid whenever he had to go anyplace that he had considered too swanky and intimidating to enter pre–taking New York by storm. So it was with this naive exuberance that Arthur bounded down the steps into the renowned and revered 21 Club on Fifty-second Street. Since he had almost immediately established himself as a regular, Harry and Shaker, the greeters who were almost as much of an institution as the place itself, welcomed Arthur warmly and by name, and helped him slip off his Burberry trench.

While making his way toward the club room, Arthur passed an easel that made him stop dead in his tracks. On it rested a blown-up, poster-size copy of the *10021* magazine cover with Olivia Weston, "The Next Mimi Halsey" caption now so pronounced it almost taunted demurral.

"Harry, what's this?" asked Arthur.

"*10021* magazine is hosting a luncheon upstairs in honor of Miss Weston."

"Upstairs? Now?"

"Yes, Mr. Korn."

"Interesting."

Olivia Weston was upstairs, right this very minute! What a strange coincidence! Or was it? Arthur paused and then distractedly greeted his friend and lunch date, Peter Hartnett. His head was upstairs in the fragrant air shared by his young novelist neighbor.

One flight up, the *10021* fete was in full swing. Olivia was sitting in head-to-toe Michael Kors, seated between her dear friends Rosemary Peniston and Lila Meyer, both of whom were frequently captured in the party pictures of the various fashion and society magazines.

"Well, the family is just in a tizzy, a *tizzy*, because Brooke's brother Harpo wants to move downtown! Her grandmother is literally having a coronary, and her mother is beside herself, I mean, *really* downtown!" said Rosemary, with her usual dramatic delivery. Rosemary was robust, and everything about her was bursting—her booming, lockjawed Connecticut voice, her big, daily-coiffed glossy brunette chignon, her large breasts barely restrained by a D cup, and her cacophonous energy. She was a genuine firecracker. And like most heavyset rich people, she collected expensive shoes and jewelry, which sated her shopping yearnings but didn't put her in a bad mood when she tried them on.

"So Brooke says to Harpo, 'Why do you want to go downtown? What in *the world* is down there that you don't have uptown?' and he said, 'I'm young, and I want to live life to the fullest.' It's astonishing. So a distraught Brooke says, 'I have to go see with my own eyes where he wants to live.' So we got in my car—luckily my driver knew how to get downtown—and we pull up to Eleventh Street and Fifth Avenue and *as I live and breathe,* what do we see? I see that there are *awnings* there! Green awnings! Needless to say, Brooke was very relieved. Who knew? There are buildings with canopies!"

"Of course there are, Rosemary," said Lila in a subdued tone. Her low-key energy and waifish body made her a marked contrast to her best friend. "It's called the Gold Coast. Very chi-chi."

"I'm down there often; it's really nice," attested Olivia.

"Well, I've never been there. I simply cannot believe that there are green canopies!"

"Haven't you ever been to the Forbes Museum?" asked Lila.

"No, what are the Forbeses doing down there?"

"I don't know, but they have a great collection of Lincoln memorabilia. You should check it out," advised Lila.

"What do I care about Lincoln memorabilia?"

"I don't know, but it's just interesting. What do you think, Olivia?"

Throughout most of the luncheon Olivia had remained quiet but attentive. Not a big talker, she chose her words carefully when she did utter something. Therefore, regardless of the content of her speech, her opinions had an elevated impression on her listeners.

"I don't know much about Lincoln, but I think I'd like to. Maybe we should take a trip down to the museum next weekend," said Olivia.

"That could be fun," said Lila. "It'll be like a field trip. We used to go on those at Brearley."

"All right, but as long as we take *my* driver," agreed Rosemary. "Fritz is large and can protect us from anything."

"Great idea," said Lila.

Downstairs, Peter was advising Arthur on the club scene in Manhattan. To most, Peter was an inveterate snob who was disdained for being both a pompous bore and a mooch. But he and Arthur had developed an unlikely friendship after an accidental meeting at the barber's and had made a habit of lunching together once a month. Arthur picked up the bill whenever they went out, and Peter provided a crash course on the ins and outs of their world.

"I think it's redundant to join the River Club and the Knickerbocker. Just pick one, for chrissakes. If you want tennis, it's the River; if you want a straight-up martini, it's the Knick. Personally, I'm a Brook man," Peter droned on. "Although, that said, I'm a member of all of the above."

Arthur took a bite of his chicken hash. This club bullshit was so difficult to penetrate. On the one hand, Arthur realized they were just blueblood breeding grounds with lousy food (WASPs didn't know how to eat) and seventeen-dollar cocktails. But on the other hand, it doesn't get any more prestigious than this. And to think that he might belong to the same club where a Rockefeller sweated it out on a racquetball court! His father would die.

"The Links membership is closed now. Seven-year waiting list," said Peter, still warming to his topic. "Tad Sinclaire's boy barely squeezed in. And McKinley Fister, now there's someone who should be a shoo-in, five generations . . ."

Normally, Arthur would be taking notes on Peter's information. But today he let his mind wander as his friend continued his snobby diatribe. He just couldn't get it out of his head that Olivia Weston was upstairs. It was okay because Peter wouldn't even notice if he didn't say anything the entire lunch; he loved the sound of his own voice that much. Was it fate that he kept bumping into Olivia? She was always so near—in the building, now in the restaurant . . .

"See, the problem now with these clubs is all the sons-in-law. The guys who marry a longtime member's daughter and then set about getting themselves onto every board and every committee—they especially love the admissions committee—so that they can run the place and let only their friends in. Then they're the first to knock legacy—trying to get new blood in all the time," said Peter, motioning to the waiter for another martini. "The guys at the Union Club gave young Higby a real hard time and his grandfather was a *founding member*, for the lord's sake. Then they opposed Matthew Nicholson simply because he'd been transfered to London for a year. They thought he'd join and not come back. Ironic, 'cause those sons-in-law would never even be allowed to set foot in those places if they didn't marry in. Now they're taking over."

The draw about Olivia, Arthur decided, was that she was both elusive and captivating. Not to mention the antithesis of himself. Whereas everything about Arthur was clumsy and ungainly, every movement Olivia made, down to the smallest gesture, was done with grace. She was an amalgamation of ease and effortlessness. Her clothes never wrinkled, her hair was never out of place. She probably did not even sweat in the gym. In fact, he would bet his money she didn't even have to go to a gym since she was so naturally gamine. She was like a serene, svelte, taffeta-draped woman in a painting—would a genteel duchess hoof it on a treadmill at Equinox? Of course not.

But the attributes that distinguished her from the rest of her social group were a combination of casual elegance, irrepressible style, and an aura of mystery. A certain je ne sais quoi. She was what his mother would have called "well put together." And obviously everyone knew that, because she was being celebrated right this very minute. Gosh, would Arthur have loved to be a fly on the wall in the room upstairs. Just to get a quick glimpse.

"Excuse me, Peter—got to use the men's room," said Arthur, rising. Peter nodded.

There was a men's room downstairs, but that didn't matter. Arthur arrived outside the door of the private room just as Clara Coste, the editor of *10021*, was preparing to give her speech. He scanned the room through the crack in the door and waded through a sea of perfectly preened young women, trying to find Olivia. Finally his eyes landed on a head of dark, glossy hair and he froze. There she was, sheer perfection.

"Ladies," began Clara. "Ladies, I'm so honored that you could be here today to help us celebrate our September cover girl."

The murmur in the room dissipated, and soon Clara commanded everyone's attention. She continued: "It's always a tough decision as to whom to put on the cover of our most important issue, and the other editors and I are usually racking our brains trying to think of the appropriate person. But not this time. We just knew. When we decided we wanted to do an issue dedicated to charitable works in the city and anoint someone as being the possible successor to the most legendary philanthropist ever—the formidable Mimi Halsey—we knew right away who could step into those shoes: Olivia Weston."

Applause erupted, and dozens of jealous eyes turned toward Olivia. She smiled slightly, with a mixture of self-effacement and shyness but also entitlement.

"Ladies, this gal has got it all!" continued Clara. "There is no young woman in society today who has the style, the intelligence, and, come on, girls, the drop-dead looks that Olivia Weston possesses. She is *10021*'s shining star, and let me tell you, she's going places. So let us raise our glasses to Olivia."

Everyone raised her glass and a few mild *here, here*s echoed around the room. Arthur watched Olivia walk up to the podium. The slight rustle of her cream-colored skirt was music to his ears, and his eyes narrowed on her delicate hands, which carefully lifted her hem so she wouldn't trip. She stood at the podium and deftly extricated eyeglasses from a small jeweled case and put them on. She looked so chicly brainy and sophisticated that Arthur gasped. He inhaled quickly, choked, and was overcome with coughs. Olivia squinted to see who was making that noise in the back of the room, and all of the women whipped their heads around to stare at him. Arthur quickly bolted into the bathroom and leaned against the bathroom door, perspiring.

"Thank you all for this unique honor," said Olivia. "What a special gathering . . ."

The bathroom attendant stared at Arthur as he ran his hands under cold water and splashed some on his face. The attendant handed him a washcloth, and he wiped his hands and mopped his brow. He straightened his tie, threw a five-dollar bill in the tip tray, and took a deep breath and composed himself before exiting. He peered into the room again and stared at Olivia. He felt her eyes lock on his as she was talking, and it was at that moment that he was lost, his head pounding like a philharmonic timpani, his heart racing like weightless jockeys at Saratoga. His vision blurred and swirled like that van Gogh painting of a night sky. He was completely smitten. Maybe even in love.

chapter 9

Morgan looked like hell. He had barely shaved, his clothes—so perfect usually—were rumpled and untucked. And the bags under his eyes—ah, the bags. They were so enormous that they could have monograms slapped on them and be sold at T. Anthony for six hundred dollars. He had—under duress—been at Maria's beck and call until she got out of the hospital. And as his fantastic luck would have it, she'd had to stay for almost six days due to some sort of infection or blood loss (he had begged to be kept in the dark regarding the details). As a result, he'd had to sneak in and out of the maternity ward in full cloak-and-dagger manner, dodging anyone who looked familiar, making up more lies to evade detection, and digging himself deeper in the gaping hole that he had created for himself.

But this was it, finally: the last haul. He was on his way to fetch his kept woman and his little bastardina, Schuyler. He had brought Maria a beautiful pasta dinner, which she could feast on while he packed her up, and had arranged with the doctors to wheel her out the back entrance into the town car waiting on the corner. As they reached her awning, he planned to present Maria with a generous check and keep his fingers crossed that that was all she was after. After that it would be adios, sweetheart. There were no other options.

So at eleven-thirty at night, Morgan trudged through the halls of New York Hospital with his head down, eyes averted, and swinging a plastic takeout bag from Gino in his right hand. He was rehearsing in his mind the words he would use to get Maria out of his life.

"Morgan!"

He thought he heard his name but he wasn't sure, so he quickened his pace.

"Mor-gan," said a woman in a singsong voice.

Shit, shit. Get me out of here.

"Morgan Vance!" bellowed a man.

There was no escape. Morgan turned around. It was Regina and Carl Bates. Shit. They were waving furiously, and he was gloriously lit by the überfluorescent lamps in the hallway.

"Morgan!" they said, approaching. "What are you doing here?"

Morgan took a deep breath and gulped. How the hell could he explain?

"What are *you* doing here?" he asked, turning the tables.

They were flushed with excitement and bursting to share their news. "Liddy just went into labor! You know our daughter Liddy? It's her first. We said to absolutely call as soon as her water broke, we absolutely have to be there, so Jeffrey called us twenty minutes ago and here we are! We don't care if it takes all night—it's our *first* grandchild and we will absolutely not miss a second of it!" gushed Regina.

"And at the rate our Preston's going it might be our last," said Carl. "Thirty-six and not married."

"Oh, Carl," said Regina, jabbing him disapprovingly. "Anyway, we are just thrilled, thrilled. This is so exciting. I mean, of course, we're not going *in* the room, because, really, that's a little New Age, don't you think? Very California, to have your family and relatives and video camera there waiting for the little head to poke out of the muffin. Not our style."

"We would *never*," said Carl, shaking his head.

"But we just will wait as long as it takes in the waiting room."

"That's why we call it *waiting* room."

"So we'll wait."

"Wonderful, send Liddy my love," said Morgan, hoping he could get going.

"Now you're not here . . . ? No, your boys are too young. What are you doing here?" asked Regina.

Their rambling had given Morgan time to think. "Oh, my uh, assistant just had a baby."

"*Oooh,*" they said in unison, looking a bit confused.

"She has no family in this country . . . she's from Mexico, very underprivileged, worked her way up from nothing, really plugs away. So I, uh, came to see her. I just thought it was the Right Thing to Do."

Those were magic words to people in his set. The Bateses nodded emphatically. It was amazing how good he was getting at this. This lying.

"Morgan, that is so lovely of you," said Regina solemnly.

"Well, it's the least I could do."

Carl touched his arm. "I'm sure her family appreciates it."

Morgan nodded. "Yes. They're good people, from what I understand."

"It must be such a shame not to have family around when you bring a child into the world," said Regina, shaking her head.

"Tough stuff," agreed Morgan.

"Morgan, good for you," said Carl.

They all paused. He could tell that Carl and Regina were itching to get back to their daughter.

"I will let you go and go bring this takeout to my assistant," he said, motioning to his bag.

"Of course! We don't want to keep you."

"Good luck to you and Liddy."

"And to your assistant," said Regina.

After they left, Morgan raced into Maria's room before he could bump into anyone else.

"Where the fuck have you been?" she said as soon as she saw him. She was dressed in the most outrageously inappropriate pink outfit accessorized with six-inch stilettos and a cotton-candy boa. She was brushing her hair furiously and barking orders at the two Mexican women who stood next to her, helping her put on makeup.

"Hello?" Morgan said uncertainly to the women.

"This is Bianca and Lourdes, my best friends. They coming home with us."

"Wonderful. So nice to meet you both," said Morgan, placing the plastic bag on the table.

They gave him a head-to-toe checkout and then started giggling. They cupped their hands and whispered in each other's ear, something Morgan had not seen another human do since he was on the playground when his sons were young. He felt immensely uncomfortable.

"I brought you pasta," he said, slumping down in the chair next to Maria.

"Give it to me!" she whined. "I'm hungry. The food here is shit!"

Morgan handed it over. She snapped off the lid and started to wolf down the penne. She motioned for her friends to pass her napkins, and they complied. He couldn't believe this scene: it was as if he were in the makeup room on the set of a Telemundo soap opera. Could this be his life? And how superb, now that his extrication plans were ruined. He couldn't very well hand Maria a check and ditch her in front of her friends. It would have to wait, and he was at his limit. His noose was tightening. The lies would continue.

chapter 10

The following evening Arthur and Melanie Korn's sleek gunmetal Bentley pulled up to Sandra and Nigel Goodyear's legendary maisonette on Park Avenue for their annual black-tie dinner dance. Jackie O's best friend had been the previous owner, so the former first lady had often been seen coming in and out of the private double-door entrance. As *le tout* New York entered, staff took their coats as Feasts et Fêtes cater-waiters offered them criss-cut potato galettes with dollops of sour cream and beluga caviar. Patrick McMullan snapped the latest threads that glided by, almost blinding Arthur, who wondered, while recovering from the flashbulbs, why anyone would invite press to a private party. Meanwhile, Melanie, eager to have her new couture Dior captured on film, sauntered by the photographers, but none snapped her. Finally, Happy Renault came up and gave Melanie a half hug and faux-admired her gown right in front of the paparazzi pack. Her greeting to Melanie was simply a ploy to get in front of the legions of lenses.

"Oh, Mrs. Renault! Right here!" one shutterbug yelled, setting off a frenzy of flashes.

"One second, guys!" Happy yelled back with a flirtatious pout as she took her perfected hip-jutting pose. "Here, take this a sec," she said, thrusting her glass of chardonnay in Melanie's hand as the cameras snapped away.

"Do you mind?" asked the photographer, making a small shooing motion with his hand so Melanie would get out of the picture.

Melanie flushed and felt at once like a peon. She was left holding Happy's wineglass, standing alone, cut out from the pictures and literally whisked aside. She looked around in a panic for Arthur or anyone to remove her from her isolation, but she was alone in her Siberia. She finally spotted Arthur and rushed over to him, setting Happy's glass down on a console table on the way. Melanie clung to her hubby as if his body warmth would somehow melt the perpetual cold shoulder she was used to receiving. They walked along the room, eyes darting in every direction, scanning the frocks and face-lifts in the crowd, all punctuated by the occasional "How are you? How was your summer?" She was hardly feeling festive but attempted to rally. As a result, her words were injected with well-feigned interest, and she flashed a fake smile honed by countless months of pandering to airline passengers.

At first Arthur was thrilled to be at the Goodyears'. It had taken Melanie a full year to cultivate a friendship and wangle an invitation, a feat more formidable than penetrating the Pentagon's security system. But now he was itching to bail and go home. He wondered if Olivia would even be at this party. Naw, she was too young—this was old fogey–land. He nodded obediently when Melanie addressed him, "Honey, you remember Cass Weathers from the Johnsons' house?"

"Yes, how ya doing?"

He stuck close to his wife. No one was truly familiar to him. Sure, he'd seen their faces everywhere, but he didn't really know them. He was still in awe of the blue-blood set, but he felt more at ease around Melanie's unflappable take-the-bull-by-the-horns approach—all the high-society pleasantries exhausted him. He caught sight of one of his neighbors, Cordelia Vance, staring blankly across the room as her husband looked at his watch. *Gee, looks like Morgan wants to blow this party too*, thought Arthur. *How weird.*

"How wonderful—did you hear that, honey?" asked Melanie, nudging him.

Arthur looked at her blankly. He had zoned out, too busy looking around.

"The Weatherses have rented a house in Tuscany for the year," said Melanie.

"Sounds nice," said Arthur. He looked at the Weatherses closely. Whenever he was anxious he had the habit of imagining what coffin a person would end up with. Cass was definitely a steel Lincoln Deluxe, red interior, and her husband would be in the charcoal Eternity Cruiser. Although if she died first, he'd probably only spring for the Cinnabar Lincoln One-Star. Men were cheap that way. Unless a man was a philanderer. Then he wanted only the best for his dead, devoted wife, who looked the other way while he schtupped the secretary. But, hey, Arthur was all for their indiscretions, as guilt wrote bigger checks.

Cordelia scanned the crowd for Jerome, who was due to arrive any second. Her hair had been blown out—rendering her ashy blond bob even more lifeless than usual—her makeup applied to perfection, her small frame dressed impeccably in Oscar's latest, but she felt naked without Jerome by her side; he always gushed about how dazzling she looked. Morgan had offered the obligatory "You look lovely, dear" in his formula monotone, and it no longer packed a punch. He was already checking the time, and it was hardly halfway through cocktails.

Cordelia finally spotted Jerome entering, and her face lit up. After kissing the hostess and a couple other grande dames good evening (and throwing Cord an "I'll be there in a second" wink over their shoulders), Jerome threw his arms open from across the parlor and came to scoop up Cordelia in a hug.

"Oh, you look *divine*! Flawless, my dear, *sans flaw*," he said, embracing his friend and shaking her husband's hand. "Morgan, hello . . ."

Morgan looked away, uninterested. He had way more significant things on his mind. Cord smiled at Jerome, who laced his arm through hers.

"Not a soul here is more exquisite than you, my dear. Now, Morgan, I need to borrow your fetching wife for a moment and fill her in on quite an interesting little anecdote I heard today. You will be simply *stunned*, my dear, stunned . . ." Jerome guided Cordelia over to the Chinese Chippendale daybeds in the corner to fill her in on the latest gossip.

It is a universally known fact that there are certain requirements that a society walker must adhere to. He must dispense effusive flattery toward his walkee, have an endless well of salacious gossip, and put to good use his acerbic tongue by contriving the wittiest malicious barbs aimed at the rivals of the woman he escorts. Jerome de Stingol fit the bill to perfection.

On the opposite side of the parlor, two other expert gossips had just arrived. Joan and her husband, Phillip, had picked up Wendy en route to the party so that she wouldn't have to go alone. Since Wendy's divorce several years ago, the Coddingtons had virtually adopted her, always purchasing an extra seat at their table at whatever charity ball they attended, including her at holiday dinners when her ex had the kids, and transporting her around the city. It had inspired some nasty innuendo. Wendy was such a constant fixture at the Coddingtons' side that many wondered if Phillip even invited her into the bedroom. But that was just talk. Joan was astute enough to know that the upper echelons of society are not very kind to a single woman over the age of forty (even a thirty-eight-year-old starts to inspire a sort of nervous energy), and therefore she made it her absolute mission not to abandon her best friend.

"It's a pretty good crowd," nodded Joan to Wendy after she dispatched Phillip to get them drinks.

"Yes, it is. Oh, I see Cordelia! And Fernanda Wingate's here," replied Wendy.

"And the Powells . . . oh, and there's Marie-Josée Kravis. Always a picture of elegance."

"No one can wear couture like she can."

"Born for it," agreed Joan.

They continued scanning the crowd.

"Ugh, there's Melanie Korn," said Wendy with disgust. "Look at how she's practically *throwing* herself in front of Patrick McMullan's camera."

"Tacky."

"She never learned the art of subtlety."

"Look how awkward Arthur looks. He already has sweat stains on his tuxedo shirt."

"Sad. He's practically panting, he's so thrilled to have been invited. Now, how did she maneuver her way in?"

"She just gave a bundle to the Robin Hood Foundation, and Nigel's on the board. It's his baby."

"Funny that he has to solicit money for the foundation when he could just forgo this party and send Harlem to school with the money he saved," said Joan.

"True."

"But that would be no fun."

"True again."

Phillip returned with two glasses of chardonnay and handed them to his wife and her friend. He stood sipping his scotch, quietly listening to the ladies. Phillip was unassuming to say the least—medium height, medium weight, nondescript dark hair, glasses. He said little, allowing his wife to run the show. The only bold personal statement he ever made was that he insisted on wearing his kilt with his family crest to every black-tie event. Joan had begged, pleaded, bribed, blackmailed, threatened, but to no avail. He put his foot down. Kilt Boy was in full effect, right down to the gigantic safety pin.

"Now, Wendy, I heard this from somewhere, and as you know it's not for sure . . ." began Joan.

"What?" said Wendy anxiously, both surprised and disconcerted that her friend might have some scoop she did not.

"Someone told me that they had seen Melanie Korn in the 741 lobby, signing for a delivery of clothing . . ."—Joan leaned in so that no one else could hear—"from a prison."

"What do you mean?"

"Well, they said it was a delivery, and the guy had a correctiions uniform and everything."

"No!"

"Yes. And I heard once upon a time that her father was a convict."

"Get *out*."

"Yup. Hand to God."

"This is amazing. What do you think, her dad croaked behind bars or something and they're delivering his things?"

"Who knows?"

"Was it a good source who saw her getting the stuff?"

"It was—Pamela Baldwin—usually reliable, however, she did just have laser eye surgery, which didn't go very well. She now sees shadows and can't drive at night."

"No!"

"Yes. They're suing. Anyway, you know I'm no fan of Melanie's, but this really seems a bit unbelievable."

"It does. I don't know . . . Pamela once told me that John Brooks was having an affair with Samantha Peters, when it was really Serena Peterson. She can get it wrong."

"Yes, she can." Joan shot her friend a sly smile. "And you wouldn't want to get a false rumor started."

"You know how people like to talk," Wendy replied archly, getting into the spirit. "The next thing you know, the gossip becomes as good as true."

They paused, watching Melanie cross the room. She was practically glued to Meredith Beringer. Pathetic.

Joan looked at Wendy, then glared back at Melanie.

"I always knew she came from the gutter," she said.

"My thoughts exactly," said Wendy, as a mischievous smile formed.

Two servants came out with crystal bells announcing dinner, and the guests filed into the long dining room. Bill Tansey and his team had been sequestered for two days, decorating the hall to resemble a picture of a party that the Lord of Westminster had hosted at his British estate several decades before. The theme was essentially El Morocco. The giant chandelier anchored the red damask panels that draped the ceiling, then flowed down the walls to the black-and-white checkered dance floor. There were ten tables for eight, covered with zebra-striped tablecloths and dotted with clusters of bursting red roses. Plush red velvet banquettes—with pillows so deep you could disappear into them—had been built around the room, creating a small, cozy effect of secrecy. And everywhere one looked were candles, candles, and more candles. Lester Lanin's band, clad in white tuxes, immediately commenced playing as guests filed in, and eager white-tied waiters clutching chilled bottles of champagne readily filled glasses. The beauty of the room was so magical and breathtaking that tiny gasps escaped the taut, painted lips of the women who beheld it. Joan and Wendy were particularly taken aback.

"What a fire hazard," Phillip muttered to his wife after one glance around. And with that terse comment, Joan's impression burst and the enchantment evaporated.

"You're right," she agreed miserably. Phillip always knew how to spoil a moment.

It was customary for the Goodyears to split up couples at a table, and although Arthur missed Melanie's social instincts, he couldn't have been more thrilled to be seated with the lockjawed drones next to him. These were some pretty powerhouse people, all right. Big-timers. He watched his wife's animated conversation from diagonally across the table and ate his food without speaking much to his partners. He just didn't know what to say. The whole setting made him nervous. At one point, as he was stealing a glance at his watch, he caught his neighbor Morgan Vance doing the same. They shared a momentary flicker of commiseration in their quick eye contact and slight smiles.

Melanie, meanwhile, was ecstatic to be sitting next to the host himself, and she congratulated herself yet again for insisting that Arthur donate the two million dollars to Nigel's foundation. On the other side of her was the tedious Paul Jeffreys, who was beyond boring as far as Melanie was concerned. She had sat next to him before, at a party where he had informed her in his nasal voice that he collected Audubon prints but his real passion was canoeing around the pond near his country club in Southampton and collecting golf balls that pathetic golfers had dunked. He explained in excruciating detail how he had tried to sell the balls back to the club but there were no takers. He had enlisted some of his son's friends to sell them, but no one wanted them, so he had bags and bags of golf balls that he didn't know what to do with since he didn't play golf, and so on. Snooze. Melanie ignored him.

Cordelia was devastated not to be near Jerome, who had been amusing her with his naughty remarks about everyone at the party; as always, he had been merciless about her neighbor Mrs. Korn, saying, "Now, where is Melanie sitting? Seat twenty-six D—is that a window or an aisle?" Cordelia spent much of the evening talking over Phillip Coddington to Fernanda Wingate, who was seated on his other side.

Wendy was once again disappointed that she was not seated next to an eligible bachelor. Yes, they were few and hard to come by, but one always had hopes. And besides, Gustave Strauss was there, and he was new to the market, as his wife had just left him for the tennis pro at their club in Nantucket. But there he was, seated next to the hostess's goddaughter, Eliza Weekes, who was a good fifteen years younger than Wendy. Drat. She looked over at Joan, who was laughing with her head thrown back at something Jerome de Stingol had said. She always got the good table.

Joan was indeed happily ensconced next to Jerome and had even coerced Ned Aldrich—her other dinner partner—into sitting with the men on the other side of the table so that Cass Weathers could take his place and join in their conversation.

"I'm not saying any names," said Joan seriously. "But *someone* we know, maybe even someone *here*, has a father who died in the can."

"Who? Who? Who?" asked Jerome with childish delight.

Joan pulled her fingers across her mouth in a zipping motion. "My lips are sealed."

"Oh, Joan, you are *sooo* naughty," said Jerome. "But I'll get it out of you by the end of the night!"

"We'll see! It's not easy to get things out of me," teased Joan.

"You'd be surprised what I can coax out of people, my dear," Jerome replied with a smirk.

Across the room, Morgan had a killer migraine, and the goddamn band wasn't helping. He had barely made it to the dinner—Maria had insisted he bring her takeout from the Palm and he hadn't even had a chance to shower before throwing on his tux. He hated these events.

The worst was that he'd have to do some dancing before he could get out of there. He leaned forward to check on his wife and saw she was rather quiet and hardly touching her food. Then he saw her get up, presumably to go to the WC. He couldn't even look at Cordelia these days without feeling enormous guilt. He had to put an end to Maria.

As Cordelia rose and left the room, Melanie noticed several of the eighty or so guests watch her admiringly. They seemed bewitched by her old-world grace and elegance, drinking in her every accessory, from her jeweled antique comb to her cabochon sapphire ring. *Barf*, thought Melanie, and asked that the Perrier be passed to her. *Everything was handed to her on a silver platter,* she thought. Everyone wanted to be her or know her. Melanie knew that compared to Diandra and Cordelia she had little social allure. Both of them were considered not only refined and glamorous, but also generous. They were on every important board in the city, and Melanie, though active in several charity committees, wanted to play in the trustee big leagues Arty's first wife has played in. It was time to get her plan into action.

"So, Nigel, you're on the board of the Met, aren't you?" asked Melanie.

"Not anymore. Nope. I resigned from everything except Robin Hood when we decided to move down to Palm Beach for the winter. I needed to focus."

Melanie was disappointed but not discouraged. "Well, perhaps you can introduce me to the board members. I am very interested," said Melanie, leaning in and pressing her breasts close to his arm.

Nigel appeared momentarily flustered. "Um, I'll see what I can do," he mumbled, then immediately turned to LeeLee Powell, who was seated on his other side.

"Nigel," said Melanie, refusing to lose her dinner partner's attention, "I am very serious about this. Please know that we are very generous."

"I know. I'll see what I can do."

"Thank you," said Melanie with satisfaction.

It wasn't until eleven-thirty that it became an appropriate time to say adieu, and Morgan Vance and Phillip Coddington were the first to drag their wives away. Melanie was reluctant, because she felt that she still had work to do, but she thought it appropriate to leave early to maintain her air of mystique. There was nothing more pathetic than being the last one to leave, she had learned early on.

When he returned home, Morgan immediately checked his voice mail at work, where there were four ranting messages from Maria, demanding to know his whereabouts. Little Schuyler Vance was crying in the background with such ear-splitting vigor that when Cordelia entered the bedroom he hung up for fear she'd hear the child's wails through the receiver. As he undressed, he realized that he had so much on his mind that he had barely made conversation with his wife all night, so he tried a topic that was likely to be of interest to her.

"How was the shopping?" he asked, feigning interest. "Any good purchases?"

Cordelia looked surprised and genuinely moved that he'd asked. "Yes, actually . . . would you like to see them?"

"Sure, I'd love to."

"I'll get them, then!"

Cordelia left the room in her nightgown and silk robe to go down the hall to her closet, which had been a fifth bedroom that was converted into a mini–clothes warehouse for all of her garments. Morgan took off his cufflinks and shirt and started to get ready for bed and the fashion show his wife would put on for him. He was exhausted. Bleary-eyed and wrecked by nerves stemming from work pressures, social pressures, and—oh, yeah—his new fatherhood, he climbed into bed and reclined on the hand-embroidered sheets while leaning against the upholstered headboard. He had lost his initial nerve to get rid of Maria, and it didn't seem like she was in any hurry to get rid of him.

"So, here we have this gown from YSL. Jerome thought it looked fabulous—perfect for the Orchid Ball. This part here is all hand-beaded." She demonstrated in a Vanna White letter-turner pose.

"It's great, darling," replied Morgan, distracted.

"And then I got these matching shoes at Helene Arpels. I also got them in white and beige. Beige is really the look right now . . ."

Cordelia noticed her husband's journey into other solar systems.

"Morgan? Morgan, did you see them?" she asked, luring him out of his orbit. "Don't you like them?"

"Yes, yes, the shoes are perfect, the clothes are perfect . . . everything's perfect, darling."

"Is something wrong?" she asked.

"No, not at all."

"You seem upset."

"No, I'm fine."

Cordelia paused. Maybe he didn't quite like beige? "Are you sure you love the shoes? Because I can take them back."

"No, don't take them back. They'll look great with the dress."

Cordelia looked down, ashamed that she didn't select things her husband liked. Morgan saw his wife's sad eyes and felt terrible, plagued with a guilt that almost split his side.

"I'm sorry if I seem out of it, honey. Things are just . . . so busy at work . . ."

"You're right. I'll take them back."

"No, don't take them back. They're beautiful, really," he protested. "I love them."

Cordelia gathered her purchases and left the room.

"Do whatever you want," offered Morgan, defeated by everything.

chapter 11

Melanie was floating in a despondent fog. She had seven women coming over in five hours and the place looked like a bomb had gone off, total Iraq. Arthur's socks were strewn everywhere, objets d'art were askew on the coffee table, and every pillow needed an aggressive fluffing, pronto. As Juanita dusted and vacuumed in a frenzied Tazmanian Devil whirlwind, Melanie stood in her slip, no outfit chosen, wanting to tear her hair out. Plus, to add insult to injury, the caterers from RSVP had yet to arrive to start their chopping and dolloping or whatever the hell they did to prepare. It was her first decorating committee meeting for the Save Venice Masquerade Gala, and as the hostess she felt poised on the brink of utter disaster.

As Melanie loitered, Mr. Guffey passed by with a slow-growing

Hitchcockian shadow projected against her toile-covered dressing room wall. In some ways, he was like a fairy godfather watching out for her. In other ways, she was spooked by his omniscience and all-knowing gloat.

"Oh, Mr. Guffey!" she squealed in her best damsel-in-distress cry.

"Yes, madam."

"I'm just a mess. I don't know what to do—nothing feels ready for this group today, and I don't know what to wear and I don't have the right food to serve. God knows where the caterers are. They always seem to show up late!"

"Calm down, madam," he said soothingly. "We will get it sorted."

"Phew," she sighed. "I just get this pre-party panic. Thank you for helping me . . . get it sorted."

"Pleasure. Although . . ." His words trailed off.

"What?"

"Nothing."

"What is it? Tell me!"

"Well . . ." He looked away.

Melanie held her breath and looked at him wide-eyed, like a Best Actress nominee waiting for the envelope to open.

Mr. Guffey finally continued, "It's just, there's only so much one can do."

"In terms of what?"

"No, nothing, just that . . . well, you see, we can clean it up and we can get the best caterers, but it's not quite the same as having the proper decor from the start, or a top in-house chef. Then everything would fall into place naturally and you'd never have to worry."

Melanie was about to protest, but then she paused and really pondered what he had said.

"Actually," she began, "I have been thinking of doing a spruce-up around here. I mean, I know I gutted and rebuilt only eighteen months ago, but I think a face-lift couldn't hurt. Right? The trends change so often."

"May I venture to offer that timeless is always better than the trend du jour?"

"Definitely, forget trends! I want something timeless. Classic . . ." Melanie drifted off into a blurry, tartan-kissed heaven, picturing her new Ralph Lauren abode swathed in equestrian chic. The she snapped out of her club chair– and cashmere throw–dotted reverie and focused back on the task at hand. "Do you have any suggestions? You know, for, uh, decorators?"

"I can set up appointments with several highly recommended people."

"Great, great. Do you think they can work fast? 'Cause Arty and I really want to entertain."

"We'll just have to see what they can do."

"Good," said Melanie, glancing around the room. "Yeah, I guess this style is a little trendy."

"Yes, madam," said Mr. Guffey, scanning Melanie's wardrobe for an outfit. "I knew you would regret ripping out all the moldings and lowering the ceiling."

"Lowering the ceiling? Well, we wanted central air," said Melanie defensively. "What do other people do when the building cranks up the radiator so high because some little old lady on the sixth floor is freezing? The whole building has to suffer? It felt like we were in Africa."

"Yes, I suppose that's true."

"But I mean, seriously. Do you think the other tenants just sweat it out?"

"Perhaps a little perspiration doesn't bother them if they have their beautiful moldings," said Mr. Guffey, pulling out crisply pressed light tweed Stella McCartney trousers and a printed chiffon blouse.

Melanie thought about it. That seemed weird. Suffer for the sake of . . . beauty? She supposed if you put it that way, it made sense.

"What do you think about the furniture?" she asked timidly.

"You have some beautiful pieces," said Mr. Guffey, flicking a piece of lint off his pants.

"Yes, yes, we do. We paid a fortune at Sotheby's, Doyle, and Frothingham's," said Melanie with pride.

"Yes," said Mr. Guffey. "Although nothing really seems to hold together."

"What do you mean?"

"Oh, it's really not my place, madam."

"No, please! Mr. Guffey, don't hold out on me," said Melanie, using a teasing tone to downplay her urgency.

"Well, you have just a hodgepodge of things, and nothing really goes together. For example, in your library, you have French provincial mixed with art nouveau and some horrid twentieth-century pieces with contemporary lighting and pop art. It's like a bloody time capsule, if you'll forgive me," said Mr. Guffey. He should have restrained himself, but the thought of it worked him up into a lather. He had been biting his tongue for too long, and he was bursting. "And the dining room has old masters mixed with folk art and rococo, the bedroom has Bavarian mixed with wicker—wicker in Manhattan! And with that garish oil painting that you bought in Venice . . ."

"That was a honeymoon gift," said Melanie softly. "Arthur paid fifty Gs for it."

"Well, he was robbed!" said Mr. Guffey.

Melanie was silent.

"I'm sorry, madam."

"No, no. Go on."

"The point is, madam, while you do have a knack for selecting some exquisite pieces, I believe that you need a little guidance in pulling them together."

"You're right."

"But don't worry, madam. Like I said, we'll get it sorted."

Her mind turned to the other missing piece of the equation. "And you think we should get another chef besides Wayne?"

"Well, madam . . . Wayne is not a chef."

What? Was he insane? He was a fantastic chef! She was sure of that. Maybe this idiot didn't know good eats when he had them, the damn Brit. I mean, since when do they know good food, anyway? When was the last time you heard someone say, "Hey, let's go out for English"? Wayne was a star in the kitchen.

"Yes he is too a chef," Melanie protested in a fevered pitch. "Whenever we need him he comes and cooks for us. I mean, he's on a fat retainer. He's our chef!"

"No, he is not."

"*Yes, he is!*"

"Wayne is a cook. Not a chef."

"What do you mean? We got him from the top, most reputable agency. He's the brother of the Mellons' chef."

Mr. Guffey sighed the sigh of one trying to explain civil rights to a swastika-tattooed skinhead.

"The Mellons do not have a chef. They have a cook. There is a difference. The cook walks their dog, Halston. A chef would never walk the dog. They tend exclusively to haute cuisine, not pooper scoopers."

"Oh . . . I see. A chef just cooks. A cook . . . does some other stuff?"

"Essentially."

"So Wayne isn't, like, what one would consider a top chef?"

"I would say not."

"But Arthur loves the food so much. It's so tasty—we always fully stuff ourselves."

"It's not about their ability to fill your fuel tanks. It's about their studies. With whom and where did they apprentice? In what Chateaux did they do a *stage*? How many Michelin stars was the kitchen awarded?"

"Michelin, like the tires?"

"Yes. But not."

"So I should get a four-star guy from France or something?"

"Three stars."

"Mr. Guffey, has it escaped your attention that we've got a ton of dough? We can afford the best, so we should get a four-star guy. I mean, what the hell? Do you think I can't tell the difference or something—I don't have the palate? Because, trust me, I know good food."

Poor Melanie, thought Mr. Guffey as he bent down to pick up some discarded outfits off the floor and put them on hangers. He knew her defensive mode. She switched it on like a chameleon abruptly changing hues to avoid becoming chomped prey on a greater beast's molars. Sometimes he felt like he was watching an episode of *National Geographic Explorer* when he watched her quake, then rage—as if a stern, solemn voiceover would accompany her actions. *Here we have a native in her local habitat. Watch as she flits about trying to avoid humiliation*

and scorn. Her eye twitches as tension mounts, and she preens in the mir-
ror to reinforce her fading sense of territorial safety . . .

"Madam. Michelin has only three stars. That's the highest."

"Oh. Right."

"I shall go check on the caterers' arrival then, and see to Juanita's straightening up."

"Thanks . . ."

Melanie sat listlessly at her vanity and took a sterling silver hairbrush to her head, combing out the snarls more and more violently while really trying to comb out the snarls of her life. There was so much out of her control, spinning away at Mach speeds: people she couldn't win over, pedigrees she couldn't buy, vocabularies she couldn't match. She wished life offered a version of John Frieda Frizz Ease that she could apply to all the coarse elements of the world and smooth out all her journey's kinks. Or if only the universe was like *The Matrix* and she could download all useful information in nanoseconds and be instantly shielded from deri- sion. Then she'd be safe. But the only armor her new milieu offered was by association. Sitting on the right boards, having the right friends and the right taste, belonging to the right clubs, being invited to the right par- ties. Each entrée was a score for her suit of armor—a gauntlet here, a breastplate there—and she fortified herself with every new rung she at- tained. But just when she felt she was encased and bulletproof, some- thing or someone would come along and undermine her and her carefully amassed coats of protection would vanish into the urban air.

Melanie felt like she was playing catch-up. If only she had con- sulted Mr. Guffey sooner! He seemed to know everything—how to dress, behave, entertain. She had been too scared of him at first to even dare ask his advice. Because, really, who would have thought that she, Melanie Sartomsky, would have a real British butler in her house! (When she wrote her cousin Dotty Hix—the only person in her past with whom she kept in touch—that she had an actual manservant from England with an accent like that guy from *My Best Friend's Wedding* waiting on her, well . . . Dotty freaked.) But now was her opportunity to exploit Mr. Guffey. He had to lead her in the right direction so she could turn a new page and get the respect she deserved.

An hour later the doorbell rang. Mr. Guffey answered it and led the first arrivals, Joan Coddington and Wendy Marshall, into the Korns' living room. Earlier Mr. Guffey had hastily removed most of the offensive furniture with the help of the doormen, shoving it all into the library and locking the door. In order to compensate for seating, he had pleaded with the Aldriches' butler to allow the Korns to surreptitiously borrow some of the Aldriches' beautiful gold-leaf ballroom chairs from their bin in the basement. It took some coaxing and bribing, but the old stiff had finally relented and the chairs were now understudying for the rest of the Korns' furniture.

In order to avoid any scandals, Mr. Guffey strongly advised that Melanie refuse all requests for a house tour by pronouncing the apartment "under construction" and promising a future unveiling at a later date.

Melanie rose from her seat in the barely furnished room to greet her guests.

"Melanie! How exciting to be here," said Joan enthusiastically. She was genuinely thrilled and couldn't wait for a tour. She and Wendy had been salivating for weeks at the thought of getting a glimpse of Casa Korn. They had been joking the entire elevator ride up about what the place would look like. Wendy had even kidded that they should both be wearing Depends in case they peed in their pants.

"Yes, Melanie—we'd love a tour," said Wendy eagerly. Her eyes darted across the room, taking inventory of every single nook and cranny. Unfortunately, there was only a pair of sofas in toile—yawn— and several ballroom chairs and a low coffee table. Nothing disastrously offensive for them to catalog. Damn.

"Oh, I'm sorry, ladies, but the house is under construction. I'm actually between decorators, so we're starting from scratch."

"Oh," said Wendy, disappointed. She glanced over at Joan. "But couldn't we just see the progress? We'd love to give you our thoughts."

"Yes, Wendy actually took a decorating class, so she knows a thing or two."

"After my divorce I thought I might dabble. But, really, who wants to wait on indecisive housewives? No, thanks."

"So, come on," said Joan, gently touching Melanie's arm to lead her into the hall.

Melanie was about to concede, but suddenly Mr. Guffey appeared with a tray of Pellegrinos.

"I apologize, madam, but the contractor has insisted that no one move about the apartment. It's simply too precarious with all of the scaffolding and beams about," said Mr. Guffey, handing each lady her drink. "He assures me, though, that in a few months' time all will be ready for display."

"Well, that's that, then. Sorry, ladies," Melanie sighed with relief.

"Just a peek?" asked Wendy one more time. She'd be furious if they left without a visual.

"Yes, Melanie. You must give us a tour, or we'll think you have something to hide," added Joan harshly. There was no fucking way she was leaving without a glimpse.

"You heard the man," said Melanie, shrugging her shoulders.

After all the ladies had arrived (Pamela Baldwin, Meredith Beringer, Fernanda Wingate, LeeLee Powell, and, of course, Mimi) and formal tea sandwiches had been set out, the meeting commenced. It actually all went quite smoothly, thanks in great part to Mr. Guffey, who somehow managed to appear from nowhere whenever Melanie was at a loss for the appropriate thing to say.

At quarter past four, after every detail had been dissected, the final guests—Joan and Wendy—were ushered out. Melanie, ecstatic that she had been able to pull off the meeting, retired to her room with a big bowl of Orville Redenbacher and the latest Danielle Steel. Joan and Wendy, meanwhile, were in a huff.

"What the hell was that all about?" fumed Wendy.

Joan looked out the window of their cab. "I don't know. I'm stunned."

"Didn't you think we'd get the tour?" asked Wendy.

"It's some sort of freaky game she's playing."

"You think she did it on purpose?" asked Wendy, wide-eyed.

Joan turned to her friend and gave her an *I cannot believe you are so retarded* look. "Wendy, it's a snub."

"No!"

"Of course it is. That little Floridian bitch has something against us. It's maddening. We've never been anything but nice to her . . ."

"We're literally Mother Teresa to talk to her at parties."

"I know. She's just got a vendetta or something. I knew she was evil."

"Evil," murmured Wendy.

They both shook their heads.

"Well, what can you do?" asked Joan, with faux resignation.

"You're right. Plus, who cares?" feigned Wendy.

But the ire and venom that bubbled under their nipped-and-tucked skin was sizzling to the surface. *That's it,* they both thought in unison. *Revenge.*

chapter 12

After supervising the kitchen staff's post-dinner cleanup and making sure that there were fresh towels in the master bathrooms, Mr. Guffey retired for the evening. His room was off the kitchen and was decorated quite simply and specifically. Mr. Guffey abhorred knickknacks, irrelevant details, and anything personal or cutesy, so the primary features in the room were a bed, a desk (with a quill pen and blotter), and a television set.

Most of his evenings were spent in a manner that Mr. Guffey considered quite indulgent: he would imbibe one Boddington's beer and watch *Who Wants to Be a Millionaire?* which he had recorded on TiVo. He would never want anyone to know that he watched such pedestrian fare but couldn't resist the smug feeling he got when he beheld those foolish midwesterners struggling with elementary geography questions.

In terms of romantic attachments, Mr. Guffey left them for the lay-folk. He considered himself sexual preference–free. Both sexes were repugnant to him (they were divided into two categories: smelly, hairy men and silly, narcissistic women). Not to mention that he considered sex so frivolous and beneath him that he couldn't be bothered. There were other ways to obtain pleasure. Yes, indeed. Currently, playing Mr. Higgins to his present mistress—Eliza Doolitle's hideously gauche American stepsister—was beyond amusing.

As Mr. Guffey drifted off to sleep under his starched sheets, he thought of the thousands of ways to improve Melanie. It was as big a feat as penetrating a celebrity wedding on Neckers Island, but possible. Yes. Possible.

Meanwhile, Melanie was sitting in her dressing room, maniacally rubbing Crème de la Mer all over her skin. Arthur had fallen asleep hours ago, but she was excited. Things were starting to happen. She just needed an extra effort to parlay herself into the top echelon of her world. Then the unflattering comparisons between her and the first Mrs. Korn would have to stop.

She glanced at the *10021* cover featuring Olivia Weston. Now *that* was press. Melanie could imagine the buzz she'd feel being compli-mented if she turned up in the occasional party picture—they would certainly justify the expense of the $5,000-plus getups she'd sport. Many women of the Upper East Side had no ambition other than to be photographed in magazines as clotheshorses or socialites, only because that was the only kind of fame they could ever hope to achieve. They couldn't ever be known for anything else, so they worked the scene to get more and more clippings of themselves. Some, Melanie had heard, even sent the social editors of magazines like *W* a cashmere sweater every time they were featured.

She remembered Mr. Guffey once saying Diandra Korn could never walk into a party without having her photo snapped incessantly, her style was so superlatively unmatched. He had also mentioned she was in *Vogue*'s Best Dressed issue "year in, year out." Plus, he had said in passing that she was close friends with many editors all over town. Melanie wondered how she could befriend these types. All it would take was one breakthrough piece and all her detractors would be forever silenced, she felt sure. Then Arthur could be not just attracted to her but proud of her too.

chapter 13

It was a typically packed night at the Upper East Side's bustling rich people's cafeteria, Sette Mezzo. Two of Ralph Lauren's kids swung by for takeout, Wall Street CEOs dined alla famiglia, and eager social observers could not walk down the street without stealing a glance through the large vitrine to see which boldfacers were dining there. Installed front and center were Arthur and Melanie, enjoying a quiet night together. Melanie, opting out of her usual order of fish, stabbed a potato dumpling as she stared at Arthur, twirling his spaghetti. Arthur noticed her wide, zoned-out eyes.

"How's the gnocchi, honey?"

"Oh, fine," she said, with a blasé air. "But I'm really looking forward to dinner tomorrow night at Cresta. It's opening night and, you know, they already have a three-month waiting list—"

"If it's opening night, how do you know if the food's any good?"

"Hello? It's Pierre Mancelle's first stateside effort. He's only been hailed as the best chef in the galaxy. Don't you remember, we went to his restaurant in Monaco?"

"Right, right. Cost an arm and a leg. Six hundred and seventeen dollars—American dollars," he said proudly. "That's half the price of a Steely Van coffin. The full price of a Harbor Island pine box—the second series."

"Arthur," she said, cooing his name sweetly, "don't be gauche." She paused and took a deep breath, ready to unload her thoughts. "So, sweetie, I have a fantastic idea."

"What's that?" he said with a mouth full of pasta pomodoro.

"I'm going to hire a publicist."

"Really? Why?"

"I'm tired of being anonymous. You work so hard and we give so much money away. You deserve respect. People should know how charitable you are."

"You think so?"

"What's the point of giving to charity if nobody knows?"

Arthur put his fork down, incredulous but smiling. That Melanie. At least she was honest. "How about to make the world a better place?" he said.

"Obviously," she said, rolling her eyes. "But is it so wrong to inform the world of your generosity?"

"I guess not. But why a publicist? Don't you think that'll just make more people come knocking for handouts?"

"Not if it's done correctly. We're philanthropists! The real thing!"

"Don't you think people know we're the real thing?"

"I know, but I want people like Olivia Weston to know that as well."

Just the sound of her name triggered the happy pain of Cupid's arrow in his heart. Arthur considered this. Maybe it wouldn't be such a bad thing to let people know they had open wallets. They should know! The Korns were generous people! They gave away their money! They spread the wealth! Melanie was right. These society people would need the information shoved down their throat. They were not good with subtlety.

"I trust your judgment," he said. Melanie's smile grew wider. "But be careful. The press can twist anything around, and they hate rich people. Especially ones who made their own money."

"Don't worry," she said, touching Arthur's sleeve teasingly. "Any press is good press."

"We'll see," he said, taking his wife's hand in his. "Just get the best publicist to handle you, then."

"Thanks, honey," replied Melanie excitedly.

She leaned across the table for a sweet kiss over the flickering votive candles, met halfway by Arthur, for all curious eyes on Lexington Avenue to see.

"Why hello, Arthur. Melanie," said Joan Coddington, waltzing up to the table with her husband, Phillip.

"Hello, Joan. Hi, Phillip," said Arthur, rising to shake their hands. He turned a shade of purple at the thought that they may have heard their conversation.

"Hi, Joan—where's your better half?" asked Melanie.

"He's right here—oh! You mean Wendy," said Joan with a tight smile. "She's at home with her children. We're joining the Weatherses for dinner."

"I was looking for you the other night, Korn. I wanted to invite you to something," said Phillip, in a rare conversational mood.

"Oh? What's that?" asked Arthur, surprised.

"I want you to be on the committee for my charity. It's for the Scottish Historical Society. I'm chairing a fund-raiser at the Waldorf, and I want you to be involved." The Scottish Historical Society was Phillip's passion in life, and he truly felt that he was endowing Arthur with a great honor by inviting him to be a part of it. Phillip was in total control of the little Park Avenue fiefdom, and he had installed all of his relatives in honorary positions (archive manager, editor of the *Monthly New York Scot* newsletter, etc.) so that they were all on the payroll. They answered to no one, received money through donations, and had complete discretion as to who used the building and when (and had been known to capriciously exercise their right of refusal to virtually everyone outside the inner circle, even members and nosy tourists). Basically Phillip used the office on the top floor as his personal space for reading historical novels when he was tired of Joan and didn't want to make an appearance at "work."

"Oh, well, I'm not exactly Scottish," said Arthur, thrilled to be asked. He just wanted to make sure it wasn't a mistake.

"Doesn't matter. We've got a special category for friends of the Scottish Historical Society."

Arthur looked across the table at Melanie, who suppressed an ecstatic smile.

"That sounds like a very worthwhile event," said Melanie. "The Scots have such a wonderful heritage . . . it's really important to preserve it. I mean, what would happen to golf without the Scottish, right?" Melanie realized was rambling, but only because Joan's piercing eyes made her nervous.

"The benefit is for the society's building, here, not in Scotland," said Joan, with the slightest hint of a sneer.

"Right, right, of course. But, I mean, I'm sure you do stuff for Scotland, right?" asked Melanie, taking a gulp of her water.

"Yes, we do lots of things. That's why this fund-raiser is really important," said Phillip.

"Super! So when's the meeting? We can have the board to our apartment . . ." interjected Arthur.

"Oh, you don't have to do anything. Just buy a table. Actually, I'll put you down for two tables, Arty. I know you can afford it. Think how many people will retire or die in the next two months!" said Phillip, laughing and slapping Arthur on the back.

"We'll do three tables!" added Melanie excitedly.

Arthur turned and gave Melanie a quizzical look.

"Fantastic!" said Phillip.

"Come on, honey—let's not interrupt the Korns' dinner any longer," said Joan, guiding her husband to the back. *"Bon appétit!"*

Melanie waited until they were out of earshot before leaning in to Arthur. "Can you believe this? I mean, the Coddingtons want us to be on their committee!"

"It's kind of ironic—me, a Jew from Queens, supporting an event that protects one of the last standing fortresses of WASPdom in this city."

Melanie gave a big sigh of relief. Maybe, just maybe, she was making a breakthrough with the society gang. "Well, you just never know, do you?"

"Peter had said it was *very* exclusive," said Arthur, raising his eyebrows.

"Oh, I'm sure."

"But, hon, how the hell are we going to fill up three tables?"

"Don't worry, sweets. It's not hard to find people to go to this sort of affair. Everyone wants in."

Arthur was excited because he knew how much this invitation pleased Melanie. He was so happy to see her recognized for all of her efforts and hoped that this would relax her a little. If it meant he had to purchase some tables from a stiff like Phillip—who should surely spend eternity in a sarcophagus etched with carvings of men in kilts and family crests—so be it.

"Good job, honey," said Arthur, touching her hand. "You've really bounced us to the top of the list."

"I feel great," said Melanie, in a show of vulnerability that she would only ever reveal to Arthur. "You know, I just—I want to show them. It's like they're the cool kids in school, the richies, and I'm still the gas station attendant's daughter who had to wait on line at a charity home to get our Butterball turkey for Thanksgiving. I don't want to be the outsider anymore. I want to be in."

The challenge that faced Melanie was an uphill battle. She had gleaned only recently that society cannot exist without a certain amount of hypocrisy, particularly high society, and New York's was no exception. Whereas the Yorkville crowd was more than willing to embrace a self-made millionaire with open arms if he was male, a female millionaire—even billionaire—was a different story. New York relished a male Pygmalion, as long as he had the cash to back it up. Who cares where he was raised, the means by which he attained the money, whether or not he attended college, or if his manners were a little coarse? Tidy him up, send him to a good tailor, teach him where to spend his money, and he was the beau of the ball. Doors would be open to him in all of New York's drawing rooms, any eligible debutante was his for the asking, and he could reside in some of the choicest co-ops in town.

But a woman who came from no background to speak of, whose pedigree was less than acceptable, had a much harder time gaining access to that world, even if she had married well. She'd either be struck down like Martha Stewart or branded an upstart, a charlatan, a trophy wife, or, worst of all, a social climber. It was unfair to Melanie. There was a tacit understanding that at the very least she had to have gone to the right schools. Had she grown up subsisting on food stamps and living in a crack den in Harlem but attending Chapin, she would be in, no questions asked. (The heads of admissions of New York's elite single-sex schools were given an inordinate amount of discretion to admit someone into a jeweled world, endowments so powerful that they reverberated for generations to come.) But had she come from a Florida recreational vehicle park, like Melanie, she just didn't have a chance. Melanie had culled this but refused to accept it.

Arthur was touched by Melanie's revelation. "We'll go to that Scottish ball with kilts on! We'll show this town that the Korns are a force to be reckoned with!"

Melanie smiled at her husband, her little teddy bear. He really understood her. "Thanks, honey," she murmured, moved by his encouragement. Joan may have the *Social Register* and all that, but she had to sleep with a creep like Phillip, whereas Melanie had her little Arthur to cuddle with.

"I love you," said Melanie leaning over and kissing her man.

chapter 14

"Look, Maria, I was with you and . . . Schuyler . . . What? Of course I know her name. Jesus Christ, you don't make it easy. I was with you and Schuyler last night. I can't come right now—I have a job to do, remember?" Morgan was hunkered down at his desk in his Brown Brothers corner office, pleading with his mistress to no avail. The wall of windows displayed a periwinkle blue sky, jagged skyscrapers, and the noisy, congested New York streets twenty-five floors below. The street lamps' glow and the shimmering pavement looked so inviting right now that Morgan wanted to hurl himself out the window. He stared off into other faceless office buildings, zeroing in on a random secretary xeroxing, a man on the phone, another eating a sandwich by the light of a PC.

Less than a few miles away, Maria was ensconced on the white leather couch in her two-bedroom apartment while a maid vacuumed the ivory-white wall-to-wall carpeting and her newborn slept in a white Baby Guess? bassinet.

"Then you'll come tonight. I'm sick of this shit! I can't do this alone. I won't! My mother was a single mother . . ."

Here we go again, thought Morgan.

". . . who raised me and my brother all alone. She moved us from Mexico to give us the better life and worked two jobs! I promised myself that wouldn't be me! Never! Did I tell you my brother is a boxer?"

"Yes, you did."

"He was in the navy, and he knows karate moves. He will kick your ass if you don't make an honest woman of me! He's strong!"

"Maria, the level of our conversation is once again deteriorating."

"Don't you talk to me about that deteriorating shit! I have your baby!"

That she did, and she had Morgan in a corner. He took a deep breath.

"Maria, what do you want?"

"I want to go out! I want to go to Peter Luger tonight! I want steak and wine and those little shrimp cocktails with the red sauce!"

"Maria, I have a benefit tonight. I simply cannot see you every night. I have a family."

"THIS is your family too! And you better not forget it!" she screamed. "You think you, Mr. Rich Man, can just fuck me and pop me up and then leave me? You loco, mister. I have a brother who knows *karate*!"

Morgan sighed. "Maria, I think we have already established that you have a brother who is prone to violence and skilled in the ancient Japanese martial arts."

"What, you makin' fun of me? Don't fuck with me! I'll tell everyone!" Maria turned to her maid as Morgan sank deeper into his leather chair. "Turn that fucking thing off, Mercedes! I have a headache!"

"*Qué?*" asked the maid. Schuyler started to cry.

"Fuck, you woke the baby! My head is splitting. This spoiled brat cries all the time."

"Maria, I have to go."

"You better come tonight and take me out. I want a big juicy steak. I want people to see me with you."

"I'm not sure that's possible." He loosened his tie anxiously.

"One phone call, Mr. Man, and you done for. I call wifey and you're in BIG trouble! You come tonight or I call."

"Maria, your tired, idle threats will not work with me. I don't have time for your petty temper tantrums either. I'll see you when I can see you. I'm doing my best." Morgan slammed down the phone.

Morgan put his head in his hands. The problem was, Maria's idle threats would work with him. The last thing he wanted was for Maria to tell Cordelia. She would be crushed; he couldn't even imagine the devastation. Maria had him by the balls.

And it had all started so innocently. Well, sort of. It was last fall, early October, Morgan recalled, because he was working on the Simonson buyout. He had been asked to mediate because there was big money involved, and although senior partners very rarely had to pull all-nighters at that stage of their career, the market was bad and this was a huge deal. It was very late and his eyes were glazed from staring at his computer screen for so long when Maria, a sweet Mexican cleaning lady whom he had barely noticed before, came banging through his door with the vacuum and her bucket of rags and cleansers. She was startled by him.

"Oh, sorry, Mr. Vance, I thought you gone for the day," said Maria, embarrassed. "I come back."

Morgan was looking for any excuse for a break and hadn't spoken to another human in several hours. "That's okay—I need a rest." He looked at her name tag. "Maria. That's a pretty name."

"*Gracias.*"

"Where are you from?"

"Mexico."

"I was in Mexico last year. La Palmilla in Cabo San Lucas. Beautiful place, great golf," said Morgan, leaning back in his chair and folding his hands behind his head.

"*Sí*, I've never been there. I'm from more central, near Mexico City."

"Oh. Well, you should try to visit. It's gorgeous."

"Okay."

Morgan stared at Maria for a second, focusing on her but lost in his reverie, thinking about his trip to Mexico. The sandy beaches, the blue ocean, the margaritas. It was a romantic place. It seemed a lifetime away.

"I come back?" said Maria, twisting the handle of her vacuum nervously.

"No, no. Don't mind me, just carry on."

"I no bother you?"

"No."

Morgan turned back to his screen as Maria bent down to plug in the vacuum. He caught a glimpse of her out of the corner of his eye and was strangely turned on by the way her gray maid's uniform tightly clung to her buttocks. He chuckled to himself. *This is absurd.*

Maria started vacuuming, and Morgan stared hard at the screen. He kept glancing at Maria and smiling, and she returned the smile. It was always a little awkward having people clean up for you in front of you, Morgan thought. He never liked to be around when his maids did their work at his own home.

Perhaps encouraged by his smiles, Maria started a conversation. "You work late tonight, Mr. Vance."

"Yes, lots to do."

"Big project?" she said, vacuuming around his chinoiserie coffee table.

"Yes, very big, Maria. Extremely important."

"*Sí.* You very important man here, I know. Big man."

Morgan liked the sound of that. He looked closely at Maria. She had a curvy figure, with firm buttocks and enormous breasts strapped into her uniform. Her dark hair was wavy and fell just below her shoulders, her black eyelashes were long and curled, her pouty lips juicy and red. She was an exotic beauty. And, maybe because it had been so long since he and Cordelia had had sex, when Maria called him "big man," he got hard.

"Sorry, I bother you," said Maria hastily.

"No, you're not bothering me at all."

Morgan looked back at his screen as Maria resumed her vacuuming. She made her way past the armchairs and got closer to his desk. All that was left finally was the patch of rug underneath his chair. Maria smiled at Morgan, who smiled back.

"Sorry—this is the tricky part," said Maria. She leaned across him and pushed the vacuum back and forth.

"No problem."

Her arm moved back and forth, and ever so slightly brushed against his crotch. They both kept smiling at each other.

In retrospect, it was hard to say who made the first move. Did Morgan push her into his lap, or did she bend her head into it first? He couldn't recall. But the next thing he knew, Maria had taken him in her mouth and he was experiencing such phantasmagoric pleasure that he couldn't even fathom that this was actually happening. It had been years and years since Cordelia had given him a blow job. They had experienced a brief period in the middle of their marriage where she was a very willing partner, but it had somehow tapered off, and it was as if Cordelia had deemed certain things too deviant for her mouth (penises and food, primarily). Maria had brought him back to life, and he was exploding with passion and, later, gratitude.

Their late-night office couplings lasted through the Simonson deal and then were moved to the Empire Hotel on Broadway when Morgan no longer had to work late. Finally, paranoid but infatuated, Morgan rented an apartment for Maria close to the office. At first it was like striking a rapturous bonanza. Maria was game for everything—no position was too demeaning, or physically strenuous, for that matter—no sex toy too offensive, no profanities uttered in the throes of passion off-limits. Morgan felt as if he was on a sex tour. He was reawakened. He'd scour the lingerie shops in remote areas of the city, purchasing whatever lascivious outfit caught his fancy. He'd rent videos that he had only dreamed of and watch them with his eager companion. And Maria had no qualms about wearing her cleaning uniform and calling him "Mr. Big Man" in the dark of their bedroom. He was on Fantasy Island.

He had thought Maria was so sweet and pretty. His inexperience in the land of infidelity had allowed him to misinterpret her silence for naivete and shyness. It was only now that he realized what a tricky creature he was dealing with. He was excited, taking her to fancy places and exposing her to nice things. She had taken notes, learned to like the high life, and decided early on that Morgan was her ticket out of her low life. As soon as she got knocked up, she changed. To this day, Morgan wasn't sure how it happened; he half believed she punched holes in his condoms or, worse, transferred their contents into a turkey baster. In any case, after that she became a shrew—a scheming, demanding, shrill nag who was threatening to ruin his life and quite possibly could. And to think that he'd once thought her attractive! He had not looked past the long lashes to see bags under her eyes so dark that a thick layer of Cover Girl base did little to conceal them. In fact, all of the makeup that she wore—and she wore a lot—did little to enhance her beauty and only cheapened her even more. Those lips that he had found so endearing were usually contorted into a demanding dark hole that spewed insults and barked orders at everyone who came into contact with her. She had been such a mistake.

And now he was stuck with her—and their baby. He didn't know what to do or think about little Schuyler. He had never had a daughter and actually always sort of wanted one, but what would she become with a mother like that? If only he could get rid of Maria, it would all be okay. Morgan sighed. If only . . .

chapter **15**

In the midtown floor-to-ceiling glass offices of the venerable PR firm Hunt & Greenberg, Melanie sat in the sleek waiting room, reading an advance copy of *Vogue*. She came across a party picture of Rosemary Peniston dressed in costume as a gypsy and Lila Meyer as a witch, but her eyes narrowed upon spotting Olivia Weston dressed as Virginia Woolf. Just as she was about to read the accompanying text, Steven Hunt's black turtleneck–clad, skeletal assistant came to fetch her for their five o'clock meeting.

She was offered a beverage and led into a state-of-the-art media/conference room, where she immediately made herself at home on the brown leather couch and began flipping through a fax of tomorrow's *Variety* that lay on the coffee table. Her nose twitched at the odor of the treated leather, which bore an unfortunate similarity to the smell of horse manure. It was the same smell those cheap cars had. That's why she would never get a Volvo. They just stank. Finally, Steven, the publicist to the stars, arrived and greeted her, his normal cool composure giving way to uncharacteristic frazzlement, for which he profusely apologized. ("Julianne Moore's water just broke—I'm crazed!") They exchanged small talk until Melanie amped up the conversation by getting to the bottom line of why she was there, taking fifteen minutes of his extremely precious time.

"So. You're the best in the world, and I work with only the best. So what do you say?"

"I understand, Mrs. Korn, but as I said on the phone, I work only with Hollywood celebrities . . ."

"That's okay—you'll enjoy working with me. It'll be a nice change working with a philanthropist," she said, putting a manicured paw through her blond hair.

Hunt's face was a mixture of confusion (*Does she not understand?*) and curiosity (*What balls!*). This one was a real character, with the ring and the fur and the hair. Why was she so desperate for a publicist?

"My clients are usually promoting a film or an album. I mean, what would your hook be?" he asked.

Melanie reached into her Gucci handbag, pulled out a large wad of cash, and slid it across the shellacked table.

"I'm such a big fish, I don't need a hook," she said.

By the end of the day, the confidential client list had a new name among its red-carpet ranks. Julianne. Charlize. Melanie.

Across town, Melanie's husband was doing some fishing of his own. Arthur's driver pulled up to the green awning of 741 Park just as Olivia Weston happened to be walking out. She was stunning in her camel coat and chocolate brown leather boots, and she burgled the breath right out of his lungs. As the wind blew her hair, she bundled a cashmere scarf around her neck for warmth. Arthur would kill to be that scarf. His eyes widened as he traced her sauntering, doelike steps around the corner. As the Bentley moved near the curb, he bolted out, quickly thanking his chauffeur, Charles, and bidding him good night. Tom the doorman rushed out to greet him, but just as Arthur was about to enter his building he paused and reconsidered.

"I forgot something," he mumbled to Tom, who stood holding the door for him. "I'll be back soon," he said, as if Tom needed an explanation.

"Yes, Mr. Korn."

Arthur turned down the block and followed his pristine neighbor around the corner. As they walked along Seventieth Street, he stayed behind for ten paces, his heart speeding to a NASCAR pace. The bounce of her shiny hair and her delicate gait were hypnotic.

There was something about Olivia that was magnetic, that just drew Arthur to her. He would be embarrassed if anyone knew that he was following her, but it was like an addiction—he wanted to gulp her in and drink until he was sated, but he could not quench the thirst. So instead he would just see where she was going and what she was doing. For someone so constantly exposed in the press, she seemed so secretive. But the cozy world in which she lived was achingly appealing.

She turned the corner onto Madison, with Arthur hot in pursuit. They walked by the fancy clothing boutiques, designer florists, children's stores, and the entire time Arthur was guessing which one was her final destination. Eventually she abruptly turned and walked into Three Guys Diner. Arthur was unprepared for this stop, so he turned and stared at the mailbox, pretending he was sending some letters, but kept his eye on Olivia through the window. He watched as she sat down in a booth with a downtownish, artsy-looking guy who had scraggly hair and a bony face and wore a vintage leather jacket. Arthur kept glancing at them, and, finally, in an audacious move that shocked even him, he entered the diner. *What the hell? It's a free country,* he thought as the waitress motioned him to a table. He walked toward Olivia's booth, but her back was to him and all he could see was her luminous head of hair. He slid into the booth next to that of Olivia and her . . . friend? Boyfriend? Brother, hopefully. He took a deep breath, knowing that he was back to back with the goddess herself.

He couldn't believe that he was right near her, with the sound of her voice flooding his ears. He could hear snippets of conversation.

"It's been really hectic . . ." she said.

"Tell me about it. I have so much shit going on I don't know what to do," said the guy. Arthur was shocked that someone could curse in front of Olivia. Disgusting. It was like cursing in a church.

". . . I have to get this done. I'm running out of time, Rob," she said.

Rob. What a stupid name. Juvenile.

"Oh, come on, you just have to lay off that society crap," he said derisively.

"You don't understand. There are . . ."

Just as Olivia was about to say something important, the waitress approached.

Arthur cursed the waitress for interrupting. The lilting timbre

Olivia's larynx produced was all the nourishment he needed. Well, he had to order something, as the waitress was breathing down his neck, chomping her Bubbilicious in the most irritating and impatient manner. He browsed the eats and finally opted for the hot pastrami on rye with mustard, and a coffee. *Melanie would die if she saw me eating this,* thought Arthur nervously.

While ordering his dish with a side of coleslaw, Arthur did not see that another young woman had returned from the bathroom and slid into Olivia's booth opposite her. The girl wore cat's-eye glasses and black tights and had a gothic, beautiful face, searing green eyes, dyed jet black hair, and five earrings up her ear.

By the time the waitress had left with his order and Arthur could resume his eavesdropping, this new girl was leading the conversation. Arthur listened intently, believing Olivia was the one talking with Rob.

"Why are we spending so much time on Plato? I think it's overrated," said Rob defiantly. "That's what I hate about our professors—it's their pretension and conceit that dead white men from thousands of years ago had all the answers."

"I totally disagree," said the girl. "I'm obsessed with dead white guys."

Arthur perked up. He didn't realize Olivia was interested in death! Now *this* was a topic he knew everything about.

"And as for Plato, I thought 'The Allegory of the Cave' was genius," the girl continued, as Olivia silently sipped water. "The concept that people climb toward the light at the top of the cave for knowledge . . ."

Arthur felt as if he were bathing in the ripples of her voice—so forceful, so ripe with opinion! The lilt of her tones was a lullaby of youth to his weary ears, which had heard only about new coffin models all day. And now, in this Greek diner, he himself felt he had been awakened from the dead by the sound of her voice right behind him.

"Once you have that knowledge, you see that the leadership is vanity . . ."

She's brilliant, he thought, consumed. Not just beautiful, but smart too. He was officially infatuated. He knew he had to go get her book, pronto.

The waitress brought Arthur his meal, a simple delight that he was never allowed to enjoy, thanks to his wife's refined taste buds at night and the stuffy club lunches by day. Should it be this hard to get a sand-wich once in a while? But Hortense the waitress had a lead-filled hand and spilled the Coke all over his pants. Great, just what he needed. As she tended to him and he tried not to berate her, the girl got up and slung her messenger bag diagonally across her body.

"Why are you leaving, Holland? I just got here," said Olivia.

"You don't need to do that—it's okay," said Arthur to the waitress, who was mopping his trousers.

"I have a class," said Holland over her shoulder.

"I'm so sorry," said the waitress. "And those look like really nice pants. Dinner's on me."

"Why haven't you called me back?" Olivia asked desperately.

"I really don't feel like dealing with you right now," replied Holland. "We'll talk later." She left.

"Really, it's not necessary. Don't worry," repeated Arthur, desperate to get rid of the waitress so he wouldn't miss anything.

"Sorry, again," repeated the waitress.

Arthur had missed the girls' entire exchange during the cola mop-up session. When he was back in the eavesdropping action, it was just Olivia and Rob at the table, making small talk about the changing leaves and getting out cash for the check. Arthur didn't want them to notice him, so he left a twenty on the table and quickly made his way out to the street. The outside air felt cold on his face, which was dewy with sweat from the nonencounter. He hustled home to change his pants so that Melanie wouldn't see the stains, badges of his mental indiscre-tions. But she didn't even notice. She threw her arms around him with a hug, blissed out in her giddy announcement that Hunt & Greenberg had a brand-new client.

chapter 16

If civilization and society exist to keep human beings from pondering death, then charity balls exist to keep rich, idle housewives from realizing that they have nothing to do, thought Phillip Coddington as he donned his kilt for yet another black-tie event. Cloaked in nobility, wrapped in generosity, and swaddled in selflessness, the real purpose of these lavish spectacles was to give husbands valid proof of why wives were not working, and to torture their spouses in the process.

Melanie Korn glanced again at the invitation for tonight's function, which lay on her dressing table. She smiled, thinking of how bizarre it was if you really thought about it. The charity gang was like a bunch of nomads traveling around countrysides, pitching tents at various mountainside nooks. Always alternating specific venues—choosing from the same top ten over and over (Lincoln Center, the Met, Botanical Gardens, the Waldorf, etc.) and setting up camp with whatever decor had caught the committee's fancy that month.

As Cordelia pulled on her panty hose she sighed deeply, unsure if she was really in the mood for tonight's gala. There were really very few surprises. Sometimes it was a black and white ball, sometimes a costume fete, sometimes a celebrity concert, sometimes a charity auction. It was usually the same gaggle of designer-clad anorexic socialites who organized the events, and usually the same crew who attended them.

Joan Coddington looked out the rain-soaked window of her car and watched pools of water drip off of store awnings. She sighed. In this day and age, where discretion and privacy were endangered traits, it rarely occurred that someone unexpected arrived at these events. And it was a real pity. Gone were the days when a recently divorced Countess Olenska would appear at the grand entrance and send a ripple through the crowds, and no one yet had stepped into the shoes of Jackie O or even Carolyn Bessette Kennedy, for that matter. In the age of shameless self-promotion, when it was *not* to one's advantage to be in the newspaper only upon birth, marriage, and death, astonishment opened eyes and lips rarely.

As Wendy waited in her lobby for the Coddingtons to come and collect her, she thought about what awaited her that night. Probably nothing—same old, same old. Society was starved for an enigma, the one breathtaking individual who would shun most benefits and press but every now and then step out of the gilded cage and let the world see her. As a result, mystique had to be cultivated, and that was why the most beautiful but somewhat evasive women, like Olivia Weston, had become the toast of the town.

So on this particularly wet and damp September night, town cars, chauffeur-driven Mercedeses, and limousines dropped off bejeweled ladies and tuxedo-clad men at the Cipriani on Forty-second Street. They were on hand to attend the Food Allergy Ball, a gala that raised funds to help people whose heads would blow up if they so much as glanced at a strawberry. Doormen with large black umbrellas lent an arm to assist ladies who were holding up the hems of their hand-beaded silk dresses so that they wouldn't sink into the puddles. Manolo Blahniks were put to the test as the ladies scurried into the buildings while their husbands placed a crisp five-dollar bills into the doorman's palm.

Inside the room, Preston Bailey had lavishly covered every surface with white lilies bursting skyward. Among a thousand white votives, the murmur of guests greeting one another was a white-noise din coursing beneath the enormous painted ceiling of the former bank. Like the critics on *The Muppet Show,* Joan and Wendy had assumed a choice perch, from where they could admire and deride the outfits and jewelry of the recent arrivals. As they stood on the grand, hand-tiled floors reminiscent of the Roman empire, they sipped the Cip's trademark Bellinis and drank in the flow of fabric and precious stones.

"Did you see Cordelia's ring? Now I know where Michelle Kwan's been practicing!" said Joan to Wendy. *I would kill someone I don't know for a ring like that,* thought Joan to herself.

"Are we sure the Hope Diamond is still at the Smithsonian?" answered Wendy.

"You know, I wouldn't put it past Morgan to buy that for her."

"Me neither. Guilty feet have got no rhythm," added Wendy.

"Are you quoting George Michael?"

" 'Careless Whispers' to his mistresses . . ."

"Do you think he's up to no good?" asked Joan, as if this were the first time they discussed Morgan's supposed infidelity.

"All I know is that Cordelia said at the Memorial Sloan-Kettering luncheon that Morgan had been playing squash every Tuesday evening with Meredith Beringer's husband, and Meredith said that Ron doesn't play squash anymore since he threw his back out. You do the math."

"Interesting . . ." Joan reflected on this with her hand on her chin, à la Sherlock Holmes. Still, it wasn't enough to indict the man. "I'll ask

Phillip what he knows," said Joan, glancing around the room. "Walter Johnson's here. It's *tres* amusing to watch him interact with his clients."

The ladies glanced at the handsome doctor, whose face was drawn into a tight grimace. His blond socialite wife was chatting and greeting everyone with abundant enthusiasm while he looked miserable. As always, he glided through the room seeing his work on chests and tightened brows everywhere and pretended never to have seen his patients before. "Nice to meet you," he said, shaking the hand of one woman he'd worked on three times. "Hello, I'm Walter Johnson," he said to another recent eye job.

"Look! There's Sebastian Little. I didn't think he would come," remarked Joan disapprovingly.

"Is he still suicidal?" asked Wendy, lighting up a cigarette.

"Probably from embarrassment. Let me ask you a question: If you want to die, why put a Ziploc bag over your head? It's the most retarded suicide method. Just jump out the window like everyone else!"

"That's what I would do. Just take some pills and take a big leap. Down fifteen floors onto Park Avenue—splat," said Wendy, who had obviously thought this through.

"I mean, it's a drag for the doormen, but it's the only surefire way. I wouldn't know what to do with a pistol."

"Well, even if Sebastian Little had a sawed-off shotgun, he probably wouldn't know what to do with it. He's not so suave with his hands," said Wendy. And she would know, since she had hopped into bed with him years ago, when she was still married and more desirable.

"Pity his wife didn't stop her affair. Maybe she could save him," said Joan.

"He's a goner."

"He must be mortified. Why in the world would he still show his mug?"

"Probably wants to put on a good face, let everyone know he's still around," offered Wendy.

"I would just disappear."

"I know. He knows that everyone in this room knows that he couldn't even get killing himself right."

"Pathetic."

"Sad."

"There's Melanie Korn," said Joan. "What a piece of work. Didn't anyone tell her that hemlines fell twelve years ago?"

"She's so inappropriate. Did you hear that she's trying to get on the board of the Met? Nigel Goodyear was just disgusted at how brazen she was about it. She practically begged him to put her up."

Joan and Wendy watched Melanie virtually assault Patrick McMullan to get him to photograph her. After he obliged, Melanie tucked her arm under Arthur's and headed over to the Lawtons, a couple she loathed. But Cindy's brother was on the board of the Met.

"Cindy! Gus!"

"Melanie! Arthur!"

There was the rapid exchange of air kisses as only cheeks met.

"You look stunning, Cindy," said Melanie.

"Great to see you, Arthur. I saw you on the racquetball court the other day. Getting back in the action?" asked Gus, laughing on the inside at how pathetic Arthur had been. It was like watching Humpty Dumpty exercise. Hilarious.

"Yeah, yeah. I play every now and then. How's business?" asked Arthur, knowing full well that it was in the shitter. The trust-fund baby had seen his hedge fund tank last week, losing millions. And Daddy wasn't going to bail him out of this one. He'd end up in a pine box at the rate he was going.

"It's such fun to be here," said Cindy, looking around. She wanted an escape plan, pronto. If anyone saw her talking to Melanie Korn, her stock would crash.

Melanie also looked around, narrowing her eyes when she saw Joan and Wendy, the second-rate peanut gallery. Although she feared them, she was slowly gleaning through other parties that they actually had no credibility and in fact everyone thought of them as malicious gossips. Remembering to treat bees with honey, Melanie waved at them from a distance, and they beamed and waved back.

"So, Cindy, is your brother here?" asked Melanie. "I'd love to have a chat with him."

"No, Martin is in Gstaad."

"Hmm. Well, is he going to be back anytime soon?"

"I'm not sure."

As Melanie did her work, Arthur glanced uncomfortably around the room. He wanted to slice through the chitchat and get to the dinner, which was always more manageable for him. He just was inept at making small talk with people he saw week after week. Melanie was great at it, but he was the dead weight. A waiter with a tray of wild mushroom ragout on polenta beds walked by, and Arthur grabbed his arm.

"Let me try this," he said, popping it into his mouth. The waiter offered his tray to the ladies, who waved him away with disgust as if he were hocking dead roaches, but Gus took one. The waiter turned to go, but Arthur again grabbed his arm.

"Not so fast," said Arthur, snagging two more. "It takes forever for you guys to come around again."

Melanie's eyes widened. "Darling, don't gobble them all up! This is not Ethiopia."

"I'm starving."

Gus turned to talk to someone else, and Melanie returned to her conversation with Cindy. Arthur took the chance to look around the room. It was a real flash crowd. In one corner nested the real power players, in another the stiffs, and in another . . . Arthur stopped in his tracks. Olivia Weston was standing in the corner with some fat girl and some really skinny girl. She was wearing a gunmetal silk dress and her hair was in a chignon, very Grace Kelly. She casually held a glass of white wine and was chatting breezily with her friends. Arthur couldn't remove his eyes from her.

"Don't look now," warned Lila to Olivia. "But there's a fat bald guy staring at you."

Olivia slowly raised her eyes and effortlessly glanced across the room. "Oh, he's my neighbor."

Arthur met Olivia's glance, realized he was staring, and quickly reddened.

"Well, doesn't he know it's rude to stare?" asked Rosemary, loudly.

"Shh . . . he'll hear you," admonished Olivia.

"He can hardly hear me across the room," boomed Rosemary. "Anyway, Liv, as I was saying before we were so rudely interrupted"—she gave Lila a look—"Jack Bellows from the *Observer* was asking me the other day when we can expect your next book. I know you've been working away on it like hell, so I said, 'Jack, good things come to those who wait,' but in truth I really had no idea. When will we be getting the next novel?"

Olivia straightened her posture. "Soon. Soon. I'm just having a little . . ."

"Writer's block?" asked Lila.

"Writer's block, yes. But I also want to make sure it's perfect. When a writer goes wrong on her sophomore endeavor, it can totally ruin her whole career."

"That's for sure," concurred Lila. "Don't want a big fat flop on your hands."

"Then the pressure's on, Olivia!" thundered Rosemary. "We're all dying for it. But I know you'll come up with something brilliant."

"If you need any help, Liv, we'd be happy to read through a draft," offered Lila.

"Thanks," said Olivia.

Bill Cunningham from the *New York Times* approached and sheepishly raised his camera to take a picture. He never spoke, just smiled, but everyone knew who he was.

All three women put down their glasses, fluffed up their hair, turned ever so slightly to the side, and thrust out their pelvises. They had been schooled early on in the art of taking a party picture.

"Thanks," said Cunningham, walking away in the direction of Cordelia Vance, who had just arrived with Jerome de Stingol.

After posing for Bill, Jerome tugged at his walkee. "Well, darling, we have to get to the bar immediately! I'm parched, I'm sure you're parched, and we simply must get this party started," said Jerome, leading Cordelia barward.

Cordelia followed Jerome faithfully. She couldn't remember what charity this party was for—wasn't that terrible? So many of them.

"What is your pleasure, the usual?" asked Jerome, realizing that he'd gone home with the bartender after last year's costume ball. There was nothing better than Glorious Food cater-waiters. He could eat them on toast points hourly.

"You know what, Jerome? I think I'll go a little crazy tonight—why not? How about a Bombay Sapphire martini?" said Cordelia, surprising even herself. She'd just seen an advertisement for the beverage, and everyone seemed to be having such a delightful time as they sipped it.

"There's my girl, steppin' out!" he said, and ordered the drinks, giving the young bartender a secretive nod.

"So, dearie, just you and me. We'd better have fun tonight!" said Jerome.

"Let's!"

Most people made the mistake of underestimating Cordelia, but not Jerome. He was aware that she could be aloof and appear absentminded or even medicated to others, including her own husband, but he knew that underneath the elusive exterior was a very clever and alert woman who actually had a great sense of humor. Jerome walked many ladies, but Cordelia was his favorite. They shared a common bond and were true confidants. Although Jerome never revealed his darker, kinkier side to her, and Cordelia would never ask, there existed a love between them, and a genuine friendship.

Wendy and Joan watched the curious pair from across the room.

"Wonder where Morgan is. He hasn't been around lately," said Joan.

"Uh-oh. She's been walked by Jerome for the last five benefits. He'll have to resole his patent-leathers."

"He's up to no good."

"Dirty bird."

"Look at Olivia Weston. She looks gorgeous."

"Stunning *comme toujours* . . ."

"But she's kind of yawn pretty, in a way. We've seen it all before."

"You're so right," agreed Wendy. "I've seen it all before."

"Did you see that article in *Avenue*?"

"Of course."

Arthur had also resumed checking Olivia out, and when she offered up a small wave he dropped his drink.

"Arthur! I can't believe you're so clumsy!" said Melanie, embarrassed.

"Uh, sorry," he mumbled.

"Look, I just studied the seating plan," whispered Melanie to her husband. "And we're at a total junior varsity table. What do you think happened? You think they didn't get our check?"

"Do you think they did it on purpose?"

Melanie shot Arthur a look. "I'm not taking any chances."

Suddenly Arthur felt nervous. He didn't want Olivia to see him at a junior varsity table. He felt like a loser.

"Well, if we're being snubbed, then let's just get out of here. I'm tired of wearing this monkey suit. Why don't we head over to Three Guys on the way home, grab a burger?"

Melanie nixed it. "We just have to suck it up. Just laugh and smile a lot. Pretend you're having the best time."

"Okay." Arthur nodded. The best time.

"Also, Guff says that if you lean in and talk in a low tone, a whisper even, people think you're saying something really important."

"Melanie, you're serious that you want me to take my cues from our butler?"

"He may be a butler, sweetie, but he has been around these people longer than we have. I think we should trust him on this one."

Arthur was about to disagree until he saw Olivia lean in to her friend and say something softly. Maybe Melanie and Guffey were right.

"All right," said Arthur, twisting his tie uncomfortably. "I'll be right back."

"Where are you going?"

"The bathroom."

"I don't want to stand alone. I'll go with you."

"To the men's room?"

"The ladies' room, silly," said Melanie. "Wait for me after."

Cordelia, although determined to enjoy herself, was having a hard time feeling festive. She could imagine her exchange with Morgan when she got home: "How was the party?" he would ask. "Fine," she would respond. "How was the meeting?" "Fine." Then they would both return to silence and retire early. It was so predictable.

Cordelia couldn't understand why the parties weren't satisfying to her anymore. All of the events were starting to blend together: same people, same band, same food. What would it say in her obituary? "Attended loads of charity balls"? And she wasn't even sure where the money went. Africa? Opera? Diabetes? Republicans?

Jerome watched Cordelia's face and could see she was in pain.

"You know what, sweetie? Why don't we do something radical? Why don't we blow this joint and head over to some greasy diner and have a cheeseburger?"

Cordelia looked at him gratefully. "Let's go!"

Arthur watched Cordelia and Jerome leave with envy. If only his wife didn't give such a shit. But at least he and Olivia were in the same room, albeit a cavernous one.

Throughout the evening, Joan and Wendy could not stop conjecturing on what had caused Cordelia and Jerome's sudden departure. There was endless speculation. Olivia spent the evening listening attentively to her dinner partner and stressing about her novel. Only Melanie truly enjoyed herself, after switching her place card and seating herself next to the Halseys.

chapter 17

As Morgan got dressed the next morning, he caught sight of his tired face in the mirror. He was wan and old-looking; he remembered when he always felt dashing and handsome. He felt his entire world had been hit by a cyclone and his whole universe was whipped into an anguished frenzy that he had started but could not stop. The night before, his wife had tried to offer her solace after his irritating day of "meetings," and he had just blown her affection off. Poor thing. What had he become? After twenty-eight years of marriage, he had deceived Cordelia, lied to her, and sent her out into the night with some escort while he fucked his whining Mexican mistress. All this was not worth it—all the lies, the growing pit in his stomach, the emotional ulcer eating away at his deteriorated, bleeding conscience. He robotically put on his Hermès tie and kissed his wife goodbye, this time with a sincere "I love you" as he headed for the door. On the elevator ride down he knew he wanted his old life back. He had to put an end to this charade with Maria. He felt his world plummeting slowly, mirroring the paneled elevator's descent.

Downstairs, another solar system was about to be hit by catastrophe.

"Madam, the *Quest* has arrived," said Mr. Guffey, placing the glossy society magazine on Melanie's walnut desk. Melanie scrutinized the cover, which was a picture of Cass Weathers and a headline that read: FUNGAL WARRIOR: CASS WEATHERS AND HER BALL TO ERADICATE THE MISERY OF ATHLETE'S FOOT.

"Oh! I was on that committee. I know they took a picture of all of us. Do you think . . ." Melanie was too nervous to finish her sentence. Would this be the moment she lost her party picture virginity? Was this the issue in which she finally entered her own race to eradicate misery, the misery otherwise known as Diandra? She didn't even want to go there mentally, but Guffey was hovering.

"I believe this could be your moment, madam," said Mr. Guffey with assurance.

Melanie carefully flipped open the magazine and hesitantly turned the pages. "Oh, there's Pamela, and there's Joan and Wendy," she remarked, her eyes gliding over the pictures.

"I believe the cover story is usually featured in the middle, madam."

Melanie turned the page and froze. There was the picture of the committee: Cass, Meredith Beringer, Mimi Halsey, Regina Bates, and . . . Melanie's arm!

"Oh my god," said Melanie.

Mr. Guffey leaned in. "You've been cropped out."

"I know."

"That's definitely you. I recognize the gold lamé sleeve."

"I know." Melanie didn't know what to say. "Is this really bad?"

"I will be frank with you, madam. Yes."

"Oh my gosh—do you think I should have worn the Dior? Was it because I didn't wear the Dior?"

"I doubt that very much."

"Perhaps they didn't have enough space?"

"That picture is almost a full page. They could have sized it to include you."

Melanie felt nauseous. "Okay, so um, tell me again—why is this so terrible?"

"If I may be frank—"

"Please!"

"Well, madam, in the society that you swirl in, having your photo featured in this sort of publication makes you validated; it confirms your existence. It's the way of the world, the fifteen minutes you get. It used to be that you had to be special to be famous, and now you have to be famous to be special."

"And, like, every who's who is in them, right?" said Melanie, knowing the answer. Every who's who, meaning Diandra. She had to get in if Diandra got in! She didn't want anyone to think Arthur had married down. Then someone would tip him off and he would get his wheels turning, and some sexy younger woman would come along and snatch him up. Melanie shuddered to think. There were so many reasons she wanted—needed—to be photographed.

"Correct. You see," Mr. Guffey said, warming to his topic, "by omitting you from these pages, they are erasing you from society. Burying you alive."

Melanie gulped. She was dead to society. As soon as Mr. Guffey left the room, she burst into tears. This whole thing sucked! Why the heck did she have to worry about this crap? On the one hand, she wanted to be everything for Arthur and make him proud, but, on the other hand, she just wanted desperately not to care. But there was no possible way to escape.

Juanita, who barely spoke English, came in to dust and found herself consoling Melanie. She could not fully understand what Mrs. Korn was talking about, but she clearly looked upset. Something about a magazine.

"No worry, Mrs. Melanie. No worry."

Melanie inhaled and exhaled mini-Lamaze breaths. Juanita was right. She shouldn't worry about this. Thank god she had someone as level-headed and astute as Juanita around to talk some sense into her.

"Well, next case. What can I do? I've done everything I think I can. They'll see . . ." she paused, pensive.

"They see," agreed Juanita.

"Thanks for listening, Juanita," Melanie said, gathering herself together to get dressed for the day and finish the rest of the mail. Hopefully Mr. Hunt would soon put and end to this misery and get Melanie her money's worth. And next week she was meeting with the new decorators to turn her house around. Things were about to start happening.

chapter 18

Cordelia had an extremely busy day planned for herself, so she asked her driver to meet her one hour earlier than usual to "get the ball rolling." She was "doing Madison," that is, popping into all of the most chi-chi boutiques and having "a look-see" at their fall collections. Unlike last autumn, when chrome and slate motifs were favored, burgundies and cobalts were the preference du jour; therefore, Cordelia had to rethink everything in her closet. Unfortunately Jerome was unavailable to shop, so she had to make do on her own, which always made her a little anxious and indecisive.

"Let's see. Shall I go with the black or white?" she asked the saleslady at Manolo Blahnik, who told her that silver was also in this season. Cordelia asked to see the look-book, and after flipping through decided to take all three colors. Armani was next, then Valentino, Carolina Herrera, and even Chloé—just out of curiosity. (Jerome had made her promise she wouldn't do Chanel without him.) There were so many stores to see, and most of them close together, so Cordelia just kept dipping in and out of them. Her driver followed her in the car so that she could throw her purchases in on the leather seats whenever she felt like it.

"Mommy, that's pretty!"

"That *is* pretty. You know what? That would be perfect for Aunt Tina's wedding."

"Yes! Yes!"

Cordelia turned around to see an elegantly dressed, very attractive woman in her thirties with her flaxen-haired six-year-old daughter, who was clad in a pressed green Chapin uniform. They were looking at a cotton candy and butterscotch smock dress on a mannequin in the window of Bonpoint.

"Shall we go inside and try it on?"

"Yes!"

Cordelia stared as they went into the store, the girl skipping with delight and the woman smiling with maternal pride. Something about the scene made Cordelia freeze. She glanced back at the window. She watched the mother and daughter talk to the saleswoman and point to the outfit, and she watched the saleswoman nod and lead them to a rack of clothing. She was riveted. It was like watching a couple fight, or a car wreck, or a really good episode of *Frasier*. She simply couldn't turn away. She had always wanted a daughter.

She got into her car. "Julio, we're going to Tiffany's."

"Yes, Mrs. Vance."

Tiffany's was not a venue that Cordelia or her friends frequented, unless they were purchasing something off of someone's bridal registry or buying lesser acquaintances holiday gifts. (They had the most delightful trinkets such as silver key chains, money clips, and Elsa Peretti earrings that were perfectly appropriate for household staff and the secretaries at Morgan's firm.) Cordelia was aware that only amateurs would buy jewelry there (even the engagement rings were meant for the out-of-towners who didn't know enough to buy estate or go to a diamond dealer to have the perfect bauble made). But there was something that she adored about the place, so she often stopped by.

Cordelia's driver opened the door for her on Fifth Avenue and Fifty-seventh Street and watched as she walked to the revolving doors. She glanced back at him as she made her way in and watched him pick up the car phone. *He really shouldn't be making social calls on my dime,* she thought.

"Hello, Mrs. Vance. How are you today?" greeted a salesgirl.

"Fine, thank you, Hilary."

"What can we do for you today?"

"I'm just looking around. Perhaps something for my niece, or my housekeeper. We'll see."

"We have a lovely new collection of diamond earrings in," said Hilary, leading her over to a counter. "Simply gorgeous."

"Let's have a look-see," said Cordelia.

While Cordelia browsed the $100,000 and up counter, she did not notice, nor would she have, that Maria had entered the store. Maria pushed through a group of Arkansas tourists and elbowed her way past some Osakans to get to the counter that displayed sterling silver rattles. She tapped her finger along the glass, smudging the recently Windexed vitrine until she found a rattle that would be perfect for her little Schuyler.

"Excuse me!" she yelled at a saleslady across the counter. "Excuse me!" she continued impatiently.

"I'll be right with you, ma'am. I'm just helping another customer."

Maria plopped her logo-covered Louis Vuitton handbag down on the case with a bang, and the saleslady looked over.

"Please be careful, ma'am," chided the saleslady.

Maria sighed deeply and loudly, and whipped her wrist out of the folds of her enormous fox-fur coat. She looked at her watch and sighed again. She glanced around impatiently. This was a fucking joke. They were treating her like scum. Did they not know who she was? She was more bling-bling than any haggy bitch in the joint! If only her brother was here—he'd demand some attention. She watched the salesladies effusively tending to other customers. What was so much better about them? Look at that old weather-beaten blonde in the corner, whom three salesladies were obsequiously throwing themselves at. You couldn't even tell what designer made her clothes. Maria moved closer to see what the big deal was.

"And this one, Mrs. Vance, is my personal favorite . . ."

Mrs. Vance? No. Fucking. Way. Was this Morgan's ball and chain? She was as old as Mrs. Roper.

Maria watched as Cordelia examined the diamond and sapphire earrings. Another customer called to the salesgirls, who dispersed, leaving Cordelia alone with the jewels. Maria was about to approach when she saw something that made her stop dead. Cordelia discreetly took one of the rings and put it in her pocket. No way! *So this is what she's all about,* thought Maria.

"Hilary, I'm just going to leave these. I don't want anything today," said Cordelia, raising her voice so the salesgirl would hear her.

"Okay, Mrs. Vance," said the salesgirl, returning and sweeping the jewels onto a velvet mat without even looking at them.

"Thank you."

Cordelia lingered a minute, casually staring at another case as if nothing were amiss. Maria decided to make her move.

"Cordelia Vance?"

"Yes?"

"It's me, Maria Garcia. I used to work at Brown Brothers. We met at the Christmas party."

"Oh, of course. It's nice to see you again," responded Cordelia, who had no recollection of this woman whatsoever.

"It's very nice to see you. How's your husband?"

"He's fine, thank you. Working hard as ever. How have you been? You left to . . . ?"

"I had a baby."

"A baby! Terrific! Congratulations. Boy or girl?"

"A girl. Schuyler."

"Beautiful name. Well, you are very lucky."

"Yes, I am."

"I always wanted a little girl."

"You did?"

"Well, yes. Of course I love my boys, but they grow up and find their own families. There's nothing like a little girl. They never leave you."

"Yes, you're right."

"I really must be running, so please take care."

"Thank you. Send my best to Mr. Vance."

"I shall."

"Goodbye."

Maria smiled. She turned back to the salesladies. "Excuse me, can I get some help here?"

The salesgirl gave her a withering look. "I'll be right with you."

Maria banged her fist on the glass. "I said I want service!"

"I'm assisting someone else. I will help you when it is your turn."

"What, I don't look rich to you? You don't think I could get you a sales commission? Well, I saw *Pretty Woman*—did you? And that is me! Without the hooker part. So you better get your saleslady ass over here and do a little song and dance for me now!"

"I will assist you when I am available."

"By the time you're available, I'll be at Cartier spending thousands," said Maria, turning on her heel and storming out of the store, pushing the doors with a heavy hand and boiling heart.

———

Morgan was deeply immersed in his spreadsheets when his secretary knocked gently on his door and entered.

"Mr. Vance, there's someone here to see you," she said nervously.

"I said I cannot be disturbed now, Lizzie," said Morgan.

"I think it's that maid who used to work here," whispered Lizzie. "She's very insistent. I tried . . ."

Morgan turned beet red. "That's all right, Lizzie. You can send her in."

Lizzie tried to suppress her surprise, but her face betrayed her.

"It's okay—it's a mentoring program I'm involved in," explained Morgan clumsily.

"I see," she said, leaving the room.

Moments later Maria burst into the room.

"I will not be kept fucking waiting! Does your wife have to be kept waiting?" said Maria, flinging her fur coat (that cost Morgan twenty grand) on his charcoal gray armchair. She was wearing an inappropriately tight black spandex top that clung to her fat rolls, and black leather pants.

"Maria, shut up and sit down."

Morgan walked over to the door and made sure it was firmly closed.

"Shut up? Why? Why you want to keep me quiet? You show me some respect! I have your baby sitting at home. It took me a day to squeeze out your fucking child, so you better show me some fucking gratefulness."

"Maria, listen. I'm tired of your antics. What is it now?" asked Morgan with a mixture of fear and exasperation.

"I was treated like shit in Tiffany's."

"*That* is why you came storming into my office? Have you no discretion?"

"Your wife was there," said Maria, an evil smirk on her face.

Morgan panicked. "You talked to Cordelia?"

Maria sat down on the chair on top of her coat and put her feet up on Morgan's desk. She folded her hands behind her head. "They were kissing her old blond ass, and you know what she did? She STOLE

from them! She's a Winona Ryder! She shoplifts! I may have no education, but I know a THIEF!"

"What are you talking about? You're crazy—"

"I saw with my own eyes! You're wife is a fuckin' jewel thief! Like in
the movies!"

"What did you say to my wife? How dare you . . ." said Morgan, rage
brewing up inside him like lava. He didn't know if he was angrier at
Maria or himself for getting in this position.

"You don't care? You don't care if your wife is a kryptomaniac? I do!
They treat her like the queen, and she is no queen!" Maria sat up and
exploded. "I'm calling Tiffany's and telling!"

"They already know," sighed Morgan, defeated.

"What?"

"I have an arrangement with them. They just send me the bill. It's
taken care of monthly, and it's none of your concern."

"WHAT? She's a fucking robber and they treat her with more respect than they treat me? Just 'cause she's a fucking Vance? I want my
last name to be Vance!"

"Maria, you must tell me what you said to Cordelia," said Morgan
evenly.

"Why should I?"

"Because I said to."

Maria and Morgan stared at each other. Morgan was fuming. Maria
had never seen him like this. Finally she raised her eyebrows and threw
up her arms. "I told her we worked together."

"You stay away from my wife!" his voice rose so much that he nervously calmed himself down so as not give Lizzie the ultimate water
cooler gossip through the door.

"It's time you make an honest woman of me!"

"This is ridiculous!" he said, almost raising his voice again but fun-
neling his ire instead to a harsh whisper. "I give you everything you
need . . ."

Maria stood up and put on her coat with the same dramatic flail she
had seen on so many soap operas. "You leave Cordelia real soon or I'm
going to make your life a living hell," she said with sheer threatening

confidence. With that, she smiled ruefully and stormed out of the office, slamming the door behind her.

chapter 19

"I'm picturing, in this space . . . medieval art; you could do so much with the richness of an ecclesiastical hall here, and perhaps painted clay tiles around this exquisite fireplace."

Vincent Delvaux, one of the city's top decorators, walked through the Korns' house, offering suggestions and mock-ups crafted by his studio. He was a screaming queen but was married with four children and lived in an extraordinary penthouse on Fifth, which was featured in every shelter mag on planet Earth. Normally he would never deign to work with the likes of Melanie Korn, but when he heard the magic words "sky's the limit" and "carte blanche," he was sprinting into his town car like a jockey-spurred Kentucky Derby racer.

"I could see some wood-carved mahogany paneling along the ceiling. And great embroidered wool and silk wall hangings and tapestries, or maybe some trompe l'oeil painted plaster to simulate crests and stonework up here . . ."

He continued with flourishing hand gestures and talk of gothic hall chairs, but Melanie's eyelids were already at half mast. *Boooring*. She wanted to have good taste and a world-class, knock-'em-dead apartment; she just didn't want to get her hands dirty with . . . choosing stuff. Mr. Guffey followed them around with a clipboard, taking notes, and once she shot him the "Get me out of here" look, he pulled out the proverbial hook.

"Madam, I beg your pardon, but your lunch date has arrived."

"Yes, yes. Thank you so much for stopping by," said Melanie, practically catapulting Delvaux out into the elevator vestibule. After slamming the door shut, she looked at Guffey wearily. Three down, two to go.

"Next."

Lilly Saint-Pierre was fluttering around the house like a decapitated bird, chirping about colors and ornate fabrics. Her skeletal frame was swathed in a fitted suit, and her pin-sized calves—restricted by her narrow pencil skirt—moved in tiny steps. As she cluck-cluck-clucked around the marble floor in her pointy shoes, Melanie knew already that this would not be a match.

"I see a single fabric here for the walls, curtains, and bedding. I love a richly festooned brocatelle. And how about a parquet inlaid floor in the living room? I love this Queen Anne, early-eighteenth-century Palladian-style cabinet, but I'd lose the rest of this and work around this piece. Maybe infuse the quarters with this kind of infinite detail— maybe some embossed leather on the walls and then maybe some Georgian carved balusters to amp up this staircase a bit . . ."

Gag. Melanie wanted to take a frying pan and bash this woman's minute face in like on a Tom and Jerry cartoon.

"And this room would be heavenly if we juxtaposed traditional elements with modern or did French and Danish! No, Swedish and English," Lilly said quickly. She spoke so fast that words just tumbled out of her mouth as rapidly as a toddler dumps over a box of building blocks. Her nervous energy was ultimately unbearable to both Melanie and Mr. Guffey, and she was eventually shown the door.

The final suitor was Jerome de Stingol, also in the AD 100, but really more because of his closer-than-close relationship to the editrix in chief than for his prowess in the decorating department. Those who had worked with de Stingol would really consider him as more of a "guide" or a "muse" who was wonderfully adept at pointing out deficiencies but not as skilled in implementing, well, anything. (His detractors, usually husbands who glanced at his bills and recoiled with horror, referred to him as "the great pillow fluffer.")

Jerome had initially been aghast when Mrs. Korn had telephoned him and explained her needs. At first he thought Joan Coddington was having a goof on him, but when he realized that it was indeed the former flight attendant herself, he was speechless. And when it sunk in, it made sense: here was a woman attempting to fit into society, and he was a man who could make it happen. Working with him would buy her a slice of the crème de la crème's teacake. As she chatted away about her ignorance of decorating, her urgency to get it all done as quickly as possible—and any cost—capped off by her almost embarrassed defensiveness about the current state of her apartment, he smiled along. He heard the ka-ching of a cash register and even felt a small burst of pity somewhere in the lower part of his body. But when she suggested they meet to discuss if they were "a match," he became irate. He preferred to be begged for a job, as many of society's followers did, shoving their checkbooks down his throat as a means to get in with him and his gaggle of glamorous walkees.

And so he was prepared to refuse the stewardess. He had his red leather Smythson address book ready in his sweaty left hand and with one swift move was primed to call all his friends and have a laugh at Melanie's expense. But when he glanced at his checkbook and thought about his recent acquisition of a Chippendale dresser at Sotheby's and the fact that he had not really worked in months, he realized he had no choice. So when he set off for the Korns' on a rainy afternoon, he was predisposed to hate. More than the other decorators, he was bitter about having to come in and pimp himself to a potential client.

When he entered the apartment, Jerome sneered at the sheer gut-churning horror of it all—such a tacky jumble of nontastes; colonial-style statuary built-ins fused with Renaissance with a dash of flowery Victorian pieces and neo-Jacobean elements. Vomit. Everything was schizo and competing and bursting at the seams. It was too much to take—he felt as if he were in a foliage-painted, mother-of-pearl-covered gingerbread house from hell. As Melanie greeted him, he could barely speak.

"God! It's worse than I thought . . ." sputtered Jerome, walking with the crazy instability one gets when disembarking the Tilt-A-Whirl.

"Well, I wouldn't go that far," said Melanie, surprised by his audacity. After all, he didn't have the job *yet*.

"Lord have mercy on my soul, the ceilings! Disaster. Sinful. It's like what happened to Yasmine Guest's apartment."

Jerome shot the butler a look after he said this, certain that he would be the only one who understood. Disgust flickered in Mr. Guffey's eyes, and they both muttered under their breath as if saying a solemn prayer.

"So," said Melanie, offering him a seat. "We looked at your sketches. Very interesting."

"We?" inquired Jerome.

"Well, me. I also asked Mr. Guffey, my butler . . ."

Jerome looked again at the butler. "Oh, yes, I think I recognize you. You were with Diandra," said Jerome.

"Yes," said Mr. Guffey.

"Wonderful woman. How is she?"

"I'm not quite sure, sir."

"Pity she moved. Wonderful, wonderful, wonderful woman. Such class," added Jerome with a sneer.

Melanie squirmed uncomfortably. "Anyway, yes—so your sketches were very interesting."

"Glad you liked them," forced out Jerome with his best saccharine smile.

"So, tell me what you have in mind for my apartment."

"Oh, you know," said Jerome, waving his arms around as if that explained it.

"I'm not sure I do," said Melanie.

Was she really going to make him explain things? "Well, I normally work in *conjunction* with other decorators. I like to oversee things."

"So what would you oversee here?"

"Whatever do you mean?"

"I mean, what is your vision for my apartment?"

Jerome stared at her coldly. Was she serious? He was about to spit on her imitation Oriental carpet and walk away when he thought about December and how he was just itching to rent Princess Margaret's former home on Mustique again. So with great effort and pain, he decided to stash away his pride and make an effort.

"I'm a fan of empire style—I did the Vances' place upstairs. Here are some photos," he said, slapping some pictures in her face. If she wanted it, she could have it. "And I think some fresh plasterwork, maybe some neoclassical columns, some French gilded consoles here, fresh colors could really open the place up." He looked at her and could see she was expecting more. What, did this slut want him to prostitute himself to her? He sucked in his cheeks and took a deep breath. He pictured the crystal blue waters on Macaroni Beach and continued.

"You see, Mrs. Korn, this apartment is crying out to breathe. It is charged with a crowded energy and it is begging, just *whimpering* to exhale. I will be the respirator. I will free it, let your home simmer in honeysuckles and moiré—use these full-height windows! Don't smother them! Let's open it all up!"

He rose and marched out of the public rooms through to the hallway, looking in the bedrooms as Guffey and Melanie followed. "See, your private quarters have as much formality as the public rooms. It's sickening, really. Did you have some queen from Miami Beach decorate? It's like they're trying too hard, with these grand pieces around the perimeter—if you like the dark choking colors of the main rooms, fine, but these should be relaxed and comfortable with a softer, perhaps paler palette. I mean, really—someone didn't know his decorating ABCs."

He promenaded into one room as Melanie and Guffey followed, and moved his arms around dramatically like a choreographer instructing the dancers with his vision.

What a fool, thought Guffey. *So condescending*.

"I want it lighter, more elegant. A portico with a fanlight, a robust William Morris wallpaper here, like Cordelia's. I did Capucine de Mendide's drawing room all in this light arts and crafts hand-pressed paper, which is more to my taste than the excesses of this more rococo era . . ."

Excesses? Was he insulting her apartment? Melanie first felt embarrassed, then angry. Who was he? Why was he so great?

Finally, Jerome must have realized that he went a little too far in the criticism department and it was time to become an obsequious sycophant. "Melanie, darling," he began in a whisper. He was trying to convey his most "we are girlfriends, you and I" mode. "We will do marvelous things! People will talk! You will be a hit!"

His words echoed in the hallowed halls, but he was not thespian enough to fool Melanie or, most of all, Mr. Guffey. It was clear to Guffey that Jerome had done his best but that he was, in fact, a hack. Plus, his seeming politesse was spiked with the most bilious undertones, and Guffey even knew what his somewhat naive employer did not: that the rivers of vitriol boiling within this snobbish man would not be contained should Melanie turn him down for the job.

"Let's do it together, Melanie. Let's make them all forget Diandra," said Jerome. He put his small, hairy hand on Melanie's wrist, as if to pat her sympathetically. He shook his head in commiseration and looked down at the floor with simulated drama.

Time was up for Melanie. She slowly raised a recently waxed brow, and Guffey got the barbed facial memo.

"Thank you, sir, for coming. Your portfolio was quite impressive," Mr. Guffey interrupted, and within moments Jerome was waiting by a lit elevator down button Guffey had pressed before shutting the large door in his face. It was as if they had a giant electric cattle prod that they used to expel him at top speed, and before he knew it Jerome had descended to the lobby. *They must be so sure I'm the one*, he thought. *That peroxide-dipped floozy wouldn't know good taste if it hijacked her Gulfstream.* He reflected on how he would face the challenge of having to see her at parties and admit she was a client. No matter, her husband's casket biz could unleash him to do whatever his heart desired, and he could just whiff the sweet smell of an *HG* cover in the wings after he had his way with their palatial spread and milked them for every red cent.

Back inside the Korns' apartment, a pooped Melanie kicked off her Louboutin mules, flopped on the overstuffed Regency sofa, and looked up at Guffey, who was carrying the pile of sketches and curriculum vitae.

"Ugh, I'm absolutely exhausted. I feel exhumed from a grave after all that! I need a nap. Or a massage. It's so much work trying to find decorators."

"Then rest, madam. But you must make a selection if you want to have the place refurbished so quickly."

"Who did you like best?"

"It's really not important what I think, madam. It is, after all, your home." Guffey glanced at the clipboard. "So, I should tell Mr. Harrington?"

Melanie watched Guffey closely.

"Tell Mr. Harrington . . ." she began, and tilted her head, squinted her eyes, and waited for Guffey to prompt her.

"No," said Guffey.

"No. Yes. Tell him no."

"And Ms. Saint-Pierre?"

Again, Melanie's head bobbed in a questioning circle. "Tell her . . ."

"No," said Mr. Guffey.

"Yes, tell her no."

"And Mr. de Stingol?"

"What do you think?"

"I think he's a no. A definitive no."

"I couldn't agree more. Geez, Guff. It's a total relief that we're on the same page! They were all kind of snobby and pretentious, don't you think?"

"I think they were ill fitted for the work at hand."

"But who in the world shall I get?"

Mr. Guffey solemnly took the sheet of notes off his clipboard and held it up before his employer. Then he smashed it up into a ball and tossed it to the rubbish.

"I think if you want the best, you should hire the *best*."

"Well, I want to, naturally. These were all listed as the top—"

"The *real* best don't sully their hands by pandering to magazines for edification. They simply don't need the business; they are constantly turning clients away. Might I suggest Diandra's two favorites?"

chapter 20

After repeated threatening phone calls, a bombardment of pages, and reams of nasty e-mails, Morgan had no excuse but to go visit Maria and the baby at their apartment. He had been avoiding it since his last encounter with her, but she was too dangerous to ignore. So after sending Cordelia off to the opera with Jerome, Morgan headed over to Maria's building on Central Park South. It had been the perfect location to sequester a mistress. Although the buildings held a commanding view of the city—some might even say they possessed a better panorama than most of the buildings on Fifth—Morgan knew no one that lived there, so he never risked running into an acquaintance. It was as if the crème de la crème of the city had decided to relinquish Fifty-ninth Street to the tourists at the hotels and out-of-towners who chose to have pieds-à-terre there. And although it had first proved sufficient for Maria, in her cunning she had gleaned that it still wasn't good enough, so she was already making noise about an impending move. Well, he knew just how to fix that.

Maria greeted Morgan in a red silk bathrobe, her hair knotted in a chignon, the diamond bracelets Morgan had given her gleaming on her wrist. She acted as if nothing was wrong, welcoming him with a "Darling!" as he walked in the foyer, taking his briefcase from him and slipping off his coat. The apartment was lit with hundreds of scented candles, a sickly lavender smell that made Morgan instantly nauseous. Maria had put a violet tablecloth on the small dining table and adorned it with a bouquet of fresh red roses and fancy china that she had made Morgan purchase for her through Tiffany's Web site. A wine stand with a bottle of champagne chilling on ice stood next to the Crate & Barrel bar stand, where Maria fixed Morgan his favorite drink of scotch and soda. She handed it to him dramatically before plopping on the sofa next to him with just enough effort for the slit in her bathrobe to fall open up to her thighs, revealing her black lace teddy and garter belt. It was all very cheesily romantic, the fact being that Maria had watched way too many soap operas and read way too many romance novels and thought that now she was finally living in one.

Morgan reluctantly played along for the evening, allowing Maria to massage his feet, inquire about his day, reprimand him for working too hard, and lick his earlobes. Maria had ordered his favorite meal from Le Cirque—filet of beef with cognac sauce and a side of garlic-infused potatoes—and played footsie with him under the table while he ate. She waited on him as if he were king of the castle, and he couldn't help enjoying himself. This was what it used to be like for them. Those were the days.

"This champagne is the best! You happy now? This is the way it should be—you and me having romantic dinners," said Maria, pouring herself another glass of red wine. (The champagne was long gone.)

"It was very nice, Maria."

Morgan was reclining on the leather sofa with a drink in his hand, his feet lazily propped on the white velvet ottoman. He remembered last winter when he couldn't wait to get there, rip off Maria's clothes, and hop under the silk sheets. It had made him feel young again. Now he couldn't wait to leave.

"See, if you come around more, this is what it's like. But you no come around, you no take the time, you ignore me and the baby, you think you can forget us!"

Maria's shrill, demanding voice jolted Morgan back to the harsh reality of the mess he'd gotten into. He looked around the low-ceilinged apartment with its tacky Burlington Leather Factory furniture and was revolted. He sat up. It was time for Morgan to enact the plan that he had brilliantly worked out over the past few days.

"This is nice, Maria, but there are going to be some changes."

"You're damn right!" said Maria, rising and walking over to the windows. It was a perfectly clear night, and the lights of the city twinkled around them. "I was thinking, there's no need for you to be married to Cordelia anymore. She's old and ugly. Your sons are away, and they don't care. So you get a divorce, and if she say no, you say, I know you a robber, I have witnesses, and you get a divorce and all the money."

"Maria, that's not going to happen," said Morgan, buttoning up his shirt and putting his tie back on.

"It's okay, I can be the witness. No problem."

"No, I mean, I'm never going to leave Cordelia. It's not an option."

Maria spun around, shocked. "WHAT?"

"But listen, I do have a solution. I've put a deposit down on a house in West Palm Beach, and I'm moving you and Schuyler down . . ."

"What the fuck are you talking about?" said Maria, approaching him with a crazy look in her eyes.

"Maria . . ."

"You think you can just ship us off?"

"Listen . . ."

"You think I some kind of Hispanic whore?" Maria came so close to Morgan that he could feel her breath on his face.

"Maria, I'm not shipping you off. I am giving you a beautiful home, and you will be a lot better off than you were a year ago."

"Does it have a pool?"

"A pool?" asked Morgan. "No, it doesn't . . ."

"You think you ship me and the baby to a house that doesn't even have a pool?" Maria bellowed and stomped over to the table. She furiously poured some more wine into her gold-dipped Versace crystal glass—spilling it slightly in her rage—and took a large gulp.

Morgan thought quickly. "Well, if it had a pool, would you go?"

"NO! I not going nowhere!"

"But what about the pool? I can find a house with a pool."

"I don't want no pool. I just want to know if you even thought of me in a house with no pool."

"Maria, it doesn't have to be this house. We'll find something you like and you can move down there."

Maria folded her arms and scowled. "NO WAY. I am never going nowhere. You can't make me. You can never get rid of me."

"Maria . . ." sighed Morgan with desperation. He was distraught and had no idea what to do. "I can make you go. I can cut you off."

Maria stared at him and, as if matching his threat, stormed over to the telephone and picked up the receiver.

"I can call Cordelia! She always wanted a daughter—and I have one and it is yours! I bet she'd like to know."

Morgan called her bluff. "You wouldn't dare."

"Wouldn't I?" Maria stared at him with venom, then started dialing. "Seven, two, two . . ."

Morgan marched over and whipped the phone out of her hand, slamming it down on the receiver.

"Enough!"

"Maybe now enough, but you know that I mean business. I'm a business lady and you're a business man, so we have to play business."

"What do you want?"

"I want you to get rid of Cordelia."

"Maria . . ."

"And no more talk about Florida. This discussion is *finito!*" Maria turned and fled from the room, slamming her bedroom door behind her. Morgan left as Schuyler started to wail.

chapter 21

Mr. Guffey was right. Jerome de Stingol had not taken his refusal from Melanie Korn well at all. In fact, he was blood-boilingly livid. He oscillated between utter shock at the fact that this trollop had spurned him and rage that he had been forced to dazzle her as if he were a peacock, and had been rebuffed. He went from mortified to offended to seething fiery rage. And as he flipped through his Island Getaway photo album, he promised to seek retribution.

Unfortunately for Melanie, he had only to make subtle inquiries to discover that the list of Mrs. Korn's spurned acquaintances and now sworn enemies was lengthy and growing. There were those who were outraged that the Korns had bought only two tickets and not taken a full table at their charity events. If they had so much money, why weren't they spending it all the time? They certainly had no problem slapping down the plastic for her cheesy sequined Versace garments. There were others who were disgusted by the way the Korns flashed their money around as a means to open doors, trying to get into the best clubs and the best parties and on the best boards. They seemed in a rush, unwilling to stoically pay their dues, and acted as if their money entitled them. And still others—primarily the older set who really didn't care about charities or boards anymore—bristled at Arthur's uncouth manner and banal work and Melanie's uncanny ability to consistently put her foot in her mouth by spewing out the most offensive remarks. The final lot concentrated on the Korns' petty indiscretions: Melanie's shorts were too short when she was the Beringers' guest at the country club; Arthur told Nigel Goodyear that he could see him spending eternity in a steel coffin; and so on.

But the gold medal in the Melanie backlash campaign would have to be awarded to Joan Coddington and Wendy Marshall, who were both still furious to have been denied the apartment tour. And when Jerome found out that the two society gossips were on exactly the same page as he, he arranged frequent late lunches to dissect and disparage Mrs. Korn.

"There was simply no way I could do the apartment," insisted Jerome one afternoon at Le Bilboquet. Joan and Wendy had made him tell the story to them for the seventh time.

"How could you? It would be as much work as building a pyramid," agreed Joan.

"Only probably would take you longer. And they didn't even have machinery back then," said Wendy.

"True. It would be easier to decorate bin Laden's cave than that disaster zone," snipped Jerome.

"And she wouldn't take no for an answer?" asked Joan, knowing the answer.

Jerome stirred the froth in his cappuccino and shook his head with feigned sadness. "I mean, I suppose I pity her. If she saw how pathetic she was—groveling, begging, tears in her eyes, as if she were a mother watching her Tibetan son go before the Chinese firing squad. However . . ."

"And how much did she offer you?" asked Joan.

"Well," said Jerome, leaning in. "She opened the safe and there must have been about . . . five hundred thousand dollars there in cash. And that was just for starters. You know, the off-the-record payment."

Joan and Wendy looked at each other. Last week Jerome had said two hundred thousand dollars. The week before had been one hundred.

"They must be up to sketchy stuff if they have that much cash lying around," said Wendy.

"I told you—someone from England called me and said something about horse whisperers, prostitution, and guns."

"It's sickening!" said Joan, reeling.

"I bet it's guns," said Wendy with confidence. "I mean, how much can you make from a coffin? I bet he stashes the guns in the coffins and ships them around the country as if he is transporting dead bodies."

"It has to be."

"Of course."

They sat back and thought about the Korns. They all were semi-aware that fiction was overtaking fact in their descriptions of Arthur and Melanie but were so hell-bent in their hatred that the little white lies seeping in became almost plausible.

"At least with Diandra, Arthur was kept in check," said Joan.

"Now there was a woman with class," said Jerome.

"She was smart. She got out."

"Sandra, darling!" said Jerome suddenly, raising his voice to signal Sandra Goodyear, who had just entered the restaurant. Sandra waved and made her way over. She kissed her friends one by one and then sighed dramatically.

"Having a late lunch after a shop, dear? Please, join us," said Jerome, motioning to the waiter for another chair.

"Oh, believe me, I'd love to. But I'm meeting someone," sighed Sandra again, deeply this time and with furrowed brow.

"Pity! Perhaps you both can join?"

"Well, I'm afraid not. I'm meeting Melanie Korn," she said with the merest hint of an eye roll. "We're chairing the Mount Sinai benefit."

"Oh, dear," said Jerome.

"I know, and it's the worst possible day to meet ever. My art curator is phone-bidding on something at auction in Tokyo tonight, and I am on pins and needles! Not to mention that it's fashion week and Oscar will be beside himself if I don't show."

A lightbulb went off in Jerome's head. Why not start revenge for his rejection now?

"Well, the reason I said 'oh, dear,' my dear, is because we just saw Melanie Korn. She in fact popped in and we heard her telling the maître d' to express her deepest regrets to her dining companion—which must be you, darling—because something had suddenly come up and she was unable to make it."

Joan and Wendy's eyes widened. They couldn't believe Jerome's audacity! What balls of steel! What hilariously cruel imagination! Both made a mental note never to get on his bad side.

"Really?" asked Sandra.

"Yes, so sorry, lovey. How perfectly evil that she didn't ring you. In this day of cell phones."

"Well, I don't actually have one. Nigel keeps asking me to get one, but, I don't know, I think it's so rude to chatter away all over the place."

"Right you are."

"Well that actually relieves me. I really should get to Oscar's show.

The traffic is probably miserable right now. Kisses to all," said Sandra. She dashed out of the restaurant.

"You're terrible!" said Joan with a laugh.

"What if she finds out?" asked Wendy, horrified.

"So what? I'll blame it all on Melanie. Deny, deny, deny. You'll vouch for me."

Joan and Wendy tittered with nervous laughter. It was funny, but had Jerome gone too far?

"Now follow my lead, ladies, when the flight attendant makes her appearance."

"It's *your* show," said Joan. She wanted to make sure she got that on the record. Deny, deny, deny.

About five minutes later, Melanie entered the restaurant and scanned the room. Jerome looked up and waved at her, as did Joan and Wendy, but it was more of a "oh, hello" wave rather than a "hello, come over and say hello" wave. Jerome bent his head down and led his dining companions in what appeared to be a very secretive and hushed conversation. In reality he was merely talking about how the Powells' shih tzus had destroyed the fringe on their velvet fauteuil, but to Melanie it appeared as if they were developing an elaborate plan to invade Cuba.

Melanie took off her coat, handed it to the girl, and was led to a table at the window. She looked at her watch, ordered a Perrier, and waited for Sandra. It was just as well that she didn't have to go over and say hi to Jerome and those gossips. She had been avoiding Jerome at all costs since she had not offered him the decorating job. It was a stressful decision, but his rudeness had made it easier. It wasn't very polite of him to praise Diandra the way he did. He should at least try to attempt to be cordial. And the fact of the matter was that he was completely untrustworthy and dangerous. The acid tongue that was attached to that toad of a man was legendary, and she was sure to somehow offend him and then be subjected to his rage. She had been so nervous to reject him that she had made Mr. Guffey call him. Mr. Guffey said that he had used a few choice words and made a sound as if he was throwing the phone against the wall. Better to steer clear.

Minutes flicked by. Melanie looked around. Jerome kept brazenly glancing over at her and offering small smiles, while Joan and Wendy barely looked her way. Melanie was getting uncomfortable. Diners left and soon she and Jerome and his little coterie were the only ones who remained. Melanie kept checking her cell phone, trying to call Sandra at home, and nothing.

Finally, Jerome lifted his head and addressed Melanie. "Been stood up?" he asked.

"I . . . I don't know. I think we must have got our signals crossed. I'm meeting Sandra Goodyear." She said Sandra's name with pride. "Have you seen her?"

Jerome shook his head. "Sorry, dear, no."

"Oh." Melanie shrugged.

"Come join us," said Jerome.

"Oh, no, that's okay," said Melanie quickly. That was the last thing she wanted to do. Her mind raced for excuses.

"Oh, come along, until Sandra shows," said Jerome in his fake English accent.

"It's okay . . ."

Jerome motioned to the waiter. "Please bring Mrs. Korn's drink over, and another chair."

Seconds later Melanie was sitting between Joan and Wendy.

"So you were planning on catching up with an old friend and she forgot all about it! What a pain," said Jerome.

"Yes," said Melanie. She didn't correct him and add that it was business, but why did she have to tell him everything?

"And how's the apartment going?" asked Jerome.

Melanie shifted uncomfortably in her seat. "Really well, thank you."

"I heard you hired the team who worked with Diandra?" asked Wendy.

"Yes." Melanie was being very cautious about what she said. She felt Joan's piercing eyes studying her carefully, examining every inch of her body, makeup, and jewelry, and felt extremely on edge.

"That's fabulous!" boomed Jerome. "Because of course everyone knows that Diandra has the most exquisite taste."

"That's what I hear," said Melanie, clenching her jaw.

"You should have never messed with it," said Wendy. "Should have just left everything unchanged."

"Well, that was impossible. She took all the furniture."

"But surely not the draperies and the wallpaper?" asked Wendy.

"No, but . . . they seemed a little dreary."

"Then why did you hire the same team to redecorate?" asked Joan.

"Well . . . they just seemed the most appropriate."

"But if it's not your style?" pressed Wendy.

"Well, I know that they have good taste. I trust them."

"And right you should!" said Jerome. "This smart cookie is finally learning. She's taking her lead from the first Mrs. Korn. Hopefully you'll have a costume party soon. Remember, ladies, that fab party that Diandra had three years ago? Smashing. I think that really goes down as one of the top fifty great parties of all time."

"It was beautiful. I think even better than Malcolm's in Morocco."

"Certainly better. Diandra really knew how to throw a party. It's funny, though, dear, because as I recall, your husband—then Diandra's husband—couldn't make it," said Jerome with a smile.

"Yes . . . he told me. He had gotten food poisoning the night before."

"That's right!" said Jerome, smacking his forehead with his pudgy hand. "He had food poisoning."

"Yes," added Wendy. "He had somehow eaten some infected meat—mad cow or something. Luckily Diandra was okay. But I think Arthur had to check into the Carlyle for the night."

"They couldn't cancel the party at that point," said Joan. "Diandra had put too much effort into it."

"I'm sure your Arthur insisted," said Jerome. "Pity, though. He missed a great party. Ah, Diandra!" said Jerome, eyes glazing over as if he were reminiscing. "What a woman."

Melanie felt her blood boiling. Who did this homunculus toad think he was? Did he think she should sit there and take this?

"It's funny that you think Diandra was so wonderful, Jerome," Melanie said, trying match his frigid tone. "Because according to our mutual acquaintances, Diandra detested you. She couldn't believe that you bilked her out of all that money for a few pillows and some ridiculous lighting advice. Now I really must go, in case Sandra has called. It was nice to see you all."

Before Jerome could rebut, Melanie rose, and with the speed of light she retrieved her coat and hightailed it home. Jerome was left even more mortified and enraged, and Joan and Wendy were aghast. Bullies aren't used to being stood up to. And when the bully gets bullied, he always breaks.

Where in the heck did that come from? thought Melanie as she walked in her front door. She was audacious, but she really surprised herself this time. It was as if she'd had a flashback to high school and just couldn't take any more jeering from the rich kids. She had to stick up for herself sometime.

She wandered into her bedroom and found Mr. Guffey steaming out the last of the creases of her duvet, which was already carefully placed on her bed. There would be no errant wrinkles on his watch.

"Hello, Mr. Guffey. Any calls?"

"No, madam."

"Really? Not Sandra Goodyear."

"No, madam," said Mr. Guffey tersely. Didn't she know that no meant no?

"Weird."

Mr. Guffey decanted bottled water into cut-crystal carafes on both sides of the bed as Melanie went into her closet and hung up her blazer. She returned and plopped down on the recently ironed bed. Mr. Guffey repressed his frustration that his mistress couldn't even wait until he was out of the room before she messed it up, and he started his retreat.

"Mr. Guffey, one question?" asked Melanie, flipping off her Manolos.

"Yes, madam."

"Did Diandra really have . . . you know, amazing, fantastic, blah, blah, blah taste?"

Melanie asked this confidently, her head cocked to the side.

"Yes, she did, madam."

What? She pays this guy and he can't even lie to her?

"Um, okay, thanks," she said, surprised. "That's all."

Mr. Guffey left the room, and Melanie lay back on her bed and looked up at the ceiling. Great. Just when she thought she was making progress with those society types and Mr. Guffey, she suffered a setback. Why did they all have to make it so difficult? Melanie was in a depressed mood all night, and drifted off to a troubled sleep.

chapter 22

It takes a tough cookie to ascend out of a life of potential pole-straddling the way Melanie did, but every so often her steely resolve would flicker and then fade to black. While she knew she couldn't compete with the ghost of her husband's departed wife, who was supremely beautiful, poised beyond measure, and oozing taste and refinement, she also knew there must've been something pretty damn magical about her. So what was this golden ring that lent Diandra this impenetrable aura of perfection? Melanie needed to figure it out. She recalled how Joan and Wendy said Arthur had been steamrolled by her flight down south, and whenever she had broached the topic of Diandra, Arthur swept it under the rug, which Melanie translated as residual lingering heartache.

So what was so enchanting about this broad? The way people gushed about her. Melanie tried to expunge the words of reverence when spoken from the mouths of poseurs like Jerome de Stingol, and yet they hung in the air like a taunting vapor over her head. She wanted to know more about this mystery woman who had so gracefully ensnared Arthur's heart.

So one rain-soaked Monday morning, Melanie's curiosity led her footsteps to the New York Society Library on Seventy-ninth Street off Madison. It was the perfect place for a private mission, situated splat in the center of a neighborhood where most denizens had their own private libraries, and even if they didn't would never deign to "rent" a book. When Melanie entered the subscription reference athenaeum, which was adorned with looming ceilings, exquisite reading chairs, and a large bound periodicals section, she was certain not to run into anyone she knew. That didn't stop her from taking a few surreptitious glances around the room before she launched into her quest.

After a quick search for Diandra Korn (née Diandra Chrysler), Melanie's computer spat out page after page of referenced party pictures in *WWD* and *Harper's Bazaar*. She was frolicking with Lee Radziwill on yachts in the South of France. She was in Paris with Susan Gutfreund. She and her bosom buddy Carolyne Roehm were at the Winter Antiques Show. Party after party, Diandra was there. There were other magazine layouts in which Diandra was featured in head-to-toe couture, and photo essays chronicling her love of garden design, and chic little themed dinner parties for thirty. There was even an article she penned herself for *Town & Country* on global fabric excursions. But what really piqued the second Mrs. Korn's interest was a Q&A-style interview, ironically in the *Palm Beacher,* which described Diandra reclining on a chaise, sipping a kir royale, and discussing the matter of offspring with a reporter named Goodie Tattinger.

Yes, this was definitely the little pearl that Melanie had been shucking oysters for. A frank discussion about Little Ones. And this was way before magazines like *Vogue* did a motherhood issue with Amber Valetta toting her giant *putti* on the cover and stories of chic yummy mummies filled the glossed pages. No, this was from the 1980s, and children were not yet the It fashion accessory. And in this spectacular find, Diandra, who was notoriously whippet thin, openly condemned tots.

"We women have fulfilled our duties to nature! There are too many people on this planet, what with China and all," she was quoted as saying.

Melanie raised a brow. Hmm.

"The way I see it, you can be the focal point of your husband's life, or you can share him," continued Diandra. "I'd rather have the attention myself. Children are simply too messy. I much prefer peace, quiet, and cleanliness to shrieks and sticky fingers."

Goodie pressed Diandra, but she stuck to her guns. "I have my dogs," she said. "Those are my babies." When Melanie turned the page, she saw a close-up of Diandra's baby poodles wearing Lilly Pulitzer dresses. Melanie reread the interview over and over until she had committed it to memory. She kept hoping to discover more about this elusive society darling, but the interview was little more than eight hundred words. She squinted and looked hard at the picture of Diandra. She wasn't that great. Nothing really glamorous or captivating. And getting up there in the age department. At least Melanie had that on her.

As Melanie walked home replaying the findings of her research binge, she figured Arthur and Diandra had spoken of children and he obviously didn't want any. It's funny, but she and Arthur had never really discussed children in a family-planning sort of way. He had said once he loved kids, but then Melanie never saw him melt when they spied a cute kid in an airport, and now she knew why; he must have shared his ex's fear of little runny-nosed runts rattling their gilded cage. And in retrospect, she remembered a conversation with Arthur in which she asked him why he and Diandra hadn't had children and he said there was no way he could do that. Maybe they were right; it would totally uproot their lives and most certainly derail the high-society express train Melanie hoped to board. But she always had a small tug toward kids and envisioned having one of her own. She'd love a daughter. Although a son would also be nice. Either or. But in her visions of little booties and fatty cheeks, it suddenly hit Melanie: Diandra was on to something; if she had a baby, she couldn't be the one who was protected and cradled anymore.

Melanie returned home to the whirlwind of hammering, sawing, and drilling that was her work in process. Her baby, if you will. Thanks to the efforts of her new decorators, the Korns' apartment was getting its much-needed face-lift, and the guts were spewing. There were exposed beams, ventilation tanks, mold removal crews, and demolition men aplenty. The frenzy sent her scrambling to her room to avoid the din and to check her agenda to begin her outfit planning for the evening. She knew she had some tedious dinner with some colleagues of her husband's, but she couldn't recall which ones.

She flipped through the pages of her Hermès datebook. Ugh. It was Milo and Roberta Tupelo, the casket distributors. Melanie remembered when Arthur had dragged her to their estate in Bayonne, New Jersey. They had enormous gold gates with swan statues that looked as if they were barfing up fountain water. Gag. The last time they had gone out in the city with them, they'd hit Sette Mezzo and the Tupelos were so incredibly loud that Melanie wished there were a volume knob on the back of Milo's head. She'd even overheard someone whisper, "Those must be Melanie's obnoxious bridge-and-tunnel friends—Diandra would *never* have dined with such . . . *colorful* creatures."

Melanie caught her breath as she saw the faxed memo from Arthur's office sitting on her bed. "Coco Pazzo, 8:30 P.M. Dinner with the Tupelos." No way. Melanie speed-dialed her husband's cell. He was already en route home.

"Arthur, there is no way we are going out to Coco Pazzo with Milo and Roberta."

"Hon, what's the problem? We have to go out. The house is under construction. It's like a tornado hit it."

"I don't feel comfortable squiring them around at our neighborhood places, if that's okay. She looks like Carmela Soprano."

"Nice."

"Come on, Arthur, it's not that I'm a snob. It's just that everyone else is. I just . . . don't want to give anyone any more ammo against me. The Tupelos are so noisy, it's like they have microphone implants in their larynxes. Please. Let's just make it a quiet night at home. I have Wayne here and everything."

"I thought you said Wayne wasn't a real chef; he was just a cook and not good enough."

"Milo and Roberta don't know the difference! They'll love the food. Come on, *pleeease*?"

"Okay, okay. I'll call Milo now."

So much for a quiet night. As Arthur's elevator rode up to his vestibule, he was greeted by hard hat–clad men covered in sawdust carrying panels, and the rattle of buzz saws making ear-splitting grinding sounds. Just as he plopped his heavy briefcase on the bench in the foyer, Melanie turned the corner in a semifrazzled huff.

"Watch out for my pillows, sweetie," she admonished. "I just had them redone; I heard Brooke Astor has this same fabric in her living room!"

Arthur picked up his stuff and looked around for a secure place to put his briefcase. Lately he felt a little uncomfortable in his own apartment. Everything was so fancy; he knew his wife wanted so badly for it to look "proper." The chair in the front hall where he usually placed his briefcase now had a little rope around it so no one could sit on or put anything on it. That was after the curator of some museum in Philadelphia came by for an appraisal and was horrified to see Arthur's somewhat plump (okay, really plump, but she was trying) sister Elaine sitting on it. Apparently it was from some important era—Louis something—and there were about two left in the world. After that Melanie forbade him from putting his briefcase on it. And Melanie had taken away the candy cane–striped bench in the front hall to be refurbished or something and wouldn't allow him to put his things on the floor because it would make them "look like the Bunkers." These days he didn't know quite what to do with it. So finally he just stood there clutching his briefcase and looking at Melanie helplessly.

"Melanie, you gotta give me a place to put my stuff," implored Arthur.

"I have found you a perfect place, darling. Follow me," said Melanie, leading him down the plastic highway that was protecting the hall rug from errant paint splatter. They passed a series of Saran Wrap–covered Matisse collages that had been hung symmetrically on the beige walls and continued past several arched doorways, which led into Melanie's office, Arthur's office, the breakfast room, the dining room. They finally arrived at the area of the apartment that Melanie now referred to as "the servants' quarters," where the kitchen and maid's rooms—and of course Mr. Guffey's suite—were located (she'd heard it called that in a BBC series and thought that's what rich people called them). There was a small closet just before the bar in the pantry, which Melanie opened, beaming. One side of the closet housed mops, brooms, and buckets, which had obviously been recently pushed together to make the other side of the closet appear empty.

"You can put your things here till the construction's finished, sweetheart," said Melanie.

Arthur sighed deeply, knowing full well that it was useless to fight Melanie on decorating issues.

"Thanks, but if I have to walk this far, I may as well just put it in my office."

Arthur's office was the one room of the apartment that Melanie had no control over. She had tried, but he had held his ground. Arthur doubled back to chuck the stuff in there and have a quick cigar before the company arrived, but only minutes after he lit up, the doorbell rang.

"*Hiiii!*" Roberta squealed at the Korns' door, and hugged Arthur and Melanie.

"Come on in," said Melanie. "Sorry for the chaos. We're redecorating."

"Gotcha!" said Milo. "Some operation ya got here!" he added, smacking Arthur, his old pal.

Of course the Tupelos insisted on a tour, and although the house was in disarray Melanie was actually pleased to indulge them. It would be practice for when important people came. So as Melanie led them around the apartment she made sure to point out every priceless artifact and mention how much it had cost and if any other distinguished people had previously owned it. Milo and Roberta kept nodding, not quite sure who "the Steinbergs," "the Paleys," or "Jayne Wrighstman" were but knowing they must be important by the flourish in which Melanie mentioned their names.

As the group sat down to dinner and talked about "the industry" (i.e., the death biz), Melanie's animation left her and her eyes glazed over. These brute creatures from across the river troubled her with their accents and big gold watches. She'd picked up a lot in New York and somehow knew now that their over-the-top, garish look wasn't refined. And it was true, Diandra would never have spent time with people like this. Melanie felt bad for thinking such snobby, evil thoughts—after all, she was from Nowheresville herself—but somehow these hairsprayed heathens threatened her. They were like a cracked-open time capsule instantly transporting her back to her own days of tawdry style, and she didn't like the journey.

"That Bobby Silverstein, he's some frickin' character!" Milo practically yelled across the table while pounding it with his fist. Mr. Guffey came around to each person with the filet mignon, and Melanie could see he was visibly put off by her crass guests.

"That fucking guy! He kills me," Milo continued, screaming. Melanie shifted in her seat uncomfortably as Guffey ever so subtly bristled. Melanie wondered why Milo was so loud.

"You know, Bobby Silverstein has this big business with the chain of funeral homes in South Jersey. And his brother, Gordy Silverstein, has a company making draperies—you know, window dressings and shit. So I says to Roberta, 'Hey, with these Silverstein brothers, either way, it's curtains!' "

Arthur belly-laughed as Roberta cackled up a storm. She had her mouth full of scalloped potatoes, which came flying out in little bits the harder she guffawed. Melanie sipped her champagne and had a full-body cringe as Guffey exited for the kitchen, clearly disgusted. Melanie desperately hoped Guffey knew these were her husband's imports, not hers.

"So, Mel!" squealed Roberta in a Fran Drescher–esque nasal foghorn of a voice. "What's the deal with kids? It's been two years now! Oh, I gotta show you the pictures of the gang. Milo junior is 'uge!"

Melanie hated it when people didn't put the "h" in *huge*.

"And little Jordan is twelve—can you believe it? Top of his class. And Jared is ten . . . little Madison is so sweet—she's my angel—she's seven now, and baby Hudson is four! Time flies, ya know? So when're you getting on the kiddo wagon?"

"Oh, well . . . we don't want kids," said Melanie.

Arthur sat up, looking surprised at his wife's cavalier announcement.

"We just think, you know, our life is very ordered," she added calmly. "I prefer peace and cleanliness to shrieks and sticky candies."

That was news to Arthur. He shrugged and looked at Melanie, feeling suddenly very far away from her.

"Really?" asked Roberta, astonished.

"Yup," said Melanie. "We prefer white couches to bean bags."

"But they're little slices of heaven," began Roberta, about to argue her case until Milo had the wits to shoot her a look.

"Next case!" Melanie said cheerfully, knowing she was squashing down the truth about her feelings toward wide-eyed little nugget faces and chunky baby feeties. But a clamoring brood was decidedly unglamorous. Exhibit A: the Tupelos. A new topic was in order.

"Milo," Melanie said with all her summonable enthusiasm, "tell us about your trip to Taiwan!" Not that Melanie truly cared; she wondered why anyone would ever want to go to Asia.

Milo happily plunged into their odyssey in the Orient and as Melanie nodded, pretending to pay attention, out of the corner of her eye she looked at the mall-frequenting mom across the table from her. Roberta was listening to her Milo with rapt attention and a doting gaze. Melanie suddenly realized how sweet and unaffected the Tupelos were. Yes, Roberta was loud and obnoxious and garish, but there was love there; for her husband and her five kids, there was love and pride bursting from her size-twelve seams. That was pretty impressive, thought Melanie. And odd. Here Roberta was in the Korns' palatial palace on Park, and it was glaringly obvious that Arthur was the much better catch, but she was still happy with her life and her hubby. You don't see that often. She suddenly felt extreme guilt for harboring such secret condescension. So they were cheesy and would make the 10021 set call central casting for the next Scorsese flick, with their *Sopranos*-esque getups, but they were good, loving people.

"Cheers to you guys!" said Melanie, who had been so far gone in her reverie that she didn't even realize she was interrupting Milo.

Everyone at the table stopped and looked at Melanie.

"Honey?" asked Arthur.

"Sorry to interrupt. I just want to drink a toast to Milo and Roberta. You seem so happy . . . and, well, you're nice people," said Melanie with genuine warmth.

Roberta and Milo seemed surprised but pleased. Arthur beamed. "Here, here," he added, and smiled at his wife. Melanie was so classy, he thought. He was a lucky guy.

chapter 23

Joan Coddington had never walked faster in her life. Perspiration was dripping down her underarms and nesting in the nook of her cleavage. She was even panting a little. She could feel the blisters bursting on her heels. With every new step in her frenzied pace, her chunky gold necklace and bracelets clanked against her body with the same pulsing movements that they make on a rapper performing on stage, minus the

Mercedes logo. It was never so urgent to get to Orsay on Seventy-fifth Street to meet Wendy. Never.

Joan burst into the restaurant, practically throwing her camel-hair coat at the coat-check girl, and made a beeline for Wendy, who was innocently sipping Perrier at a front table.

"OH! I'm *dying!* Do I have goodies for you!" said Joan, untangling her Hermès scarf and sitting down dramatically.

Wendy at once gauged the situation's urgency by the glint in Joan's eye and immediately implored her friend to get down to business. "Don't make me wait! Spill it!"

"You're going to *die,*" said Joan, nodding to the waiter, who poured her a glass of the Perrier. "I'd also like a glass of chardonnay, and please, I'd like a lemon with the mineral water, not a lime. If I have even a drop of lime on the rim of the glass, I will turn purple, so please, lemon." She turned back to Wendy.

"What is it?" asked Wendy, practically panting in anticipation.

Joan, who had been waiting for this moment for seven blocks, when she would inform Wendy of the latest hot gossip, suddenly paused, realizing that once she told her captive audience this dish it would no longer be her secret. And secrets were like currency for Joan, valuable when fewer people had them. But, oh well, it wouldn't be worth anything unless others knew you had it.

"I almost want to savor this morsel . . ." said Joan, drawing it out.

"Spit it out, Joan!"

"So. Last night my daughter was out with some friends, including one of the Vance boys . . ."

"Drew or John?"

"Drew. They went to some faddish club downtown."

"I get nosebleeds if I go below Fifty-seventh Street."

"Who doesn't? But they're young . . ."

"Continue."

"So, who does Whitney see sitting at the bar with some exotic woman?"

"Ted Wingate?"

"No."

"Gustave Strauss?"

"No."

"That man from the Goodyears' . . ."

"Morgan Vance," said Joan, sitting back in her chair with an air of benevolence, as if having endowed her best friend with something more important than a kidney.

"NO!"

"Yes. And they were obviously together."

"What did she do?"

"Well, naturally Whitney is a pearl of discretion—she really is her mother's daughter if I do say so myself. She herded the group off to the side so Drew wouldn't see his father with some south-of-the-border slut. Can you imagine?"

"I'm in shock," said Wendy, mentally going through the list of people she could get to quickly in order to relay this information before Joan did.

"Whitney. Always thinking."

"Thank god. Drew doesn't know how lucky he is."

"My question is, what was Morgan thinking?"

"He's really lost it."

"Gallivanting around with some trollop . . ."

"Do we know who the woman was?"

"Very ethnic is all Whitney said. Dressed like a harlot."

"Interesting. I wonder who it could be."

"We have to find out, just to be prepared, of course."

"Of course. If we know her, we want to make it clear to her that we disapprove."

"It's bad form."

"Nauseating."

"Poor Cordelia."

"Yes, poor Cordelia."

Not that either lady could have cared.

Morgan had been forced to go to great lengths to deceive Cordelia last night, as Maria had staged a first-class temper tantrum, forcing him to cancel with the Powells at the very last minute, pleading a work crisis. When Morgan finally acquiesced to Maria's demand to go out, he insisted on finding some obscure place listed in the *Village Voice* that no one he knew would frequent. Maria was jovial and victorious as he led her into the bar, only elevating Morgan's wrath.

"This is my first night out dancing since the baby. All she does is cry. She's a real pain in the neck. I get no sleep!" Maria had whined.

"Well, you're the one who wanted her," said Morgan, downing two drinks in a row.

"I'm a Catholic! What did you want me to do?"

"I don't know."

"I so sick of your complaining—you think you did me a favor! You are lucky to have me! You get all the sex you want!"

Morgan tuned her out and glanced around the bar. It was dark and dank and seemed like the type of place where rats would set up camp. There was a scraggly band putting up their instruments on a small, sticky stage and some punky-looking twenty-somethings swigging beers. The whole place stank of a fraternity basement and kitty litter. In fact, come to think of it, the band was called Kitty Litter. Morgan couldn't wait to bolt. It was at that moment that all the color drained from his face. Of all the places in the world! It was his son Drew, with the Coddington girl and two other kids who looked familiar.

"Oh my lord, Maria, we've got to get out of here," said Morgan, slamming down his drink on the bar and grabbing Maria's elbow in an effort to push her toward the door. Maria jerked free from his clutch.

"We just got here! I'm not going anywhere!"

"Maria," said Morgan leaning in with urgency. "I see people *I know*. We have to go."

"If you see people you know, you have to introduce me. You introduce your wife. I'm just as important as her—I have your child!"

Morgan's palms were getting sweaty. He looked over at Drew, who was lodged now in a grimy, ripped red leather booth, doing shots with his friends. Morgan pulled Maria behind a pillar.

"Maria, please. Let's go. I'll take you to Peter Luger instead," begged Morgan.

Maria was enjoying making Morgan squirm. She folded her arms. "I won't go. Introduce me!"

"Maria, I'll get you that diamond bracelet you want."

"If you don't tell people the truth soon I will send a birth announcement to everyone you know!" Maria turned on her heel and stormed into the bathroom. Morgan took a deep breath, glanced back at Drew, who was totally engrossed in the band, and took a seat on a bar stool in the corner behind the pillar. As Morgan sat down, he noticed a man with a slight smile sitting two stools down, who had obviously heard the whole interaction between him and Maria. How embarrassing. Discretion had always been one of Morgan's mantras, and Maria was slowly tearing that apart. The man, who was about forty-five, with greased-back hair and a black leather jacket, looked over at Morgan and nodded. Morgan nodded back as he took a shot that the bartender placed in front of him. Morgan looked around again to make sure Drew didn't see him.

"I see you're having a little problem," said the guy, lighting a cigarette.

"It's okay."

"Doesn't look okay to me," said the guy, leaning back in his stool. "Looks pretty bad."

Normally Morgan would have avoided any form of conversation with a stranger in which he would reveal anything about his emotional state, but for some reason—maybe because Maria had worn him down—he decided to open up.

"It is."

"You know, a guy like me can help a guy like you in a situation like this."

"That sounds very cryptic," said Morgan, taking another sip of his drink. He wanted to drink the whole bar and cloud away his nightmarish errors.

The man slid across the bar stool between him and Morgan and sat down next to him. He had very large hands, Morgan noticed, and a big blue and gold signet pinkie ring.

"It's not cryptic. I'm a problem solver, you see. You've got a problem; I can help you."

"What are you implying?"

"You know what I'm implying."

There was a pause. Morgan wasn't sure that this guy could possibly be talking about what he thought he was. Perhaps the liquor was getting to his head. Either that or he was having a full-on Tony Soprano moment.

The man looked Morgan up and down. Expensive pinstriped suit, sterling silver monogrammed cufflinks, horn-rimmed glasses, steel gray full head of hair. This guy had probably never stepped foot in a joint like this. He realized that he would have to spell it out for him. "Difficult mistress, twisting your nuts. Wants it all. I can tell you're a successful guy. You don't need this shit."

"What 'shit' are you referring to?"

"Come on, don't insult me. I wasn't born yesterday. But let me tell you, don't beat yourself up. I've seen a lot of guys like you—feeling old, not getting any, some tramp comes along and wags her pussy in your face and you can't resist. Next thing you know, you're roped in. She's got you by the balls."

Morgan chuckled. "Isn't everybody roped in?"

The guy glanced toward the bathroom and saw Maria bang open the swinging door. He stood up.

"They don't have to be," he said, handing Morgan a card. "Here's my business card. Give me a call, and I'll make your life a whole lot easier."

He walked off.

Maria came up and tugged on Morgan's suit. "Well, let's go if we're going to go! Those bathrooms were dirty. What kind of a place did you bring me to? Take me to the Pierre. I want caviar."

"You wouldn't even like caviar if it wasn't expensive."

"What?" said Maria, straightening out the sides of her satin skirt. "Did you say something nasty? You better not have!"

"You know what, darling?" said Morgan, leading her by the arm. "I've had enough of you. We're going home."

chapter 24

"So, Mr. Guffey. Did, uh, Diandra have a Kelly or a Birkin?" asked Melanie with feigned casualness. She didn't even look up from her correspondence.

"Neither, madam," said Guffey, pulling a dying branch out of the flower arrangement on the hall table.

"Really?" asked Melanie, surprised.

"Well, actually, if memory serves, she did have a crocodile Kelly in a couple of shades, but they just collected dust, really."

"Oh," said Melanie, licking a stamp with dramatic nonchalance. "So what kind of purse did she carry?"

"Mr. Della-Valle would make her a one-of-a-kind *handbag* for every season."

"Oh."

It had been going on for weeks but was only getting worse. Melanie was constantly hinting and alluding to All Things Diandra, trying to gauge how she behaved, what she bought, and who did things for her, somehow wishing for a handbook on how to do things properly. Mr. Guffey indulged her—he genuinely did want to help and improve Melanie—but it was getting out of hand with all this detail-scavenging. Finally he dropped his shoulders and turned to his mistress, evaluating whether or not he could be so brazen. When he met her eager face, he decided that he could be.

"Mrs. Korn, may I be frank with you?"

"Yes, of course," said Melanie nervously. She couldn't handle any more insults today. She had already seen Meredith Beringer roll her eyes at Joan Coddington when she entered the Lowell for tea.

"I've noticed that you've inquired about the first Mrs. Korn quite often of late—"

"Well, I . . ."

"And I beg your pardon, but I understand. She was a very . . . correct woman. And it is only understandable that you inquire about her in matters of society's whims. But I could also be of less subliminal service if you allowed."

"What do you mean?"

Ten minutes later they were in Melanie's office. Guffey was pacing back and forth, brainstorming, while Melanie was taking copious notes in a leather-bound pad.

"All right. A few things."

"Ready," said Melanie.

"You must stop saying 'I'm going to the *Hamptons*.' Say 'I'm going to the country.' If they press you, say *Southampton*. Always specify. This is not a time-share house with crashing kids dancing on tables. And you don't want anyone to think that you're off to *Westhampton*. God forbid."

"Right." Melanie sketched a tiny devil next to the word *Westhampton*.

"Also, never say 'Meet me at the Union Club' or 'I'm off to the Ladies' Club.' Just say you're going to the club, and if they don't know which one, then they don't deserve to."

"Are you sure? There are so many!"

"Trust me, madam. Have I ever led you astray?"

"No," said Melanie with complete faith.

"A funny aside: the Ladies' Club is the ultimate bastion of WASP-dom and mannered propriety. And those ladies are so far gone that they completely miss the irony of the giant beaver on their flag," said Guffey, raising his eyebrows.

Melanie was so busy taking her notes that she almost missed Guffey's small attempt at humor. She looked up and laughed. He was immediately back to business.

"Now this is important: if you want to be photographed when making an entrance at a ball, don't shout out to the photographers. Especially not Bill Cunningham, who prefers not to engage in chitchat when he is on the job."

"But what am I supposed to do? They totally ignore me!"

"The preferential decorum is for one to casually stop by the throng of the photographers to catch up with a friend or acquaintance. You admire her dress. She will admire yours. Then you pull out your dress a little when you say thank you, and perhaps even smooth it down. The photographers will notice. Let them approach you."

"I don't know why they're not up our asses by now. Arty and I throw money at these events. The least they could do is recognize us for it."

"Well, that is another point, madam," said Guffey, pausing. "If you want to be renowned for your philanthropy, then make large donations to public charities under the name 'Anonymous.' You'll get more attention than if you splatter your name all over everything. And, trust me, you won't be anonymous for long."

"Really?"

"For certain. Everyone tries to find out the secret, and no one can keep a lid on it."

Melanie thought about that and finally agreed.

"And continuing in that vein, I must add that discretion is paramount," said Guffey with grave seriousness. "Don't say 'Do you want a ride in my *Bentley?*'" said Guffey, shuddering. "That is considered gauche. Rich people don't advertise. Let me rephrase that: people with *class* don't advertise. 'May I offer you a ride in my car?' is most proper."

"Oh, this is good, Guff," said Melanie, furiously writing. "This is real, real good. Hit me again."

Guffey spoke briskly in his clipped British tones while Melanie's hand started to hurt from writing so fast.

"Take down that hideous portrait of you in the library," he commanded.

"But Arthur loves it!"

Guffey exhaled in frustration. Some people just don't know art. How should he phrase this?

"Madam." He cleared his throat. "It belongs in a pizzeria. Never hang a portrait or commission unless Francesco Clemente is a dear friend and presents one to you unsolicited."

"What else?"

"Write thousands of thank-you notes. For every occasion."

"Everything?"

"There's the obvious—if you attend a party or an event at someone's house. But also if someone donates to your charity, refers you to an excellent tailor, or even vomits on your carpet! Write them and thank them."

"Okay. That's good to know. What else?"

"Let's see . . . clothes. Yes, you do need some advice there."

"Why?"

"You break the cardinal rule."

"What's that?"

"You should wear only *one* easily identifiable designer article of clothing. That includes accessories. You are not paid to advertise those brands; you are not a human billboard. There is no reason you should have four million LVs running around your person. If you are carrying a

Chanel bag, that's enough. If your purse says 'Prada,' which it never would—leave that to the Euro trash—then that is enough. Don't get carried away with the logos. You'll look like a Spice Girl."

"What about outfits? I overheard someone once saying my hemlines are too short."

"Disaster, madam!" said Guffey, giddy be so forthright.

"That bad? But I've got the legs! Why hide them with these granny hems?"

"May I suggest an excursion, madam?"

Twenty minutes later they were driving along Madison, Guffey pointing to the various fashion boutiques and barking out instructions.

"Versace, usually no, unless they have a conservative-for-them pastel. And wear it wisely, like to a theme party, not to some country club event."

"Got it," nodded Melanie.

"Valentino, always. Be careful with Armani—he has a penchant for appearing too much like Talbots of late. And you don't want to dress like your cleaning woman."

"No, thanks."

"Carolina Herrera, flawless. Gianfranco Ferré is grand I suppose, yet I've yet to know one person who shops there."

"That could work to my advantage."

"Or disadvantage, if you run into a grandmother wearing the same frock. Michael Kors, perfection. Stella McCartney—"

"Love her!"

"You're too old, I'm afraid, madam."

"I'm thirty-five!"

"Sorry. La Perla is noxious. Cheesecake Factory, if you will. Victoria's Secret for the rich."

"Are you sure?"

"Chances are if the general public has heard of them, so have the ladies of the night."

Melanie made a mental note to trash her entire top drawer.

"Prada! You can't tell me they're bad."

"The hoax of the nineties."

"Really?" said Melanie, with sadness.

"Yves Saint Laurent is magnificent, but try not to wear something that some starlet has been photographed in. You can afford to demand exclusivity."

"Yes, I can," said Melanie earnestly.

"Buy only estate jewelry. Give monogrammed silver frames from Tiffany as small gifts. Don't purchase wedding presents from somebody's registry. Buy something more extravagant than what they are registered for. Asprey and Garrard is good for that. You also can never err with a silver tray. Baby gifts should come from Au Chat Botté. And if need be, pregnancy outfits from Veronique."

"Oh, that will never be an issue," said Melanie confidently.

"Mr. Korn should not appear on a beach unless he is clad in Villbrequin trunks. They're very smart."

"Yes, smart, okay—"

"No to Frette—go around the corner to Porthault. Smythson is grand for everything. You could purchase anything there and you wouldn't go wrong, but it's Mrs. John L. Strong for monogrammed stationery."

"Got it."

Guffey turned to look at his adept student. He was excited. She really, truly seemed to be getting it.

"You'll do well, madam."

Melanie turned and looked at him gratefully. "Thanks, Guffey."

chapter 25

Jerome had bumped into Joan and Wendy at Nello's and was escorting them home. It was a beautiful afternoon, and he had little else to do.

"So did you hear that Mrs. Korn has been buying up a storm at the auction houses?"

"Doesn't surprise me," said Joan.

"The funny thing is that she is outright purchasing *collections*. She bought Penelope Mayhew's baby rattle collection, Bill Blass's shrunken staircase collection, and Monique Burden's tea caddies. She's in such a rush that she won't even take the time to *collect*. She just goes about buying up other people's lifelong passions."

"Pathetic," said Wendy.

"So sad," echoed Joan.

They walked along, shaking their heads at Melanie's idiotic ways. Just as they passed Seventy-second Street, an elderly homeless man thrust a coffee-stained paper cup at them.

"Good evening, ladies and gentleman. What's the richest nation? A *do*nation! What's the richest city? *Genero*city. I'm not being greedy. I'm just a little needy. You don't have to be a Rockefella to be a Good Fella!" he said, the routine down pat.

Jerome turned to Joan and Wendy. "Here's my good deed for the week," he whispered. He gently kneeled and smiled softly at the man, whose eyed widened at the scent of Jerome's aftershave and the sight of his gleaming white teeth aligned in a perfect smile.

"Everyone goes through hard times, and it's at those times that we need a little extra help," began Jerome.

The man's face brightened with hope. Was this guy about to hand over a crisp twenty? A fifty? He'd scored a fifty once in front of St. James on Christmas Eve.

"But you have to be a fighter. And get off your ass and do something!" said Jerome, handing him an envelope. He wagged his finger at the man and motioned for Joan and Wendy to continue on with him.

"Wow, Jerome, I'm amazed. That was *sooo* generous!" said Wendy, gloved hand on her heart.

"How much did you give him?" asked Joan.

"Money? No, no, no, no, no, ladies," said Jerome, laughing.

"What?" asked Joan and Wendy, confused.

"It's a McDonald's application," Jerome said with a flourish, as if it were a satchel of gold ingots. "A job is a better start than some cash he'll blow at the next crack house, do you not agree?"

"What?" asked Wendy, floored.

"He needs to get up and get a grip! It's not as if he's that quadriplegic in front of DKNY. This guy has full limbs and everything. He can work."

"But, Jerome . . . it's freezing and he's *homeless!*" said Wendy.

"He had all summer to walk to Florida. Besides, I didn't see you doling out the bills." Jerome sneered in their faces. "Now let's carry on. It's getting nippy."

chapter 26

"Yes!" said Melanie, shrieking with delight as she hung up the phone.

"What?" asked Arthur, who was slumped in his dimpled leather club chair, totally engrossed in *The Honeymooners*.

"We just got asked to be on the committee for the Dysmorphia Association."

"Aren't you already on that committee?"

"No, silly. That's dysentery."

"Geez. What do we have to do?"

"Just buy a few tables."

"How much?"

"I don't know, Arthur," said Melanie, irritated. "Why do you always ask?"

"Just curious."

"Well, what do you care? We have the money."

"I know we do. I just don't even know what the hell dysmorphia is, and so I'm wondering how much I have to pay to help cure it."

"I'm sure it's something pretty bad. I think she said it's something like when you see your body different from how everyone else sees it."

"What? You mean like when fat people wear skimpy outfits 'cause they think they look good?"

"No, silly, the opposite! Like when anorexics look in the mirror and see Roseanne Barr."

"Jeez," said Arthur, shaking his head. "Who knew there were all these crazy diseases. I love it—the richer you are, the more diseases you're surrounded by."

"It's true," Melanie said, laughing. "And a little odd that some are more fashionable than others. I had no idea that the Myopia Association is the thing to go to, but the Myopia Network is for total losers. It all depends who has myopia and which charity they give to and then who they rope in to donate. It's complicated."

"Right—well, it all depends on which high-profile person has it. I bet there's not a long line supporting the Syphilis League."

"Right."

"Listen, sweetie, by the way, speaking of money . . ."

"Yes?"

"I'm just asking, so don't get all broily. But how come your AmEx bill this month is for sixty grand?"

"Oh, that," said Melanie, getting up to stretch. "I had to buy new clothes."

"You look great! What did you need new clothes for?"

"They were all wrong, Arty," said Melanie with loving condescension. Men could never understand what it cost to look good in this town.

"They looked all right to me," he said, rubbing her knee.

Melanie pecked him on the forehead. "I love you for saying that. But, sweetie, it's work to keep up with all the trends and stuff. Apparently, my clothes were a little . . . tacky I suppose. My hemlines were totally inappropriate."

"Who said that?"

"I heard murmurs, and then Guffey confirmed."

"You're taking fashion advice from the butler?" asked Arthur, finally looking away from the TV.

"Yes," said Melanie, fluffing up the pillow her buttocks had just flattened.

"Isn't that a little weird?"

"No. He's actually provided me with some valuable insight."

"I don't know, Mel. I thought you were doing fine."

"So did I. But he really made some valid points."

"Like what?"

"You know, like silk is meant for curtains and wedding dresses, not sheets."

"What's wrong with silk sheets? I like them."

"They're very Mafia-esque."

"I don't know, Mel. Everything hoity-toity is so goddamn uncomfortable! Those new chairs in the dining room don't even fit my fat butt!"

"Come on."

"I guess that's the point," said Arthur, teasing. "To keep you from lingering over your dinner. God forbid you stuff yourself."

"I thought you liked the improvements I made."

"I trust you. If they make you happy, and this is how we're supposed to look, then I like them."

"Thanks, babe."

"Just don't go crazy following everything the butler says. It's like reverse *Jetsons*, where you're the robot."

"Okay," said Melanie, smiling. "I won't follow."

" 'Cause if he's so damn smart, why is he still a butler?"

Arthur had a point. He was still a lowly domestic. Yes, he'd given her a few tips, but she was the one who was out there making it happen. Time to listen to her gut a bit more. Hell, it had gotten her this far. Melanie vowed that she'd trust herself and not waver anymore. After all, her instinct had always been her best weapon.

chapter 27

At ten-thirty at night, the line outside of Dorrian's was already wrapped around the block all the way down Eighty-fourth Street, but Drew and John Vance ignored it and went straight up to the entrance.

"Hey, man," said Drew, high-fiving the three-hundred-pound African-American bouncer.

"Yo, what up, Drew?" answered Steve. "Who are you with?"

"Him, him, her, and her," responded Drew, pointing to his brother, Chester Winthrop, Whitney Coddington, and Cynthia Whitaker.

"Come on in," said Steve, opening the door for them as the cold and envious New Jerseyites watched them prance up the stairs and into the restaurant.

"It pays putting Steve on your Christmas list," said Drew over his shoulder to Cynthia. "I gave him a Burberry scarf."

"I'm friends with Jimmy Dorrian, so I never have to wait," said Cynthia, immediately swiveling her head from left to right to survey the crowd.

From the scene inside one would think that boarding schools and small liberal arts colleges had dumped their preppiest, richest, most socially connected students off for the night. Blond waifs in Seven jeans with small Gucci bags hooked over their shoulders and tucked tightly into their armpits mingled with baby-faced boys in Brooks Brothers oxfords clutching large pints. Small klatches of friends sat at a smattering of tables adorned with red-checkered tablecloths and were digging into french fries to cure their "munchies." The music was loud, the crowd was attractive, and pitchers of beer were being poured throughout the restaurant. It was a holiday weekend.

"Look, Whitney snagged a table," said Cynthia, pointing to the corner, where Whitney had already installed herself at the prime spot by the window. She waved, urgently motioning them over so she didn't look like a loser sitting alone.

"That girl can get a table in record speed," said Drew, impressed.

"Thank God," said Cynthia. "Get me a chardonnay, please."

"Chardonnay?" repeated Drew. "What are you, forty?"

"Ha, ha," said Cynthia, who turned and made her way over to her friend.

"Dude, check this out," said Chester, who was leaning against the bar with his arm extended and a twenty in his hand, trying to flag down the bartender. "Remember that chick I told you about last weekend? Well, she's here again."

"Where?"

"Down there, end of the bar," said Chester, tilting his head to the right to point in her direction.

Drew peered down the bar and saw a Latina woman sipping some sort of pink concoction through a straw. She appeared to be alone, and older than the crowd. Her eyes were darting around.

"Nasty!"

"What are you talking about? She's hot."

John came up behind Drew. "Who's hot?"

"That skank at the end of the bar," said Drew. "Chester's the one who thinks she's hot."

"You can't deny she's got that Salma Hayek thing going on," said Chester.

"So what? I don't think Salma Hayek is hot."

"You're whacked, man."

"Oh, come on, it's just really PC these days to pretend you think chicks like Salma Hayek and Penelope Cruz are hot. They're fugly."

"This girl is smoking."

"Gross, man. Who knows who's dipped his prick into her? She looks dirty, dude," said Drew.

"No way, man. She's sexy," insisted Chester. "What do you think, John-o?"

John stared at her carefully. She could go either way. She was definitely exotic-looking, with dark, cascading hair and thick lashes, and she did kind of look like Salma Hayek. But she also looked a little beaten down.

"Naah, not my type," he said, grabbing his drink.

"You guys are wrong."

"If you think she's so great, you can have her."

"I will, dude," said Chester, grabbing the two pitchers of beer. "Oh yes, she will be mine."

The hours flew by at Dorrian's, as they always did. Throughout the night various people joined the Vances' table and then moved on. Whenever anyone left, everyone air-kissed the person goodbye, even though they would see each other tomorrow. It was a subtle mimicry of their parents' societal movements. By three-thirty, Drew had left with Stephanie Morissey, Whitney had gone home, Chester had struck out with the Latina and was hitting on a seventeen-year-old Nightingale student, and John was left at the table with Cynthia and some geek named Mike, who was hitting on her.

"I know an underground off-hours place that's just jamming. Any interest?" asked Mike, addressing Cynthia more than John.

"Where is it?"

"The meatpacking district."

"The meatpacking district? I don't want to go all the way down there."

"Why not? It's rocking."

"Rocking with who? Triple-pierced headbangers and runaways? No, thank you."

"Well, do you want to come back to my house? My parents are in the country," asked Mike.

"I don't know . . ." said Cynthia, looking at John before she'd commit. John got the hint.

"I'm going to get another drink—does anyone want anything?" asked John, rising.

"No, thanks," said Cynthia and Mike in unison.

John wandered over to the bar. The place was only about a quarter full, but there were still people determined to make it until last call. Chester was now playing backgammon with the girl, but she kept glancing over at her girlfriend, imploring her to pick up on her ESP SOSes.

"What'll it be?" asked the bartender.

"Sam Adams," said John. He put money down on the bar and glanced around.

"Hi," said the Latina, who had sidled up to him out of nowhere.

"Hi," said John, surprised.

"I was hoping I would get to talk to you," she said, dipping her eyes down and taking a sip out of her straw.

"Me?" asked John, surprised.

"Yes, you."

"Do I . . . have we met?" he asked.

"Not yet. But I was hoping."

"Oh, I'm John."

"Just John?" she asked, teasing him with her accent.

"John Vance."

"John Vance. Nice name. Can I sit?" she asked, sliding onto the bar stool next to him.

"Sure. Can I get you a drink?"

"Do you want to?" she asked, batting her eyelashes.

This was weird. This chick was coming on to him. At least, he thought she was. But since he'd had about six beers, he realized he was wrong about her. She was his type. With fun bags like that, she was every man's type.

"Of course I want to," he said, assuming a deeper voice. It was hot when chicks made the first move.

"Then let's have champagne. To celebrate," she said, crossing her legs so that he could see the slightest hint of a garter belt on her thigh. She must be cold.

"What are we celebrating?" he asked as he motioned to the bartender. "A bottle of champagne, please," he asked, then turned to the Latina.

She leaned in so that her large bosom brushed against his hand, and whispered in his ear. "It's a secret."

"A secret," said John. "I like secrets."

"You do?" she said, flirtatiously swirling her straw around in her glass.

"I do."

"Well, we should have a secret together, no?"

"I think that sounds like a good idea," said John, chugging the bottle of Sam Adams while the bartender uncorked the champagne.

"You didn't even ask me my name," she said, pouting.

"Do I need to know?" asked John, smiling crookedly. He knew chicks dug him. And this one was definitely in heat.

"Not if you don't want to . . ." she said, turning and picking up her champagne flute.

"Just kidding, of course I do. What's your name?"

"Now I no tell."

"Come on, I was just teasing."

"No," she said, frowning. She took a sip of her champagne, then ran her tongue along her lips.

"Please?" he asked, smiling. She was fun. First eager, then hard to get. He knew the drill. Chicks wanted to be appreciated, at any age.

"Why should I? You don't care."

"On the contrary," he said, leaning in so that he felt her breath on his face. "I care a lot."

By the time Maria had finished the champagne bottle and gone down on John in the men's bathroom, she still had not told him her name. John watched her snap up her garters with expertise and reapply her bright red lipstick.

"So, John Vance, you have fun?" she asked.

"It was amazing, baby," said John, who was having trouble getting his fly up. He fell a bit to the side and had to hold himself up against the sink. The alcohol was finally making him wobbly. "Will I see you again?" he asked.

"I don't know, John Vance."

"Why do you keep calling me John Vance?"

She smiled. "I don't know . . . maybe because I know other Vance. I worked with a Morgan Vance."

"Holy shit—that's my father."

"No!"

"Yeah," said John, practically sliding down the wall of the bathroom. He was feeling really nauseous.

"You better go home. You look like you ready to pass out," she said, applying more red lipstick to her mouth.

"Yeah."

She turned and looked at him and smirked. "Goodbye, John Vance," she said, leaning in and kissing him on the forehead. He could feel the loose strands of his hair nestle into the sticky lipstick stain she left on him.

"Say hi to your father for me."

"Sure," he said, sliding down to the floor. He was now splat on top of discarded wet hand towels. She turned to leave.

"Hey, what's your name?" he was able to muster.

She turned at the door and smiled. "Maria."

chapter 28

As Arthur's car pulled up alongside the Lexington branch of Barnes & Noble, he felt his heartbeat quicken. He looked down at the card in his hand for what must have been the hundredth time. It had Olivia's perfectly airbrushed picture on it and said, "*Rhythms of Fisher's* reading by author Olivia Weston, Wednesday, October 21, 6:00 P.M."

"Okay, Charles," he said, stepping out of his car, "no need to wait. I'll walk home."

He entered through the large, green revolving doors and glanced around. Already the rows of chairs were pretty much filled, and there were even some people standing in the back. A large poster of Olivia's book cover sat on an easel with a banner that read BY POPULAR DE-MAND.

She must really have a following. Arthur looked around at the crowd and noticed it was mostly men who filled the seats. He used his handkerchief to wipe the sweat from his forehead, and he glanced at his watch. Any minute.

The B&N special events coordinator took the podium to introduce Olivia, who was standing behind him. She looked ravishing as usual, this time in a cream cashmere twinset, taupe scarf, and black pencil skirt. As Arthur drank her in, he thought for a moment about how he loved his wife dearly, but Melanie was so desperate to have the class and breeding that Olivia was born into. Olivia was the real thing. Real lineage, and what a looker. He looked away, almost ashamed; she'd never be interested in a schlemiel like Arthur.

Olivia said a quiet hello to the crowd and then opened her copy of the well-worn book to a page marked by a crimson velvet ribbon. She delicately cleared her throat and took a sip from the glass of water next to her. She looked up, flashed a lightning-fast half smile, and began.

"The ice clinks in the tumbler at the Goodrichs' annual Fourth of July soirée, and I know there is no escaping the monotony of another patterned dinner party. Through the rooms, the women come and go, buzzing like honeyed flies at a golden lantern . . ."

As the words spilled from her lips, the rapt male listeners were vir-tually drunk in their amorous haze. Arthur was entranced.

"Lipstick-stained brandy glasses recline beside drooping baked brie. I sit on a striped chaise beside Preston, who has been breathing down my neck since Memorial Day . . ."

Preston? Who the hell was this Preston guy? Arthur's eyebrows were among several others that raised. Olivia glanced off to the side mid-read, and he followed her gaze to see the guy she was with in the diner, plus some girl he was seeing for the first time. What was *he* doing hanging around her again? Certainly he was just a platonic friend. Probably the girl with him was his real girlfriend. He could never land a gal like Olivia. Interesting, though—these two weren't the stuffy Upper East Side types, they were . . . funky, edgy, cool. She was class blind! Yes, she didn't care about such nonsense as lineage—look at these two East Village types! Woman of the people. And really, because these friends looked like they crawled out of a gutter.

After the reading ended Olivia closed the book and gave a gracious nod to the crowd, acknowledging the rapturous applause. Arthur decided to linger for a little while, and he walked behind a bookshelf in the travel section. As he pretended to leaf through the colorful snapshot pages of *Let's Go India!*, he heard Olivia's feather-soft voice greeting her friends, Rob and Holland.

"Great job, sweetie," said Rob. Arthur peeked around the corner and saw them embrace.

"Thanks, Robbie. Hi, Holl—"

"Hi, Liv," the girl in black replied coldly.

"You guys, I've gotta jet," said Rob apologetically. "I have a lecture at Cooper Hewitt in like twenty minutes—"

"No problem, thanks for coming," said Olivia.

" 'Bye babe, see you later," said Holland warmly to Rob, giving him some kind of hipster handshake. He raced off.

"So Holl, listen—"

"I don't think so," replied Holland, back to her icier tone.

"I just . . . want to talk—"

"There's really nothing to say."

"But—"

"But what? This is all getting ridiculous . . . look, I should go."

"No," Olivia pleaded. "Can't we just get a cup of coffee?"

"A cup of coffee won't solve the problem. I'll see you around."

Arthur peeked out again and saw Holland sling her bag over her shoulder and walk out. Olivia ran a hand through her hair and received compliments from awaiting fans who approached her. Arthur listened from around the bookshelf corner and then looked at his watch, realizing he should probably head home. As he started to walk toward the door, Olivia turned around and practically bumped into him.

"Oh—hi . . . thanks for coming," she said to Arthur, who bristled with the shock of sudden interfacing.

"Great read! I mean, nice, uh, excerpt. Well, the whole book is wonderful," he said, guiltily holding up his copy. "I'm halfway through . . ."

"I'm glad you like it so far," she said with a smile. "Shall I sign it?"

Arthur resembled a beet. "Of course, yes." He nervously handed her the precious tome, which he held in his tight grasp as if it were the Guttenberg Bible.

She took an elegant silver fountain pen out of her bag and wrote simply, *"Enjoy the rest—See you in the elevator, O.W."*

"Ms. Weston," interrupted the special events coordinator, "I need to steal you for a moment."

"Of course," she said, snapping the book closed and handing it to Arthur. "See you," she said to her neighbor over her shoulder as she was led away.

As Arthur walked home through the brisk evening air, his John Lobb shoes never hit the pavement. He felt as if someone had laid out all the world's cotton for him to bounce home on, his every fevered step alive with longing and admiration. Her book was so engrossing, so charged and radiant, her rarified world was so present on the pages in her airtight descriptions and velvety adjectives. But wait—what about that weird exchange with that girl? He began obsessing on her "problem" with "Holl." What could possibly be wrong? Her dulcet tone seemed so wounded and damaged by the girl with all the ear piercings who spoke so harshly to his angel. Whatever was upsetting her, he wanted to make it better.

That night Arthur lay beside his wife in the giant upholstered canopy bed they shared, each absorbed in their reading. Arthur held a *Newsweek* magazine up on the comforter, which shielded what he was actually reading—the rest of *Rhythms of Fisher's*, with the occasional flip back to her inscription.

Melanie was too engrossed in her read of the *Social Register* to notice. Arthur ran his finger over the cobalt ink of Olivia's exquisite penmanship. He felt himself getting turned on just recalling her scent and smile. *In the elevator* . . . what did that *mean*? Maybe she wanted him to nail her standing up in the elevator. They could have that *Fatal Attraction*–style hot sex while ascending the floors; it would be a heated secret affair, minus the boiling bunny rabbit. Naturally, she was sane. She was honest and good, a youthful flower whose fragrance filled his lungs with new life as he inhaled it.

As his eyes closed while recalling her smell and the fold of her scarf that warmed her soft neck, the jolt of Melanie's outraged voice scissored through his fantasy.

"The McFaddens! They weren't in here last year! Bullshit."

Arthur tried to soothe his wife, but she was too dejected.

"I don't know. It's always when I think I make progress, I suffer a setback."

"Don't take it personally, sugar."

"I know," she sighed. "I just have to trust Guffey's tips."

"If they work for you."

"And I've got to call my publicist and whip his tiny hiney into gear. That is turning out to be money *not* well spent."

"Don't worry about it."

She sat up and tied her new robe over her lacy nightgown. "That magazine? journal? is such a crock."

She chucked it toward Arthur on the bed and walked into her bathroom. Arthur looked at the book and could almost see the blue blood leaking out of it. He opened it and looked through the pages. He had already read the entry on Olivia, but now he was combing for someone else. He eyed the P section for Preston. Damn, only last names.

"Honey," he yelled toward the bathroom. "Does this thing have a first-name index?"

Melanie opened the door and hopped back into bed.

"No. But tell me the name and I'll probably know who it is."

"Oh, no one, just there was some kid Preston somebody who is applying to the Racquet Club—"

"Preston Bates? Regina and Carl's son? Around twenty-nine, thirty-ish?"

Arthur gulped. "Yeah, that must be him." Little cocksucker.

"Has he gotten over his drug problem?"

"He has a drug problem?"

"He's been 'vacationing' in Minnesota for three months, so you do the math."

"Oh," Arthur said, relieved. A junkie! Ha. As if she would ever be with a needle-toting maniac. "Maybe it wasn't him. Never mind."

Mr. and Mrs. Korn kissed good night before they turned out the lights and rolled onto their pillows for sweet dreams, which were in totally different realms.

chapter 29

Cordelia and Jerome, with arms linked, made their way up Madison from Fifty-seventh to Seventy-second in over three hours, enjoying the chilly air and brisk pace as the Vances' driver slowly moved alongside them, carrying the day's purchases. It was the pair's favorite activity, like a special date they both loved each season, with the dynamic combo of her money, his taste, platinum plastic, and garment bags.

But that day, even when the ready-to-wear gown fit as if it were couture or a brand-new piece from the Cruise collection was being unpacked in the store, Cordelia's usual sparkle was muted and dulled. When Jerome ran across Valentino, spying the ultimate beaded top, her normal yelp was this time a nod and forced smile, which quickly evaporated as her eyes belied a grayness inside her. Jerome said nothing. He knew. He had already heard rumors the day before at Swifty's that his poor friend's husband had a girlfriend.

As they strolled across the street to Armani, Cordelia looked at her pal, who seemed to want to help her so much. She knew she was being a bit of a downer, but she couldn't even manufacture enthusiasm for new things when she truly wanted something else altogether.

"Jerome, I . . ."

"What, dear?"

"I . . . feel like . . . something is missing in my life. I've been feeling this for quite some time now, and I've come to realize what it is."

"A new bauble from Fred Leighton?"

"No. A daughter."

"That's fabulous! That's the best news I've heard since Jerry Zipkin died!"

Cordelia smiled, the first real one all day; she was relieved her dream wasn't thought foolish.

"It's not that my sons aren't great—they're wonderful. But they're all grown up now, and I still feel like I have so much to give. It's like this wave of energy trapped inside me. I really want to adopt a baby girl."

"That's fabulous. Fabulous! You know, there are so many underprivileged children in this world crying out for a home. You could take one in."

"We have plenty of room. I could do up a nursery in no time." She drifted off with visions of pink chintzes and a white crib with custom linens. Maybe she should swing by the D&D building in the morning. Just uttering the words aloud gave her a new hope.

"I think it could be really chic to do a mulatto," said Jerome. "Blends are the way of the future. So modern. It's good to have a little bouillabaisse of genes."

"You're right! I'm so glad you agree with me!" said Cordelia, now beaming.

"I'm very proud of you, Cord. Not many people would take in a needy youth. It takes real humanity and sensitivity to care about the forgotten children and let them be a part of you."

"Oh, Jerome, thank you," she said, hugging him. "You always know just what to say."

When they got to the canopy of 741 Park, the doormen immediately rushed out and started unloading the car. Cordelia squeezed Jerome tightly, and as she looked into his eyes before heading into the lobby, she felt completely understood.

As Cordelia went up to her apartment to start envisioning the new nursery, Jerome had children on the mind as well. He went up to Harlem in his own car that afternoon and whistled out the window to a Puerto Rican boy, then waved a wad of cash. The boy, not a day older than fifteen, swaggered over and hopped in.

Downtown, Morgan Vance was working at his desk, for once without distraction, when his assistant came in.

"Mr. Vance, John Vance line one."

Morgan picked up the phone, happy to hear from his son. "Hi, John."

"Hey, Dad. Just wanted to confirm about squash this afternoon."

"Looking forward to it."

"Great, see you at five. Oh, by the way, I met this chick the other night at Dorrian's. She said she knew you. Maria? Spanish girl."

Morgan turned sheet white. Casper.

"I don't recall a Maria."

"Oh. Well, she was kind of hot. Chester Winthrop was scamming on her."

"How strange. I don't know any Maria. See you later, son."

Morgan got off the phone and reached for his handkerchief to wipe the cold worry sweat from his brow. In a panicked frenzy he rustled through his desk in search of the small card handed to him by the leather-wearing self-professed "problem solver."

chapter 30

It was the gala of the season: the New York City Ballet's perpetually oversold opening night. Dinner and dancing were preceded by a three-act performance, during which women scanned the room scoping the outfits and their husbands squirmed in their seats with hunger noises emanating from their stomachs. Then, after the ethereal flurries of chiffon and tulle, when the last prima ballerina curtsied in front of the curtain and got her roses, the hordes flowed into the vast lobby of New York State Theater. Tonight's extravaganza boasted a kitschy Hawaiian-themed, flower-filled fantasia of dramatic lighting, sexy music, and Glorious Food catering. As paparazzi snapped Miller sisters, Hilton sisters, and Boardman sisters, Melanie Korn watched curiously from the side as Arthur talked up some Wall Street zombie.

If she only had a sister. *These gals ain't all that*, she thought. She had calves like them, and carbon-copy killer threads. But the sister phenom was all about the Doublemint hot twins campaign—one can be just okay, but when you have two or three, the eye bounces off the other and makes them an alluring, magnetic unit.

As the guests took their seating cards, Melanie was let down to find that their table, one of the most expensive, was not bordering the dance floor. And not only that, they were tucked away from all of the swans she wanted to dazzle.

"Arthur, what do you think this means? Our table may as well be in Botswana."

"Hon, it's fine. At least we can hear each other talk. It's a zoo by the dance floor."

"A zoo with the best animals. I feel like we're the skunks."

The Korns walked toward their table, past the sequined and brocaded guests, and drank in the bustling, enormous room. Mixed perfumes filled the air and glamour never felt more present than in that glistening venue. Melanie was very disappointed that she would be unable to put any of her Guffeyisms to use. They had practiced a little chitchat before she blew him off to get ready. She'd had enough playing Julia Roberts in *Pretty Woman* to the instructive bellhop. She felt red carpet–ready.

As Arthur and Melanie were about to sit down, Pamela Baldwin pulled her aside.

"Um, Melanie, can I have a word with you?" said Pamela gravely.

"Sure, Pamela. Is something wrong?" asked Melanie with concern.

"Look, I'm sure you found your seating card and are not very happy . . ."

"Well," said Melanie, unsure how to proceed. "I'm a little surprised. I mean, we've been very generous, and I think that should buy us a slice of the dance floor."

"And I agree. So I just want to make sure that you know *it wasn't me*," said Pamela, bobbing her head.

"What do you mean?"

"I didn't put you there."

"Who did?" asked Melanie, her stomach sinking with a thud.

Just as Pamela was about to respond, a waiter clad in the most garishly tacky Hawaiian shirt tucked under four plastic leis interrupted to hock his cocktails.

"Now those look interesting . . . Oh, look at those coconuts. And the little umbrella is darling. What are they?" asked Pamela.

"Coconut breezes. Our speciality."

Melanie was getting impatient. "Just have one, they're great." She grabbed two and thrust them in Pamela's face, eager to be rid of the waiter. "So you were saying?" she prompted. Pamela put her finger up for Melanie to wait as she took a sip of her drink.

"Yuck," said Pamela. "This isn't very good. He should have said it had Kahlua in it. I always get a rash from Kahlua."

Could she get to the point for the lord's sake? "Yeah, you shouldn't drink it," said Melanie, grabbing Pamela's coconut out of her hand and dumping the contents down her throat. She then took a large swig of her own drink. She rarely imbibed at these sort of events, but if it would expedite her torture she was more than willing.

"Be careful—mixed drinks can be sneaky!"

"I'll risk it. So, was there someone who didn't want me near the dance floor?"

Pamela sighed deeply. Melanie looked into her cracked–China doll blue eyes and realized she was face to face with the stupidest woman alive. All that WASP inbreeding had produced this Pine Manor dropout who was unable to fill her own gas tank or have a normal conversation.

"Yes, Melanie. You know . . . well, Chauncey Goodchild, my cochair, is very tight with some of the other ladies, and I don't know why but they just don't like you."

Melanie felt numb. She took another gulp of her coconut breeze before she could respond.

"So, what, they made sure I sat in the Urals?"

"What's the Urals?"

"You know, they made sure I had the worst table?"

"Oh!" said Pamela, still not getting it. "Yes. Shall I tell them you're upset?"

"No, please, definitely *do not*." Melanie took another sip and continued with determination. "I'm here to have a good time, and I will."

"You have such a great attitude!" Pamela waved at someone across the room. "Gotta dash. But I am so impressed that you are such a great sport."

"Yeah, maybe it will win me an award one day."

Pamela scurried across the room in a flash as Melanie took her seat next to Arthur.

"What was that all about?"

"Bullshit," said Melanie. A mixture of anger, humiliation, and frustration was bubbling under her skin. Sometimes this social hike was so tiresome and childish she felt like opting out. Despite all her social ambitions, her desire to parallel and exceed Arthur's first wife in society, this was the kind of gut-churning snub moment that made her want to give up and pull the rip cord. She wanted to escape and float back down to the real world, landing in some unchallenging, rectangular M state in the middle. But if her life in a small town taught her anything, it's that the social jungle has vines everywhere. There were probably even social hierarchies in face-painted pygmy tribes and stuff. It was everywhere. Even in rectangular states in the middle. *Look at Nellie Olsen and her rich, store-owning family ruling the roost on* Little House, she thought. Class and climbing and desperation for acceptance were global phenomena. But, like Sinatra said, if she could make it here . . .

"Thank you so much for having us. What an event!" squealed Lil Broady, the wife of one of Arthur's Addams Family–esque go-to guys. "Did you see who's here? That's Sarah Parker!"

Melanie realized she had been zoning out with the poor Laura Ingalls school-supplies-in-a-bucket reverie. She still had guests to entertain and had to at least pretend she was having a good time. But she was in such a crushed mood that only lots of alcohol could help her through this event. She was already feeling a bit buzzed as she took another gulp.

"Who?" asked Melanie.

"Sarah Parker! From that HBO *Sex in the City* program! We love that program. Don't we, Bob?"

"Love it," her remote-controlled hubby answered while staring at the taut thigh of a dancer like a starving Ethiopian would behold a bucket of KFC drumsticks.

"Sarah *Jessica* Parker," Melanie corrected, agitated. Did these people know anything? "I mean, that's like saying 'Michael Fox.' "

"Who's that?" asked Lil.

"Exactly. It's all about the J," said Melanie. "Michael *J.* Fox."

Just then the chairwomen took the microphone to do their endless laundry list of thank-yous—to corporate sponsors, the *faaaaab*ulous dancers, the florists, director Peter Martins, and so on. Melanie examined her newfound nemesis closely. Chauncey Goodchild was a sexless, bland, middle-aged woman. She had her little note cards for her speech—so prissy and perfect. *How in hell did she get to be a chair?* Melanie wondered. She could easily answer her own question. It was because she wolfed down muffins every morning at Payard with that bitchy coffee klatch that included the likes of Joan and Wendy. They all had too much time on their hands and too many enemies. After the tenth and final burst of mechanical applause for so-and-so's boundless generosity, Melanie addressed her table.

"That Chauncey Goodchild makes me *ill.*"

"Uh, sweetheart—" Arthur tried to calm his visibly wounded wife.

Melanie knew she was tipsy and probably shouldn't continue, but she was not in the mood to feel charitable to anyone.

"No, Arty, do not edit me on this one. That woman sucks."

"Why?" asked Polly Puccini from across the table. "She seems nice."

"Nice? NICE?" asked Melanie. "Let me tell you about nice. Her husband's estranged trust-fund cousin bit it on some adventure-travel freak accident in rural Hawaii, and Arty kindly offered to take care of all the unpleasantness through one of his subsidiaries, fully absorbing the cost of the casket and funeral and flying the body back and everything. And those assholes barely said thank you."

"Wow, that is nice, Arthur," said Lil.

"Wait," continued Melanie, with a silencing jeweled hand. "Then, after we eloped, we decided to have an intimate wedding reception at Doubles."

"Oh, that was such a lovely evening! Your dress was spectacular," said Lil, swooning.

"I had it copied from Stephanie Seymour's in the 'November Rain' video. Anyway, guess what the Goodchilds got us as a wedding present? Just guess. And keep in mind, they are loaded."

"Melanie—" Arthur shifted uncomfortably in his seat. His wife was really on a rampage this time.

"Babe. Don't *Melanie* me. I want everyone to know how lame they are."

"So what did they give you?" asked Polly.

"We literally got an e-mail saying, *Dear Melanie and Arthur, In honor of the momentous occasion of your marriage, as a wedding gift for you to cherish, Chauncey and Frick Goodchild have adopted a goat from a rare South American breed that is tragically facing extinction. Funds have been set aside in your name to raise the goat at Hacienda Las Cabras in the hills of Peru, and one day it shall breed . . .*"

"No," said Lil.

"*Yes.* I mean, is that not a Fuck You or what?"

"That's the kind of gift you give to someone you hate," Polly thought out loud.

"No shit," said Melanie. "I mean, that was a five-hundred-a-head seated caviar dinner. And they give us a goat we'll never meet from near *Lima*?"

"Well, hon, would you have rather had them ship it to our apartment?" Arthur asked teasingly. He knew Melanie was drunk, and he wanted to lighten the subject, but Melanie tossed him the glare she had used on the airline when lowlife shower-curtain salesmen pinched her butt.

"Obviously not. But I'm saying big whoop if some goat croaks in another country. Plus, that's not the point. The point is, you helped them in their time of need, shelling out thousands for that idiot who died swimming with sharks. Which was his own stupid fault."

"He was swimming with sharks?" asked Bob Broady, suddenly tuning in after removing his face from the salmon appetizer.

"Yes. Courting death. It's a Greenwich thing."

"Greenwich, like . . . Connecticut?" asked Lil.

"Yeah. You know, all those kids of privilege that kick the bucket doing these insane rich-people sports? Like there aren't enough problems and dangers in the world—they have to cough up ten thousand dollars to go charter a skydiving plane."

"Why, are there a lot of Greenwich deaths with extreme stuff like that?"

"Polly, where have you been?" asked Melanie, exasperated. "The Goodchilds' cousin, he was in that massive heli-skiing avalanche three years ago that wiped out, like, half of Round Hill Road! And THEN, after looking the Grim Reaper in the face, he gives it the finger and swims with sharks!"

"The Grim Reaper doesn't have a face," said Arthur. "He has that cloak thing."

This time Melanie didn't even dignify Arthur's observation with a comment.

"I mean, there were literally snowballs rolling by, packed with the severed limbs of his Hobart pals, and he still went heli-skiing up until he was chowed by Jaws. It's just a cavalier sense of entitlement, like they're all untouchable."

"That's amazing. How awful that there is this trend," said Lil.

"Whatever," said Melanie. "I'm not shedding any tears. Feel bad for people who get diseases, not for those who who plummet off bridges with bungees on purpose. I think the feng shui in Greenwich is all screwed up, 'cause no one's happy there. That's why they seek out this adrenaline crap, to wake themselves up from their spoiled comas. Anyway, it's all very Darwinian. Those inbred kids wouldn't have done anything anyway."

"Honey, why don't we dance?" Arthur suggested, trying to put an end to his wife's wild theories and impassioned rants. It worked.

"I'd love to dance! That's a great idea."

Melanie loved a dance floor. And she had all the moves. She used to practice in front of her mirror and knew in her bones she could out-shimmy any crappy *Dance Fever* contestant. Arthur took her hand and led her to the crowded floor and she coiled coyly around him and giddily tossed her head back with laughter.

"Babe, have you had, maybe, a little too much to drink?" asked Arthur.

"Maybe." Melanie giggled.

"Just be careful. You don't want to say anything you'll regret."

"I have no regrets now! But if you want, I'll dance it off."

Arthur and Melanie danced up a storm, until he had to hit the john.

"Oh come on—I love this song," she cried in protest.

"I have to go, Mel—"

Just at that moment, a stunning star of the company, Albert Evans, walked by and overheard.

"Well, I'd be happy to cut in," offered Evans.

Melanie's face flushed—he was a celeb. And wanted to spin her around!

"I'd be honored," said Melanie.

Evans gracefully dipped her and spun her around the floor as onlookers gathered. A photographer from PartyPicturesOnline snapped their photo, and more and more heads began to turn. As Melanie realized the pairs of eyes were on her, she bumped it up a notch, shaking her moneymaker and sexily sliding down Evans in a full-on *Solid Gold* move.

Needless to say, Joan and Wendy were aghast.

"Look at what we have here," Jerome de Stingol mused, arching a brow at Melanie and the statuesque dancer. "She's really pouncing on that sexy African-American gentleman. She's writhing in ecstasy! Look at her."

"Jerome, he's gay," said Wendy.

"I know it. But clearly she is loving the ride."

"She's loving the attention," added Joan. "It wasn't enough we had Chauncey put her table in Antarctica. She had to march back into the limelight and take it."

"Well, she sure is having the time of her life," said Jerome, dying of jealousy.

She was. Melanie felt like a million bucks. And it drove everyone nuts. Until the next morning, that is, when Melanie awoke with an aching head and an overwhelming sense of panic about what she might have said. It took six phone calls to Arthur to assuage her fears, and seven Advil to eliminate the pain. She swore never to drink again.

chapter 31

The line at Clyde's Pharmacy was *ridiculous,* and Joan was in no mood to wait. She was in the throes of a crisis, a real-life crisis, and all these Upper East Side ladies refilling their Valium and Vicodin prescriptions needed to move aside and let her through. Things were so bad she had even enlisted Wendy to hop over and keep her company in line before she fainted from impatience.

"Don't worry, you'll be fine," said Wendy, reassuringly patting her arm.

"I'm in agony, Wen. Agony," moaned Joan.

"Why don't you let me wait? You go home," offered Wendy.

"No, thank you, dearie, but I absolutely cannot be forced to wait another *second* after this damn prescription is filled to pop those babies in my mouth and smooth that cold cream on my face."

Joan had gone for her usual Monday morning swim at the Colony Club. The procedure—her acid skin peel—had been on Friday, and she had been certain it would heal by Monday. She was wrong. Some sort of sixth-grade science lab chemical reaction had taken place between the peel and the chlorine, and the result was a horrifically red, blistery, scaly face. It was a disaster, and an agonizing one. She needed that face cream and those painkillers. Now.

Wendy decided to distract her friend. A nice pure dose of gossip was always the best medicine.

"It's so thirdhand . . ." began Wendy.

"What?" said Joan, immediately sliding down her dark glasses and peering over her nose at her friend. "What happened?"

"Nothing happened. It's . . . it's merely, and again, very he said, she said."

"Wendy," said Joan in a singsong, reprimanding voice. She loosened the Hermès scarf knotted under her chin.

"I've heard more rumblings about the"—Wendy leaned in and whispered—"salsa girl Morgan Vance is seeing."

"Really? From whom?"

"Meredith Beringer said her husband said he thought he saw Morgan with what he called a 'hot little red pepper.' See, I'm not sure it sounds plausible."

"It doesn't. And besides, it would just be too juicy. It's like out of a movie, no one would believe it. Plus it would be around by now."

"You know, there have been a lot of situations where things happen to people in our little world that no one would believe if it wasn't true."

"You're right," said Joan, thinking. "Like when you-know-who's husband caught her cheating with the black governor."

"Or when you-know-who married the former prostitute," added Wendy.

"And how about the time when you-know-who was caught in the Pierre with you-know-who?" said Joan, nodding.

"Don't forget about you-know-who gallivanting all over Europe with that much-married woman," said Wendy.

"Or what about when you-know-who's husband married his children's nanny?" said Joan.

Wendy froze. "Joan, that was me."

Joan froze. She was right. *That was Wendy. Oops.* "Oh, Wendy, don't be silly, I'm talking about the Cosgroves, from Chicago."

"Oh," said Wendy quietly. "I don't know them."

As sore and raw as Joan's face was from her chlorine-tainted acid peel, Wendy's tiny little feelings with regard to her husband's departure several years ago were rawer.

"Wendy, seriously, I'm not talking about *him*." Wendy didn't even like her ex's name to be mentioned in front of her. "He's not even important enough to be a you-know-who."

Wendy remained silent. It was just so depressing! She never ever thought she would be divorced, living alone, and relying on female friends for a social life. It was so pathetic. And her poor children had to live with the fact that their skunk of a father married that harlot named Tracey. And was breeding with her! And she was using his money to buy houses in Quogue! To go to Bali!

"I think you're next, Joan," said Wendy, dropping the subject.

"Wendy, thanks for coming to wait with me," said Joan, hoping to cheer her. "You're a great friend."

Wendy put on a smile. "Thanks, Joan."

Wendy waited with Joan while she got her prescription filled. She *was* a great friend. And she was a great mom. So screw Tracey. Joan turned to her.

"Lunch, on me at Daniel?" she asked.

"Deal," said Wendy.

<h2>chapter 32</h2>

"Mr. Guffey!" said Melanie, slamming the front door with excitement. "Mr. Guffey?"

Her faithful servant appeared out of the shadows. "Madam?"

"Oh, Mr. Guffey, you won't believe it! I am walking on air. Guess what?"

"I have no idea, madam."

"Guess!"

"I'm . . . unable. It appears to be positive news . . ."

"The best." Melanie cleared her throat dramatically, as if bracing her manservant for the ultimate relaying of good fortune and blessing from heaven, sent down by God himself in a radiant bolt of lightning. "My picture is in *WWD*!"

Melanie thrust the trade paper in his face. "ME! Dancing with Albert Evans!"

Mr. Guffey took off his dusting gloves and peered closely at the picture. "Wonderful, madam. A step in the right direction. Up."

"And that's not all. Just this morning I got a handwritten letter from Meredith Beringer asking me to be on the Fighting Irritiable Bowel Syndrome committee! Can you deal? I'm part of FIBS! It's only one of the most glamorous committees in the city."

"Things are happening for you, madam."

"They are, aren't they?" gushed Melanie, overjoyed. Her name would appear next to *Condé Nast* fashionistas and celebs alike on the invitation. She had the world's most sought-after decorators doing a carte blanche tune-up on her apartment, she had the best charities chasing her ass for dough, and with her publicist busy in the trenches, she'd soon burst on to the scene and be in everyone's surgically en-hanced, cheekboney face. This was a blast.

"So, I need your advice. I'm going to Olivia Weston's this afternoon for a meeting. It's with the younger set. The swans, as you call them. Any thoughts?"

"Perhaps I could fetch something from Mason du Chocolat for you to bring to Ms. Weston, or something from Neuhaus . . ."

"I agree with the whole bringing something, but I happen to know that Olivia Weston and her 'rexi cronies would never touch a bite of them for fear of powdered cocoa on their manicured fingers, or more important, butter and sugar on their skeletal asses."

"Touché."

"What about potpourri?"

"Too 1980s."

"A Votivo candle?"

"That's what people in the West Village give."

"Well, any ideas?"

"I'll fetch some gold almonds."

"Perfect!" said Melanie, straightening her skirt. "So, any um, thoughts in terms of convo?"

"The young, the rich, and the idle take great pride in their burgeon-ing art collections and decor. They generally purchase through an art consultant and feel semi-insecure about their choices. Compliments go a long way."

"I can do that. Just like the old, the rich, and the idle," said Melanie, smiling. "Thanks, Guff."

"Good luck, madam."

chapter 33

Olivia opened her front door, and although her face didn't convey any emotion, she was extremely surprised to find Melanie Korn stand-ing on the threshold.

"Hi, how are you? I can't wait to see your apartment. You must give me a tour, pronto. Who did it?" said Melanie as she waltzed into the sweet-smelling home and looked around the front hall. She wanted to be breezy.

"Um, a friend . . ." said Olivia, not sure what the hell Melanie was doing there.

"It's very original. Oh, I see you have a Twombly chalkboard painting! It's *faaaaaaab*ulous. I wanted one of those for a while, but Arthur said absolutely not. Reminded him too much of school and what a terrible student he was. Although, not that it mattered—he was more successful than any straight-A nerd I ever met!" said Melanie.

She glided her hand along the Biedermeier chest and fondled a silver letter opener, running her finger along the sharp edges. Olivia watched curiously as Melanie peered down at the neat stack of letters in the silver dish. "You're also invited to Joan Coddington's tea party, I see. Should be a snoozefest, but I suppose you've got to go to these things. I'll tell Joan that we should be seated next to each other, so we're not bored to tears."

Finally, after using the full extent of her photographic memory to imprint the decor of Olivia's foyer onto her brain (toffee walls, mushroom-colored sisal carpeting, a Campbell's soup can umbrella stand signed by Andy Warhol), she turned and faced her host. Olivia was wearing camel slacks, an ivory blouse, and a Van Cleef flower necklace. Olivia in turn faced Melanie, who was dressed in a short black skirt and blazer, with a chunky tourmaline bead necklace that she bought at auction.

"Melanie, I just . . . I'm expecting the junior committee for BAMAM here any minute," said Olivia.

"I know! That's why I'm here! You know I want to battle against Mumps and Measles! I told my butler, sure, they were eradicated outside the Congo years ago, but the ball was so great, they kept it going! I'm so excited to be a part of such a fun gala. I just decided to get here early so we could have a little chat. Plus, I live in the building, so it's obviously not a stretch for me like it is for other people. I really hate it when people are late, one of my pet peeves. It's all about respecting other people's time. But anyway, you and I don't really know each other, and I thought to myself last night, Why is that so? We're both philan-thropists . . . I mean, you won't see anyone else's name appear on more invitations than ours, so we're two peas in a pod, really. It's about time we bonded."

Olivia's class and elegance would never allow her to reveal how rep-rehensible this statement was to her, so she chose to ignore it and let it float up into the air like fairy dust. "But I thought you were on the regu-lar committee of Fight Against Mumps and Measles, not the *junior* committee."

"No, I'm on the junior committee."

"But . . . it's really for people . . ."

Melanie stared at Olivia, waiting for her to spell it out. "What?"

"Well, I suppose for the . . . ones who are responsible for bringing in the junior crowd."

"Oh, I know that people think I'm older because my Arty is middle-aged, but I'm actually closer to your age than Cordelia Vance's. And I don't want to hang around with those old fogies. They're super boring. I want to be with the gals!"

Fortunately for Olivia, the doorbell rang. "Well, you can just have a seat in the living room while I get the door. Please help yourself to tea or coffee."

"Great."

The apartment was almost the identical layout to Melanie and Arthur's, although some walls were moved around. Melanie wondered why in the world Olivia, a single woman, would need all this space. Really, five bedrooms? For what?

Melanie walked into the capacious living room and gauged at once the motif, that very minimalist Ian Schrager hotel lobby meets Calvin Klein home furnishings decor so trendy with the younger set. Of course, the pieces were more important than the ones at the Delano, but the theme was pretty much the same: a palette of muted colors, Eames chairs, Dunbar sofas, crystal vases bursting with fresh calla lilies, the drill. Pencil-pleated champagne silk curtains with white pip-ing adorned the windows, which looked north, providing a sweeping view of Park Avenue and all of the little arterial side streets coursing into it. A marshmallow and coffee Stark carpet covered the chocolate stained floorboards. Some gold-framed charcoal drawings of women in various positions of repose hung above a Chinese lacquer chest, and a few interesting bronzes on a commode. But Melanie's eyes were immediately drawn to the Jasper Johns American flag over the mantel—pretty much the sole burst of color in the room. She could sniff out the cash prizes a mile away.

"Hello, Mrs. Korn," said Brooke Lutz, the housewares heiress (really pots and pans if one was being technical), as she pranced into the room in her Gucci pantsuit and Jimmy Choos.

"Oh, please, call me Melanie! I'm your age—don't make me feel like an old hag."

"Okay. Melanie. Did you enjoy the Botanical Garden party? Wasn't as good as last year," she said, plopping on the sofa.

"That's because Fernanda Wingate was the chair. Really, they have to get some new blood into these organizations, shake it up a little. Dullsville!"

"Why don't you try and become chairman?"

"I really could breathe some life into it."

"Why don't you call Royton Carlson? He's the man who runs it."

Before Melanie could answer, Olivia entered the room with a pregnant Charlotte von Peltz (everyone knew she had forced her husband to add the "von" when she married him). She was soon followed by Adriana Pierce (emerged out of nowhere and quickly ascended the social ranks—oodles of moolah) and Jenny Grossberg (a dog, poor thing— the sister was so much prettier—but at least she possessed a family brokerage account more impressive than the Rothschilds'). Their eyes widened when they saw Melanie, but they said nothing. Melanie chitchatted with Charlotte and Adriana for a while, learning about Adriana's impending move to London ("The Brits are so much more civilized. Plus, we've done New York") and Charlotte's decision to send her daughter to Sacred Heart rather than Spence ("The girls at the convent have more morals than the Spencies . . . While, yes, it's true the Hilton sisters did go there, the fact is we want Serena to go to school with all types of girls, not just children of billionaires"). Melanie made a mental note of every accessory, every jewel, and every label the ladies in the room were wearing. She also watched carefully as Rosemary Peniston and Lila Meyer made their entrances. A cow and a worm. If Melanie were Lila, she would be scared that Rosemary would eat her for dinner.

A fully uniformed maid appeared from time to time to refill cups and make sure the coffee was still hot. There was a plethora of William Poll crustless tea sandwiches (because really, who can deal with that change in texture with crusts?), Greenberg cookies, and Payard petits four laid out on china platters, but none of the women touched a thing.

At long last Jane Roberts, on whom they had been waiting, assumed Melanie, arrived. Jane had elbowed her way onto all these committees by virtue of force. She had been a complete nerd at Chapin and in order to make up for the cool girls' rejection had spent every weekend immersed in breeding and showing her Airedales. When she got older and learned that money was a lot more powerful than going to third base with the hottest guy at Collegiate, she threw it around, hired a publicist to photograph her extravagant parties, and became a queen bee.

"Charlotte, I have to talk to you," said Jane with great urgency. She nodded to Melanie and Adriana but focused all of her attention on Charlotte.

"Okay . . ." said Charlotte awkwardly, aware of Jane's rudeness.

"It will only take a minute. It's *very* important."

Melanie watched as Jane led Charlotte to the corner. They were both about six months pregnant, but you could tell only if you looked at them from the side, and even then you had to strain your eyes. Melanie leaned back on the sofa in order to find out what was so important.

"So. I just came from Schweitzer Linens, and I was in complete *shock* to find that the monogrammed crib linens set takes sixteen weeks to arrive! I couldn't believe it. There's just such a backlog. So you have to run—I mean, literally, right after this—and put your name down. It's just chaos. It's imperative that you get down there before it's too late."

"Jane, my goodness—thanks! You're a *savior!*"

"Seriously, you don't want to miss out. And they're almost all gone."

Melanie rolled her eyes. What lame-o's. These gals had just too much time on their hands. But that would change when they had sobbing tots in a few months, not that they'd ever see them. Melanie knew women like that just wanted a new accessory, a toy doll to spice things up since their husbands were tedious suits from hell.

The conversation buzzed for another ten minutes, and more tea was consumed. Melanie realized, listening to their snippets of chatter, that she was just as bored with this crowd as she was with the older folks. What a letdown. So they came out of the womb a little later—so what? They were still the same stiffs yakking about the same meaningless stuff. But this group had a faux seriousness that irritated her. Jane monopolized the conversation about the coffee table book she was doing about Upper East Side libraries. Virtually every girl in the room would be featured. When Charlotte left the room, everyone whispered about how her daughter was not accepted to Spence, and *that's* why she was going to Sacred Heart. Plus, there were some eyebrows raised over little Serena's mental capacity at her kindergarten interview (poor little thing had apparently been trying to jam the square block in the triangle-shaped hole). Brooke talked about how hard she worked, when everyone knew that although she had an "office" at her family's company, she did jack. Rosemary talked about her purebred poodle having puppies that she had no idea what to do with. Lila moaned about no single men in New York. Adriana complained that she couldn't find a costume for Jane's Madame de Pompadour party. There was the usual banter as well, and every cutting remark was couched in concern, every snide barb followed by a "just kidding." The only one who didn't really partake in the conversation was Olivia, Melanie noticed. Smart cookie. That's probably why no one really said anything bad about her.

"So, when do we get down to business?" Melanie finally asked loudly. She had to get out of there soon or she'd fall into a coma.

"What do you mean?" asked Rosemary, surprised.

"I mean, this is a committee meeting. When do we talk about the gala?"

The women all looked at each other. Lila smiled slyly.

"Oh, well, what's there to talk about?" asked Olivia.

"Well, don't we organize something?"

"Not really," said Adriana.

"Then what is the meeting for?"

They all glanced at one another. "Well, to catch up, regroup," said Charlotte.

"That's all?" asked Melanie.

"Yes," they all said, almost in unison.

Bizarre, thought Melanie. And a shame. It seemed like this group could really put not only their wallets to use but also their brains and think up some creative charitable events. Something radical for them, like maybe actually visiting the sick patients or underprivileged children that they raised money for.

"Well, then, I've got to be going," Melanie said, rising. "Great to see you all."

Olivia walked out to the foyer with Melanie. "Can I use your restroom?"

"Sure," said Olivia, wondering why she couldn't just go at home. "It's through my office," she said, pointing down the hall.

"Thanks, and don't worry, I'll show myself out," she said, turning around. "Oh, and let's have lunch soon."

Melanie entered Olivia's office and looked around. The peanut butter–walled room was definitely set up like a writer's dream office—rare leather-bound first editions lined the shelves; a collection of antique globes (as if for research purposes) were displayed on a large Campaign chest, and a reclining chair sat in the corner. An arty-looking drafting table hosted a laptop, a Tiffany glass lamp, a silver cup full of architect's pens, and a diary. Melanie walked over to the desk and spied a bright-colored piece of cellophane poking out from the slightly open top drawer. *Hmm, what's this?* Melanie reached for the pewter handle and pulled it open. Wow. Not Percocet, not Demerol, not Valium, but Ding Dongs, Reese's Pieces, and Twinkies were her drugs. Grinning and in shock, Melanie moved her hands over the Entenmann's explosion of chocolate-coated doughnut holes and half-eaten cookies next to picked-at pound cake and cinnamon filbert swirls. It was as if Sara Lee herself had stocked the carb- and candy-loaded drawer. Melanie's eyes widened as she beheld the gazillion-calorie extravaganza. Interesting, very interesting. And the chick was a twig. Bulimia? Obviously. So this was what Olivia Weston was all about. Who would believe it? So graceful and perfect on the outside, and yet if a coroner were to slice her open he'd find er refinedreve hostess

a sea of M&M's and Ho-Hos. Her refined, revered hostess was an addict of Hostess. And *Melanie* was the one they all called white trash?

chapter 34

Eddie and Tom, the doormen of 741 Park, were standing side by side, their wide eyes looking right and left as if following a tennis ball at the U.S. Open. But it was not that kind of moving sphere they followed so carefully. It was pairs of breasts. Watching the posh women of the tree-lined avenue balancing on their high, pointy shoes, wrapped in sensuous fabrics, and ornamented in fineries the porters' combined salaries couldn't dream of acquiring was a never-ending intoxicator. A high school girl sauntered by with a cigarette and a pleated school uniform rolled up at the waist to hike the school-enforced dreary hemline, revealing her coltish thighs.

"Look at that little nymphet," said Tom, practically salivating. "I could teach that student a thing or two."

"Come to papa," echoed Eddie under his breath.

Olivia Weston strolled out, every silken hair in place, in a cropped Prada bomber and swirly Marc Jacobs skirt.

"Hello, Ms. Weston!"

"Hello." She never learned their names.

Her exit was followed by more girl watching, then helping batty Mrs. Cockpurse out of her car. Drew Vance then came in with his tweed jacket and cocky swagger. Just the daily upscale foot traffic at the swankiest residence in town.

"Cowabunga," said Eddie, drooling over a Euro-trash trophy wife with platinum Donatella locks and amped-up boobs. Keeping her in his leering gaze, he followed her stride around the corner.

"Good afternoon, mademoiselle," said Tom, straightening his posture respectfully.

A small dog in a full Burberry outfit entered the lobby. It was Mademoiselle Oeuf, the sole heir to an infinite fortune, prancing across the marble to the elevator, led by her trainer.

"That bitch is so unfriendly," said Eddie.

"Which, the pooch or the dyke trainer?"

They shared a hearty laugh until a distinguished-looking African-American gentleman approached them, interrupting their harmonic chuckle.

"Deliveries at the back," said Tom before the man could say a word.

"I beg your pardon?"

"Just around the corner. You'll see the door," said Eddie.

"I'm here to see Mrs. Korn. It's not a delivery."

"Oh, uh, hold on. What's your name?" As soon as the man said it, Eddie put up his hand sternly. "Stay right here," warned Eddie before going inside to buzz his tenant. He came back out and offered an unspoken "oops" with his guilty, doofus smile, then said, "Go on up."

Melanie was doing some last-minute pillow fluffage when she thought she heard the doorbell.

"JUANITA! Can you get the door? JUANITAAA!"

She couldn't even hear her own voice over the vacuum cleaner racket. Melanie rolled her eyes and walked toward the door to answer it herself. In an unfortunate coincidence, it was Guffey's day off. Melanie was in a panic that she would have to be interviewed by the *Observer* without him, but Arthur calmed her down. He reminded her that Guffey was a butler, after all, not Emily Post or Albert Einstein. Let him get back to dusting and pouring, and Melanie could handle the rest. Melanie was unsure, but she had no choice.

"Hi, welcome!" She flashed her best newly whitened smile.

"Hello. I'm Billy Crispin from the *New York Observer*."

"It's nice to meet you—come on in. I have a whole lunch set up for you. Feasts and Fêtes catered. Daniel Boulud's company . . ."

"Splendid," he said, looking around curiously.

"But first, why don't I give you the grand tour? It's going to be in all the magazines."

"I'm sure it'll be photographed as many times as the Boardman sisters."

She laughed, hoping he was right. What a compliment! She led him across the hall to the grand parlor, decorated by Ann LeConey, who was Diandra's favorite. She was so proud of the massive renovation she'd had done in less than two months; she'd paid triple the normal rates to rush everything, but what's money for if you don't spend it? And while the armies of decorators has been installing, she had been all over town swinging paddles relentlessly at all the auction houses, amassing a new collection of artworks that would make everyone foam at the mouth. She proudly led the way like the *Price Is Right* girls through a showcase showdown, past the mahogany balustrade of the large staircase into the massive drawing room, swimming in silks and satins.

"Of course, you may have read that we purchased this chair at the JFK auction. Such a tragedy about the son. And the wife! Caroline Bessette!"

"Carolyn."

"Right. Such a horror. People with real class like that are like an endangered species. There are very few women of taste left," she said, unconsciously counting them on her fingers.

"You're obviously including yourself in the glittering pantheon," said Crispin, baiting her.

"Oh, you!" said Melanie, flattered and unsure how to react. Crispin stared at her, waiting for her response. "Well, everyone aspires to be the best," she offered.

"You're absolutely right," said Crispin, amused. "And I believe Olivia Weston will carry the torch for the future. Doesn't she live in this building?"

"Yes, she does. Such a sweetie. I was at her house the other day."

"Oh, you two are tight?"

"No, er . . . no."

"But you are friends?"

"I like her very much," said Melanie.

"You seem like such opposites."

"Well, I guess . . ."

"I suppose people are more alike than you think," offered Crispin.

"Yes, that's true!" responded Melanie with alacrity.

Crispin squinted and scribbled something down on his notepad. Melanie decided to move on by highlighting the exquisite provenance of various decorative objects around the room ("This bar cart was

Pamela Harriman's"; "And this ashtray was Babe Paley's!"). She guided him into the ornate library complete with the rare leather spines of a bibliophile's first-edition fantasy.

"And this, this was Slim Keith's cigarette case—" She held it up to him, smiling, hoping for a reaction as if to say, "Love me, Daddy!"

"You smoke?"

"No."

Silence.

"Um, let's go into my office!"

She led him up the stairs, passing a large painting in a gilded frame.

"This is a Claude Monet. There's one at the Met just like it, but ours is better, scholars have said."

"Lovely. What scholars?"

"Um . . ." Melanie was flummoxed. "I'll have to get back to you on that."

As they ascended, two cute (but not that cute) twenty-somethings walked down, holding various notebooks and invitations.

"Oh, Billy, this is Susie, my assistant."

Susie nodded politely.

"And this is Emma, Susie's assistant."

At the top of the stairs, there was another large entrance hall with eagle sconces she and Arthur had bought at auction for four hundred thousand dollars. She showed them to Billy, who couldn't help but realize that she was pointing them out in the very same way a flight attendant would demonstrate where the emergency exits are.

She stopped by a pair of micro mosaic side tables.

"These were in the Rothschilds' country estate in England. Not the suicidal Rothschilds, mind you, a different branch. Provenance is very important to us."

"Pedigree is primary."

"That goes without saying. We have a similar one at our home in the Ham—" She'd caught herself, thank god. "At the beach. We were foolishly planning on living out there full-time. I mean, it is twenty thousand square feet, forty acres—we'd be fine! But we scrapped that idea."

"I see."

"I used to think I was a country girl, but I soon realized I was a country house girl."

They made their way back downstairs, pausing by a Degas statue of a forlorn-looking ballet dancer in an aged yellow tutu. Melanie was leading him toward the dining room when Billy stopped.

"What's this door?" Billy asked, leaning for the filigreed antique knob.

"Oh that's—"

Before she could answer, he turned it and opened the door.

"NOOOOOOO!" screamed Melanie, as if being stabbed by a machete-wielding maniac. Billy was alarmed by her ear-piercing shriek. But the damage was done: before his eyes was Arthur's private office, complete with his black leather Jennifer Convertibles furniture from his days across the river. Yankees memorabilia lined the walls, and autographed balls and jerseys were displayed in lit glass cabinets. Melanie, unable to recover in her momentary shock of The Press seeing her husband's sports garbage, caught her breath and swiftly closed the door.

"Oh, this junk is all just Arthur's loot. His hideout, you know."

Trying to paint over the visual faux pas that was her husband's lair, she swiftly led her guest into a stunning chamber with painted rococo panels and a Georges V desk.

"Voilà! This one is my office."

Billy looked around. Clearly he was impressed, thought Melanie.

"What do you do, exactly, Mrs. Korn?"

"I'm a philanthropist," she said, as is she were saying, *I bring water to ailing souls in a hospice*. "I work entirely on behalf of the people who are less fortunate than Arty and myself."

"How does your work compare to say, that of Joan Coddington or Blaine Trump?"

"Well, Joan Coddington works out of a phone booth at the Colony Club. She doesn't have a setup like this!"

"Is there any . . . rivalry among women in your philanthropy scene?"

"No, no, no . . . I mean, not on my side, that is. Most of these socialites are all talk and don't actually do anything but coast on the Roman numerals at the end of their husbands' names."

"So you fancy yourself as different."

"Different compared to whom? I mean, I don't just want to throw money around so I get good tables at charity balls. I mean, I'll be honest—I want good tables at events as well, but it actually is really important to me to make a difference. 'Cause if you don't, then what's it all about?"

"So whom do you compare yourself to?"

"Well, I really admire Brooke Astor. Everything she has done has been so incredible."

"So you consider yourself the next Brooke Astor?"

"As far as my charitable ambitions."

"So, yes?"

"If that's the case, then yes, *I'm* the next Brooke Astor."

As the sides of his mouth slowly lifted to a bold smile, Billy's small cassette recorder in his breast pocket was lovingly reeling the thin brown tape in, printed with her every murmured word. It sucked all her stridently confident banter into little audio codes, ready for playback and transcription in an hour's time at the East Sixty-fourth Street *Observer* offices, to be savored forever. And Crispin was smelling a cover story.

chapter 35

It had been a busy morning for Jerome de Stingol, who had spent hours—hours!—rearranging the Bateses' toy bank collection in their new Carnegie Hill apartment, which had a spectacular view of the Jackie Onassis Reservoir. When he finally took his leave, the weather had cooled considerably and he was quite chilly in his light Barbour jacket. As he was miles away from Bergdorf's and even farther from Paul Smith, he made an emergency detour and pushed open the blue door to J. McLaughlin. He almost gasped as he felt seasick from all the whales embroidered on the Nantucket reds, and he even put a calming hand to his throat, though none of his ladies were on hand to smile at his dramatic gesture implying need for an emergency Dramamine.

"Scarves, please?" he bellowed to the smarmy, pleated-front

khaki–wearing prepster behind the counter, who was reading *Handbag Designing for Dummies.* Hmph. *Everyone thinks she can be the next Kate Spade these days. She's probably named Penelope.*

"Right on this shelf," she gestured, leaving her entrepreneurial satchel dreams for a moment to escort the impeccably dressed de Stingol to the cashmere wares. He selected a plain cranberry one and studied the hue in the store light and then again by the window.

"No need to wrap it," he said.

He emerged swathed in his new acquisition, which protected his delicate throat from the cold. As he passed the perfectly squeegeed windows of Carnegie Hill on his way to lunch with the girls, he glimpsed at his smart reflection off the shiny glass of the casual café Island. Then, through the glass, he spied Melanie Korn getting up from her table to leave. She was wearing way too many jewels for daytime.

Jerome had hoofed it in his Stubbs & Wootton loafers almost twenty blocks when he burst into RSVP, where Olivia Weston and Brooke Lutz awaited him at a charming table by the window, overlooking Lexington. And more important, overlooking all those who entered for lunch across the street at Swifty's—Dominick, Mimi, Pat, Mario—and the girls were so pleased with the divine sport of people watching, they hardly noticed their friend was ten minutes late.

"Oh, I'm *mortified* to keep you two lovely doves waiting!"

"*Gerôme*," Brooke pronounced in a parfait French accent. "Do not worry, love. We were having a delightful time spying."

He embraced Brooke, then her delicate compatriot Miss Weston.

"Liv, darling," he said, kissing her pale hand. "How art thou? Ugh—guess who I just saw?"

Jerome took a seat, ready to dish. The waiter inconveniently approached for his order, which seemed to frustrate the group. "Seltzer and gazpacho," Jerome said, almost dismissing the young man from their space. The girls added their salad requests and Jerome launched.

"Your neighbor, Mrs. Korn. So tacky. And I have Pentagon-worthy news: I hear Billy Crispin's working on a profile of her in the *Observer*."

"No! He has an acid tongue!"

"I refuse to talk to him. So indiscreet."

"I know, this town is *full* of indiscretions. As a decorator, I am privy to them all, you see—I mean, installations in Greenwich where the husband was screwing the babysitter! And I did a maison in Sagaponack, and I needed to measure the grounds for the rock wall and found the wife snogging the pool boy. I mean, nothing surprises me!"

"Vulgar," said Olivia.

"Well, I can't wait to see the article," said Brooke, with a huge grin. "I have to tell Mummy to look out for it. She is literally stalked by Melanie! She so wants to be friends with my parents, it's scary."

"She's my neighbor," added Olivia, taking a small sip of water. "She and her husband live just above me."

"Poor you!" Jerome laughed. Jerome looked over at Brooke, who looked beautiful in her perfect suit, fur collar—a perfect size two.

"Looking *ravissante,* my dear Brooke. Tiny as can be."

"Well, that was the upside of all my nausea throughout the pregnancy. Everyone felt horrible for me as I ran out of the town car to get sick in a Madison Avenue trash can, but meanwhile I stayed skinny the whole time!"

"You had a C section, right?" asked Jerome. "Does that take longer to recover from?"

"So they say, but who cares? I scheduled my C section in advance. I always knew I wanted one. I got the Demerol so the healing was painless, and, trust me, my husband's thanking me for it!"

"Well," said Jerome in a hushed tone, "the last thing you need is a vagina the size of the Midtown Tunnel."

The girls blushed and cackled.

"True. Plus, C section kids are always much cuter," said Brooke, as if all naturally birthed babies were hideous cone-headed freaks. "It's totally the way to go. That Caesar totally knew what he was doing."

"Good for you! You look just fabu," said Jerome, proud of her. "Poor Amy Freston—she really put on the ell-bees, I must say."

"I know," said Olivia, looking downward.

"Everyone thought she would produce septuplets at the very least, and just one hideous creature popped out! She looked as if she had eaten Canada," said Jerome with disgust.

"It's so sad," said Brooke. The trio had a moment of silence for Amy, as if it had been announced she had been diagnosed with Lou Gehrig's.

"What did she name her son?" asked Jerome.

"MacAllister. But they're calling him Ster."

"Anyway, Brooke, thank goodness you don't have on the weight she does. I mean, looking at you, no one would know you just bore fruit."

"Ugh! The fruit is driving me crazy! Thank heavens for my Icelandic babysitters. I tell you, it's all about Iceland these days. I would never have some stupid island person near my little Carrington. I tell you, these girls are saviors. I don't know what I would without them. I mean, the child cries and cries!"

"Well, this is normal," said Jerome. "It's a baby."

"I know, I know." Brooke laughed. "It's just frustrating, because when Montague comes home, it's just all about the baby and I'm, like, invisible!"

"That's why I don't want children," said Olivia, matter-of-factly. "I could never deal with that. Also, I'm just not a baby person."

"Or they love the nanny too much," continued Brooke. "I mean, sometimes I have to pry little Carrington's fingers from Gröotie's arms!"

"Well, maybe he's a ladies' man; he's certainly not taking after his Uncle Jerome!" the decorator cried.

"You kill me!" exclaimed Brooke.

"I'd rather have that Ashton Kutcher as my caretaker!"

"Oh, Jerome!" squealed Brooke, who had never laughed harder. "You're hilarious!"

chapter **36**

Cordelia was putting in an earring as Morgan poked his cufflink through the hole in his dress shirt with irritation and glanced at his watch.

"I can't believe you got us roped into this," he said, shaking his head.

"Darling," said his wife apologetically and defensively, "what was I supposed to do? Melanie was very persistant. She stopped me in the elevator a hundred times, and I offered every excuse in the book. But what can I do when she leaves seven dates on our machine? I can't possibly tell her we're booked for every one."

"There are ways, Cordelia. Just keep canceling at the last minute. Then she'll get the hint."

"She doesn't *get* hints, Morgan. She doesn't *get* anything about what people think of her."

"I just can't believe we have to endure dinner there. Arthur's fine I suppose, harmless."

"There will probably be tons of people we know so we can just go off in a corner. I'm guessing they'll have fifteen couples, maybe twenty."

Moments later, after first riding the elevator to the lobby so that Luca and Fred on the evening shift could unlock the Korns' floors, the Vances arrived in the hand-painted vestibule. But there was no familiar din coming through the front doors, as there usually was at New York dinner parties—no excited bustle or music or cocktail chitchat . . . just silence.

"Are we early?" asked Morgan.

"I don't think so," said Cordelia, ringing the bell.

A black tie–clad butler answered the door to an empty foyer and shortly Melanie appeared, relieving them that they hadn't come on the wrong night.

"Hel*loooo,* neighbors!" she said, leaning in to kiss Cordelia. Cord wasn't the kissing type.

"Are we early?" asked Morgan.

"No, no, no, no, no!" said Melanie. "It's just us and Paul and Miriam Lutz. They're in the living room with Arthur. It'll be nice, just an intimate dinner for the six of us! I thought it would be more fun that way, you know, with all the crazy packed parties we all go to every night. This way it's just relaxed. We like doing things very, very casual."

Casual consisted of three Tentations chefs, one sommelier, and three servers, resulting in a one to two ratio of waiter to guest. Mr. Guffey actually enjoyed fetes such as these, when he felt like a conductor directing a world-class symphony. With his magical ability to be invisible and yet everywhere, he oversaw every last detail on its course toward perfection.

The Lutzes, noticeably relieved to see the Vances, ran across the dining room to greet their semi-acquaintances. At least they were not alone.

"So, we're all here!" said Arthur.

The sommelier poured everyone an exquisite pink champagne. "It's Crystalle Rosé, 1972," said Melanie, making sure everyone noticed. She wanted her guests to know they were getting the best, but it actually worked against her. In a world where tact was a virtue, Melanie was a constant sinner, and her pronouncements—which came off as bragging to her acquaintances—took her guests aback. Mr. Guffey shot Melanie a look, and she realized at once that she had erred. No more name-dropping! One of the cardinal sins. It wasn't her fault; she was just nervous.

"Is there a ladies' room?" asked Cordelia, setting her flute down delicately.

"Oh, I'll join you!" said Miriam.

A servant directed them down the hallway into a gilded powder room. Miriam looked at Cordelia, who had never been the warmest, but she had never been happier to see someone.

"You know how you could be in, say, Rome," Miriam started, "and you bump into a couple that you sort of know in New York, but you say hello and perhaps even have a drink even though you never would at home?"

Cordelia paused. "Yes, yes, I know what you mean."

"Well, I know we're not the best of friends, but we have a trillion friends in common, and when we saw you tonight it was like you and Morgan were our brethren who we ran into on foreign soil. I mean, I am thrilled to see you!"

The two women smiled and held hands for a moment.

"You know," Miriam continued, "that Melanie has been itching to have Paul propose her for the Met board. She's just dying to be a Some-body. I said *hell,* no to this dinner, but she called and left eleven dates on our machine! What were we supposed to do?"

Cordelia smiled, feeling sorry for her neighbor: everyone truly detested her. And she wasn't *that* bad. Maybe a little rough around the edges.

"I'm sure it will be great," said Cordelia, trying to put on a positive front. "Let's just have fun," she suggested as they made their way into the dining room.

They all gathered around the table, and Melanie took on the role of conversation guide.

"So," she said, as everyone lifted their sterling spoons to the bowls of white truffle–infused mushroom soup, "so Cordelia, you and Morgan have been married for, like, ever and ever! Morgan just said twenty-eight years? How did you two meet?"

Cordelia, even with only five people in company, felt suddenly as if a huge laser beam were being shone on her face, and she almost squinted from the glare. Her husband felt tightness in his neck as well. He knew Cordelia loathed being the center of attention, and he wanted desperately to protect her. But his fragile little bird was forced to venture out and give an answer to the beast shaking the tree.

"Well," she began, looking at Morgan for comfort, which he gave in the form of a supportive smile, "we were at the Cosmopolitan Club at Deirdre Pearce's cotillion. I was seated at the same table as Morgan, next to Higby Sommers, but I never stopped staring at this one." She blushed, looking down at her soup. She felt reckless, admitting that.

The way her lashes flickered downward at that moment reminded Morgan of her bashful glances back then, in her strapless lilac gown with a flower in her hair.

"But he seemed more interested in our hostess . . ."

"Not true! I couldn't even pick her out of a lineup."

"Well, I was under that impression. He danced the night away with her."

"Her older sister was very bossy. She kept coming over to me and telling me I was being terribly rude not to ask her sister," explained Morgan apologetically.

"Well, thankfully there was one dance that her father insisted on dancing with her. And for some reason—I believe Higby had gone to the bathroom . . ."

"Or gone out back to have some scotch out of his flask . . ." interjected Morgan.

"Whatever happened, Morgan and I were suddenly alone at the table. So Morgan slid over the seat next to me and we started talking . . ."

"And I tried to gather the courage to ask her to dance," Morgan added, smiling at his wife with nostalgic love into his voice.

"And he finally did." Cordelia paused, remembering. She could still picture the table decorations, taste the lemon meringue cake, smell the hyacinths draped around the patio in the yard.

Morgan paused as well. Normally he would never have confessed all these intimate memories in front of a room full of people; it wasn't his style. But he didn't care. And it all came back to him now. He remembered that Chuckie Lyons had given him a ride and scratched his father's car when he pulled in the driveway. And that he hadn't gotten home until two and his nanny—yes, she was still around then—had been worried. And that he had thought Cordelia was the most perfect creature he had ever laid eyes on.

Melanie stared at them. "And then what?" she interrupted.

Cordelia and Morgan returned back to present day.

"And I knew, that first time Morgan swirled me out and twirled me back in, that he would be my husband." She smiled that enigmatic, wistful smile that had first melted him.

Morgan's heart ached with love for his wife. Her goodness was almost too much; his already mounting guilt was approaching epic, intolerable proportions.

"Isn't that just great!" squealed Melanie, clapping her hands together. She motioned to the waiters to clear the first course.

Meanwhile, Mrs. Lutz knew damn well how their host and hostess had met but wanted to see what they'd offer as answer. See how they liked the spotlight.

"How about you two?" The corners of Miriam's mouth went up mischievously, but she was trumped.

"Oh, we met while Arty was traveling. We were seated next to each other in first class," she said. Melanie knew Miriam knew the truth. But the Korns had been asked this before, and they knew how to play it.

"Really? Where were you off to?" asked Miriam.

"Florida," said Arthur quickly. He knew this was Melanie's least favorite topic. Well, that and her past. "How about you two? How'd ya meet?"

The Lutzes explained rather didactically how they had been set up on a blind date by a mutual friend who told each about the other and how they were both from "good" (read: loaded) families. They conveyed little emotion.

As the filet was served, the talk turned to the world of finance.

"I am just so sad for poor Ben Holden," said Miriam. "To be pushed out of his own company!"

"It's terrible," said Paul. "He built that from the ground up."

"But I mean, the poor dear! He just seems so sad!" added Miriam.

"It's awful," agreed Melanie.

"Whattaya talking about?" interjected Arthur. "The guy raked the company through the coals, screwed the shareholders, and is leaving with a billion bucks in his pocket. He should be happy he's not in prison!"

Miriam looked stricken. Who was this odious man? "How can you say that? He's a huge contributor to New York Hospital!"

"What I think Arty means . . ." began Melanie, worried. *Don't fuck it up!* It was going so well.

"So what?" Arthur said with his mouth full. "He gave away money that wasn't his to give. Hell, I can do that! Here, Cordelia, would ya like some of Paul Lutz's three hundred million?" Arthur burst into laughter.

Cordelia smiled politely. Melanie watched Miriam's eyes narrow and tried in vain to diffuse the situation. "Arty, I think they mean that he was generous and the shareholders should have some mercy."

"I don't buy that, Mel! Come on, the guy's a crook! He was skimming off the top! He oughta go to jail."

Melanie cursed herself. She should have told Arty to abstain from red wine. It made him too loquacious. He was embarrassing her! He should not offer opinions at any time.

"You know, I think Arthur's right," said Morgan. "People should be held accountable. That's what we lack in our society. Accountability."

Morgan became Melanie's personal hero. "True," she murmured. Miriam, meanwhile, raised her eyebrows yet again.

"See, I knew I liked you, Vance. We're on the same team."

Morgan felt emboldened. Perhaps it was the wine. "Yes, we are. People need to pay for their sins. You have to stand up and be a man. The time has come. If Ben Holden cheated the shareholders, then he's out! That's all there is to it. What's that saying that the African-American lawyer always said?"

"If the glove don't fit, acquit?" offered Melanie, unsure.

"Oh, yes. No. Maybe it wasn't the African-American lawyer. Hmmm . . ." thought Morgan aloud, as five sets of eyes egged him on. "Oh, yes! If you can't do the crime, no, no. If you can't do the time, don't commit the crime!" Morgan leaned back with satisfaction.

"Thatta boy!" said Arthur, raising his glass. "Here, here."

Melanie raised her glass eagerly, and Miriam and Paul followed halfheartedly.

Cordelia stared into her glass, and then took a very large swig of the wine. "Why, Morgan," she said finally, "I never knew you felt that way." And with that, she finished her glass.

After the magnificent five-course menu, the three couples retreated into the living room, where Miriam's eyes grazed every single painting and objet d'art in the joint, estimating its value. She was an auction-aholic and had memorized every hammer price for years. She raised a knowing eyebrow and gave a quiet nod of recognition when she came upon a piece she knew the Korns had acquired despite escalated bids. And with each piece, her inner accountant's calculator tabulated the grand total, as the mental white receipts rolled on and on until hitting the floor. Melanie tried to give her a tour, but Miriam brushed her off and instead embarked on her own private excursion of the apartment, her mental data processor ready. She liked to assess in private.

It was tasteful, you had to give Melanie that. She had been coached well. That was one thing she at least had the smarts about, to hire a decorator who knows furniture. Too many of them just fill the house up with reproductions and then when it's estate sale time the heirs are left with loads of fakes that may have fit well in an obscure corner of a room but are ultimately worth nada. Miriam reluctantly approved of the wall art in the study and the decor of Melanie's office, but she still searched for a fatal flaw. Finally she was in luck: in the library she spied a pair of blue and white Ming Dynasty vases on the mahogany mantel. She immediately returned to the living room and approached Melanie quietly as the others were conversing. She took Melanie's hand.

"Darling Melanie," she said. "Come here."

"Is everything okay?" asked Melanie. Miriam Lutz unnerved her. She had a supercilious air that was impenetrable, and she was one of those people who seemed to relish finding faults in others. Miriam didn't deign to answer her hostess and instead dragged her to the library and stopped in front of the vases. She sighed deeply and pointed.

"Do me a favor," she implored.

"A favor?" asked Melanie. "Sure," she said hesitantly. "What is it?"

"It's about these vases," she said, pausing dramatically.

"What?" asked Melanie. She had no idea what Miriam meant.

Miriam sighed deeply. "They really do not belong in this room," Miriam pronounced. "They ought to be in the living room. It's a much more suitable color palette for them."

At first Melanie felt humiliated, as if she had been slapped. How could she be so stupid? These vases—in here—it was just so stupid. And then she thought, *Wait a second . . . who the hell are you?* Suddenly, Melanie felt her blood boiling. What was Miriam saying? Had she never heard of ANN LECONEY? Who the the hell was she to march in and give decorating tips! Just because she was some housewares doyenne didn't mean she knew shit about collecting. What a sense of entitlement! Here she was, sauntering in and being served a caviar and white truffle dinner that was five hundred dollars a head, and she was doling out advice? Melanie was working herself into a frothy frenzy and was about to blow her lid. But instead she took a deep breath and counted to three. With "Mississippi" between the numbers. She took a final exhalation.

"Thank you for that thought," she said finally. "Oh! Just look at the time! I must put Arthur to bed. He turns into a pumpkin at midnight!"

Melanie tried to chuckle politely, but her heart wasn't in it. Miriam smiled at her while thinking that finally she could get out of there. Despite its size and lavish decor, the Korns' apartment still felt to Miriam like one of those coffins that Arthur hawked in Queens.

When they returned to the room, Cordelia and Morgan were

squeezed tightly into the settee, looking like honeymooners. Paul sat alone on a fauteuil, and Arthur was on the couch, regaling the guests with death stories.

"We should be off," said Miriam, with pretend sorrow. Paul shot up like a cannonball.

"Yup, great supper, Arthur," he said, patting Arthur on the back.

"Wow, I suppose it is late," said Morgan, glancing at his watch.

"This was such fun," said Cordelia with sincerity. It was. It was nice to break out of their boring little social circle every now and then. Shake it up a little.

"I hadda great time," said Arthur, walking them to the door. "And Vance, if that person you mentioned does die, I got the perfect coffin for ya," said Arthur.

"What's that all about?" asked Melanie.

"Oh, just someone I know," said Morgan. "Someone on the brink of death."

"Come on, sweetie, time for bed," said Cordelia.

Mr. Guffey appeared out of nowhere with coats for the Lutzes. There was a flurry of thank-yous and kisses good night and finally the two couples left. When Mr. Guffey closed the door behind them and returned to the kitchen, Melanie and Arthur looked at each other and gave a shared sigh of relief.

"I think it went well. What do you think?" asked Melanie.

"Fun," said Arthur, ripping off his tie. "You know, those Vances are not as boring as I thought. They're actually nice."

"I agree. Really down to earth. I never would have expected that."

"I bet Vance would be fun to go to a ball game with."

"I wish you hadn't said that about Ben Holden . . ." began Melanie.

"Don't start, sweetie," advised Arthur. "It went well. Be happy."

"You're right. It went well. I think they loved us."

"Here we are, hobnobbing with witty and fashionable society! Who'da thought?"

And with that they went to bed. Melanie was excited. The dinner party was a coup, and except for Miriam's snide little comments, everything had worked out well. The meal was impressive, of course the apartment was impressive, and, actually, the Vances were nice. Melanie was tired and ready for sleep. Tomorrow was a big day. That night her dreams would be filled with something better than sugar plum fairies— the sugar-candy land of Fame. And tomorrow, after much delay, the profile that would launch her as a bona fide society maven was hitting the newsstands. Fuck you, Miriam Lutz! After tomorrow's *New York Observer* article, she and the rest of her Met trustees would be salivating to get Melanie on their board!

chapter 37

The stenciled elevator doors opened with a bell into the grand lobby of 741 Park Avenue and Melanie ran out, eyes darting in all directions. Last night had really been a success, and today was to be her ultimate triumph: the *New York Observer* featuring her interview would be released.

Olivia Weston walked into the lobby, holding a copy of the *Observer,* and looked at her neighbor with an amused glance before stepping into the elevator.

"Oh good, it's out!" yelped Melanie, thrilled. Finally Olivia would see what it's like to read press about someone else, for a change. She could already tell Olivia was looking at her differently. Now she'd definitely want to be friends.

Emma Cockpurse was plopped on her usual perch, the lobby's slate blue overstuffed velvet couch, and the doormen were trying to coax her to go back to her apartment because she had come down in only her late husband's blue bathrobe. Melanie waited impatiently for Eddie and Tom, but they clearly had their hands full. Finally, kooky Mrs. Cockpurse got back in the elevator, escorted by Tom, and Melanie was free to inquire about the day's mail. Olivia seemed to have brought her paper in from the outside.

"So, Tom . . ."

"Eddie."

"Right. Is the mail in yet?"

"Nope, not just yet."

"Oh, well—I'll get it at the vending machine."

"It's cold out there, ma'am."

"Oh, that's okay. It's worth it," said Melanie, who was nearly knocked over by the huge gust of wind that came in when they opened the door. She bravely stepped out and buttoned her cashmere sweater. She folded her arms and hugged herself against the cold as she battled the wind to get to the corner.

Tom came back down and asked Eddie where Mrs. Korn had gone.

"She's in for some surprise when she sees that newspaper!" said Tom, laughing.

Eddie whipped out his already dog-eared copy of the *Observer* from under his coat. "Tell me about it. Quite a scandal."

At the corner, Melanie nervously fed quarters into the slot, opened the box and ripped out the top copy of the peach-colored newspaper.

Shrieks. The trees down Park Avenue bristled. Horrified pigeons flew from their roost. In a three-block radius, every human heard her cry, plus some pets. A huge caricature of Melanie in a full stewardess uniform holding wads of fanned-out money was emblazoned on the front cover, above the fold. In a state of shock, she began to hyperventilate, then gathered herself up enough to look both ways and take out the rest of the papers in the machine. She walked furiously at Mach ten speed and marched into her lobby. She carried the stack of thirty papers past her mischievously amused doormen and couldn't even acknowledge them, as her head vibrated with the rattle of mortification, vaulting her into a black realm of surreal panic. This could not be happening.

Second to the births of their children, the time Joan and Wendy were enjoying was the happiest of their lives. It was as if rays of light shone down on them that morning, and they were falling over themselves thanking their lucky press stars; it was too good to be true. In their corner booth perch at Daniel, they counted the copies of the *Observer* around the room. Wendy spied twenty-six so far, which meant twenty-six jaws on the floor. Everyone was agog.

"*Oh!* Listen to this one!" said Joan, rereading Crispin's piece for the seventeenth time, selecting the greatest nuggets from Korndom. "Quote: 'I want the best tables at events . . .' and then two seconds later she calls herself, and I quote, 'the next Brooke Astor.' Can you *believe this*?"

"Imagine what Brooke would say."

"Listen to this," said Joan, practically licking her lips. " 'Mrs. Korn counts herself in the glittering pantheon that includes Olivia Weston and the late Mrs. John F. Kennedy, Jr. She talks often of Olivia, whom she refers to as "such a sweetie" and keeps track of how recently she was invited to Ms. Weston's home. Although Ms. Weston refused comment, her inner circle insists that she loathes the coffin heiress.' That's just humiliating! What does Arthur think?"

"Can you believe she refers to him as her little Jewish cowboy? Gagsville."

"Billy Crispin is genius. Listen to this line: 'The more that Melanie Korn tries to claw her way up the social ladder, the farther down she slides. Her critics say she is her own worst enemy; her lack of tact, unwavering determination, and notoriously uncouth remarks make people physically recoil.' "

"The man has a gift. He fully captured her essence," marveled Wendy.

Just then, Joan noticed heads turning as lunch partners leaned in with wide eyes and whispering tongues. She turned to see who was entering: was it Brooke Astor with Kenneth Jay Lane? Aerin Lauder? No: it was the man of the hour. Arm in arm with Mimi Halsey, Billy Crispin strolled in, beaming. As every head turned to gaze at him, one socialite began to clap slowly, rising proudly from her chair. Her claps were met by a second pair of hands, then a third, until nearly the whole restaurant joined in the chorus of thrilled palms and approving smiles, which then snowballed into a full standing ovation worthy of La Scala. Butternut squash soup was left for the moment, Bibb lettuce with chives abandoned. As the writer walked to his booth past all the lunchers, he was greeted with approving nods and winks, visual high fives celebrating the brilliance of his oeuvre.

One woman boldly left her table altogether to pay homage.

"Billy, you're a genius; you've made Melanie Korn into a laughing stock! Hilarious."

"Billy, you were naughty naughty!" fake-chided another.

"I was *nice*," said Billy as a hush fell over his neighborhood of tables and everyone lent an ear, as if listening for investment advice from Alan Greenspan. "That article was charity. You should have heard the other things she said! I didn't skewer her," he said. "I *spared* her."

Spared her? What other tidbits had Melanie spewed that fell by the wayside? Joan waved over Gustave, the maître d'.

"Gustave, please send Mr. Crispin a bottle of your best champagne."

"*Oui*, Madame Coddington, *tout de suite*."

On their way out from lunch, Wendy and Joan walked through the grand revolving doors onto Sixty-fifth Street, still reeling. It was as if their lunch had evolved into a full happening, an *event*. And to think that Crispin had been gentle!

But before Joan and Wendy could make it to Park Avenue for cabs, the very same TAG maniac—that odious, fat, stinking man in a greasy army jacket and dirty blue overalls who had accosted Lady Harvey at Swifty's—came charging toward them with a bucket of paint. Leaving no time for them to brace themselves, the bearded demon hurled blood-red paint on their fur coats as they tried to recoil. As if in slow motion, Wendy saw the thick liquid fly toward her as she opened her throat for her life's biggest scream. But it was futile; she knew her sable was toast.

"MURDERERS! ANIMAL KILLERS!" he yelled with an almost drugged slur. "YOU'LL ROT IN HELL WITH DENNIS BASSO AND THE FENDI SISTERS!"

Joan fainted as the TAG maniac chucked the empty bucket and ran.

chapter 38

There are so many options as to how you want to spend eternity. Pine box or steel coffin. Cremated or buried. In a casket with silk lining or velvet folds. Ashes thrown over the edge of a boat or placed in an Oriental urn on the mantel. There were a thousand choices, and Arthur was an expert on every one of them. If there was a new technological advance made in the death business, Arthur knew about it first. He enjoyed being very hands-on in his work. That's why he had the third largest rest home and funeral home business in the country. His retirement homes, Rest 'n' Eaz, and his funeral homes, To Die For, were like the McDonald's of elder care and death services in the United States. And his custom coffin business was also a huge up-and-comer, according to the most recent issue of *Fortune* magazine. And hey, death wasn't going to go out of style anytime soon.

One of Arthur's favorite things to do was to make impromptu visits to all of his outlets just to make sure all was going well, and that is what had brought him to the Lower East Side branch of his funeral home on a particular brisk November afternoon. Three funerals and four cremations were scheduled that day. Not bad, but they could do better. Arthur gave the employees a pep talk about ways to promote the business and was then on his way to his next stop. As the manager held open the door for him, Arthur took two steps onto the pavement and then stopped dead in his tracks. He was face to face with Olivia Weston.

"Oh, hello," she said with a slight smile on her face. She flipped her eggshell cashmere scarf over her shoulder.

Arthur was so surprised to see her that he barely mumbled hello. She looked up at the sign of the building he was exiting and her face immediately changed from forced formality into genuine concern.

"Oh, I hope everything's okay," she said in a worried tone.

"Yes, sure. I was just surprised to see you," Arthur said quickly.

"No, I . . . are you coming from a funeral?"

"A funeral?" Arthur looked around. "Oh, no! This is my place, I mean, not my place, my place of business." Arthur flushed. Why the hell did he get so tongue-tied around her?

"Really?"

"Yeah, I own retirement and funeral homes."

"Interesting."

Arthur looked around. It was not the best neighborhood. He wondered what the heck she was doing there.

"Can I give you a lift?" Arthur asked, motioning to his car.

"Oh, I would love it, but I'm supposed to meet someone who lives

over there," said Olivia pointing across the street at a brick, loftlike building with a giant black door covered in graffiti. "My friend's not home yet,
so I was just going to head to that diner on the corner and wait."

"Oh."

Arthur looked down at the diner, where there were a few sketchy
guys smoking cigarettes and a skinhead with tattoos over every visible
part of his body drinking something out of a paper bag. They were being
really loud and seemed a little dangerous. It was getting dark, and this
whole 'hood was creepsville. Who would Olivia know who lived there?
Maybe Preston was out of rehab? He really didn't like the idea of leaving her alone there.

"You know, I don't think a young woman such as yourself should be
unaccompanied here. I have some time—if you'd like, I could join you
for a cup of coffee," said Arthur in his most formal tone.

"I don't want to impose," said Olivia, glancing around. It was scary
there, and although it might be awkward to sit with a virtual stranger,
she didn't want to be raped.

"It's no imposition."

"All right then, thank you. You're a real gentleman."

After they had been seated at a booth and ordered coffee (Arthur
also asked for a cheese Danish), they gave each other an embarrassed
look. Arthur couldn't believe they were sitting together. She looked
beautiful—her cheeks were flushed pink from the cold, her hair had
been gently tousled in the wind, and she had on an ivory cashmere
turtleneck sweater. He looked down at her beautiful fingers, which
clasped the chipped white coffee mug. She had pale pink polish on
them, so dainty. Sometimes he hated those very red nails that Melanie
favored. They looked like claws. Every little detail of her interested him,
and yet he had no idea what to say to her still.

"Oh! I read the rest of your book. It's great." His enthusiasm was
more about his having thought of something to say rather than about
the novel itself.

"You're sweet."

"Is it autobiographical? I mean, I . . . er, know the woman drowns
herself at the end, but I meant, I mean . . ."

"Parts of it are. Tolstoy said to write what you know, so that's what I try to do."

"And this Preston character? Who's he?"

"He's really a composite."

"I see. Well . . . it's really inventive. That's great that you can think up stories and stuff."

"For my entire life, I've kept journals and scraps of paper where I would jot down little ideas, essays, even poems. Some may say it was foolish or nerdy . . ."

"Who'd say that?" asked Arthur, irate.

"Oh, my friends. They're just kidding, though."

"They'd better be, or maybe it's time to get some new ones." The nerve of those society dilettantes.

"No, they're very supportive."

"They should be. You're great at it. You shouldn't quit just because some boob tells you it's not fashionable."

"Oh, I would never. I love to write."

"Did you always know ya wanted to write?"

"Yes," she said, smiling. Arthur watched her blow on her coffee. Her lips were a perfect shade of pinky red. She opened one of those tiny buckets of half-and-half and swirled it in with her spoon.

"How about you? Did you always want to . . . own funeral homes?"

"Me? No. I was a terrible student. I wasn't going to be a writer, that's for sure. I'm terribly dyslexic."

"Oh, that's too bad," she said, lowering her perfectly plucked eyebrows in sympathy. "So how did you get into your line of work?"

"It's a funny story," said Arthur, taking a bite of his Danish. "I grew up in Flushing—not the good part, the wrong side of the tracks part. Anyhow, one day I was at my friend's house—he lived in the nice part of town—and a big Cadillac pulled into the driveway across the street and a guy got out in a fur coat. I said to my friend—Lenny Shipman, I wonder whatever happened to him?—anyway, I said to Lenny, 'I'm going to do whatever that guy does.' 'Cause it seemed to me like he had so much money. Anyway, he had a funeral home. And that's how it started." Arthur chuckled to himself a little, remembering the old days.

"Well, I guess *Six Feet Under* has made your industry a little chicer," said Olivia.

Just then her cell phone rang. "Excuse me, this may be my friend," she said. She fumbled in her monogrammed tote and pulled out her phone.

"Hello?" she asked in her demure voice. "Holland! Where are you? . . . I'm right on the corner of your block . . . What? Listen, I need to see you." Olivia looked at Arthur, who was staring, and then turned away to the side and whispered into the phone. "It's urgent. Why are you avoiding me? . . . All right, I'm leaving now." She closed her phone and put it back into her bag. She turned back to Arthur.

"My friend's back, so I should be going."

"Sure, no problem." Arthur looked at the check and put down a twenty.

"Oh, no, let me pay! You were so nice to sit with me."

"No way. A lady never pays."

They got on their coats and walked out. Arthur's car was waiting for them.

"Can I walk you to the door, make sure you get in?"

"I'll be fine."

"I'll watch you go, just so I make sure."

"You really don't have to."

"I insist."

"Thanks very much, Mr. Korn."

"Call me Arthur."

"Arthur." Her voice was like whole milk—heavy cream, even—cascading over his ears. He watched her walk down the street in her fur-lined white parka, her bag swinging in the air. He felt as if he had melted into a giant vat of creamy chocolate.

He practically floated uptown, but when he arrived, his mood was immediately ruined. He entered his darkened living room to find Melanie and Juanita heaping piles of the *New York Observer* onto the fire, the only source of light in the entire apartment. The room was about five hundred degrees as the fire raged, but Melanie was completely oblivious and in a manic frenzy.

"Where have you been?" she asked, wild eyed.

"What's wrong?"

"I've been calling and paging you all day. Where were you?"

"I was at the funeral home—I don't keep my pager on there, you know. I don't want to interrupt a ceremony." He put his overcoat down over the edge of the sofa.

"They're *dead*, Arty. You can leave your goddamn beeper on, for chrissakes."

"Melanie, what's going on?"

"What's going on? I'll tell you what's going on. That Billy Crispin is the *devil*. So malicious! He destroyed me—he destroyed *us*."

"What did he do?"

Melanie was so consumed with rage that Arthur didn't know if she had heard him. Her hair was a disaster—as if she had stuck her finger in an electric socket. Her clothes were stained with newspaper print. Her mascara ran down her face from the tears and perspiration. This was not the Melanie he knew. She threw more papers on the fire, and the shadows in the room danced off the walls, making the entire atmosphere seem like a carnival fun house.

"You know what's so annoying? It's that I showed him kindness and generosity. I arranged a gourmet meal, catered, served by waiters. We're talking white truffle risotto and lobster salad. We're talking caviar *amuses bouches*. I gave him a tour of our *home*, and he dragged me over the coals! I still have char marks!"

She burst into convulsive sobs, and Arthur walked over and tried to embrace her. She allowed him to finally, and her heaving chest rested on his. Juanita continued hoisting the papers into the fire, faster and faster.

Arthur patted Melanie on the back. "So I'm assuming the article came out."

"It came out, all right. And I am the talk of the town."

"But isn't that what you wanted? That's why you hired a publicist."

"You don't hire a publicist for *bad* publicity."

"It can't be that bad."

"It is."

"Come on."

"Everyone slammed me. That Jerome de Stingol said, quote, 'She was too cheap for my services, and I refused to renegotiate.' I was not cheap! I was just under the assumption that that disgusting man was a *decorator*. Excuse me for expecting him to *decorate*. The guy just fluffs pillows and charges twenty thousand dollars for one room! What an ass-hole. And some unnamed source—probably Wendy Marshall—bashed me for trying to get on the board of the Met."

Arthur rubbed his hand through her hair. "People are jealous of you. I've told you countless times to expect that. They're twenty years older than you and not as beautiful."

Melanie pulled back and looked him in the eye. "Arthur, this is something different. This is a vast right-wing conspiracy."

"People will forget about it. They're too narcissistic to care about an article on you."

"Maybe." She sniffed.

Arthur walked over to the stack of peach newspapers. "Let me see it. Wow, you have a lot."

"I've had the driver take me all over town—we hit every newsstand on the Upper East Side, every vending machine. Every deli. I think I cleared out the entire Yorkville distribution, too."

As Arthur perused the article, Melanie threw more stacks on the fire. "Juanita, there are more in the foyer. Please go get them."

"Yes, ma'am." Juanita raced into the hall.

Arthur's supportive smile slowly started to turn into a grimace as he read the article.

"WHAT?! Melanie! You said, 'Arthur always refers to all those Up-per East Side party picture people as the Walking Dead.' I can't believe you said that! Melanie!"

"It was out of context, Arthur." Melanie started sobbing again.

"You have to be careful! The press are vultures." Arthur was not thrilled. He had been having such a nice afternoon with Olivia; it had felt like lying on a bed of feathers. And now Melanie, with her blind ambition and stupid remarks, made him feel as if he were writhing on needles. He didn't want Olivia to see the article. What would she think? What does she think in general? He couldn't figure her out.

"Oh, Arthur, I'm sorry. I'm so ashamed. I never want to leave the house again," said Melanie, collapsing in his arms.

Arthur patted her on the back. "Don't worry, kiddo. Don't worry. People will forget."

But they both knew that it would take a very long time or another very big scandal for that to happen.

chapter 39

"Hello, Mrs. Vance. I bet you didn't expect to see me here," said Maria, who was standing on the threshold of Cordelia's front door.

"No . . ." said Cordelia, not quite remembering who this Mexican woman was. The Powells' domestic? The saleslady at Wolford? The manicurist at Frederic Fekkai?

"You don't remember me," said Maria.

"I . . ." said Cordelia, trailing off, hoping that Maria would fill her in before it became embarrassing.

"Maria Garcia—I worked at Brown Brothers. I saw you at Tiffany's the other day."

"Oh, Maria, of course!" said Cordelia, still wondering what this woman was doing here and how she could afford such an enormous fur coat. Perhaps she had been doing a bit of unfair racial profiling, but she had assumed that Maria was on the cleaning crew.

"I'm here for the flower arranging lesson!"

"Oh! I didn't make the connection that it was you."

"Yes, I know somebody who works at the Harbor who went to the auction and got me your lesson. I had to have it! I had to check out your house—oh, and I love flowers."

"Why, thank you . . ." said Cordelia. Could she be Colombian wealth? There were some fine families in Argentina too.

"Not to mention that we're pals now. We shop at the same fancy stores, you and me," added Maria.

"Right," said Cordelia.

Maria had pressed Morgan for the money, claiming that Schuyler had a heart murmur and needed a small operation. There was no way Maria would let an opportunity to see the inside of Morgan's apartment and hang with the missus slip through her fingers. Nah-uh.

"Well, please come in. Welcome," said Cordelia. A maid appeared out of nowhere and helped Maria off with her fur. "What a lovely coat," Cordelia said.

"Thanks. My boyfriend got it for me," said Maria, beaming. When she unswaddled herself, she revealed her interpretation of an appropriate flower arranging outfit: fire-engine red glittery pants with black stiletto boots, a gauzy low-cut black blouse, and a huge eighteen-carat gold chain. It was as if Miami threw up on her. She also had several thick, clanging gold charm bracelets on both of her wrists.

Cordelia raised her eyebrows. She was in her uniform: beige slacks with a pencil-thin black belt, an ivory blouse, and suede loafers. Her only accessories were a watch and her wedding ring.

"Well, shall we get started?"

"I really want a tour first, if you don't mind," said Maria, looking around the foyer. All this big, black, ugly old furniture and pictures of frowning old people that looked like pilgrims. She could tell immediately that Cordelia had no style. Where were the crystal statues? The gold figurines? The big gold-framed portraits of naked ladies with fairy wings?

"Oh, all right," Cordelia said, sort of taken aback. "I hope it's in order. We haven't really entertained lately."

Of course the house was in order. *House Beautiful* could enter the Vances' houses at any second of the day and it would be picture perfect. Cordelia led Maria into the living room and watched her scrutinize every inch. Cordelia, who never set foot in the room unless they had company, turned to look at it with an outsider's eyes. The walls were lemon, with elaborate moldings, adorned with gilt-framed Fragonards and Mary Cassatts. The curtains were Colefax and Fowler, the Jubilee Rose design. There were two eighteenth-century powder blue velvet fauteuils, a trio of Louis XVI bergères, a George Smith sofa upholstered in pale persimmon. There were silver-leaf consoles, regency tables, and a Russian pedestal table. Famille rose vases on chinoiserie brackets were sprinkled on the walls. Yes, she could definitely see how someone could be impressed.

Although Maria murmured "It's nice," she really wanted to barf. It was a load of crap—all mismatched chairs that looked too uncomfortable to sit on, a tiny couch that her Aunt Lupita's ass wouldn't even fit on, and all those flowery fabrics. The woman clearly had no taste; that was probably why Morgan was fed up with her.

Cordelia led Maria through the apartment, which just confirmed Maria's distaste, until they finally arrived at the Boston lettuce–walled solarium. Tons of flowers were laid out, as well as elaborate vases, scissors, gardening gloves. Maria realized that she was going to ruin her Lee Press-ons. Great. They took three hours to get on.

"So what do you know about flower arranging?" asked Cordelia. She was an expert and had even been pressed to write a second book on the topic by her friends, but she had demurred.

"I know that it's easy to dial one-eight-hundred-flowers," joked Maria. Cordelia didn't smile.

"So we'll start with the basics."

Cordelia began a detailed discussion of the ins and outs of flower arranging while Maria's mind wandered. *This old bag is a frickin' bore!* She looked at Cordelia's cornflower blue eyes and counted the wrinkles. She wore very little makeup—she really needed to spice it up a little, make an effort. After all, pretty soon she'd be searching for a new husband.

"I think I get it now," said Maria, cutting Cordelia off.

"Oh, okay. Sorry, I get a bit carried away. It's really a passion."

"Yeah, so, uh . . . you wanna go sit down and talk? My feet are killing me."

"Oh, okay." Cordelia led Maria into the spinach green library. More chintz, more mismatched chairs. And with all that money, you'd think they could buy some new books. Every one on the shelf looked used and old. Geez, these people needed serious help.

"So tell me about your family," said Maria, plopping onto a couch and immediately sinking into a sea of tasseled pillows. Way too many pillows. Maria chucked some on the floor. Cordelia looked disconcerted.

"Well, I have two sons."

"And what about your husband?"

"Well, you know Morgan."

"Yeah, but how did you meet?"

"We met at a cotillion."

Maria stared at her blankly.

"A friend's deb ball," Cordelia added.

"So you've been happily-ever-after since?"

"I suppose," said Cordelia, surprised by this woman's audacity. But it was actually kind of refreshing to speak with someone who was so blunt. Social doublespeak could be so tiresome.

"You suppose?" asked Maria, scooping out a handful of mixed nuts from in a silver dish. "You're not sure?"

"Well, it's been twenty-eight years. Everyone has a few bumps."

"Really? So it's bumpy."

"No, things are fine."

"Then what were you saying?" Maria looked at her as if she actually cared, and for some reason that emboldened Cordelia.

"I think . . . I think I may be going through a little—I don't want to say crisis, but I definitely am at a strange time in my life. It's . . . you know, well, you're still very young and attractive, but you get older, the kids grow up and leave home, everything changes but everything stays the same. There's really no sense of liberation or purpose. I guess I just feel really restless."

"Well, all those old farts you hang around with are probably pretty boring."

Cordelia laughed. This Maria was kind of a hoot. "That's true."

"You need to rev it up a little. I bet you never had a Latin man. You need a Latin lover. Someone who fucks you hard."

"Maria!" said Cordelia, more amused than appalled.

"It's true. You WASPs are all frigid! You need some cunnilingus! Get a guy to go down on you."

Cordelia turned bright red. "Maria, you really are too much."

"It's the solution."

"I was thinking of another solution entirely, but you may be right . . ."

The sound of a key opening the front door interrupted the talk of Latin sex habits. It was Mr. Vance.

He walked in and saw Cordelia and Maria. His heart stopped. The Venn diagram of his world had collided completely now, and his whole universe swirled with confusion and fear.

"What's this?" said Morgan, entering the room like a wind-up doll, stunned and stiff. His face displayed no emotion, but he was bubbling with fury inside.

"Hi, darling. What are you doing home?" asked Cordelia, turning her head to look up at him.

"I have a match nearby, needed to get my gym bag. What's going on?"

Maria gave Morgan a wicked smile, and then she actually winked at him. It was fun to see him squirm.

"This is Maria Gonzales—"

"Garcia."

"Excuse me, Garcia. She won the flower arranging lesson lot at the Harbor auction."

"I see."

"You remember Maria from Brown Brothers?"

"Yes, I do . . . hello."

"Yes, I was a working girl until I got myself a rich honey. He takes good care of me." She pierced Morgan with her sly gaze.

"How wonderful," said Cordelia with sincerity. Good thing she was blessed with the looks to lure a man who could take care of her; she'd probably worked her way out of the barrio.

Meanwhile, Morgan hadn't seen his wife this gay in months. What the hell was going on here?

"Cordelia, I really need to talk to you. *Now*."

Cordelia could tell there was something wrong. Maria stood up. "I guess I be going now. Thanks for the lesson, Cordelia. We'll have lunch sometime?"

"That would be fun!"

Morgan was seething. He scowled at Maria as she took her leave, and waited impatiently for the elevator to come and collect her. When he was sure she had gone, he turned to Cordelia.

"What's wrong?" she asked.

"I don't like that woman. I don't want you to see her again."

"Why not?"

"She's a thief. She stole from the company and she was fired. And she's a liar. Don't trust her."

"She seemed charming."

"Don't let her fool you. *Never* contact her again; do you understand?"

"Yes, dear. All right."

"Good. Now where's my gym bag? I've got to go to a match."

If Morgan had ever had any doubt about what he was about to do, it had dissipated the second he saw Maria at his apartment. Her evil, taunting looks over his innocent wife's shoulder made any former feelings for her evaporate; she was a horrible, manipulative, insidious little tramp. And she could bring down his entire world. The audacity. She was in his home; she had crossed the line into the sacred—where his wife sleeps and his children were raised, for god's sake! The stakes were getting way too high.

An hour later, in a cold open field in Battery Park, near a piece of modern art, Morgan paced back and forth, looking at his breath as it hit the air. On his shoulder he carried a Brown Brothers gym bag, and as he spied passersby he thought of what they'd think if they had X-ray vision to see the piles of cash that sat in his sack instead of squash clothes. Would he even remember the man's face? It had been dark in that nightclub. There was a red glow to everyone's face—even his son looked different. He stopped mid-stride and looked at his watch. Damn this. What was he thinking? He turned to walk back to his office, then froze again. Cordelia. What about her? This would be to help them, their marriage—she didn't deserve any of this. No wonder she's so lonely; he had tuned out ages ago. Maria was too dangerous to be allowed to continue.

The thuglike goombah from the club sauntered over.

"Hey."

"Hey."

Morgan handed him the bag, grimacing. Was this his life?

"Don't worry," comforted the man in the floor-length, belted leather coat. "You're doing the right thing. Life's too short to deal with shit like this. And hers is even shorter." He laughed, but Morgan did not match his smile. He simply shook at the reality of this moment.

"I've gone insane. She has driven me insane."

"You gotta save yourself, everything you've built," the man said. As his arms moved, Morgan could hear the leather of his coat rubbing against itself, and he wanted to throw up. "You don't want that bitch nagging you and threatening you in twenty years, do you?"

"No. I love my family. I've got to protect them. My wife—I . . . I realize now that I love her more than anything."

"So you know it's the right thing. That bitch I saw you with, she only sees the money in you. I mean, no offense, you're good-looking guy and whatnot, but if you were a pharmacist in Passaic, she'da never been on her back—you know what I'm sayin'?"

"I suppose."

"That bitch has dollar signs in her eyes. Like the cartoons."

"She totally used me," agreed Morgan. "I made a terrible, terrible error of judgment. It was a moment of weakness, and now it's just spun way out of control. I almost destroyed my whole life. I can't hurt my wife. I just can't."

"Hurt that bitch instead."

"It won't . . . be painful, will it?" Morgan thought back to her spread legs and ear-piercing screams when their daughter was so violently born. The echo of her cries still haunted him. Clearly she had zero tolerance for pain.

"She won't know what hit 'er."

Morgan nodded and stood there, silent.

"I've seen situations like this before," the man said, now slinging the gym bag over his shoulder. "If it ain't dealt with, you know, it gets too messy to deal with . . ."

". . . and it all unravels."

"And then everyone's a loser."

chapter 40

The sagebrush raw silk curtains were drawn to a close, and the white-noise machine was on the highest setting. A Georg Jensen tray with dill-dappled poached salmon and balsamic-splattered mixed baby greens topped with goat cheese and toasted almonds lay untouched next to the firmly shut door. There was a pile of discarded European fashion magazines (American being too painful right now) and unread Judith Kranz novels next to the bed. But everything was ignored. Melanie was in too much agony to face the outside world, so she lay in her apricot peignoir under her Porthault sheets and stared at the ceiling. She had remained in this torpid state for the past four days since she had read the article. And she was hoping to remain there until it was off the newsstand. Three more days. But then, what about the newsstands of the mind? There would be no trucks to come around and erase what the city's readers had already seen. The electroshock-torturous words were already emblazoned in the memories of everyone, engraving her in the tome of scandal for all eternity.

She had a gallery of emotions and visited them at various intervals. The first, her favorite, was victimization. How could this be happening? Why was everyone against her? Because she was young? Because she was beautiful? Because she was from Florida? Did these people really think they were so great because their ancestors thumbed an earlier boat to America than her ancestors? It was ridiculous.

Her second emotion was humiliation mixed with paranoia. What did the Lutzes think? What did the Vances think? What did Diandra think? And—oh, god! What did Mr. Guffey think?

Her third, remorse. Why did she have to show off? Why did she have to name-drop? Why did she try so hard to impress everyone? Why did she humiliate her beloved Arty? Her final emotion was despondency. Because with her datebook empty, the mail void of invitations, and the phone silent, she was really on her own.

Melanie's mind wandered back to the most humiliating episode of her life prior to recent events. She was in eleventh grade and not in the "cool clique," which primarily comprised the richest girls with the best clothes. One morning the leader of their pack—Sandy St. John, whose daddy owned the Toyota dealership and who was head of the cheerleading clique—decided to stand up and write on the blackboard: *"These are the people I hate."* And underneath was only one line: *"Melanie Sartomsky: Hillbilly Trash."* Melanie never knew why she had singled her out. She felt the same way today.

As Melanie tossed and turned, running through possible scenarios in her mind, there was a soft knock on the door.

"Yes?" asked Melanie, annoyed. Didn't "Do Not Disturb" mean "Go The Fuck Away"?

"I'm sorry, madam, but may I please have a word."

It was Guffey. Damn. Melanie had been avoiding him in particular. She knew she had failed him. She was like his errant student who hadn't heeded his lessons and had flunked out of school.

"It's not really a good time, Mr. Guffey."

"I do apologize, madam, but I really must speak to you as soon as possible."

Melanie sighed. She knew what was coming and couldn't bear to hear it. "All right, you can come in," she said, clasping her satin robe closed.

Mr. Guffey opened the door and looked around at the mess. She could see him recoil in his retinas, but his face betrayed no emotion.

"I do beg your pardon, madam. I know you're under the weather. It's just that something really rather urgent has transpired, and I do need to inform you."

"Oh? What's happened?"

"I won't bother you with the irrelevant minutia, madam, as it's quite trivial, but the fact of the matter is that I need to request a leave of absence, effective immediately."

He paused and waited for Melanie's reaction. *So this is what happens,* she thought. *When the shit hits the fan, even the butler clears out.* Her own frigging servant had turned on her. But then, how could she blame him?

Although her voice had disappeared somewhere into her trachea, she managed to get out, "May I ask why?"

"It's really quite trite, madam, so I'd rather not burden you, as I know you've had your own . . . concerns of late."

"I see," said Melanie, rising. She walked across to her mirror and squinted her eyes. She'd bet all the SARS in China that this poof was galloping down to Palm Beach to shack up in Diandra's servants' quarters. He should at least forgive her. People make mistakes. His departure was treason. He was a friggin' Benedict Arnold.

"Fine, Mr. Guffey. And how long is this . . . *leave of absence* supposed to be for?"

"Unfortunately, I cannot say. I do apologize, but there are some matters that need attending to, and I am unsure as to how complex it will be to settle them."

"Right, right," said Melanie, pouring herself a glass of water from her etched bedside decanter. "Matters. Yes. Important matters can take a long time."

Mr. Guffey raised his eyebrow. "Perhaps, madam."

"All right, Guff," said Melanie, taking a swig of water. "Off you go! You can take all the time you need. We'll be just fine here. Me and the rest of the gang."

Mr. Guffey paused, wanting to say more but realizing it was really not the time. "Thank you, madam." He gave a slight bow and walked out of the room.

That was it, thought Melanie. If her own butler was hotfooting it away from her scandal-ridden life, the whole situation had devolved into a Turkish sitcom. Enough lounging around in her nightie: she had to go have a gulp of New York fresh air.

An hour later Melanie was briskly walking along Second Avenue, perusing the windows of Banana Republic and the Gap. She had her sunglasses on and knew that in this locale (east of Lex) she was safe from detection. It was good to be outside. Arty—who had immediately forgiven her after she'd shed her first tear—had been begging her for days to get back into the swing of things, but she had resisted. But now she had become ready from going through not only her four grieving stages but also three boutique boxes of Puffs Plus. She had no more tears. She was hardened and strong. Stronger, at least. She was in "to hell with it" mode. She strolled for close to two hours and headed home.

As Melanie was turning the corner to her building, she could have sworn that she saw Regina Bates entering under the canopy. But she was nowhere to be seen when Melanie entered the lobby.

"Luca, was that Regina Bates?" asked Melanie.

"Yes, I believe, ma'am," said Luca, the doorman. He picked up a clipboard that was on his desk and scanned down it. "Yes indeed, ma'am. Regina Bates."

"Where was she going?"

"To Mrs. Aldrich's, ma'am."

"Oh my god!" said Melanie, realizing at once that she had made a terrible error. "Please let me see that list, Luca, because if it is what I think it is, I'm in big dog doo!"

Luca handed her the clipboard and Melanie scanned through all the names as quickly as possible: Joan Coddington, Cordelia Vance, Eve Masterson . . . and so on. It was the FAD group.

"This is the Fight Against Dysentery committee."

"I'm not sure, ma'am. I know that it's a committee meeting at Mrs. Aldrich's. Yeah, some sort of charity—"

"I'm on that committee!" said Melanie, interrupting. "I must not have gotten the message when I was ill!"

Luca didn't quite know what to say. "Oh, ma'am."

"This is beyond embarrassing, Luca. What floor is Leslie Aldrich?"

"Five, ma'am."

"I should go right up."

"Sure, ma'am."

Melanie looked down at her clothes. She was dressed completely inappropriately for a FAD meeting, but it would be more humiliating to miss it.

"Do I look okay?" she asked Luca out of sheer desperation.

"Yes, ma'am," sputtered Luca, surprised. "Wonderful."

Melanie walked to the elevator and asked Fred, the elderly doorman, to press five. He complied. When the door opened into the glazed foyer, Melanie walked along the marble floor and pressed the doorbell.

Leslie Aldrich opened the floor with a beaming grin, which immediately dissipated the second she saw Melanie.

"Melanie!"

"I am so sorry, Leslie. I can't believe I'm late. You know I pride my-self on my promptness. I didn't get the message somehow."

"Oh, well, Melanie—you see, this is very awkward."

Melanie felt herself redden. "Uh-oh. You mean, this isn't a meeting for the FAD ball?"

Leslie's eyes darted as if she was unsure whether to lie or tell the truth. Finally her shoulders sagged and she sighed. "Well, yes . . ."

"I'm not sure I understand."

"Well, Melanie. You see . . ." Leslie looked at Melanie pleadingly, but Melanie was still confused. Leslie cleared her throat. "Well, I didn't leave you a message, Melanie."

Melanie still didn't get it. What was going on? "I am on the Fight Against Dysentary committee, right?"

"Well—"

"Sometimes I get all these diseases mixed up. I mean, I know they're all very serious and important, but it gets a little confusing. Any-way . . ." *Stop talking, Melanie.* She hated how her mouth would run off without her. She looked at Leslie, who was silent and not amused.

"Melanie," Leslie said, sighing dramatically. "Regarding your role on the committee. You've been released."

"Released?"

"Melanie, it's . . ." Leslie looked at her imploringly, hoping she would be discreet enough to catch on and take her leave. But Melanie stared at her. "You see, Melanie, it wasn't my decision. But we won't be needing your services on the committee anymore."

"Oh," said Melanie. Her heart dropped and she felt dizzy. She started walking backwards and pressed the elevator button with the back of her palm. She wanted out of that vestibule ASAP.

"Oh, Melanie, I am sorry. But my hands were totally tied. I really didn't want to exclude you."

Melanie nodded, in a daze, until Leslie's words finally registered.

"Your hands were tied by whom? You're chairman of the steering committee."

"I know," said Leslie, biting her nail nervously. "It's all really silly, and I know it will work itself out. Don't worry about anything. It's just a really awkward situation . . ."

"Well, what's the situation?"

Leslie appeared as if she'd rather jump off a cliff than continue. "It's our corporate sponsor," she finally offered. "I don't know why, but they don't want you involved with the event anymore. It's so infantile . . ."

This was so humiliating! There were corporations who wanted to disassociate themselves with Melanie? That *Observer* article was getting more damaging by the minute. When the hell was it going to go away? Just as Melanie was reeling, the elevator door opened.

"Going up?" asked Fred.

"Yes, she is," said Leslie.

Melanie felt nauseous and was about to step onto the elevator when she remembered something.

"Leslie, isn't Frothingham's the corporate sponsor?"

"Yes."

"Phew! Because we're great customers. I'm sure if they made the connection, there wouldn't be a problem."

"No, Melanie. They know exactly who you are."

"And they said they didn't want me involved?"

"Something about recent . . . you know, press surrounding you. They don't want to be . . . mired in any kind of scandal."

"*Frothingham's* doesn't want scandal?" said Melanie, almost laughing. "Didn't their chairman and president just do time in prison? Their company is fraught with felonious activity! And yet I, I who have appeared in one teeny, tiny disaparaging article in a local weekly newspaper, am the one they don't want to associate with? Come on, Leslie, agree with me that it's absurd."

"They have their standards . . ."

Melanie shook her head with shock. "I mean, I've literally raised my paddle at their auction house more times than Venus Williams has volleyed at Wimbledon! This seems really ridiculous."

"It's not an ideal situation, but as I said, Melanie, our hands are tied. They want you off the committee," said Leslie, shifting her stance. She clutched her front door as if Melanie was going to slam it down and burst into the meeting anyway.

"It's really sad. Because I could have done a lot of great things to help eradicate dysentery."

"Next time," said Leslie, closing the door.

With that, Melanie retreated back over to the elevator. Fred pressed the button without a word. On the ride up there was an awkward silence. Melanie knew that Fred had heard everything. Great, now the doormen could all laugh at her behind her back. Fred kept looking at her sideways, as if he wanted to say something. Finally, he broke down.

"You know what, Mrs. Korn? Don't think twice about those cheapos. You and Mr. Korn are the nicest in the building. With your Christmas gift, I took my whole family to Disney World."

Melanie looked up at him and smiled. Kindness always came from the most unexpected places. "Thanks, Fred," she said as she stepped onto her floor.

It was an odd feeling to realize that she'd rather hang with the doorman than those society bitches. Odd, but kind of liberating.

chapter 41

"Hold the elevator!" shouted Drew Vance just as it was about to close. A white hand with the long, slender fingers of a musician wrapped around the door to prevent it from shutting.

"Thanks," said Drew, stepping in.

"No problem," said Lila Meyer.

"Sorry, I thought you were the doorman," said Drew.

"He told me to go ahead."

"Hey, I know you," said Drew, cocking his head to the side. His baby blue eyes blinked twice, as if he was remembering. "You're Jimmy Meyer's sister."

"Lila."

"Right. So how's Jimbo? He still at Georgetown?" asked Drew, pressing the button for his floor.

"No, he graduated. He's working in the mailroom of some agency in L.A."

"Rock on. He was always into that Hollywood stuff."

"I know."

"So who you are going to see?" said Drew, scanning the floor panel. "Nine. Olivia Weston?"

"Yes."

"Cool. She's a writer, right?"

"Yes. Well, she wrote one novel."

"One more than me," he said, laughing. He looked at Lila. She was definitely a hottie, even though she was, like, thirty. She was really skinny, in that "I'm rich so I've gotta starve myself" kind of way. And no boobs to speak of. But her face wasn't that bad, and she had pretty long brown hair. Plus, she smelled nice.

Lila, in turn, studied Drew. He was her brother's age, which would make him roughly twenty-two. She could totally tell that he was a player, used to getting what he wanted. He had the act down perfectly, the way he cocked his head to the side, played up his long, thick eyelashes, and how he wore that dorky wool hat with the ball at the end. Only a really good-looking guy could wear a hat like that. He was definitely confident. And he was really tall.

The elevator stopped unexpectedly on five, and when the doors opened Mrs. Cockpurse shuffled on in her pink terrycloth bathrobe and fuzzy slippers.

"Ah, Mrs. Cockpurse, I'm not sure you want to get on the elevator," said Drew.

"Yes, I do!" she screamed back at him. She pressed every button on the panel.

"You want to stop at every floor? Now, come on, Mrs. Cockpurse."

Lila held the elevator door open as Drew tried to gently guide Mrs. Cockpurse back into her foyer.

"Get your greasy paws off of me!" she snapped, and grasped on to the door of the elevator as if it were a life jacket.

"Mrs. Cockpurse, where do you want to go?" asked Drew.

"I wanna get the hell out of here!"

"But you can't . . ."

"Why the hell not?" she screamed.

"Because you're in your bathrobe."

"So what? I got to get away from that crazy doctor! That crazy doctor wants to give me an enema! I told him to stick it up his own ass!"

Drew couldn't suppress his smile. He turned to Lila and raised his shoulders in a sort of "What can we do?" way. She just smiled back and shrugged.

"Now, Mrs. Cockpurse, is anyone at home?"

"Just that crazy doctor! That ass-crazy doctor!"

Drew walked into the foyer and pressed the doorbell. "I'm sure we can work something out with the doctor."

"Tell him to get away from my ass!"

The door opened and a two-hundred-pound, white-uniformed nurse stood on the threshold. She folded her arms and shook her head.

"Now there you are, Mrs. Cockpurse. We were looking everywhere for you," she admonished.

"She wanted to get away from the doctor," said Drew, leading Mrs. Cockpurse by the hand to the nurse.

"The doctor has left, honey. No need to worry."

"You tell him to stay away from me!"

The nurse rolled her eyes at Drew as he got back on the elevator. "Take care."

When the doors shut Lila and Drew burst out laughing.

"Gosh, what a nutter," said Lila.

"Yeah. It's actually sad. She kind of lost it when her husband died. He was really nice, used to give out the best Halloween candy in the building. And she totally filled our UNICEF boxes."

The floor opened on six. "I guess we're going to be stopping on every floor now," said Lila.

"Yeah, looks that way. The doormen are supposed to lock each floor so you can't access them, but they're usually too lazy."

"Yeah."

There was a pause. "Hope you're not in a rush," said Drew, looking Lila in the eye. Girls melted when he did that.

"No, no. Just going to read some of Olivia's new manuscript."

"That's good," said Drew, as the doors opened on seven.

"Yeah, I'm kind of not psyched. Just not in the mood today. But you know, she's a friend."

"Right," said Drew, giving Lila a crooked smile.

They both stared at the panel and watched as each floor lit up when the elevator ascended. They looked back at each other and smiled.

"So," Drew said, slowly moving toward his co-captive. "I know a good way to pass the time."

"Oh yes?" she said coyly.

"Hmm," said Drew, glancing down. He pressed the Stop button on the elevator. Lila was startled but completely exhilarated, and she could feel her heart start to pound. He leaned in for the kill, grabbing her and kissing her forcefully against the elevator wall. She was in heaven. Gosh, this guy was practically a fetus! What was she doing? Whatever it was, she kept doing it.

After they had had the first vertical sex of her life, Lila took a gulp of air, exhausted, and Drew pressed the button to restart their ascent. The next floor was his.

"Care to . . . come in?" Without saying a word, she followed him into the grand apartment to his room. It was as if the home department of Ralph Lauren had been cut and pasted into his bedroom. It was really an incredible reproduction—wintergreen walls, enormous dark wood bed, snapshots in silver frames, leather armchair, Audubon prints, tweedy throws.

"Jesus, was Ralph himself your decorator?" asked Lila.

"He had nothing to do with it. My mom did it all."

He attacked her again, and they rolled onto his pillow-lined bed and had sex a second time. Afterward, the two were silent.

"Can I smoke in here?" asked Lila.

"Sure," said Drew, passing over an ashtray with some cigarette butts in it. Lila took her pack of Marlboro Lights and her lighter out of her bag and lit up. When she went to tap her ash she noticed that one of the butts in the tray had lipstick on it.

"So, what do you do, Drew?"

"What do you mean?"

"I mean, did you graduate? Do you work?"

"Oh, you mean livelihood," said Drew, smiling. He walked over to his bureau and picked up a half-eaten bag of Cheez Doodles. He started munching and stopped to stretch and let out a long yawn. He then rubbed his stomach, which was perfectly ripped. "Yes, I did graduate. And yes, I work. Part-time at a hedge fund that's run by a family friend."

"Where'd you go to college?"

"Middlebury."

"So, what, you don't plan on working full-time? Is that too much for you?"

"Yes, someday I do plan on working full-time," he said, plopping down on the bed and offering her some Cheez Doodles.

"No, thanks," she said, waving it away with disgust as if he had offered her an al-Qaeda dirty bomb.

"Come on, they're good for you!"

"Please, nauseating."

"Really? I like them," he said, stuffing ten into his mouth.

"So, you just . . . what? Are hanging out?"

"No, I'm not just hanging out. My, aren't we the Spanish Inquisition?" he said, smiling. He started flicking the cheese dust off of his orange-coated fingers. "I'm joining the army."

"Ha-ha," said Lila, putting on her bra.

"Or the Coast Guard, I'm not sure."

"Come on, seriously—what are you planning on doing?"

"God, you sound like my mother!"

Lila gave him a dirty look.

"Okay, I'm going down to Florida in January to get my pilot's license."

"You want to be a pilot?"

"No, but I want to get my license. We have a plane, and I want to be able to fly it."

"Can't you just go somewhere on Long Island?"

"I wanna be able to fly the big ones, baby! The commercials! In case of emergency, it'll be Drew Vance to the rescue!" he said, rising and pounding on his chest like a he-man.

Lila swung her legs over the side of the bed and started to slide on her skirt. "And then what?"

"And then . . ." said Drew, pausing dramatically. "I don't know."

Lila rose and buckled her belt. "Well, you should think about it."

"Why?"

"'Cause you should." She walked over and used his hairbrush. She wondered how many girls had done the same.

"Yes, mama."

Lila turned and looked penetratingly into his eyes. "Well, I should get going. Olivia's going to wonder where I am."

"Okay," said Drew.

Lila paused and stared at him. What now? "So, I guess, goodbye."

"I'll walk you out," said Drew, opening his bedroom door.

Lila gathered her coat and bag and followed Drew—who was in just his boxers—out to the hall. He led her to the front door and opened it.

"So . . ." began Lila.

Drew leaned in and kissed her crisply on the cheek. "You're the best."

Lila wasn't sure what to do, but at that moment the elevator door opened and Mrs. Vance got off.

"Hi, Mom!" said Drew, opening his arms wide.

"Hi, sweetie," said Cordelia, kissing her son. Drew took the packages out of her arm. Cordelia looked at Drew in his boxers and then at Lila.

"Mom, this is Lila. She's a friend of Olivia Weston's."

"It's nice to meet you," said Cordelia, sticking out her hand. Lila was mortified. She shook it.

"Nice to meet you, Mrs. Vance. Gotta run," she said, jumping on the elevator before the doors closed.

"'Bye!" said Drew.

"'Bye" was all Lila could muster.

The entire time Lila was at Olivia's, all she could think of was Drew. Luckily, Rosemary was there as well, and with her endless yammering Lila didn't have to say a word and could let her mind wander. *So he's only eight years younger,* she thought. *That's not so much. Madonna and Guy Ritchie are ten years apart. Goldie Hawn and Kurt Russell are also, like, eight years apart or something. It's not that strange. Drew's definitely a ladies' man, but maybe with the right girl . . . ?*

Drew, meanwhile, didn't really think twice about Lila after she left.

But he knew she was thinking about him. He was aware of his power: he had looks, money, and a charming personality. But above all, he had girls all figured out. They loved the bad boys; they wanted to tame them. It was like a game to them, and they all felt that they were special enough to be the one. And he learned this all from George Clooney and his cousin Eleanor. When George—gotta love him—announced he would never marry again, he made every girl in America fall in love with him. Eleanor was in tears for weeks (as if she could get him!). But now George gets more ass than anyone in Hollywood, because every girl thinks she'll be the one who changes his mind. Fucking genius, man. But Drew didn't plan on settling down until he was thirty-five or forty. What was the point? Life was good.

chapter 42

Melanie Korn was officially in exile. When she wasn't holed up in her apartment, which felt like a prison (though most people would kill for a "cell" like that), Melanie hid out in places where she knew she'd never bump into anyone. She frequented haunts no acquaintances would be caught dead in: tourist attractions, movie theaters, Liberty Island, the Upper West Side. She decided to forgo the visible Bentley rides and opted for solo walks through the park. She wore oversize Jackie O glasses and, during occasional bouts of extreme Garbo-worthy paranoia, an Hermès scarf on her head. As the days flowed into weeks, the acute, piercing shame almost morphed into a dull, familiar pain—a pain she had grown up with, an insecurity that was sadly recognizable to her.

She would often walk down the street and spy a matron who she knew would report the sighting (Melanie's appearance, outfit, etc.) to the whole Swifty's set. When she saw one of these women, she'd casually dart into a random store or coffee shop, and she accidentally discovered many new places as a result. Example: a little day spa when she decided to get a pedicure without fear of some society hag sitting in the leather throne next to her. And believe it or not, the little Korean nobody who cut her cuticles was actually better than Mila at Frederic Fekkai. Who would have thought? Another time, she thought she saw Pamela Baldwin on Columbus Avenue (she must have been on her way to pick up her son at Collegiate), so Melanie popped into an avant-garde art gallery that featured Romanian bronzes, which were actually quite original. Melanie purchased nine, then later rethought it and gave them to Juanita.

One afternoon, Melanie decided to walk around Midtown and see what the world was like south of Fifty-seventh Street. She crossed Thirty-fourth Street and suddenly saw Maggie McSorley, a Met trustee, heading toward her. Before she could even wonder what the hell a woman like that was doing in the land of Denny's and Dunkin Donuts, she turned into the grand revolving door of the Empire State Building. Relieved to have avoided the close call, she walked in a lemming trance down the marble foyer, through security, and up in the majestic elevators. She stood in line—incognito—for what seemed like an eternity, and, zombielike, followed the crowd up to the busy observation deck.

Wow. This glittering vista that spread out before her was truly awe-inspiring. She could see everything. Amazing. Melanie even put some quarters in the telescope and found her apartment. Who'd have thought the Empire State Building was so neat?

Melanie walked toward the goosebump-inducing view and drank in the flea-size cars and the collage of silhouetted rooftops. An hour went by. She stood there, bleary eyed, thinking of all the cinematic kisses set here, which she had seen flickering on Floridian Mall Multiplex screens. Those embraces always made New York beckon as if it held the promise of romance and escape, no matter who you were or where you came from.

"*Melanie?* Oh my god! Is that you?"

She was snapped abruptly out of her reverie to see a weathered blond mom of three looking at her quizzically.

"Yes."

"I knew it! Hi, it's Sandy! Sandy Braddock! Formerly Sandy St. John? I haven't seen you since high school!"

"Oh, yes—right, of course."

Sandy St. John. Melanie's former nemesis, who'd made her life a

living hell. The one who led the gang and convinced everyone that
Melanie was a big slut from a little trailer park. Well, today the tables
were turned. Here Melanie was, decked in jewels and looking . . . well,
fabulous.

Melanie looked at her former classmate. What was it about high
school hierarchies that always dragged you back by the knapsack to the
tenth-grade hallway? It was as if the twenty years that had gone by had
never happened and—poof—she was back in the bleachers, watching
Sandy's posse swooning over the football jocks. And now look at Sandy.
There she was, wide in the hips and with three towheaded tots that
looked right out of a *Children of the Corn, Part* 7 casting call.

"It's *soooo* good to see you!" squealed Sandy. "You look fantastic!"

"Thanks. You do too." Lie. She looked like ass. Her blond, once-
shiny hair sported dark roots that were in dire need of a bleach job. She
wore too much base, which didn't match the skin tone of her neck. And
it was obviously time for Weight Watchers.

"So what happened to you? What have you been doing for the last
twenty-something years?" said Sandy, who then honked with laughter.

"I live here in New York. On Park Avenue."

"Park Avenue! My, my, look at you, little miss fancy pants! Well, you
were always pretty. You must have landed yourself quite a gentleman!
'Cause I see by that giant rock that you're married."

"Yes, I have a wonderful husband."

"And what does he do?"

"He's an entrepreneur."

"Well, that's wonderful! We were always wondering what happened
to you, Melanie Sartomsky. But you seem like you've really arrived. You
look, well, terrific."

Sandy was always a haughty little bitch, but here she was almost
kissing Melanie's butt. How odd. One of Sandy's little kids yanked her
skirt, and Sandy had to depart with her brood, Le Sports Sac in hand.

"Okay, okay, we're going," she said to calm her kid. "Great to see ya,
Mel. Time is on your side!" she shouted as she wandered away.

"Right! You too," said Melanie, halfheartedly. Her kids sure were
cute, though. Minus the JonBenet leopard-print leggings.

Melanie exhaled and gazed out on the magnificent rooftop buffet.

She shook at the coincidental flashback to high school, another miserable moment in her life. It was as if on that deco deck there was a wrinkle in time transporting her back through the years, back down to her shitty home, her father's sentencing for thirteen counts of fraud, her complete isolation, the gossip in the hallway. She was now, thanks to the scandal she got herself wrapped up in, right back in high school. There used to be whispers in the locker-lined hallways, and now there were whispers in velvet-lined banquettes. The only difference was that in high school there was a light at the end of the tunnel; she knew things would get better. And they did . . . for a while. Now, in the face of total solitude, she was experiencing the same pit of despair, this time without the hope of being lifted out.

Melanie left the famed building and walked. She kept walking and walking until the light turned darker. The sun set, and the sky went from burnt orange to azure blue as she walked through a rush hour–packed Columbus Circle. She walked by a lit-up Lincoln Center and watched a gaggle of New York City Ballet dancers run across the marble, pitter-pattering the expanse of white with their little steps on their way backstage. At Seventy-second Street, she made a left and walked west. She strolled up Riverside Drive, surveying the stunning Gothic buildings and charming townhomes, watching the children come and go and play in the park as their daddies came home with briefcases. She saw fit women in yoga clothes making their way home with ripe groceries from Fairway, Citarella, and Zabar's. She spotted busy Columbia students looking brainy in their Elvis Costello glasses, hustling to study groups and seminars on Foucault and rallies for women's reproductive rights.

And that's when it dawned on her.

New York was not just her tight-ass zip code. It was a whole world. She wasn't "ruined"! She always thought because her life with Arthur had been, by her design, a revolving door of the same faces at the same benefits, the same restaurants, the same salons, that the world was tiny. But here she was in this gorgeous neighborhood she had never even seen, and she had it all to herself. She knew most of the supposedly glitzy socialities would break into hives if they stepped one Louboutin-covered foot west of Central Park West. And what a loss it was for them.

And for her. All these years and she'd never walked this tree-lined, river breeze–filled avenue. It had taken this scandal sequesterage to get her here. The looming gargoyles overhead didn't just scare off the evil spirits—they scared off her fears. Miraculously, with this revelation, all her cares and nervous energy seemed to flow out with the tides of the Hudson.

She felt as if she had jetted to some weird, foreign, European city. Forget forking out buttloads of money to go abroad; people should just hop over the park. She glanced around her and there was . . . life, as usual, just in a new locale. Perhaps this was a life better than everyone knew. They didn't even sell Billy Crispin's crappy paper here. She inhaled the crisp air and began to walk home, feeling armed with a new hope of getting over her whole wave of worries. Life was just too short. And her city was too big.

chapter 43

Wendy was nervous. Why was she nervous? It was so silly, really. She checked her reflection again in the mirror. Joan had said to wear her sexy black V-neck dress and her diamond pin that her ex had gotten her for their seventh wedding anniversary. She had wanted to wear the one she received for her eleventh (and final), the diamond and emerald, but Joan said, "You don't want to dazzle him too much."

Joan was setting her up with an old friend of Phillip's from Tuck Business School. He had recently been divorced, had recently moved to New York, and recently made a billion dollars in some sort of telecommunications thing of which he had been lucky enough to get out early. Joan had been pressing Phillip for months to get things moving and make the introduction, but Phillip had been noncommittal in his usual way, until Joan finally had to pick up the phone and do it herself.

The doorman rang up and announced that Joan and Phillip were waiting in the car downstairs, and Wendy walked into the family room to say good night to her kids.

"So how do I look?" she asked them.

George and Nina barely glanced up from *Friends*. "Fine" and "Good" were all they could muster.

"Don't sit so close. You'll ruin your eyes," said Wendy, walking over and pecking them on the forehead. "And don't stay up too late. Love you."

"Huh," they murmured.

After one final glance at her reflection, she was off. This was the first thing that she had looked forward to in ages. She couldn't remember the last time she had been set up, and she felt out of practice and strange. She crossed her fingers that it would go well. How great would it be to find a man? Even if she didn't get remarried, just had someone to go to foreign movies with and maybe take in the theater. Have late-night suppers at cozy Italian restaurants and maybe visit the south of France together. Maybe rent a house on the Vineyard and . . . *Stop, Wendy,* she reprimanded herself. Her fantasies were getting ahead of her, and she hadn't even met the man! As she descended in the elevator to meet Joan, she pushed all of her hopes to the back of her mind and took a deep breath.

"Now, don't be nervous," advised Joan as they entered Elio's. "Tom is a very nice man. His ex was a bore—a total bore—I couldn't stand her. *Very* Fairfield County, just dullsville. I think she had too many electroshock treatments. I mean, she was a real mute and very frowny. The children I believe take after her—the daughter is really a dog—but don't let that put you off; you wouldn't have to deal with them that much. They're off at boarding school somewhere—and somewhere good, by the way—at least they're smart and ugly. Because ugly and dumb is just a curse, as we both know. You know who I'm talking about: yes, those Goodyear children. Sorry, but true. They're as dumb as rodents. But these girls get the brains from Tom, not from the mother. How funny—I can't even remember her name anymore: she made that much of an impression on me! That cat ran off with her tongue, because the woman was a virtual Helen Keller. Now, what was her name? Something silly and stupid like Libbitz. Hopeless, really hopeless. And you should have seen their house in Darien! Oh, my, a total disaster. She used the same green chintz fabric on the sofas, chairs, and curtains! Can you imagine? Like a set from one of those suburban sitcoms on television. You'd expect to find the Newharts there! Good thing he got out of there. You'll do fine, just don't worry."

Throughout Joan's diatribe they had been following the hostess to a prime table in the back. Tom had not arrived yet.

"Now, Phillip, you sit there, and Wendy, you are there," ordered Joan.

Phillip and Wendy followed her instructions.

"You know what? That's not good. We need Tom to face the wall so he's not distracted. There are so many attractive people here tonight. If he's over there, he will only be able to see the tables on his right, and we'll just hope some old fogies are seated there. So Wendy, switch places with Phillip."

They followed her instructions.

"Hmm . . . now I'm not sure . . ." began Joan before Phillip interrupted.

"Joan, I'm not moving again. Now, I'd like a scotch," he said, turning to the hostess. "Neat, a double."

"And what can I get you ladies?"

Before Wendy could say anything, Joan answered for her. "Two chardonnays."

"Lovely."

"Now, Wendy, just remember not to talk with your head lowered. Keep it raised at all times. Otherwise, that little extra flesh under your neck pops out a bit."

Wendy immediately touched her chin. "Really?"

"Nothing to worry about, really. But just make sure your chin is the same level as Tom's eyes. And look who's here!"

Wendy turned to see Tom Fairbanks approach their table. He was in his mid-fifties, with the lean body of a tennis player and a full head of steel gray hair. Very handsome. Wendy felt her heart quicken.

"Hello, Joan, Phillip," said Tom, kissing Joan and shaking Phillip's hand. "And you must be Wendy. Tom Fairbanks."

"Nice to meet you."

He had an appealing sense of confidence, and Wendy approved of the way he sat down, ordered a drink, and didn't pussyfoot around. He was no Phillip. Wendy watched him curiously as he engaged in the usual perfunctory persiflage and nodded with approval when he gave his order to the waitress. It was going well.

"So, Wendy, Joan tells me you're a writer," said Tom.

"Writer? Oh, well, I used to be an editor at *Mademoiselle*; that is, before my marriage, quite some time ago," said Wendy, nervously laughing but at the same time shooting Joan a look.

"But Wendy, you have been working on your memoirs," reminded Joan.

"Oh, yes, well, that was really more just keeping track of my ex's whereabouts and the expenditures of our previous life together—the life I became accustomed to—for the divorce lawyers. Our settlement took a long time."

"I see," said Tom. There was an awkward pause.

"Tom, Wendy, you both go to Millreef Club."

"Really?" asked Tom. "When do you go down?"

"Every March."

"We'd go every Christmas," said Tom, taking a sip of his drink. "But actually, I won't be going anymore. My ex got the house."

"Oh. That's a shame. It's beautiful down there."

"Yes. Great golf course."

"Oh, do you play?"

"Every chance I can. I'm going next week to golf camp, actually, down in Florida."

"Oh. Fun."

"Do you golf?"

"No."

"Oh."

"But I've always wanted to take it up."

"You should. Great game."

The hostess brushed against Tom's sleeve as she seated a middle-aged couple. "I'm sorry," she said, touching Tom lightly on his shoulder. "No problem," he said, turning his head. He glanced at the couple she was seating next to him.

"Tom! How are you?" the man asked.

"Great, Frank. Hi, Liz," he said to the couple.

"We're here to celebrate Ginny's graduation from law school. Second in her class at Yale."

"That's wonderful."

At that moment, a stunningly beautiful woman approached. She had long blond hair and green eyes, and was wearing a slinky red top and a short skirt that showed off her fabulous legs.

"Here's Ginny now. You remember Tom Fairbanks?"

"Of course I remember Tom Fairbanks," she said, pecking him on the cheek. "Even though you canceled out of our Labor Day party at the last minute," she said teasingly.

"I'm sorry! I had to go out of town. Please forgive me!"

"Okay, but you'd better come next year," she said, flirting heavily.

"I will."

There were brief introductions all around. Wendy watched Joan watch Ginny, who had seated herself at her parents' table with an air of youthful self-assuredness that she knew would put Joan off. She watched Tom study Ginny and felt uncomfortable.

"So, Mr. Fairbanks, my pop here said you just made a bundle on the sale of your company," said Ginny from her seat, again in a teasing voice.

"Ginny!" said her parents in unison, laughing.

"Oh, Ginny, you always were one to say what was on your mind," said Tom with amusement.

Tom turned back to his table as Joan raised a disapproving eyebrow. As they returned to their conversation about the usual—golf, whom they knew in common, what clubs they belonged to, holiday plans, and so on—Wendy had the strong sensation that Tom had checked out. His mind was on Ginny and the table behind him. Wendy looked over again at Ginny out of the corner of her eye. She was one of those girls who had it all—looks, brains, confidence. And she also definitely had that only child thing going—her parents worshipped her, indulged her, thought that she was God's gift to the world and that everything that came out of her mouth was the most witty and fascinating utterance possible. Wendy could not compete with that.

"And her son flunked out of Choate. I mean, really . . ." Joan was saying.

"Excuse me," said Tom, interrupting. He stood up and Wendy watched him walk to the back to go down the stairs to the men's room. Joan leaned in.

"So, what do you think? Handsome, right?" asked Joan.

"Very. But not interested."

"What are you talking about? I think he is."

"Joan, he's had his eye on the young lady behind us for the entire evening."

"Nonsense!" said Joan vociferously. She twisted her neck to catch a glance of Ginny. "Don't you think it's nonsense, Phillip?"

Phillip shrugged. "She's attractive."

"Phillip! You are useless. Men, Wendy. Please ignore my husband. He—like others in his breed—catch none of the subtleties."

"Yes, just ignore me," repeated Phillip sarcastically. "Doesn't matter what I say anyway."

"Besides, that Ginny is too flashy," said Joan, attempting to whisper but incapable. "She also wouldn't be attractive if she didn't have blond hair. That face only a mother could love."

At that moment, Wendy watched Joan watch Ginny stand up and prance across the restaurant to the restroom.

"Not at all pretty," said Joan confidently.

Several minutes later, neither Tom nor Ginny had returned from downstairs. Joan was in the throes of her favorite topic: Melanie Korn. It had become almost a parlor game for her to conjecture where Melanie was spending her expulsion from society.

"I've heard lots of things, lots of things. But what I can tell you both is that with this level of ostracism, there's just no recovery. None what-soever. She's over, ruined." Joan was about to continue, but she noticed Tom and Ginny walking up the stairs, laughing and appearing as if they were enjoying a secret joke. They gave each other a sideways glance and then both sat down at their tables.

Wendy shifted uncomfortably. This was embarrassing! This guy wasn't even that attractive. He was just loaded and single. Pathetic. She hated having to compete with people half her age.

"Ran into some friends downstairs," said Tom apologetically.

"Really? 'Cause we thought you fell in! We were about to send for the Coast Guard to fish you out," said Joan, angry on behalf of her friend.

Tom gave a half smile. "So, Phillip, tell me what's going on in the Scottish Historical Society these days."

And that was it. Once someone got Phillip on that, his favorite topic, the rest of the night was over. Joan kept interjecting what she thought were subtle barbs at Tom, such as "Oh, now you've got money, so you're trying to get into New York society" and even the desperate "You Connecticut folk are so provincial," but they only fell flat and made her seem bitchy and drunk. And anyway, every time Joan said anything, Phillip just talked over her in his loud, nasal voice. For someone so completely taciturn in most aspects of social interaction, the man was positively loquacious on the topic of his society.

Wendy, meanwhile, couldn't wait until the dinner was over. She was completely mortified, but more than that, profoundly sad. Was this it? She would end up alone, always tagging along with Joan and Phillip to some dinner or interminable event. It would be better to be like Joan— in a loveless marriage but at least with a companion—than to be a single middle-aged woman in New York. That was for sure.

chapter 44

Cordelia, for all her usual sedated calm, was in a state of sheer mania. There was a looming task at hand, a project in which it was time to get knee deep. She would have to roll up her cashmere sleeves, take a deep breath, and follow careful procedure. When the phone rang, she answered with a nerves-charged "Hello?" and dismissed the caller, a lunch pal from the Colony Club, with great haste.

"I'm so sorry, Candace," she said, looking at her watch. "I am simply crazed today; it's my son John's birthday and I have to bake a cake." Yes, unlike many Park Avenue matrons whose assistants put in a call to Fauchon to have a gleaming personalized birthday cake sent right over, Mrs. Vance was determined to do it herself. She was not like those cold, high-maintenance moms who took no care in their family members' special day—she was hands on, and she would bake all her love into the confection.

She walked into the kitchen, nodding to her staff, who were busy cleaning, chopping vegetables for the evening's supper, and assisting the Poland Spring man with his new delivery of water.

After signing for the new shipment, Madge came over and guided Cordelia into the pantry. There, laid out with such perfection that one would think cameras from the Food Network were soon to swoop in, were all the ingredients in their measuring cups and spoons, next to a shiny, big red mixing bowl. Cordelia surveyed the immaculate vessels and looked at all the different textures—flour, oil, chocolate: they were so beautiful in their simplicity. She looked nervously to Madge, who nodded, and Cord slowly reached for the first glass cup and dumped it into the bowl. Relieved, she smiled, looking at Madge for a thumbs up. She kept going, daintily dumping each of the ingredients from container to bowl. Madge then transferred the contents into the mixer, and when the batter was finished, Cordelia held the bowl as Madge poured it into the cake pan.

Cordelia was hypnotized by the ribbons of chocolatey mixture that fell cascading into the pan. She felt so whole, so back to the olden days when time was spent by the hearth and home.

"I love cooking," she said.

Downstairs, Tom and Eddie were in a similar state of calm, as foot traffic was slow due to the threatening charcoal clouds overhead.

"God forbid these people get their fuckin' hair wet," said Tom. "It's like they think it's acid falling from the sky!"

"Tell me about it," replied Eddie. "Especially Miss Weston; I don't think I've ever seen her go out if it's not crystal blue skies out there."

"I wonder what's going down with Mrs. Korn. You think she's still cooped up in there?"

"Naw. After she hid out in the Hamptons, she came back. Luca said she's even been going out now."

"Damn, she still is a foxy bitch, though. Maybe since she was so disgraced with all her fancy people she wouldn't mind a shag from the old porter, huh?"

Tom laughed as Eddie punched him teasingly.

"Dream on, buddy," he said, kidding, slash not. "Dream on."

chapter 45

Joan and Wendy were walking on East Eighty-sixth Street, sidestepping street fashion vendors, hot dog hockers, and a clogged strip of pavement coursing with thousands of weary worker bees and boom box–toting, rowdy "yutes."

"Ugh, I'm allergic to Eighty-sixth Street. East of Lex, you might as well be south of the border," said Wendy, fanning herself as if to make room between her and the unseemly pedestrians in oversize parkas and flashy gold jewelry.

"I know—second to Canal, it's the most hellish street on the island," added Joan as she was shoved out of the way by a pack of young Hispanic teens.

The two had been on East Eighty-fifth Street and York in a quiet shop near the mayor's residence at Gracie Mansion. It was out of the way, yes, but the old Italian proprietor sold the best mantels in the city, and Wendy was looking for a new decorative marble piece for her living room. Blocks later, after much huffing and puffing and bitching about their less-than-pristine company on the sidewalk ("Not to mention all these grungy junk shops!" said Joan), Wendy stopped and grabbed her pal's fur-covered arm.

"Oh! look . . ." Wendy was gazing across the street.

There, as Joan followed the point of Wendy's gloved finger across the street, was the most famous recluse of recent weeks, Melanie Korn. In sunglasses and a long, trenchlike camel coat, Mr. Crispin's human voodoo doll was coming toward them.

"Hi, Joan. Hi, Wendy," said Melanie calmly.

They were silent for a moment. Joan had no idea what to say. Wendy paused to follow Joan's lead.

"Mel! What are you doing here on Eighty-sixth Street?" asked Joan.

"Oh, errands and stuff. How are you guys?"

"Oh, fine," said Joan tentatively. "How about you?"

Melanie knew they were tiptoeing around the elephant that was the profile, and she didn't care. *Bring it on,* she thought. "Well, since the article I've been holing up a little. You know on the 'D.L.,' as the kids are saying . . ."

"What?" asked Joan.

"The down low," explained Wendy. "Ghetto speak."

"Oh."

"Well, nice to see you two," said Melanie politely, with a new, serene, "I don't give a shit" confidence that she never had before. Her openness about the article's aftermath disarmed her two biggest critics and piqued their interest even more.

"Where are you off to?" asked Wendy, thirsting for more, for amusement and curiosity's sake. "Would you like to join us for lunch? We were just going to have a bite at Demarchelier . . ."

"Oh, please do join us," added Joan courteously.

Melanie paused. Why were these two being nice to her? Was it a trick? Should she bolt? She was hungry, though. What the hell.

"Well, okay. I am starvatious," said Melanie.

"Great!"

"Fabulous!"

The unlikely trio walked another two blocks west to the famed Parisian bistro. Plates of steamed artichokes and moules marinières floated by on the lifted hands of aproned French waiters, as Wendy's mouth watered when a platter of pomme frites sailed by and landed on the adjacent table.

"Ooooh, look at those fries!" she said, her hand on her chest. "I'd better not."

"Why not?" said Melanie. "Life's short." She summoned the waiter, who took their order for three salades Niçoise and an order of french fries.

"So," ventured Wendy, "you said you were 'holed up'?"

"Oh, yeah. I've been, you know, in recovery. Don't worry, I'm not popping pills Melanie Griffith–style. It wasn't a meltdown or anything, but I was, well, dragged through the mud a little and now I'm all cleaned up."

"Wow, you're taking this all so well," said Joan, impressed.

Melanie knew she was playing the trauma way down, but despite her not caring as much anymore, she still had her guard up. These two may have been all smiles, but they were still vultures stuffed into Givenchy suits.

"Oh, you know. As I said, life's just too short to worry about all that nonsense. As Arthur says, we'll all be dead in forty years, so what does it matter anyway, right?" She laughed casually as she sipped her glass of chardonnay.

"You're amazing!" said Wendy. She knew if she was decimated in print like that she'd be in shatters, having to be spatulaed up off the floor. And that caricature? Get the noose ready.

"No, not amazing. I just listened to my husband," said Melanie. "He said, 'Honey, you've gotta have a little more Fuck You in you,' so I took a little of his these last few weeks. It's all just meaningless social stuff, you know. So much matters more."

Joan and Wendy were thrilled that they had asked their former archenemy to join them. When the salads were through, Melanie left some cash (enough for everyone's lunch) and said she had to dart off to a doctor's appointment. Joan and Wendy, who were staying for dessert ("Oooh, that tarte tatin looks so good I can't help myself!" cried Wendy), watched Melanie walk out. As soon as she turned and was out of sight, they rolled up their sleeves and launched. But this time, it was with a newfound . . . almost . . . respect. Not respect, exactly, but a loathing dulled by the new humility of their former punching bag.

"Metamorphosis," pronounced Wendy. "Sheer transformation."

"Forget Jeff Goldblum in *The Fly*."

"Did you see how calm she was? It was like a new human. She always used to try so fucking hard. She didn't name-drop once—did you notice?"

"Or money-drop."

"Exactly! It was like this whole debacle brought her back down to earth. Maybe this was what she really needed, a little shake."

"A smack in the face," added Joan.

"Yes! It's like she was drunk on all this new money and lavishness and drugged on vanity and clothes and jewelry, and this whole episode just sobered her right the hell up."

"True. True."

The pair ate dessert and stopped talking for a moment. Wendy thought about how much she had loved to loathe Melanie Korn. And today, that big brassy rottweiler was a perfectly friendly puppy. Now that Melanie wouldn't be their hate magnet, who would be? And if she wasn't scandalized anymore by the article, could they still be? Something new needed to go down.

chapter 46

"Adorable! Really great structure, and you can tell this one will age well," said Jerome, flipping through the look-book. He looked at his pal Cord for thoughts.

"Beautiful," she answered. She was sincere but in a daze.

The woman sitting across from Jerome and Cordelia stared in astonishment. She was speechless.

"Oh! Now what a unique look. I haven't seen that before," added Jerome, on to a new page. "Wow, this is really going to be difficult to decide."

"Um, I think you really have to be sure," said the woman.

"Oh, I know. It's not something to be taken lightly," said Jerome.

"Right . . ."

"Should we go with white or brown?" Jerome asked.

"I can't really answer that for you."

"What do you think, Cord?"

"I'm not quite sure."

"I know, I know. I mean, white is more practical, of course," Jerome thought aloud. "More natural. But then brown is tempting, different. I have serious inclinations toward brown, but am I too radical? Let's face it, white is more appropriate for your country club. They're not very modern."

"I don't think that should really be the deciding factor," the woman said.

Jerome continued his flipping through the book as Cordelia looked on dreamily. "Ooooh, I think we have a winner!" he said at last, showing Cordelia his find. "This one is so cute, perfection!" he said, pointing to a picture. "What do you think?"

"Could work," said Cordelia, looking on.

"I think this might not be a good idea," said the woman, snatching back the book. "You should not rush into this! This is very serious." What were this people thinking? These were not shoes. These were living, breathing human beings!

"We here at the Spence-Chapin adoption center are committed to finding the best families possible for our children, and we will not allow one of our babies to enter into a home based on a bored, rich housewife's capricious fits. I suggest that you adopt a dog, not a child."

And with that, Jerome and Cordelia were shown the door. Cordelia did feel bad—Jerome seemed to be making a fashion statement out of the adoption, as if she were acquiring an accessory, but that really wasn't the point. She truly wanted to be a mother again. She wanted to feel loved and needed and relied on. She wanted to feel relevant. Perhaps Jerome wasn't the best person to advise her on this front.

While his wife was toying with the fate of a helpless bambino, Morgan was at his home office, determined to make his situation less helpless. The instructions from the man as to how to proceed had been strict, concise, and professional. Now all Morgan had to do was to call Maria.

"Where have you been?" whined Maria when she heard his voice. "I called you three times. I was going to call your house!"

"I had a meeting. Listen," began Morgan quickly, so he wouldn't lose his nerve. "Let's meet on Friday night. There's a new restaurant I read about in *New York* magazine. Now, it's in Brooklyn, but it has been getting incredible reviews. And Shirley Rockefeller told me I had to go," he added the last part, a lie, because he knew that Maria would be suspicious about his taking her to Brooklyn. There was no Shirley Rockefeller, but she wouldn't know that.

"It's about time you take me out. You never take me anywhere nice. I need some time away from that brat."

Could she have a better attitude? Schuyler was just a baby. But he didn't want to argue, and he wouldn't need to after Friday. "Well, this place is supposed to be really nice."

"Yeah, I'll go," she said, as if doing Morgan a favor. "Why don't you ask the Rockefellers to come with us? I wanna meet your friends. We'll have fun!"

Yeah, right. "I'll ring Shirley and see if she's free."

"I'll wear my Versace. They'll love me—watch out!"

Uh-huh. "So, I'll have my driver pick you up at seven. It won't be my usual guy—he's on vacation. But this one knows where to go." *And you'll go straight to hell, baby.*

Morgan heard Cordelia enter the apartment, so he quickly hung up the phone and went out to the front hall to greet her.

"What are you doing home so early?" asked Cordelia, putting down her shopping bags.

"The boys were coming for dinner, and I feel like I've been completely preoccupied with work lately, so I wanted to spend more time with all of you," said Morgan quickly, pecking her on the forehead.

Cordelia was touched, so she reached out and clasped Morgan's hand. "Speaking of family, there's something I want to talk to you about. It's very serious," she said solemnly.

The color immediately drained from Morgan's face. "What's that?" he asked nervously.

"Let's go in the living room," said Cordelia, leading the way.

The living room? *Shit, this must be bad.* Could she have found out about Maria? Morgan felt sick.

After Morgan was seated, he patiently waited for Cordelia to straighten a painting she insisted was askew, run her finger across the Steinway to check for dust, and rearrange the jade cocks on the mantel before she would tell him what was on her mind. He grew more and more nauseous as she stalled. Finally, she turned to him.

"I've decided that I want to adopt a baby girl. I've always wanted a daughter. And in China they leave them on bridges and things . . ."

Morgan was both confused and relieved. "This is new. I've never heard you say that."

Cordelia played with her pearls. "I've had a hole in my heart for some time now, and I've thought about why. Finally I realized what it was, and now I know that it's something I truly want."

"It's not like shopping, Cordelia. You don't just decide one day that you want a kid and then just give it to Goodwill when it goes out of fashion."

"I wouldn't do that! I don't return things."

John and Drew came noisily bursting into the room, banging open the doors behind them.

Morgan turned to them. "Boys, your mother's gone crazy. She wants a daughter."

John and Drew looked at their parents and realized they had entered at the wrong moment. "Cool," muttered John.

But Drew was not pleased. "What? A sister? Damn."

"Drew!" said Cordelia.

"Yes, now that she's bought everything else in New York, she wants a child," said Morgan in a harsh tone that he never used in front of his wife.

"That's not why . . ." began Cordelia.

"I don't know, Cordelia. This just seems crazy. You want a fur coat one minute, the next you want a Regency desk, the next a kid. Are you going through menopause?"

Cordelia was mortified. She never expected this reaction. Why was Morgan being so cruel?

"I know it sounds impetuous to you, but I've given it a lot of thought."

"Oh, yeah? Have you thought about how babies scream all day? How they whine and fuss? Have you thought about what you will do when you get tired of it?" Morgan couldn't even think of babies.

"I have! I'll take care of her. In China they leave them on bridges!"

"You say you want one now, but who knows . . ."

"You all have left and have your own lives," she said, looking not only at her sons but also at her husband. "And I'm here with still a lot of love to give. There are so many needy kids in the world—shouldn't a family as privileged as ours give back?" Cordelia stood up and stared at her family. They were surprised to see her so passionate. It was if she had been defibrillated from a flat line back to life.

"Cordelia—" began Morgan.

But before he could finish, she interrupted him. "I know you all think of me as someone who just shops all day, but I'm more than that! I am!"

Cordelia burst into tears and ran out of the room. Morgan turned to look at his boys, who glared at him. He felt guilty. It wasn't Cordelia he was mad at.

"Boys, be nice to your mother. She's having a hard time."

Morgan gently rapped on Cordelia's dressing room door. He thought he heard a muffled "Hello," so he slowly opened the door. Cordelia was lying on her peppermint-striped divan, her back to him, a bunched up ball of tissues clasped in her fist. Her shoulders rocked with her sobs. Morgan sighed and sat down on the armchair beside her.

"I'm sorry, Cord. I shouldn't have snapped at you."

Cordelia didn't respond. Morgan looked around the room, at the peach skirted vanity table with the silver dresser set. All of the brushes and mirrors were carefully aligned in front of the row of Cordelia's antique perfume bottle collection. He felt sad thinking of Cord sitting there, primping to go out to a party, looking at herself in the mirror.

"Make me understand, Cord. Where is this coming from?"

Cordelia still did not face him. But her small voice murmured, "Is this what it's all about? I can't believe that this is my life . . ."

"What do you mean? I think your life's pretty good."

"No, no, no," she whispered.

"You have two healthy kids and everything your heart desires."

"I don't mean that, Morgan. I know I'm privileged and lucky."

"Then what is it?"

She turned toward him. "I feel like I'm floating in emptiness," she said, her eyes dancing around the room, blurred by a veil of desolate tears. "I feel marooned."

Morgan took her in his arms. Her thin body went limp, and she seemed so frail and helpless. How could he have done this to her? She *was* marooned. He had forgotten her. This was all his doing. "Don't worry, sweetie. You're not alone."

"I'm gasping, Morgan. I need something more."

"I haven't been here for you, Cord. I'm sorry."

Cordelia broke into heaving sobs. Morgan held her until she fell asleep in his arms. He brushed his lips against her hair and vowed that he would make her happy. It was about time.

chapter 47

Joan was sitting at a booth at RSVP, absentmindedly browsing the lunch menu while waiting for her cohort. Cheese soufflé? No, too fatty. Hmm, what would it be today? Okay, leeks vinaigrette—she'd be a good girl. She looked around the normally packed café, and today it was oddly sedate; there were three tables of women, and they were all speaking in hushed tones. Was something amiss? Just as Joan was starting get suspicious about something being up, Wendy burst in dramatically and took her seat across from Joan, poker faced. She exhaled before opening her lips to speak. The news was that shocking.

"Joan. Something horrible has happened."

A few blocks away, Morgan was opening the bedroom door and looked upon his sleeping wife. She had been through so much, and now he was about to rouse her from her comforting slumber only to deliver news that would certainly make her want to crawl back under the covers and hibernate forever. Morgan was at an early squash game that morning when he heard. Instead of going back to the office, he went to tell Cordelia in person before the barrage of phone calls woke her and thrust her into drowning hysteria. He needed to be by her side when she was told. He could barely believe it himself. In a Harlem flophouse, bound and gagged, on a soiled mattress, Jerome de Stingol was found dead.

"Cord, honey, wake up," he whispered softly, putting a hand on her hair. "Cordelia, something horrible has happened."

Two floors down, Melanie soberly wound up her phone conversation.

"Gosh, what is the world coming to? This is such a tragic loss, what a shock . . . Yes, I'm just floored . . . Right, okay, well, thanks for calling . . . Take care. Okay, 'bye." She hung up the phone quietly. Wow.

If she had sat down with the pantheon of scandal gods herself, she couldn't have asked for a better eclipse of that Crispin article. Kids, there's a whole new disgrace in this town, and it's rocked by a lot more seedy darkness than her boring life. That bitchy asshole Jerome de Stingol was gonzo. Poor thing, he probably never knew what hit him. But even though Melanie was relieved by Jerome's demise, she didn't relish it the way she would have several weeks ago. It just didn't affect her life in any way, and that was odd to her.

Cordelia's screams of agony were deafening. Her quivering sobs from the night before paled in comparison to this world-toppling catastrophe, as the hole that was usurping her life was now gaping. She pounded her pillow, screaming "WHY?" and Morgan told the housekeeper to please ring for a doctor. He rubbed her back soothingly, though nothing could mend her twice-shattered heart.

At RSVP, Joan was also in a state of shock. "No! It cannot be possible! He was the last great walker!"

Wendy paused dramatically, inhaling and closing her eyes. "He shall walk no more."

Across town, Arthur walked from the carport lined with hearses to the main entrance of To Die For, his vast empire serving all your death needs. Hearse drivers bent over playing craps stood and saluted Mr. Korn, whom they revered as a leader but related to as if he were one of their own. He was loaded, sure, but he was always down with the peeps.

"Hey, boss!"

"Hey, guys—slow day?"

"Yeah."

He walked through the reception hall leading to the seven different funeral parlors, down the stairs to the embalming lab. Makeup artists did the finishing touches in one section, reconstructive surgery took place in another, and new bodies entered the refrigerated room from a doorway on the side.

"One, two, three," said a coroner as a command for his assistant to help him lift a corpse onto the gurney. Two seconds and one groan later, the body was in place and the bag unzipped.

"Holy mackerel. I knew that guy!" said Arthur, amazed. Was it some friend of his wife's? He'd seen him around.

"Forensics just got through with him," said Sal, his head of operations. "He was found last night, and they did some rush autopsy. They said he was some big deal in Manhattan."

"Wow."

"Homicide victim—some gay porno sex slaughter in Harlem."

"How strange," said Arthur. It was starting to come back to him that his wife thought this guy was a real phony.

"It took two hours just to get the dildo out of his ass."

"Is his service in one of ours?"

"Naw, we're just preparing it. It'll be in some fancy schmancy church on Park Avenue."

"Shit. I'll probably have to go to his funeral."

"You run with quite a group of people, Mr. Korn."

"Yeah, Sal, I do," he said, walking farther down the hall. "And the funny thing is, I don't even like most of them. They're all very snooty and not so much fun. I don't know why that is."

"They can play all high and mighty, but they all end up on the same slab as you and me."

"Ain't that the truth."

Arthur noticed a new coffin coming out of the shipping department.

"Hey, is that the new DX7000?" he asked, as exhilarated as a child bursting bows and ripping wrapping on Christmas morning.

"It just arrived, boss." Sal beamed with pride.

"What a beauty. Look at the finish," he said, stroking the glazed exterior with awe and appreciation.

"Burl."

"Fabulous. The brocade lining is terrific," Arthur noticed, fondling the interior. "Lavender was a good choice for this."

"We've also got burgundy and hunter green."

Arthur stared at the coffin lovingly, rubbing his hand back and forth on the polish. He sighed deeply.

"It's sad that no one will appreciate all this hard work and craftsmanship; it's all in vain. It doesn't count, really."

"Well, we do. And we count."

Arthur looked at him and smiled. "Yes, Sal, we do count."

chapter 48

At lunchtime Cordelia was still unbathed, unbrushed, unrouged, and wrapped in her ecru cashmere peignoir. Not that she cared. She tried to lift her arm to comb her hair, but after one stroke her hand fell limply to the vanity table. What was the use? Nothing mattered to her now. Nothing, that is, except writing the best eulogy that the Upper East Side had ever heard. She owed it to her Jerome. Oh, Jerome. What could he have been thinking? What could he have been doing? To end this way was so unseemly, so sinister, so seedy. There must be an explanation; he was obviously abducted, no matter what the police said. It just didn't make sense that he would be in Harlem of his own volition. And in some dirty apartment . . . no. Everyone knew Jerome was the biggest germaphobe there was. He wouldn't even swim in the pool at the Bathing Corp., for fear of toddler feces. And he went ballistic at cocktail parties if someone double-dipped the shrimp. No, not a chance he'd be up there in some vulgar tenement by choice.

He had walked her to the Memorial Sloan-Kettering benefit just last week, and now he was gone. Flashes of Jerome in his tux, gently guiding her into a grand ballroom, raced through her mind. How could she exist without him? How would she know when it was time to re-wallpaper? How would she know what to wear? Her life was torn apart. She would have done anything to bring him back. But all she could do was walk to her Queen Anne's desk and furiously try to write something that captured the man she admired, the sad irony being that he would have been the one she would have turned to for advice on precisely this sort of endeavor. Every time Cordelia tried to compose something, pulling at her hair, the tears blurred her eyes and she was unable to see the paper. Balls of Easter-egg Tiffany stationery lay crumpled on the oatmeal carpet—glaring failed attempts at heralding the man she adored. She looked outside the large French windows at the frenzied, fevered pace of traffic and pedestrians. She was offended that the world was going on outside. How could Park Avenue continue as if nothing was amiss? It was vile.

"I hear Cordelia Vance is chained to her desk, convulsing," whispered Joan to Wendy, her bright red–lipped mouth full of foie gras.

"They should never have asked her to write the eulogy. She's probably ripping her hair out," agreed Wendy, wiping her mouth with her napkin.

They had arrived at Swifty's early, in order to get the best table, in order to catch all of the lunching ladies on their way in, in order to make sure they were not left out of the loop in any way. And, yes, while Cordelia was ripping her hair out, furious at the world for existing without Jerome, Joan and Wendy had made it their mission to find out every dirty little detail of his demise.

"Who decides those things, anyway? I mean, he has no family, right?" asked Joan, waving to Cindy Briggs and Fernanda Wingate.

"Except for that nephew in Minnesota," said Wendy, putting a forkful of frisée in her mouth.

"What nephew?"

"I don't know, a nephew," said Wendy.

"So he asked her to do it?"

"No. Cass Weathers told me that her husband's firm is handling the estate. Apparently Jerome left a ridiculously long, detailed will, with all these last wishes down to the songs to be played at the funeral and the hors d'oeuvres to be served at the reception."

"No."

"Yes."

"Well, at least we know we'll be well fed! Oooh, and I know he loved caviar! Maybe there will be some," said Joan with a raised brow.

"Oh, definitely. And not only that—his stipulations were so particular that it took three lawyers to arrange everything. Apparently flowers could only be white calla lillies arranged by Renny, Lawrence Powell was to read the Lord's Prayer . . ."

"Lawrence? But he barely knew him!"

"Come on, dear, we're talking about *Jerome*. It was all about status."

"Good grief."

"He specified who would be his pallbearers."

"I can imagine that list."

"And he even wrote the pamphlets to be handed out to the guests, specifying the *font* to be used."

"Such a diva!"

"And of course, Cordelia *had* to do the eulogy. No ifs, ands, or buts about it."

"It's interesting that he said he wanted his precious Cord-Cord to eulogize him, hmmm? He would know that she would never be up to the task—"

"I know, it's unfortunate, because Cordelia is not the type who can handle this," said Wendy in a solemn whisper. "She's so fragile."

"Fabergé egg."

They paused, lingering over Cordelia's weakened condition in their minds, and then moved on. Wendy switched the subject to one of their faves.

"Anyway, on to more important things: what are you wearing?"

"Black Valentino, and you?"

"My Chanel matelassé suit. What do you think? Last season, but I'm not going to splurge on a new one for Jerome."

"No need. He would have been the only one who noticed anyway."

As Joan and Wendy headed into a full-on debate as to which shoes to wear for the ceremony, Morgan was dealing with his own trifling affairs. Namely, Maria.

"I'm so sick of your excuses!" she screamed into the phone. "I will *not* be ignored."

"We're going out on Friday!" said Morgan, exasperated.

"I don't care. I want to see you now!"

"Listen," said Morgan, making sure the door of the library was closed tightly. "My wife has suffered a tragic loss. A great man has died. He was a dear friend."

"I read all about your 'dear friend' on *Page Six*. Now I know what psychos you hang out with. You and your friends are *loco*! You put freaks on a pedestal and you treat me like yesterday's shitty diapers!"

"Maria, it's not like that. It's complicated."

"It's not complicated! It's simple! You prefer lunatics to your daughter!"

"That's not true."

"It is! And I wonder how *Page Six* would feel about that!" Maria slammed down the phone.

"You wouldn't dare," Morgan said into the empty phone.

Oh, she was a nightmare. But she'd be over soon, and hopefully he'd put to rest that little chapter of his life. It had to end, finally. Cordelia would need him now more than ever.

chapter 49

Arthur had left work and was driving home when he spied Olivia Weston exiting their building with a worried face. She wrapped her caramel shawl around her, wincing from the cold, and tried helplessly to hail a cab. All off-duty. Arthur was about to pull over and offer her a ride when a cab slowed down and asked for her destination. Agreeing to take her, the driver gave a nod and she hopped in. Arthur paused. Should he follow her? Wasn't that a little stalkerish? But before he could even think, he was pulling around the corner in her direction. At least his driver was off that day. He would have felt too idiotic saying, "Follow that cab!"

He followed her down Park, around Union Square, down Broadway, and left on Twelfth Street. Where the hell was she going? He kept his eyes glued to the medallion number on the top of the taxi so as not to lose it. Q6X8. They suddenly became magic numbers to him. Around a garbage truck, around a stalled car, he kept the number in his vision; it was the code that brought him to her, the signifying mark of her chariot, a yellow swerving vehicle that carried precious cargo.

When the cab finally slowed, Arthur was surprised, since they were back in no-man's-land, on Avenue D between Eleventh and Twelfth streets, right across from To Die For number 487, and right back to where he'd run into her before. He watched Olivia get out of the cab and walk up the shady steps of that creepy building dappled in fire escapes, where her friend lived. There were a couple guys having a smoke on the landing three floors up, and music was playing out the window of another floor.

She buzzed and waited until the ringing sound allowed her slight push to open the door. Arthur was worried. Here she was, this total knockout, wandering into this fleabag of a building. She could be the next Jerome de Whatever. Panicked, he parked, flipped on his hazards, and walked out toward the building. Just as he was approaching the front door, his cell phone rang. Arthur fumbled in his pocket to turn it off and walked over to the building Olivia had entered. The front door was still ajar, so he walked in and followed the soothing sound of her voice. He could hear Olivia up one more flight, but he lurked below under the staircase by an open utility closet where he could hear most everything. She was talking with someone in the hallway. When he peered out momentarily, he saw that friend of hers, Holland, from the reading. She was framed by a doorway with pieces of chipped paint falling off, and she seemed to be in sweatpants and a T-shirt, with those same cat's-eye glasses. She seemed mad. Furious. And his dreamgirl, the beautiful and brilliant Olivia, was now somehow reduced to tears by this venomous girl.

"Please don't do this to me, Holland!" she said, her soft voice breaking. "We had such a good thing going—"

"Forget it. You're way too high maintenance. Not to mention dishonest."

Olivia started to cry. "But I need you—"

Whoa. Was this some kind of lesbo action? Holy shit. Arthur couldn't believe his ears.

"I'm not ghostwriting for *Sweet Valley High,* Olivia," said Holland, with so much force on the word "Olivia" that it sounded as if she were saying "Bitch."

"But—" Olivia tried to interrupt feebly.

"Your novel took a shitload of research and work, and I'm not writing one more chapter until you pay me the fucking fifty thousand dollars you owe me!"

Arthur was . . . stunned. He literally put his hand over his heart, which was racing and breaking at the same time.

"Holland, I'm begging you," said Olivia, near tears. "I need those two chapters for my editor by the weekend. Please—"

"Fuck the editor. I want my money. I am not writing another word of your bullshit sequel until I get it." Holland tried to slam the door, but Olivia caught it. Suddenly the fragile, quivering timbre of her voice metamorphosed. The new iced poison tone was a spear through Arthur's midsection, unseaming him from neck to navel.

"I wouldn't slam that door in my face, Holland," she said coldly. "I am wired."

"Ooooh, I'm terrified."

"You should be. I can ruin you. I'm the next Mimi Halsey!"

"Listen, Mimi, go ahead and try to 'ruin' me! No one in the East Village knows who you are or could give a shit about you. I wouldn't have even known who you were if Rob hadn't met you in writing class. You're not capable of 'ruining' me."

Olivia lifted her arm and smacked Holland across the face. Both girls seemed stunned, especially when they realized that Olivia's ring had drawn blood. Arthur, witnessing the violence from his staircase hideout, thought he might have a coronary. His little dove was officially a witch.

"*You psycho!*" said Holland, aghast. "Fine, fucking hit me, you freak. I'm happy to call your editor—or better yet—one of your glossy uptown rags—and tell them you didn't write *one word* of your society bestseller. And the whole truth, including your wallop across my face, will be in the papers if you don't give me the money you owe me by tomorrow."

Holland slammed the door, this time successfully, in Olivia's face. Olivia stood silently for a moment, then turned to go down the stairs. Arthur hid in the shadows by the utility closet and lurked there until he heard her familiar step go by. The front door closed and she was off, and that was it. He stood, frozen, in the closet for what seemed like an hour, pondering the surreal haze of his shattered ideal. He felt drugged by reality, slain by the truth. He was bowled over, weakened by what had unfolded. With a crush, it's more about hope than reality. But now all dreamy walks through that perfect realm were over, and it was painful to him because all the things he cherished in this paradigm of grace and brains and beauty vanished in a slammed door. And his fantasy was dead.

The door upstairs opened and Holland's sneakered feet skipped down the stairs. Arthur didn't mean to startle her, but when he said, "Miss . . . ," she shrieked.

"Don't worry—"

"Who *are* you? What do you *want*?"

"I'm Arthur—I-I-I swear I'm not a criminal. I just wanted to ask you—"

"What?" she said, hesitating. Okay, he didn't look like an ax murderer.

"You're Olivia Weston's friend?"

"Not a friend. Who are you?"

Arthur looked at her face. It was still red around her mouth. He pulled out his handkerchief. "Are you okay? Wow, she really slugged ya."

"I'm fine," said Holland, waving the handkerchief away. "What do you want?"

"I, um . . ." He may as well just blurt it out. "Did she write *Rhythms of Fisher's,* or did . . . you?"

Holland paused. Who the heck was this dude? Probably one her uptown jack-off followers. Probably brought her book into the john and whacked it to that Scavullo portrait on the back cover. Ew.

"I need to know," he said, his face crumbling.

Was he, like, crying over this? Sheesh.

"Okay. I wrote it."

Arthur was shocked all over again to hear it from her lips, face to face.

"I can't believe it . . . I just can't believe it was all bullshit."

Holland walked down and he followed her outside, in a daze. They walked down the street, Arthur virtually comatose, Holland sad for him but mildly amused. Jeez, her work must have really touched people.

"Why are you so upset?" she asked him.

"Because . . . I believed her. There's no truth anymore."

"I'm sorry. I really am. Don't worry." Poor shnook.

"I'm so disappointed."

"Most people are disappointing."

"But . . . I thought she was different from all those country club bores. She stood out from the crowd," Arthur said wearily.

"She pretended to."

"Why?"

Holland paused. This guy really was crushed! He seemed sweet enough. Another victim of Olivia's weird spell. Holland remembered when she first thought Olivia was so glamorous and mysterious. What a load of steaming crap that turned out to be.

"Listen, Olivia wanted to be different just as badly as everyone else wants to assimilate into society. It's ironic. They aspire to be her. They think she's the real thing."

"I don't know what the real thing is anymore."

"I'll tell you." She stopped and put a comforting hand on his shoulder and smiled gently. "The real thing is the person you have a true, meaningful connection with. Someone who exposes their flaws, their fears, everything—that's how you get to know someone, from their cracks. When there's nothing for you to fill in, no flaw, no problem, how can you ever know a person?"

"I suppose."

"No, think about it."

"I can't. I'm just stunned. Olivia, a plagiarizer! A bully! A fake! I don't know what anything is anymore."

"Yes, you do. The real thing is someone who is open and honest and not afraid to show what's at the chewy center. And Olivia has no chewy center. She had to pay me to invent one for her."

"I just thought Olivia was different. I hoped . . ."

"No. Olivia Weston is a fantasy, a myth cobbled together by your dreams. She's a white screen and people project what they want on it, their desires for class or beauty or whatever."

"But she's . . . I just thought she's what I dreamt about. She was everything good."

"You know what's ironic? She holds none of these illusions, because she doesn't even know who she is. She is lost. She's nothing without her lineage or that face or a camera to snap her newest gown. She's nothing but a party picture."

And with that, Holland walked away, leaving Arthur standing idly on the street.

chapter 50

Melanie entered the lobby with two bags of groceries from Fairway. She had selected them with care after deciding to make something other than reservations for dinner. And she was going to make it herself, much to her chef's astonishment. Hey, if Nigella could make it look so easy and sexy, couldn't she?

While awaiting the elevator, Melanie saw Dr. Herb Stein exiting, toting an old school–style doctor's bag for house calls. He was the head of internal medicine at New York Hospital, and his patient files were like a carbon copy of the Fortune 500 CEO list, which was a good thing, since he did not accept insurance and got north of two grand for a checkup.

"Hey, Fred," Melanie said to the doorman after Dr. Stein was out of earshot. "Is anyone sick? Why was Dr. Stein here?"

"Yes, ma'am," he replied in a whisper, looking both ways as if he were revealing classified information to someone with top clearance from Quantico. "It's Mrs. Vance. She's taken ill. Death of her friend. Hasn't left her bed in days."

"Oh," said Melanie, thinking of her own despondent spell mired in the stagnant sea of sheets and pillows. It was not a distant memory. Poor Cordelia. "That's terrible."

As she watched the lit numbers of the ascending floors, Melanie felt a pang for her neighbor. Sure, she hadn't been a fan of Jerome's. That was putting it lightly. He sucked. Literally. And frankly, he was snobbishly cruel and spewed poison into the world with his toxic gossip and bitter, bilious words. She had been, in fact, relieved and even a little glad that he had died. One less person on a mission to ruin her life, and not only hers, but others'. He left a long list of people whom he had set out to destroy. But for some reason he was devoted to Cordelia, and Melanie knew he'd left a gaping hole in her life. And that was sad.

It was odd, because the more she thought about it, the more she realized that Cordelia wasn't like the other women in his flock. Sure, she was weirdly adrift and spacey, but compared to everyone else and the mean barbs they'd chucked Melanie's way, Cordelia wasn't bad at all. In fact, she had a sad serenity in her tone, a kind of zoned-out nurturing thing, as if she had the muscles to be warm but just hadn't flexed them in a long time.

After Melanie and Juanita had put away the wild mushroom ravioli and a battery of sauces and vegetables, Melanie sat down at her enormous desk and thought she'd finally put it to good use for once. She pulled out the first crisp piece of her new Mrs. John L. Strong stationery and drew a casual line through her last name so as not to seem too formal. *"Dear Cordelia,"* she began. She was about to write a very formal condolence letter full of very correct Guffeyisms, but then she reconsidered. Why not put down her real emotions? Why not say, "You know what? I know right now sucks for you, but it will get better"? That was more to the point anyway. And that was what she truly believed and felt.

An hour later, with a flower- and cookie-filled basket in hand, Melanie got off the elevator to leave her package in the Vances' vestibule. But just as she turned to get back into the elevator, the Vances' front door opened. Melanie turned around slowly and was startled to see herself face to face with Cordelia, who had emerged in a robe, her face pale and her eyes weary from cataracts of tears.

Each seemed equally shocked to see the other.

"Oh, Cordelia, I'm so sorry—I just was leaving this for you."

"Oh, hello. I just . . . was coming to collect the mail."

Melanie turned and saw the pile on the upholstered bench against the wall. She handed it to her neighbor and was about to retreat when she felt emboldened.

"Listen," Melanie said warmly. "I know we don't know each other very well. But I see you're in pain right now, which is something I know a lot about. I just wanted to bring you some stuff to . . . maybe make you feel a little better and say I'm sorry for your loss."

Cordelia was not too out of it to be deeply touched. Even through her Percoset haze she was moved by the kindness this woman (whom so many people bullied) was offering her, in a moment when she felt thoroughly forsaken.

"That is so kind of you." Her eyes began to water just looking at the pretty basket. "So thoughtful. I really appreciate it."

"My pleasure," said Melanie. "If there's anything you ever need, I'm right downstairs. I know what it's like to lose people. And to feel . . . alone in grief."

Cordelia looked at Melanie. She had never before been seen looking like such a mess. Even by her help. But for some reason she was not mortified. She was actually very relaxed. This woman got it.

"Thank you so much, Melanie. It's hard—every hour without Jerome has felt like an eternal battle." Her voice broke. "He was my best friend."

"I know. And you think you won't get through that blackness of the void, but you will."

"I hope." Cordelia gave her a soft nod. "His funeral is tomorrow. I'm supposed to write a speech, and I just stare aimlessly at the paper."

"I'm sure you'll think of something beautiful to say."

Cordelia wiped a tear from her eye. "How do I summon the language? How can I reduce him to a page of words?"

Easy, thought Melanie. *Try two*: ass *and* hole. No, Jerome's wickedness aside, she sincerely felt for Cordelia. She knew this soft-spoken woman had a special rapport with him. Not to mention a whole other armoire of issues at home.

"I'm sure you can do it, Cordelia. Just think of all the good times you shared. Trust yourself and don't edit."

Cordelia looked at Melanie. She never paid much attention to the gossips, but she seemed to recall some silly banter about Melanie when she and Arthur wed. But she now saw that Arthur was truly quite fortunate.

"Arthur is very lucky to have you, you know."

Melanie was surprised by this pronouncement. And flattered.

"Thank you."

"Really. I don't really know him, although I vaguely knew his first wife . . . um?" Cordelia couldn't recall her name. How odd. She'd been on so many committees with her, and yet for the life of her she couldn't think of her name.

"Diandra."

"Yes. She was . . ."

Melanie took a deep breath and waited to hear the superlatives that everyone used to describe how fantastic Diandra was. *Brilliant. Witty. Stylish. Classy. Gorgeous.*

Cordelia looked at Melanie carefully. "Well, she was not the wife you are. She was . . . a little tough. Brittle."

Melanie was stunned. Cordelia was . . . bashing Diandra? This was a first.

"No, no. Completely wrong for Arthur. He's a very sweet man and a lucky man. You're a very caring woman."

Melanie smiled gratefully. Cordelia was really nice. For the last two years, Melanie had chalked her up as a robotic Stepford beauty without a beating heart, and here she was breaking through, even in her sorrowful state.

"You know what? There are givers and takers in this world. Diandra is a taker. And it doesn't surprise me that her current marriage is collapsing."

Diandra was once again headed for divorce court? Interesting.

"You're caring as well, Cordelia. Take care of yourself, and good luck tomorrow with your speech. I know you'll honor him beautifully."

Before Melanie turned to get back into the elevator, the two women looked at each other and shared a silent, mutually comforting smile.

chapter 51

Jerome would have been very pleased indeed with the turnout at St. James Church on Madison on a glittering, snowflake-blanketed Wednesday morning in early December. All of the pews were filled with

designer-clad socialites whose names had appeared in bold print in
WWD. Although it was mostly women, a few bereft wives had forced
their husbands to zoom up from Wall Street for the occasion and offer
their arm in place of the arm that Jerome had so lovingly lent them to
cry on. As predicted, everything was exquisite and in good taste, none of
the evidence of Jerome's sordid or lascivious extracurricular side repre-
sented in any shape or form.

Cordelia clasped Morgan's hand so tightly that he felt the blood in
his wrist clotting. But he deserved the pain, dammit, for what he'd put
her through. When the minister finally nodded in Cord's direction,
Morgan had to physically heave her up onto her wobbling Sergio Rossi
heels and practically carry her to the podium. He wasn't sure she would
make it through the speech. He just hoped she wouldn't faint.

Cordelia had never looked frailer. She was practically swimming in
her black size-six Gianfranco Ferré suit. Her emerald and diamond earrings and matching necklace appeared to engulf her, and her face was
positively gaunt. (Jerome, knowing his best friend to a tee, had delin-
eated in his will exactly what Cordelia should wear to eulogize him, taking into account, of course, the seasons. If it had been spring he would
have had her in the black crepe Calvin Klein, and summer would definitely have been cause for the linen Yves St. Laurent. The accessories
rotated as well. He amended this part of his will every year to take into
consideration new purchases.)

Cordelia stood at the podium and began to speak, but she was so
far away from the microphone that the minister had to go over and ad-
just it and she had to start over again.

"As you all know, Jerome was my best friend. He was one of the
most unique and genuine people I ever met—so true to himself. There
was nothing contrived or dishonest about him," she began.

Joan turned to Wendy and rolled her eyes.

Cordelia continued. "We spent so much time doing Madison and
the all the Bs—Barneys, Bergdorf's, Bendels, Bloomingdale's, Bonwitt's
in the old days—though never B. Altman's. Jerome forbade it. Not even
for underwear, he'd say.

Wendy mouthed "Can you believe this?" to Joan as Cordelia sighed deeply and whipped her head back dramatically. She was consumed with emotion.

"For Jerome. He was my north, my south, my east, my west. My gallant walker, the most wanted guest. My shopping companion, my sweet confidant, I will miss you dearly, best friend one could want."

Cordelia broke down in gasping sobs and had to be helped back to her pew. When the mourners filed into the Knickerbocker Club for the reception immediately following, there was plenty of fodder. Guests were swarming around the food, gobbling up canapés, and with feigned sincerity worrying about dear Cordelia—*how will she survive?*

"Joan, I just talked to Cass again. She said Jerome was found with a leather dog collar and chained in some S and M position," said Wendy. She had returned to the prime corner table where Joan had ensconced herself in order to attain the most spectacular vista of the affair. Wendy placed a Bloody Mary in front of Joan and slid into the booth.

"I just heard even better from Fernanda. She said there was all sorts of gruesome paraphernalia around him, really vile stuff."

"How could he?"

Sandra Goodyear approached the table and greeted her friends. "It was a beautiful ceremony," she said solemnly.

"Divinity," nodded Joan.

"Perfection," agreed Wendy.

"Jerome would have been so happy," said Sandra.

"Thrilled," agreed Joan.

"Ecstatic," murmured Wendy.

"The minister's speech was so profound," added Sandra.

"Touching," said Joan.

"Wise," agreed Wendy.

There was a pause. "So, what are you doing after? Do you want to go downtown?" asked Sandra.

"You mean, like, Saks?" asked Joan.

"Gosh, no, not that far. I was thinking more like Chanel. The spring trunk show has arrived."

"It's a date," agreed Joan.

"I can't wait," said Wendy.

"I'll find you later. We'll take my car."

"Fabulous!" said Joan as Sandra walked away. Joan turned to Wendy. "She'll have a good scoop if we pump her hard. Nigel is BFs with Jerome's executor." Joan crossed her fingers to show how tight they were.

"Good," said Wendy, surveying the room. "I just don't want to walk anywhere."

"I wonder where Cord is," mused Joan.

"She was so distraught, Morgan had to take her home to bed. It's such a pity—she would have loved these canapés." Wendy took a bite of a peppered goat cheese puff.

"Jerome would be so upset she missed this little shindig."

"I'm sure that he planned for that in his will. That's why it's being videotaped," said Wendy, motioning to a discreet camera propped up in the corner.

"What, does he think they have VCRs in hell?" scoffed Joan.

"Oh, Joan, you're too much!" said Wendy, bursting into giggles.

"The good news is, Jerome would have wanted us to laugh."

"And to dish," said Wendy, glancing around. "Wonder if Melanie Korn will come."

"Of course she'll come!" said Joan confidently. "For her, it's poetic justice to have her worst critic, the very one who had recently vilified *her* in the press, drop dead of a heart attack in a fleabag with some guy's penis in his mouth. She couldn't have dreamt of a better scenario. She'll probably wear an orange dress."

"But she's been absent from the scene for a lifetime."

"She'll recover very well from her obliteration," said Joan. "She got lucky yet again. This is the best thing that ever happened to her. Jerome's salacious death has eclipsed her scandal. She's been ex-humed."

"Well, we always knew he'd go out with a bang."

"A bang that will bring one social climber back to life," added Wendy.

"It makes me shudder," said Joan, shuddering.

chapter 52

After tucking Cordelia into bed for the afternoon, Morgan had gone out to get her favorite chicken salad from William Poll. She had refused to eat since she had heard of Jerome's demise, and Morgan was increasingly worried. He had ordered in every one of her favorite dishes—arugula salad from La Caravelle, artichoke vinaigrette from Le Cirque, chilled melon and prosciutto from Daniel, but to no avail. Those lips would simply not open to ingest anything except pills. The chicken salad was a last resort. When Morgan returned to 741, Tom the doorman greeted him with a serious face.

"Mr. Vance, I thought you should know, there's been a death," said Tom somberly.

"I know, Tom. I was at the funeral today."

"No, not Mr. de Stingol. I'm afraid one of our own has passed on."

"Oh?"

"Yes," said Tom, looking down gravely. "Mademoiselle Oeuf."

Mademoiselle who? Oh yeah, the dog. "That's terrible."

"Yes. She was walking on one of those expandable leashes and, well, got too far ahead of her walker. You know how it is. She fell down the open chute leading to the basement of Nello's."

"Horrible," said Morgan. He bent his head down. A walker dies dressed up like a dog, and then a dog dies because of his walker. Were the gods trying to tell them something? "Well, it's been a sad day all around," said Morgan, walking toward the elevator, where Melanie Korn was waiting.

Melanie was holding a newly purchased yoga mat and a stack of brochures on European bicycle tours.

"Hello, Melanie," said Morgan. He looked carefully at her. Something was very different. Her face appeared to be freshly scrubbed. He wasn't sure, but he could have sworn that she wasn't wearing any makeup. Whatever it was, she looked fabulous.

"Hello, Morgan. I'm so sorry about your loss," she said with sincerity.

"My loss? Well, I didn't know the dog that well."

"No, I meant Jerome. I know he was a dear friend."

"Oh! Jerome. Yes," he said, putting out his arm to let Melanie enter the elevator first. "He was very nice to my wife."

But truth be told, he really hadn't been all that crazy about Jerome. He had always seemed slimy. And he charged exorbitant sums for his "decorating" work.

"Was he a friend of yours as well?" asked Morgan.

"No."

"Oh." That made sense, he thought. Jerome was such a snob. The Korns would never have made his cut.

"How's Cordelia feeling?" asked Melanie.

"She'll be fine, thanks. How's Arthur?"

"Great."

Morgan cocked his head and again studied Melanie. He really couldn't pinpoint the change, but she just seemed genuinely *nice*. She'd had a dash of the tramp factor before, but now she seemed truly at ease and calmly put together.

"You know, you and Arthur should come up for dinner one night. Something casual."

"That would be great," said Melanie, getting off on her floor.

"I'll have Cord call you to set it up."

That was sweet. With an exuberant flair in her gait, Melanie leapt into her apartment and found Arthur sitting in the dark living room, reading a book with only the small glare of the Tiffany lamp. Arthur had been acting a little quiet and strange in the past few days. Depressed, even. Maybe he was coming down with the flu.

"What's up, buttercup?" asked Melanie, moving his feet off the coffee table and sitting down on the sofa beside him.

"Nothing much."

"Morgan Vance just invited us to dinner."

"That's great," said Arthur, gloomily. "Didn't you go to that guy's funeral?"

"You know, I thought about it, but it would have just seemed dishonest. I mean, for lord's sake, we detested each other. Just because it's a big whoop-de-doo social event doesn't mean I should parade my mug around his funeral."

"Makes sense."

Melanie flipped over his book to see the cover and scrunched up her nose. "Why are you reading Olivia Weston's book?"

"I don't know."

"I heard it sucks."

"No, it's . . ." Arthur began to defend it and then stopped. "Well, it does suck. It's really overwritten and bad. A disappointment."

Melanie snuggled up next to Arthur. She put her head on his shoulder.

"Those people really don't impress me anymore," she said, yawning.

"Me neither."

"I mean, a few weeks ago I would have been ecstatic to be invited to the Vances', because of who they are. Now I'm just excited because I think they're pretty nice. And if they never even call and follow through, I'll be fine with that. Isn't that strange?"

"Yeah," said Arthur, staring at the wall.

"You seem so far away, Arty. What's up?" asked Melanie, cocking her head to see his eyes.

"Nothing."

"Are you sure?"

"Yup."

"Don't lie to me."

"I'm not."

Melanie kept looking at Arthur strangely. He went back to his reading, but she wouldn't stop staring.

"What is it?" he asked finally.

"I want to ask you the same question."

He sighed. "I don't know. I'm just thinking about things . . . it's just strange how much you can change your impression of people."

"Like who?"

"No one in particular. It's just, don't you sometimes think people disappoint you?"

"All the time," said Melanie. "That's why I don't expect things from anyone. You've got to do things for yourself or be disappointed. People will always let you down. Especially this crowd we hang around with."

"Why do we hang around with this crowd?"

Melanie was about to launch into her spiel of how these people were the crème de la crème, the elite, and how once you wined and dined with them you were *something*. But she stopped herself and realized that she didn't believe that anymore.

"I don't know!" she said, laughing. "Why do we hang with these . . . jerks!"

Was it because of Diandra? If so, that was pathetic. Diandra was a fool—she had given up Arthur. *Why would I want to be anything like that idiot?* She giggled at how absurd she was.

Melanie's laughter was contagious, and soon Arthur was laughing his ass off.

"Come on," he said, kissing her forehead. "Let's go get some Chubby Hubby."

chapter 53

The morning had not started well for Joan. Actually, that was not entirely true, because she had woken up in a great mood, but things had only deteriorated from there. Stupid stuff was the first source of irritation. The dry cleaner had failed to get the balsamic vinegar stain out of her tan skirt, her housekeeper had thrown out yesterday's *New York Observer* before she'd had a chance to read it, and she'd found a small tear in the fabric on the love seat in the den. Vexing, but manageable. It was Phillip who'd really set her off.

"Did you ask Larry Powell to write a recommendation for Camilla?" she inquired over breakfast. Larry was on the board of Hamilton College, which was their daughter Camilla's first choice.

"Nope." Phillip didn't even look up from his newspaper.

"Phillip, we have to get that done. Applications are in, and already seven people from Camilla's class have declared it as their first choice."

Phillip didn't respond.

"Can you please call him and ask him?"

"If I have time."

That was annoying. If he had time? "And what, pray tell, are you so busy with, Phillip, that you don't have time to make a call on behalf of your daughter?"

Phillip lowered his paper and stared at Joan. He didn't say anything and finally returned to his paper. Joan was irate. He was useless, useless!

"Phillip, I want you to answer me."

"Oh, come on. Don't start . . ."

"Don't start what?"

"You know, your usual nagging, whining. What, are you bored? Why don't you run off to tea with Wendy?"

Joan was seething now. "Phillip, I'm getting pretty fed up with you."

He looked her in the eye. "So, what? You're going to leave me? Ha," he scoffed.

"Why do you always bring that up when we discuss anything important?" He didn't answer. "If we ever get into a discussion that you don't want to have you bring up leaving me or divorce or something like that. It's childish," Joan complained.

"Here we go." Phillip sighed and took a swig of his coffee.

"Well, I do think it's important to discuss things."

"Like what?" he said with sarcasm.

"Like the fact that you don't do anything, Phillip! You spend all day at the Racquet Club, where you sit around, read the paper, get a massage, take a nap, play backgammon, and maybe, just maybe, play some racquetball! Or you go to your Scottish club, where you sit and fiddle around on the Internet or yak with those other bores! It's pathetic, Phillip, really pathetic. Work means nothing to you—you don't even bother with the guise that you have a real job. Sure, you put on a suit, but that's only because the Racquet Club requires one! You do nothing! Nothing! I am supporting this family, and I am getting tired of it!" After Joan had finished her rampage, she took a deep breath. She had really worked herself into a lather.

Phillip stared at her. "Are you finished?"

"Yes."

"Thank you," he said, and returned to his paper.

"Don't you want to say anything?"

"What do you want me to say, Joan? It's the same old argument."

Joan purposely took deep, loud breaths, in and out, in and out.

"Well, do you think it's true?"

Phillip threw down the business section and shrugged. "So what? I like going to the club."

"But don't you think you should be out supporting the family?"

"We have money."

"But it's *my* money. And you lie around and do nothing!" Joan was hysterical now.

"Well, Joan, yes, it is *your* money. But if it was *my* money, you probably wouldn't hesitate to spend it. And by the way, don't forget that you did not earn that money yourself. You *inherited* it. Some distant relative hauled his ass to work and you are reaping the benefits. So don't start with me about work ethic, because you have none."

"You are not a man! How can you be so comfortable sitting idle? Don't you want to contribute to society?"

"Like you?" he said, venom in his voice. "Now let's call a spade a spade, Joan. What do you do that's so important? So different from what I do? You just run around in your five-hundred-dollar shoes from one fancy restaurant to another, where you eat twenty-five-dollar bowls of lettuce and gossip about every woman that walks in the door. You're petty, you're two-faced, you're jealous, you're bored, and no matter what happens, you are stuck with me. Because you see Wendy and her little lonely life and you wouldn't wish that on your worst enemy. So stop criticizing me, stop nagging me, and get up, get dressed, and go do whatever it is you waste your time doing!"

There was nothing else to say. Joan did as he said, and dreamed of a life where she had a rich, successful, uxorious husband who bought her diamonds and didn't care about her love handles.

Hours later, in the elliptical stenciled room at the Carlyle, Joan enjoyed a quiet tea with Mimi Halsey. As they sipped cinnamon and red zinger brews and sampled crustless sandwiches, Joan broached a subject that she had wanted to talk to Mimi about.

"We're having it on Tuesday at the Pierre. With full high tea. It's a done deal."

"Another shahtoosh party? Well, Joan, my dear, perhaps you should wait—"

"Why? It's all set. I just would love it if you'd spread the word with some of your pals whose addresses I don't have. It'll be fabulous."

Before Mimi could answer, Wendy burst into the room in a frenzy of apple cheeks and panting breaths.

"You'll never guess what happened!"

Joan almost gagged on her watercress. "My god, what?"

"What? Pray tell," said Mimi calmly.

Wendy cleared her throat dramatically.

"Divulge this instant!" said Joan, with rising anticipation. For Wendy to race over here with her hair looking like that . . . well, it had to be juicy.

Wendy looked both her attentive listeners in the eye. "Cordelia Vance has been arrested."

"No."

"Oui. I can only chalk it up to the grief she's been suffering from Jerome's violent and untimely death."

"What happened?" said Joan, about to shake the gory deets out of her friend.

"Apparently she casually strolled out of her building—no makeup—and went—on foot—to Cartier."

"No," said Mimi.

"On foot?" asked Joan.

"She asked to look at some rings, put them on her fingers, and walked out of the store, but not before being apprehended and forced to the ground by security. She was cuffed right there on Fifth Avenue. Can you think of anything more humiliating?"

Joan thought back and recalled an episode when one of her three-inch Chanel heels snapped off in a metal grate in front of sidewalk lunchers at La Goulue. Wendy revisited a ghastly moment when she'd come out the ladies' room at La Caravelle with a trail of toilet paper attached to her calf. Mimi thought about the time when she had accidentally eaten a crouton that had somehow landed in her salad.

"No," said Joan confidently. "I can't think of anything worse."

"Me neither," said Wendy.

"Not I," said Mimi.

"So what's going to happen?" asked Joan.

"Well, I don't know. I had to tell you, and now I'm dashing back home to get on the phone. Poor Cordelia," added Wendy, remembering that it was appropriate to show concern at this stage.

Immediately Joan and Mimi's faces fell on cue.

"Poor dear," they both murmured.

"Well, I'm off. I won't interrupt you anymore," said Wendy.

"Oh! Well, we uh . . ." said Joan, desperate now to depart and hit the phone lines.

"We were just finishing," said Mimi. And although they still had another tea cozy coming, they quickly paid the check and taxied home to get all of the juice.

chapter 54

Morgan paced anxiously in his foyer as his lawyer, Sy Hammerman, wrapped up a call to the D.A., who thankfully happened to be a law school and squash buddy from their New Haven days.

"Thanks, pal. Okay, Jasper, sounds great . . . and send my love to Ellen . . . Terrific, see you then. 'Bye." He hung up, sighed, and turned to his client, giving him a supportive pat on the back and a look as if to say "no sweat." Morgan looked relieved.

"We're in the clear," Sy said, smiling. "Let's go get her."

The two walked from the Vances' apartment three blocks to the Nineteenth Precinct on Sixty-seventh Street between Lexington and Third. The red-brick facade was accented by cop-car blue window ledges, and walking up to the attractive building one would never guess there were thugs inside. (Although the hordes of parked squad cars might be a giveaway.) This wasn't a standard New York *Law & Order*–style precinct with greasy perps being dragged around in cuffs— there were the occasional violent criminals, sure, but mostly it was the jurisdiction where the white-collar ilk resided. As Sy walked up to the officer at the front desk to inquire about Cordelia, Morgan surveyed the scene and noticed a man who seemed familiar. Racquet Club? No. Hmm . . . Lyford? He couldn't place him.

"Mista Vance?" a tough, Staten Island-y voice bellowed. "Detective Doherty. Right this way." He led the pair up the stairs, where Cordelia had been placed in custody.

"Normally I woulda put your wife in the holding cell, but we got a few nasty ones in there today, so she's been sittin' at my desk."

"I appreciate that," said Morgan.

"No prob. Say, who are you guys, anyway? A call from the mayor's office? Sheesh. The D.A. dropped this case faster than a hot coal. Cartier called us personally to say they were dropping all charges!"

"It's not who my client is," said Sy firmly, "it's that she is completely innocent and that this was all a terrible mistake."

"Oh, yeah? We got camera footage of her stealing a boatload of loot!"

"She didn't steal!" burst out Morgan.

"Morg—" said Sy, trying to calm him. "Don't listen. She's fine!"

"No," continued Morgan. "We have an arrangement with Cartier. The salesgirl who normally is aware of our house account was on vacation, *okay*?" He put a hand to his brow, wiping the sweat, which was not caused at all by Cordelia's actions but his own.

Had he driven her to it? Clearly the jewels and the clothes and the benefits were all plugs to fill the gaping holes he had punched into their marriage. The poor woman, and now some Staten Island schmuck was berating and belittling her. This was not their life! He was picking her up in a jail? Deep breaths.

He calmed down, and as the three rounded the corner in silence Morgan saw his wife looking sullen at the detective's desk.

"Cordelia!" Morgan ran to her, throwing his arms around her to get her out as soon as possible.

"Oh, darling," she cried, hugging him. "Thank you—I'm so sorry."

"Never, don't say a word. This was all a terrible misunderstanding."

"I'll say," interrupted Detective Doherty. "We misunderstood that it was okay for you to steal."

"That will be enough," said Sy.

It took several minutes for Sy to sign the necessary documents, and Cordelia spent the time huddled in Morgan's arms. This was a big deal, she realized. She was in jail! She was getting out, but she was lucky she had a fancy lawyer who could save her. What had she been thinking? Sometimes she felt as if she were possessed or sleepwalking. She remembered going to Cartier and taking the jewels, but it was as if she had been under water, or somehow watching herself do it, while at the same time remaining very detached. How did she get there? She really had to throw out some of those pills in her medicine chest. They were playing tricks on her.

"All done," said Sy reassuringly. "Now let's get out of here."

They all three turned on their heels and scurried down the stairs. As nice as an Upper East Side precinct was, it was certainly not a place one wanted to linger. On the way out they passed some high-class prostitutes, an old lady complaining about some disruptive dog, and a guy filling out a form about a lost cell phone. The air outside had never felt fresher.

"Thanks so much, Sy," said Morgan, shaking his hand.

"No problem," he said, getting into a taxi.

Cordelia was leaning on Morgan as they walked home. She was shivering and shaking, from the cold or her actions, he didn't know.

After Cordelia and Morgan got to their bedroom, he asked what those three hours were like in there. "Oh, not too bad, I suppose," she said, trying to keep her composure, dreamily staring out of the window as if in a semitrance. The tears had been caked onto her cheeks, making the skin feel taught over her bones, but she hadn't shed any over the actual incident, only over the weight of the pressure that led her to it.

"It was funny, actually. I wasn't embarrassed at all. It was fine," she said, putting on a fake smile. She had to be strong, for herself and for Morgan. If she let herself collapse again . . .

"Oh, and I saw Lamar Crabb being booked!" she said.

"That's who that was. I knew I recognized him!"

"He didn't see me, thank goodness," said Cordelia. "They told me he was indicted in a stalking case! There was this poor girl just out of college—I mean, young enough to be his daughter—who was getting called incessantly at all hours. She was getting these obscene and threatening calls for months, and it turned out it was him, her boss! Or, rather, her boss's boss—he's the CEO. She was an assistant or something at his firm—can you imagine? Poor Beatrice."

"That's appalling. He must be praying this doesn't get out."

"Well, the good news is I'm back home."

"Yes, you are, darling." He stroked her hair lovingly. "Why don't we get some Coco Pazzo takeout and eat at home?"

"That would be lovely," she said, wearily but with a smile. "Just perfect."

Her forced smile was betrayed by the welling tears that made her eyes grow shinier and shinier. *Be strong, be strong!* She chanted to herself, but to no avail. Finally, she all but collapsed into a quivering mass of choking sobs, her life spiraling out of control, and her body following suit.

"It's okay, darling," Morgan said, comforting his wife with hugs.

"I'm so sorry, Morgan, for humiliating you. I don't know what came over me."

"Don't worry, honey. It's been a traumatic week. You have to let yourself rest. Let's go lie down."

Morgan tucked her into the crisp sheets and sat beside the wife he loved so much. He fluffed up the monogrammed pillows around her and made sure she was comfortable. Despite the tragedy of Jerome's death and her own propensity for jewel snatching, he felt this was all his fault, that the unraveling of Cordelia was all due to his adultery, the initial yank of her threads.

"I'll get you a sedative. You should sleep," he said, patting her head.

"Thank you, Morgan."

He brought her a pill and a glass of water. She stared off, glaze-eyed, at the curtains. "What is happening to me? I feel so . . . aimless. Nothing means anything to me anymore."

"Don't think that. It's not true," he said, desperate to fix all that he had destroyed in her.

"I . . . I feel like I'm just going through the motions—another party, another lunch, shopping. I'm half dead."

"Just calm down, honey. Don't worry about all this. Everything's going to be all right."

"I don't deserve you, Morgan. I'm just a shell. You . . . you're such a good man. You're such a good man . . ." she began to cry again, and

Morgan felt a pain that knifed through his chest, his guilt a blade that sliced him into shards.

"Cordelia," he said, taking her hand in his. "I have not been as good a husband as I could have been to you. But I am going to change that. I want to be a better husband for you, and a better person."

"I've always loved you, Morgan. You've never let me down."

"I promise I never will."

As Cord slowly fell asleep, the echo of her words calling him a good man hung above him. He, a good man? He was about to have his *mistress murdered*. No, he was not a good man. What was he thinking? He had been temporarily insane. Ending up in jail would not be a great way to be a good husband to Cordelia. She needed him by her side, and no matter what, he knew he would be.

He went into his study and retrieved Vince's card and dialed the cell.

"Hello, it's me, Morgan. Listen, I've reconsidered what we discussed. Call it off. The . . . whack, or whatever you call it . . . Yes, I'm sure . . . What do you mean, it's in motion? Look, I've changed my mind . . . Can't you just not go? . . . Then who is it who does it? . . . No, no, you know what, you're right not to tell me. Can't you just call that person and tell him no? They can keep the money."

Morgan began pacing, and sweat was dripping from his brow. He had to call this off. "Call back tomorrow? What kind of organization are you running? I know, I know, but look, I want you to cancel my order . . . Okay, I'll call tomorrow. Please. Please!"

Great, this was great. He had to make sure this goombah didn't kill Maria. He couldn't have another thing on his conscience. And even though he wished her dead, he couldn't be the cause of her annihilation.

"Who was that?"

Morgan turned around, startled. It was John, standing on the threshold, clutching his weekend duffel bag.

"Oh, a business acquaintance."

"What's going on with Mom?"

"She's had an accident."

"Is she okay?"

"Yes. She's suffering from posttraumatic stress disorder, due to the loss of Jerome, so she got a little confused in Cartier and took some things and forgot to pay for them."

"She stole?"

"Not intentionally," said Morgan defensively.

"Shit."

"Why don't you go in and cheer her up? I'm sure she'd love to see you."

"All right," said John. He left the room. That was a close call. Indiscretion could be his downfall. That and murder. He had to call off the kill. Now.

chapter **55**

Melanie woke up and stretched herself across the bed in an X like a fluffy Persian cat who had happily happened on a strip of sunlight. Arthur was sitting at the foot of the bed, putting on his socks.

"Well, hello there, miss. You're finally awake."

"My god," said Melanie, looking at the clock. "I'm so lazy today! I must have slept, like, ten hours."

"It's okay, babe."

Arthur scampered over across the bed and kissed his wife on the forehead. Melanie giggled, pinned under him, and bashed him with a pillow to free herself. Feigning pain as if impaled with an Acme anvil, Arthur staggered to his shoes. Melanie, meanwhile suddenly looked ill.

"Arty, I think I'm going to barf."

"Ha-ha. I'm sure you're so sick, Sarah Bernhardt."

"No, seriously—"

Before he could say a word, she was doing a Flo Jo sprint for the bathroom.

"Oh, my goodness—" Arthur darted after her to put a calming hand on her shaking back as she violently chundered her tummy's contents into the porcelain, Linda Blair–style.

"Holy moly," said Melanie. "That was horrible."

"It's okay, sweetie," Arthur said, trying to soothe her by patting her head. "Maybe you should get back in bed."

Arthur tucked her in sweetly and looked down at his wife, who was safely wrapped in a cozy thousand-thread-count Porthault eggroll. He said he'd be happy to stay home by her side, but she knew he was swamped gearing up for Casket Week in Vegas. So she bid him farewell, and before long her eyes were at half-mast and then closed for business as she entered a deep, downy morning nap.

About two hours later, she heard keys in the door and man's shoes across the marble foyer floor.

"Sweetness? Is that you?" Arthur must've come back to check on her. What a mensch she married.

"No, madam," a familiar, crisp voice chirped. "It is I. I've returned."

Guffey! Returned? Melanie had been convinced he was lying on a chaise longue in Palm Beach with his former mistress, who had so much class it was coming out of her ass.

"Guff, you're back? I'm in here!"

He appeared in the doorway.

"Yes, madam. I am sorry my troubles kept me from you for as long as they did . . . Are you all right?"

"Well, I'm a little under the weather. But yes, I'm just fine. Everything's fine."

They shared a smile, and Guffey left to go to his room and unpack.

Later on, over tea, Melanie sat in her robe in the kitchen as Guffey got back into the swing of things, putting the kitchen in order and making the necessary shopping lists for Juanita.

"So, Guffey," Melanie said gently. "I know you said you had . . . troubles. Is everything okay?"

"Nothing to worry about, madam. I'm fine. We are only dealt what we may handle, as they say."

"Well, I was worried. I didn't know what went wrong or if . . . it was my fault."

"*Your* fault? Why, no!"

"I just thought . . . maybe it was something I did. Or said. Or an embarrassing combo of both. 'Cause that *Observer* piece—"

"Nonsense! I don't care about a foolish article."

"You don't?"

"Lord, no!"

"I thought . . . I thought maybe you left because I humiliated you."

"Not in a million years," he said, shaking his head. "Madam, I left because sadly my brother's latest bout with fairy dust had left him temporarily incapacitated. It was a dark family matter, nothing more."

"Really?" said Melanie, her face lighting up, as if she were thrilled Guff's bro was on the smack. "I mean, that's awful. But I'm relieved. I know things were much smoother with Diandra, and that I don't always know what's what. But I'm glad I wasn't the cause of your sudden departure."

"Heavens, no," he said, smiling softly. He was touched that he had so much of an impact on her. She must have simply crumbled when he fled. As if the pressure of the damning article wasn't enough, she probably felt abandoned by even him, her trusty servant and advice giver. And one thing was for sure: the harsh words from Billy Crispin's pen-as-sword had most certainly deflated her swollen pride. In fact, his mistress seemed more relaxed and real than ever before. He looked at his sick charge in her new robe—he had noticed her new sheets and the new conservative clothes on her dressing chair earlier—and he felt a parent's pride. She was listening, absorbing; she was trying so hard, all this time. And it was out of this touched and compassionate place that Guffey decided to tell her the truth about her looming predecessor.

"Madam," he started, not knowing quite how to broach the subject. "Something you should know about the first Mrs. Korn . . ."

"Hmm." Melanie smiled. "Funny you should mention her. I was so paranoid after the article, I actually thought you went back to work with Her Majesty."

"Not at all," he said, nodding. "You see—how should I say this?" He paused. "I made her."

"What?"

"I knew her before she was Diandra Chrysler."

"She had another husband?"

"No. I knew her before her reinvention."

Melanie was quiet. Guffey continued.

"I knew her when she was Diane Buick."

"*Buick?*" Melanie was stunned. A cheap car clearly was not name enough for her, so she thought it was only a minor change if she switched to a more luxe brand? No way.

"Diandra isn't *Diaaaandraaa?* You mean, she changed her name? From Diane?"

"I'm afraid so."

"And *Chrysler?* Well, god, at least she had the good sense to pick a name that had a mark in the New York skyline. And here I thought she was this great pinnacle of breeding and taste!"

"She was. Because of me. I buttled for the Viscountess of Havorshire before I left the U.K. I knew it all: I was the eyes and the ears of the castle, of the social season. And when I came to the States to work for Prince Casius of Greece, Diane was one of his . . . well, women."

Melanie sat with bated breath, stunned. Guffey continued.

"We became fast friends. She was desperate to win his affections, and I spied her attempts to be refined and worthy of him, but she suffered tremendous class anxiety and sought my help to hone herself. And I did the best I could. But his heart was led to greener pastures, to the young daughter of a derby horse breeder in Kentucky. And Diane was devastated. So I decided to help her. She became my little project, and before long she was a social force to be reckoned with, and shortly thereafter she was on the arm of every millionaire on Fifth Avenue. She brought me with her on her ascent, but we parted ways when I took a liking to Mr. Korn and I saw how she mistreated him. When she took up with another man and said she might move, I knew I could never leave New York. Our winter season in Palm Beach was torturous for me. Florida is my least favorite state in the Union."

"Tell me about it," said Melanie, her eyes glazed over in a flickering montage of screen doors slamming, cheerleaders' pom-poms, teased, bleached bangs, Dairy Queens, and El Caminos rocking in the parking lot out back.

So, there it was. The famed, renowned, revered Diandra was just like her. Only Melanie had made it out of that putrid peninsula and the first Mrs. Korn was put to pasture there. Sunshine shmunshine—Melanie would take the darkly sparkling, edgy bustle of Manhattan any day. And the diamond-esque glimmer of the Chrysler Building's sharp spire was a nightly sight she'd never give up for all the money in the world.

chapter 56

"Make a left here. Yes, this should be it," said Morgan, glancing down again at the address that he had scratched out on the Post-it.

The cab driver turned and looked back at him. He could tell this guy was, you know, sophisticated. This wasn't a place he should be hanging around.

"You sure you wanna stop here?"

Morgan looked at the less than enticing darkened building on the deserted corner of this Bronx neighborhood and thought, *No!* But, alas, he had no choice.

"I don't want to, but I have to."

"All right."

"But do you think you could wait for me? Keep the meter running and I'll give you a fifty-dollar tip."

"Sounds great. Don't jerk me around."

"I promise," said Morgan, getting out of the taxi. He had intentionally not called a town car or used his own driver because he did not want anyone to be able to trace his steps. Vince had been so vague about calling off the hit that Morgan had been compelled to go and meet the guy in person, just to make sure it would not happen.

Morgan walked up to a door that at first appeared to lead nowhere, until he noticed a small sign that read, FRANK'S. He took a deep breath and pushed open the door.

There was a bartender behind an old-fashioned bar, and two men sitting at a table, smoking and drinking. The place itself was not bad, just an average bar, but it seemed all the more sinister to Morgan because of his reasons for being there. He approached the bartender, who stared at him without saying anything.

"Hi, um, I'm looking for . . ."

"Me," said someone behind Morgan before he could finish.

Morgan turned around. There was a skinny man with a pockmarked face, revealing surprisingly perfect teeth as he smiled.

"You're . . . ?"

"That's right."

"All right. So," said Morgan, taking a deep breath. He was prepared to sit down, lay out his life story, and explain why he first chose to and then decided against killing his mistress. He'd go into detail about her relentless whining and demands, how he had forgotten how fantastic his wife was, how he had experienced a midlife crisis but had come to his senses. How Maria had first been great but was now evil, but regardless, he couldn't be responsible for the death of another human being. But the pockmarked man stopped him.

"So, you want it off?"

"Yes," said Morgan, looking around. He had thought he'd be led to a small dark room and made to plead and beg.

"Okay."

"Okay, and as I said, please keep the money."

"Sure."

Morgan looked around, uncertain. This was it?

"So, is this it?"

"Yup. You can go."

"All right," said Morgan. He looked at the bartender, who was busy watching the Rangers game on a small screen on the wall.

"Great, thanks," said Morgan, relieved.

The man returned to his seat with his friend.

Morgan exited the bar with excitement. That was so easy! He'd just walked in there and called off the hit. Hooray! It was only after he was back in the cab and crossing the bridge that his elation burst. He had done the Right Thing. Too bad his reward was to have to endure more suffering from Maria as he squirmed in her tyrannical, blackmailing hands. Christ.

chapter 57

"Are you sure you're feeling okay?" asked Rosemary for the fifteenth time.

"I swear," replied Olivia, earnestly.

"Anything we should know about? Something happen with your family?"

"No, no, they're fine."

"What about Henry? Are you still going to Lyford with him?" asked Lila.

"Yes, I think so."

"So it's not your love life?" asked Rosemary.

"No."

"Is it that you lost out on the Childe Hassam painting?" asked Lila.

"No."

"'Cause you can't blame yourself. Frothingham's always messes up with the phone bids."

"No, I just called the dealer who bought it and purchased it from him directly."

"No sicknesses, no ailments?" asked Rosemary.

"I already said, I'm fine."

There was a pause.

"Oh! Is it winter bloating? 'Cause you look great," said Lila.

"Why?" asked Olivia, panicked. "Do you think I look fat?"

"No, you're a stick."

"I mean, I haven't had carbs in two weeks. I'd better look good."

"You look great."

Olivia lifted up her arms and squeezed them to make sure there was no extraneous fat. There wasn't. Rosemary gave Lila a look and they both turned to Olivia. She looked very regal sitting on the pistachio armchair in her library. But something was up.

"Listen, Olivia. We're just very worried about you," began Lila.

"About me? Why?"

"Because you've skipped the last two charity balls and you haven't been out to dinner in days," said Rosemary.

"I guess you'd call this . . . an intervention," said Lila.

"We just can't imagine what's amiss. If you're not sick, or lovesick, what could possibly keep you holed up in your apartment?"

Olivia sighed deeply. She knew it was only a matter of time before people came asking questions. She just wasn't in the mood to party or socialize, and although that sounded strange, it was true. For the first time in her life she was seriously stressed—she had a deadline and no writer to help her. Holland wouldn't return her calls, and even Rob—who'd introduced her to Holland—refused to intervene. Perhaps she shouldn't have slapped her.

"You two are so sweet to be worried about me. The fact is, it's work related. I'm just very stressed about my deadline."

Rosemary and Lila turned to each other and then erupted in laughter. "Is that all?" boomed Rosemary. "Good lord, we thought it was something more serious. Sweetie, deadlines come and go. Nobody pays attention to those things."

"Frankly, we thought it was strange that you were in such a rush to get your second book out. You should enjoy your success for a while," added Lila. "Plus, writers are *supposed* to be flaky. That's part of the image, you know?"

"You really think so?" asked Olivia, both relieved and perplexed. "But there's been such a demand—everyone is asking, begging to read my new pages, wanting to do follow-up pieces."

"Well, all you have to do to solve that is write a little article for *Town and Country* or *Elle*. Write about shoes or something. That will keep them sated for a long time," said Lila.

"That's a great idea," said Olivia. She could do that. She knew about shoes.

"Well, thank goodness we got that taken care of," said Rosemary, leaning in and grabbing some of the Greenberg cookies that she had brought over to cheer Olivia. "Now listen to this: Ashley Sommers is getting married."

"Ashley Sommers?" snapped Lila, quickly. "But she's . . . much younger than us. Who is she marrying?"

"Some guy from San Francisco. She has to move there."

"Nightmare," said Lila.

"Oh, I don't think Frisco is so bad," said Olivia, pouring herself tea.

"I don't mean Frisco, I mean marriage," said Lila. "I mean, gross, to be tied down to one person. And really, once you marry a guy he refuses to go out. It's so pathetic. Brooke Lutz's husband will go out with her only twice a week. He insists on staying home with the kid the other nights."

"Boring!" said Rosemary. "That's why I am so grateful I got out when I did." Rosemary was referring to her own brief starter marriage that lasted only seventeen days and three hours longer than her ten-hour, five-hundred-person wedding at the Pierre.

"Totally. I am so not into that," said Lila.

"I know what you mean," agreed Olivia.

"Did you hear about Rupert Wingate's wedding?" asked Rosemary.

"Who'd he marry?" asked Olivia.

"Some little nobody from nowhereville. Anyhoo, of course the Wingates paid for the entire wedding, since the girl didn't have two nickels to buy a box of Cracker Jacks, and she was very, very bossy. Fernanda almost had a coronary. Plus, the girl has no taste. Anyway, it was at the Vineyard, and she insisted—and, I mean, gag me with Dr. Phil's tongue depressor—that she wanted a live butterfly release at the end of the wedding, so everyone got a handwoven basket and got on the dock. They were all ready to release them at the same time and they all opened their baskets in unison and all of the butterflies were dead! Can you imagine?" Rosemary burst into laughter.

"Isn't Rupert best friends with Drew Vance?" asked Lila. She hadn't told her friends of her little sex romp; they wouldn't understand. But she had been on the lookout for Drew everywhere. She walked by 741 as much as possible, went to a cocktail party at the Racquet Club. She even went to happy hour at Dorrian's one night when she was going to dinner at Elio's with her parents, but he wasn't there. She thought for sure he would call, but he hadn't.

"I don't know," said Rosemary. She stood up. "Anyway, Livy, so glad you are feeling better. I've got to get home. Sergio comes in one hour to do my makeup, and he just did Jane Roberts's, so I will get loads of scoop! You are going tonight?"

"I suppose," said Olivia. It was time to end her exile. The public was waiting.

"Fab. It'll be a blast."

As the elevator doors opened in the lobby Lila came face to face with Drew Vance. And the pretty blond girl whose hand he was holding.

"Drew!" blurted Lila, without thinking.

"Hey, doll," said Drew, pecking her on the cheek and then suavely guiding his blonde into the elevator. "How are you?"

Rosemary stepped out of the elevator and stared as Lila froze. "Great" was all Lila could get out.

"Fan-tastic," said Drew, giving her a big smile. "Don't be a stranger," he said, and then winked just before the elevator doors closed.

"How do you know him?" asked Rosemary. She tied her scarf tighter.

"Friend of my brother's," Lila mumbled.

"He's a cutie," said Rosemary.

"Yeah, but did you get a look at that child with him?" asked Lila, turning a pale shade of green. "Tacky."

"Such a prepube. He must have plucked her out of kindergarten," said Rosemary.

"Yeah."

"I hear he's an unconscionable cad," boomed Rosemary. "But at least a handsome one."

They exited the building, and a huge gust of wind slapped them in the face. Lila felt mortified. She never wanted to go there again.

chapter 58

The buzzing, frenetic spin of Wall Street was silent within the thick plate-glass windows that walled Morgan Vance's Brown Brothers office, but the headache-inducing noise of his phone call with Maria paralleled (if not surpassed) the din from outside. Her nasal screeches bore a hole through his brain, her voice like a cheese grater in his ear. Her ceaseless complaints, her Rosie Perez–times–ten timbre, her rapacious demands, and her credit card craziness were getting to be too much for him to handle. And yet he would have to suck it up, because he had no choice. This was his fate, from now on.

"Maria, I just opened a huge bill from AmEx for eleven thousand dollars at Cartier," he said, his rage pumped into every whispered word. "What in the world were you buying? You cannot be spending like this."

Maria sat twirling the phone cord in her French-manicured fingers as she lay on a settee upholstered in one of the new selections from the Versace Casa line of fabrics. As the receiver rested between her cheek and shoulder, she held her hand in front of her, admiring the recently acquired bauble in question, loving the glint of the sunlight off the ruby in the center.

"What are you talking about?" she asked flippantly. "I have your child, remember? We have our expenses."

"Maria, I hardly think you were spending all this on Pampers. Last time I checked, Cartier didn't hock baby bottles."

"I don't want to talk about this. I'm late for a shahtoosh party."

Morgan's old desire to snuff her spoiled ass out rose to the surface again. Fuck this little whore. His ire snowballed, and he wanted to dive through the phone wires *Matrix*-style and strangle her with the cord.

"A *shahtoosh* party? You'd be filing nails in Astoria if I hadn't rescued you from your janitorial life, and now you need *shahtooshes*? You didn't even know what they were when you were picking trash out of cans in Asunción! You'd better not be going near Cordelia or any of her friends—do you understand?"

"I can do what I want, Morgan. It's a free country. Fuck you."

With that, she hung up, leaving Morgan only to bury his head in his hands once more, trapped in the exitless labyrinth that he had erected.

But he'd had to call off the hit. Too messy. He had to live in purgatory forever. Only a miracle could save him now.

Maria sauntered out of her building to hail a taxi. She was off to Joan and Wendy's shahtoosh party at the Carlyle, to benefit the Narcolepsy Institute. Maria had been lucky; her cousin Santiago was a temporary elevator man at the Coddingtons' building for the holidays, and she had coerced him into purloining one of Joan and Wendy's invitations. No one would know how she got it. But she was determined to start ingratiating herself into high society. They would get used to her, dammit. She was the next Mrs. Vance.

Uptown at the Carlyle, Joan and Wendy were holding court, playing the hostess with the mostest to the extreme, bending over backwards to make sure everyone had what she wanted to be happy and get in the shopping mood. The scores of ladies sampled the deluxe array of finger sandwiches catered by Fauchon, and sipped teas from a luxurious lineup of fourteen flavors shipped in by Mariage Frères in Paris. Joan surveyed the scene; all were fluttering around, rubbing the soft wares, comparing hues, and already throwing pieces over their arms to take with them. She smelled a good bunch of sales.

Melanie Korn took a deep breath when she entered. She didn't even know why she was going or why she was invited. But she knew that if she was going to be seeing these people for the rest of her life, there was no better time than the present to return to social engagements. She had been totally nonchalant about it until she got to the door. And then she felt very, very weird. Because for the first time she didn't have an agenda. She didn't care about showing off or impressing people. It wasn't important to her whom she chitchatted with. She was there to have a good time.

When she checked her coat she noticed the small Tibetan women—obviously flown in for the occasion—spinning away in the corner. Ladies were gawking at the various colors of wool and barking orders to these confused non-English-speaking people. It seemed a little sick, thought Melanie, who bypassed them and entered the room. Joan and Wendy were grazing at the buffet. Melanie's first thought was that they looked like two Hoover vacs snarfing up the petits four, but she immediately dismissed that thought. She was trying not to be bitchy. As she made her way over to greet them, they braced themselves for a barrage of tact-free exchanges.

"Oy," said Wendy.

"Here we go," said Joan, pasting on her best saccharine smile.

"Hi, ladies!" said Melanie brightly. "What a wonderful party. You seem to have oodles of shahtooshes. How are sales going?"

"Can't complain," said Joan.

"We've already made a tidy sum for Narcolepsy—that's where the money goes after the vendors are paid," offered Wendy.

"Yes, there will be no excuse for people who fall asleep at the dinner table!" said Joan.

"Super. Well, thanks for having me."

"You're welcome," said Joan and Wendy, surprised.

"I guess I'll go check out the goods," said Melanie.

"Yes, we know we can count on you to buy, buy, buy!" said Wendy.

"Those spontaneously drowsy people depend on you!" said Joan.

Melanie walked over to the corner, and Joan and Wendy watched as she bent down and talked to the Tibetan women. She didn't even stop to accost Sandra Goodyear or Fernanda Wingate. Bizarre.

"Listen, sales are not going as well as I thought," whispered Joan.

"I know. How embarrassing if we only have one grand to offer up to the institute? Cass Weathers made fifteen when she had hers," said Wendy.

"We need a big spender to come," said Joan with great seriousness.

Just then, the double doors to the suite opened and heads turned as Mimi Halsey walked in bedecked in floor-length fur, an attractive woman with her. Both were dressed to the nines. Joan and Wendy, dollar signs in their eyes, rushed over to greet them.

"Mimi! You look to die! So thrilled you could make it. And who is this?" asked Joan.

"Joan, darling, this is my very dear friend Alice Martinez."

"Hello, Miss Martínez," Wendy said obsequiously, pronouncing the name as if she were a local news reporter of Latin descent who uses an accent even for *taco.* "Any friend of Mimi's . . ."

"Thank you," said Alice, surveying the scene. "Beautiful. Is this your party?"

"Yup. Wendy and I organized everything, down to the last smoked turkey with cranberry relish tea sandwich," said Joan.

"Lovely shawls you have. What are they?"

"Shahtooshes. Haven't you seen them? Feel one. They make cashmere feel like emery boards. These really are the must-haves of the season." Joan leaned in closer to Alice, whispering, "They're very hard to get, and not to be so tacky as to talk about money, but we spent a pretty penny making connections at the airport to get these all through."

"Why? Are they illegal?" asked Alice.

Wendy rolled her eyes at the nonsense that, yes, they were. "They're 'endangered,' " she said, making finger air quotes. "It's all politics, if you ask me. Some laws are made to be broken, like that Cuban cigar idiocy. You only live once, right?"

"I hear you," said Alice.

Mimi then led her friend to scope the luxurious loot. Joan and Wendy looked around at the busy bees loving their wares as they socialized, fingered plenty, and thanked them profusely for the sublime afternoon.

"Hopefully this will encourage others to buy. Some people are already leaving empty-handed!" whispered Wendy, worried.

"Just relax. People are just biding time. They'll all follow Mimi's lead," answered Joan.

"I hope so."

"And there's always Melanie. She'll probably empty our trunks. She always wants to spend the most."

Joan and Wendy continued their way around the party, delicately suggesting to their guests that they buy the wraps "for a good cause," eat the food, have a great time.

"Melanie, how many are you getting?" asked Joan with faked indifference.

"None today. Just browsing," said Melanie, sifting through the piles of shawls.

"Browsing? Come on, you of all people. It's for charity!" said Wendy.

"They are completely exquisite, but the reality is that I don't really need any more," said Melanie.

"Really, Melanie! I didn't think you were so stingy!" said Wendy, desperate to make a sale.

Melanie turned and looked at Wendy. She'd never win with her. "Oh, Wendy," she said, for lack of anything better to say.

"What about these Tibetan women!" said Wendy, waving her arms. "You don't want them to go hungry, do you?"

"No, I don't," said Melanie.

"Good. So, how many?"

"That's why I invited them over to my house tonight to give me a private weaving lesson. I promised them a thousand each," said Melanie, walking away.

Across the room, Joan was desperately trying to make a sale.

"You know what the beauty is of these things? That you can fit the entire shahtoosh through your wedding band. That's how you know it's real," said Joan, whipping off both her engagement and wedding rings and gliding an ochre shawl through them. She looked like a magician's assistant performing a trick. "Come on," said Joan to Mimi and Alice. "Don't you want to buy a shahtoosh? Don't tell me those goats croaked for nothing."

Mimi looked at Alice. "I'll purchase one," said Alice steadily.

"Now we're talking! And remember, it's for a good cause."

As Joan took Alice's cash, she watched Melanie air-kiss Mimi on her way out the door.

Joan handed Alice her shawl. "Enjoy," she advised, and then walked over to Wendy.

"Is our whole social set going to hell in a handbasket? First Jerome keels over leaving no heir apparent, then Cordelia commits a felony, and now Melanie Korn, the fellatrix of the friendly skies, is embraced by the upper tiers of society? What's going on?" asked Joan.

"It is spiraling out of control. What's next—the Clintons get into the Bath and Tennis?" responded Wendy.

Joan burst out laughing. "Oh, Wendy, you are too much."

"Oh, I'm short of breath at the thought."

"Okay, listen. The Winter Antiques Show is in January, and it's a time when everyone regroups and we weed out the undesirables. Hopefully things can get back on track," said Joan sternly.

"I hope so. Otherwise I don't know what I will do," she said with a frustrated sigh. "We need some excitement to shake things up."

chapter **59**

Mindy Greenbaum did not know what hit her. She was gasping for air, choking on noxious fumes, struggling to keep from vomiting onto the floor of the taxi. The driver, an odious, greasy-haired, dirty little man, had obviously not showered since the seventies. And now his BO was strangling her throat like a noose, making her wonder if she really did need to go to Macy's to buy her boss a Christmas present. And not only did he reek, but he was a fanatical animal activist to boot; he'd been on a cosmetics testing tirade since Ninety-fifth Street.

"And those bitches, man, with their fur coats! They have dead corpses draped on them all for the sake of vanity and fashion! It makes me fucking SICK!" he raged.

Mindy was starting to get a little nervous. He was really on a roll.

"Yeah, I know what you mean," she said softly, in the futile hope that she could shut him up.

"Oh, do you? Well, they don't! Those poor, precious animals are cooped up and farmed in order to make slippers and ponchos! It is a TRAVESTY! Those fuckers need to be taught a lesson."

"Uh-huh," Mindy mumbled.

The driver kept staring at her in the rearview mirror, making sure she was on the same page. He barely kept his eyes on the road, but he would raise his voice and gesticulate louder when they passed either a woman in fur or a man in a leather jacket. Mindy was now convinced he was on drugs.

"I try and show them a lesson, those fucking fashion designers and rich bitches! I throw blood on them, but they don't care! It's going to take more! I want to teach them a lesson! They SUCK!"

"You know what? I think I'll just get out here," said Mindy nervously. They were only on Sixty-fourth and Fifth, but she couldn't take any more of this freakish David Koresh–ian rampage.

"Look at that BITCH out there!" he said, referring to a woman waiting on the corner, clad in a sable. He furiously rolled down his window and shouted at the lady. "FUR KILLS!"

She gave him the finger and the car behind him honked. "Fucking slut. Inhuman bitch!"

"This is great," said Mindy again, throwing ten bucks at him. He pulled over and let her out. There was a woman waiting to get into the cab, but Mindy gave her a warning look. It didn't matter anyway, because when the driver saw her shearling coat he yelled "Fucking killer!" and hurled a Coke can at her, nailing her in the shin. "This is just a fraction of the pain those animals on your back felt, you murderer!" he said before tearing off down Fifth.

The driver was in a foaming-at-the-mouth fury. He beeped his horn, gave other drivers the finger, and practically mowed down a group of tourists before turning onto Fifty-ninth. As he cruised along past the horse-drawn buggies, he yelled at the drivers, "You fucking treat animals like shit!"

Those poor horses. They should be on a farm, not fucking hauling white trash from Kansas around Central Park. They must be so cold. And they put blinders on their eyes so they couldn't see! So cruel. It was insane. It was shocking. He would have to write George Dubya again about this crap. How could people do this? Where was the ire? Was he the only one who cared? He was so worked up by now that his wrath blinded him. As he accelerated down the street, he noticed a doorman hailing a cab for another rich bitch in a fur coat on the opposite side of the street. That was it. That was fucking it. Those fuckers needed to be taught a lesson. He whipped his car around in the middle of the street, practically knocking down a pretzel vendor and causing several cars to jam on their brakes. He found his target. She was a tarted-up, spoiled whore in a fur coat so huge, he could see the souls of the seventy-five martyred sables it took to make it.

"Die, die, my darling!" he muttered before accelerating full-force into her. Her eyes widened as he took aim, but it all happened so very quickly. With one hit and a final "AY!" Maria was dead.

chapter 60

It was beginning to look a lot like Christmas. Wreaths festooned with red ribbons and bows were placed on the front door of every grand apartment building in Manhattan. Sweaty workers heaved Christmas trees to align every cross street on Park Avenue. The teams at Barneys and Saks had spent hours and hours mounting festive themed windows to give those Wyoming tourists something to make their eyes pop out. Elijah and Betty Ann Mackeral had beamed with pride as the team from NBC hacked down the seventy-two-year-old pine tree that had stood on their property in Stowe, Vermont, and was now gracing Rockefeller Center for Katie and Matt and all the world to see. But for the high-society crowd, complimentary eggnog and reindeer-shaped cookies at department stores and the aroma of cider and mulling spices at Williams-Sonoma did not herald in the holidays. Neither did the relentless renditions of "The Little Drummer Boy" and "Let It Snow!" over the intercom at Frederic Fekkai, nor the tinsel on the plastic trees at Elizabeth Arden. No. For them, it was and only was Lawrence and LeeLee Powell's annual Fête de Noël that officially ushered in the season.

The party was always held on the Tuesday before Christmas, at their triplex apartment on the tippy-top of 741, and everyone planned their mass exodus out of the city for the holidays accordingly. This year, Robert Isabell and his crackerjack team had been working on the event since December 26 of the previous year. The instructions had been terse—"Think stained-glass window"—and Isabell had taken the concept and run with it. The results of his efforts would make Martha Stewart appear lazy. Over the course of a year, he had carefully assembled colorful celluloid-paned lanterns from the 1920s to hang from the ceiling. He had found—through a Hermitage connection—yellow enamel Fabergé ornaments to adorn the tree in the foyer. An art dealer had led him to stained-glass ornaments that dangled from the tree in the dining room; they had been specially commissioned from Louis Comfort Tiffany for a Washington, D.C., debutante at the turn of the century. He had successfully outbid a German newspaper tycoon at the Druot in Paris for the seventeeth-century Santa Claus figurines that were purported to have once been owned by the Hapsburgs. And he had even gotten his hands on a dilapidated, grease-stained cardboard box of red and green puppets that a good source told him were made by John-John and Caroline for their mother, Jackie Onassis.

But Isabell not only purchased decorations, he commissioned them as well. Shellacked pinecones that had been gathered in Acadia National Park in Maine were discreetly clipped onto the ropes of fir branches that snaked around the mantel. Seamstresses from a Very Important Italian couture house had been enlisted to make raw silk and crushed velvet stockings in their off-hours. Exotic fruits like red tamarillos, deep purple eggplants, orange tangelos, and cherry lipstick bell peppers had been ordered in advance from Mexico and California, and glazed or spray-painted and arranged in epergnes. Freshly plucked and redolent small nosegays of red spray roses tied with subtly monogrammed ribbon were placed in small bouquets throughout the apartment. But perhaps the most whimsical decoration was the live creche that had settled in the living room. A set designer from Lincoln Center had constructed the manger, and the New Haven Repertory company had rehearsed their pantomimes for months. Isabell had been careful and precise, and the result was magnificent. So as the Harlem Boys Choir softly sang Latin carols in the ballroom, and Tony Bennett—the surprise guest of the evening—warmed up his magical voice in the visitors' quarters of the apartment, guests started to arrive.

By seven-thirty, approximately three hundred people had checked their furs and evening coats in the lobby, accepted a glass of champagne from a tuxedoed waiter, and wandered around the apartment to inhale the fantastic decorations.

"They really outdid themselves this year," said Joan with approval.

"Magnificent," agreed Wendy.

They of course had arrived early and cased the joint in order to plant themselves at the best viewing location. That was in the spectacular reception room, where Bobby Short had been coerced to sit down at the Steinway and tinkle out a few songs.

Joan and Wendy continued scanning the crowd. "I don't see Cordelia Vance," said Wendy.

"Still in seclusion."

"Wise," said Wendy, eyes darting. She narrowed them when she saw Melanie Korn, in a red dress with a plunging necklace. She was chatting away with Nigel Goodyear, and he couldn't take his eyes off her boobs.

"I really hate that Melanie."

"Now, now, Wendy, Santa's watching," chided Joan, looking Melanie up and down. "But I know what you mean."

Melanie laughed, then touched Nigel on the shoulder and wandered away. Joan turned away in disgust. Melanie spotted her husband and went up to give him a hug.

"Now, will you look at Cindy Briggs," said Joan. "She most certainly has had work done. And before Christmas—so stupid, really. Everyone would know. Why not do it after Christmas, when you're gone for so long that everyone forgets your face? Some people are just clueless."

As Joan babbled on, Wendy continued guest scanning. She saw Gustave Strauss arrive with a leggy blonde and plant a wet one on her under the mistletoe. *Another single man bites the dust,* thought Wendy, averting her eyes. In the corner, swaying to the music, was Cass Weathers, who really seemed a little bloated. Perhaps it would have been prudent to have forgone the turkey at Thanksgiving. Holding court in the corner was the latest toast of the town, Billy Crispin. A small sycophantic group was gathered around him, hanging on his every word, and it was obviously already going to his head. When he'd seen Wendy earlier he'd looked at her as if she were cellophane. Whatever. He'd be over in, like, two minutes.

Suddenly, shock registered on Wendy's face. Something mega was going down. Right here. Right now. Right over Joan's shoulder.

"Oh my god," said Wendy.

"What?" said Joan, turning desperately.

"Look!"

A full team of police had entered with Lawrence Powell, who was frantically looking around the room.

"Do you think they're here for Cordelia?" asked Joan, excited.

"Couldn't be. The doormen would have told them she's holed up in her own apartment."

Joan and Wendy's peripatetic eyes danced around the room.

"You think the grand Dr. Johnson's prescription drug abuse caught up with him?" asked Wendy.

"I doubt the police would be out in full force for a little misdemeanor."

They watched as Lawrence Powell's head bobbed up and down, searching for someone in the crowd. Finally, he spotted his prey and whispered to a police officer. He then pointed in Joan and Wendy's direction. Wendy and Joan immediately whipped their heads around to see who was standing behind them. It was Melanie Korn. She had her back to them, chatting away with Pamela Baldwin. Wendy and Joan turned back to each other, mouths agape.

"It's Melanie!" whispered Wendy with glee.

"I *knew* she had sketchy background. Her father croaked in the can," said Joan, ecstatic.

"Maybe they're arresting her for bad taste."

They watched as the stream of officers moved through the crowd toward them. Joan looked back at Melanie, who was still yakking away.

"Mrs. Korn is still oblivious," snorted Joan, loving every nanosecond.

"All I can say is, I thank you Jesus for letting me be here to witness this with my own eyes," said Wendy, looking skyward.

"We just won the scandal lottery."

"We have been called on. Now we have to spread the gospel."

"Unfortunately, everyone's *here*," said Wendy.

"Not Europe. Not London. We must get to them *first*."

This would be a hoot! Suddenly, in unison, both women squinted. Why, the woman in the ill-fitting, masculine police uniform with a gun strapped to her belt looked a lot like . . .

"Isn't that . . . ?" asked Wendy, turning to Joan.

"It couldn't be," replied Joan. "But it looks just like her."

"Wendy Marshall and Joan Coddington?" the woman asked.

"Yes?" both replied, confused.

And sure enough, the leader of the pack was none other than Alice Martinez, Mimi's "guest" at Joan and Wendy's little shahtoosh tea, no longer in the borrowed Dior suit but in head-to-toe New York's finest blue. Forget the Fendi baguette. This time her only accessories were a badge, pair of cuffs, and hip holster.

"Wendy Marshall and Joan Coddington, you are under arrest."

"Alice?" Joan asked incredulously, making out the seemingly elegant matron under the navy getup.

"Yes, Alice Martinez. *Detective* Alice Martinez. And I have warrants for both of your arrests."

There was a gasp and a hush. Bobby Short abandoned the piano, the Glorious Food waiters stopped passing the hors d'oeuvres, and the gentle purr of voices that had enlivened the party came to a dead silence. Was this part of the festivities? Or was this . . . god forbid, no. A real scandal?

As Detective Martinez started Mirandizing the newest felons on the block, Joan and Wendy entered panic zones.

"Under arrest? For what?" Joan asked, her voice rising to a shrill decibel.

"For illegal trafficking of contraband goods, importing without a license, customs fraud, and two counts of bribery," Alice replied robotically.

Wendy, her vision blurred by on-deck tears, glanced around the room at the astonished onlookers. This was absolutely mortifying. There must have been a mistake. No.

"It can't be," said Wendy.

"It is," said Alice, clasping the cuffs over the black satin band of Wendy's Cartier dinner watch.

"Phillip? Phillip?" shouted Joan over the crowd. Her eyes wildly moved through the aghast guests, searching for her spouse. But Phillip was nowhere to be found.

Joan was beside herself. This was all horribly unfair. Why were they the ones who got pinched? Every Fifth Avenue bitch had thrown a shahtoosh tea, including Mimi! She must have turned state's evidence, the sellout! THE RAT!

"It was a setup!" yelled Wendy.

"We're patsies!" shouted Joan.

Out of nowhere, Mimi appeared. "I tried to warn you," she reprimanded. "I had no choice."

Traitor!

"Come on," said Alice, pushing Joan through a throng of slack-jawed socialites.

"Do you have to?" asked Joan.

"Yes," said Alice gruffly.

"This is a mistake," said Wendy, bursting into tears.

"It is no mistake. You two are crooks, you hoity-toity Park Avenue snobs who think you are above the law. I couldn't wait to bring you down. You both are worse than pond scum!" shouted Alice.

Wendy and Joan didn't know what to do. They stared at their "friends." Everyone either glanced away, embarrassed, or stood mute, enjoying their comeuppance. Finally, Alice dragged the offenders away. The din in the room grew louder and louder with mouths flapping over what had happened. Finally, Bobby Short returned to tickle the ivories and everyone soon forgot about Joan and Wendy.

chapter 61

"Sweetheart?" Cordelia called out, sitting up in bed. "You there, darling?"

She looked at the clock—10:34! She couldn't believe the healthy dose of sleep she'd won, without one frustrated toss or anxiety-ridden turn.

"Out here, Cordelia!" Morgan shouted from down the hall. She smiled and rose to wrap herself in her soft cashmere robe. It was nice, it being just the two of them for Christmas. At first she was devastated when the boys announced at Thanksgiving that they'd be renting a house on St. Bart's with a group of friends, but now, in the quiet of her home with her husband down the hall, she felt cozy and warm. Of course, it would have been nice to have the children, but she focused on the positive—that would be her New Year's resolution.

As she walked down the hall into the paneled den, Morgan came out and closed the double doors behind him.

"Good morning, sweetheart," he said, kissing her cheek.

"Hello, my darling. Merry Christmas," she said. They embraced and Morgan looked at his wife with tears in his eyes.

"Cordelia, you are as beautiful today as the day I married you, you know that?"

"Oh, Morgan . . ."

"Listen. I have a wonderful surprise for you."

"Oh?"

"It's your Christmas present."

"Don't tell me—does it come in a red box with white writing?"

"No. No, it doesn't come in a box."

"Really? Does it come with a parking space?"

"No. But . . . you will need a car seat."

"What?"

Morgan took his wife's hand and opened the den doors. He led her into the room, and on the couch sat a nanny holding a baby in a pink blanket, sleeping soundly.

"My darling, meet Schuyler Vance."

"Oh, Morgan!" she said, throwing her arms around him with glee. "You didn't! You knew it was what I truly wanted!"

"I took care of all the adoption papers. She's all yours."

"This is a dream," she said, rushing to relieve the English nanny of her duties so she could hold her new daughter in her arms.

"It will be wonderful to start again with you. In so many ways." He put his arms around Cordelia and the baby. Tears streamed down Cordelia's chiseled cheeks.

"Oh, Morgan! We're a family again!"

"I love you."

"I love you too."

As Morgan watched his wife nuzzle their new daughter, he gulped and almost looked skyward as a thank-you to the gods that had rescued him. He had truly dodged a bullet and was graced with a second chance. And he swore he would be the best husband and father he could be this time around.

Everything was confirmed for Cordelia as soon as she heard Morgan utter the name "Schuyler." She had heard that name before. God bless Morgan for not even having the foresight to change it, but then, he would never have known she'd heard it at Tiffany's. It was nice to see him relaxed, not squirming anymore. There was something to be said for those TAG maniacs.

chapter 62

Melanie rounded the corner of Seventieth Street with a giant Burger King bag in her hand. She had a hankering, and as she knew that Arty loved Whoppers, she had gone out to get some for dinner. Mr. Guffey, who had become a lot mellower now that his "madam" had stepped off her social-climbing ladder, offered to whip up fried candy bars for dessert, a favorite from his early years in Brighton. It was going to be a fun night; Melanie and Arthur had a date to watch one of their favorite movies, *Three Men and a Baby*. Melanie ran toward the elevator just in time to climb aboard with her neighbor, Olivia Weston, who clearly was annoyed to have to share the small space with her.

"Hi, Olivia," said Melanie, in a chipper tone. "Happy New Year."

"Same to you" was her chilly reply.

"Did you do anything fun for the holidays?" asked Melanie warmly.

"Antigua," she replied, without even looking at Melanie.

"Oh, I hear it's beautiful there."

"Yes" came her terse response.

Normally Melanie would have continued kissing this bitch's ass, but why should she? Olivia was a total snob, and for all her fancy education had no manners if she treated people this way. Melanie noticed she didn't even say hi to the doormen.

"You know, Olivia—I finished your book. It was very interesting."

"Oh, thanks," she said, sort of smugly. "I'm glad you enjoyed it."

"Yes—what I found particularly intriguing was the similarity of your pill-popping heroine named Keely to the pill-popping lush named Neely in Jacqueline Susann's *Valley of the Dolls*."

"I—" Olivia was stunned.

"You might want to check out the copyright laws now that you're

having this big reprint. Someone might pick up on it, and you could run
into some hot water."

The elevator slowed to Olivia's floor and the door glided open. She
didn't move. Holland! She must've done this on purpose!

"This is you," said Melanie.

Olivia nervously exited, looking back coldly.

"Plagiarism is no small offense," said Melanie as the door was
closing.

When she arrived upstairs, Arthur was reading the paper in the den
by a roaring fire, feet up.

"Hiya honey," he said, truly happy to see her.

"I just rode up in the 'vator with your former flame Olivia Weston."

"What?"

"Oh, come on, sweetie, you can scratch the babe-in-the-woods routine with me! I knew about your little crush on her. Don't worry. I always had her number."

"What crush?" Arthur said, guiltily laughing. How cool was his
wife? She didn't seem to give a shit.

"Arty, it's okay! You're married, not dead."

"Do . . . you have crushes?"

"I have a crush on you," she said, pulling his sweater so he'd come
closer. She kissed him passionately.

"We make a good team, you and me," said Arthur, touching her face.

"We do. I knew you'd come to your senses. Plus, that chick couldn't
suck a dick to save her life."

He laughed heartily. "These people," he said. "They all seem like
this big force, but it's crap. I know that now."

"Screw society. They're all a bunch of gossiping hags. And Olivia
and her group of little Coddingtons-in-training . . . please. You think I
don't know what they're saying about me? I don't care."

"They think they've got you pegged, but they don't."

"They're very sad, sad women. Joan has to live with the most boring
man in the world, who whittles away his time in a club and lives off of
his wife's dime. And Wendy, well, she's just alone. Alone with her inse-
curities. That's why they're so angry and unhappy."

"You're right."

"And what do I care if they say things about me? It used to bother me, because I wanted their validation so much. But now that I know who and what they are, I couldn't care less what they think. I've got something better than all their fancy friends and little clubs."

"What's that?"

"You."

Arthur kissed his wife.

"And there's another reason why I can't relate to Olivia," said Melanie with a smile.

"What's that?"

"Well, aside from the fact that Olivia is a closet binge eater, I happen to know that she never wants kids."

"Really?"

"Really. Just like Diandra."

"Diandra? Mel, honey, what are you talking about?"

"Well, both of those women didn't want children. And I . . . well, Arty . . ." she trailed off nervously. "I'm pregnant."

A shocked expression flashed across Arthur's face as Melanie bit her lip. She felt a pit. She knew Diandra had said "they" didn't want kids, but she had hoped . . .

The look of shock on Arthur's face morphed into the biggest smile his wife had ever seen. "Babe, that's the greatest news I ever heard!" said Arthur ecstatically, pulling her into an all-engulfing embrace.

"Are you sure?" she asked, tears welling up.

"What do you mean, am I sure?" he said, pulling back and looking her in the eye. He brushed a stray hair from her forehead. He was charged with unbounded joy and love for her. "I would love to be a father. And I want you to be a mother."

"But I thought you didn't want kids."

"Where'd you get that idea?"

"Diandra."

"No! Diandra never wanted kids. That's one of the reasons we didn't work out."

"Seriously?" asked Melanie, surprised.

"One of the many, many reasons. Diandra was a cold, selfish, evil woman."

"But I thought she broke your heart."

"Broke my heart? No, just my bank account. You're the love of my life, sweetie."

"But you once said there was no comparison between me and Diandra. I thought you were pining for her . . ."

Arthur hugged Melanie tight. "There is no comparison. You're the best. You win game, set, and match against Diandra. And I can't wait for the baby. I just hope it gets your looks!" He kissed her passionately as he shook with awe.

All that time wasted to try to live up to Diandra, and she didn't even mean jack to Arthur? What a waste! But Melanie was beyond relieved, and she breathed a long sigh of relaxed bliss. She and Arthur could relax and finally live happily ever after, the way they were meant to.

Arthur picked Melanie up and twirled her around the room. That night they rocked to the sounds of Arthur's Rao's Restaurant CD, the soft swoon of Tony Bennett's voice framed against the crackle of the logs in the fireplace. Their lavish apartment was the biggest either of them had ever lived in, but in that moment, they never felt cozier.

Epilogue

Two Baccarat champagne flutes clinked like little bells as Joan and Wendy, dressed for friends and flashbulbs, ushered in the new social season at the Winter Antiques Show's opening-night benefit. It was the post–St. Bart's and Aspen see-and-be-seen extravaganza that had the social set falling over themselves (literally, as they often had to travel through a fog of sleet, hail, and snow) to get to the Sixty-seventh Street Armory on time. Next to old master vanitas paintings, antique suits of armor, medieval books of hours, and Chippendale furniture, cheeks were air-kissed, hair complimented, and outfits looked over. There were the fake-interested questions about how the vacation was (the holidays were a complete shutdown uptown; Park Avenue was so empty you'd think an H-bomb had been dropped on it).

Wendy and Joan, who had fortunately been able to get the charges against them dropped if they promised to be good girls, were determined not to suffer any social setbacks due to a small "misunderstanding." They'd talked of lawsuits against the city and how they had been set up and then quietly dropped the matter, hoping that everyone else would as well. So, with determination and confidence, they strutted into Leigh Keno's booth, where, after thirty-five minutes of being open for business, there were already red dots on half the loot. Joan drank in the scene; there were aggressive shoppers anxious to fill their new co-ops with top-of-the-line pieces, trophy wives scoping vintage jewels, and people who didn't give a shit about art but didn't want to miss a photo op.

Wendy looked at the crowd as it poured in. She had been nervous about showing her face around town after the embarrassing shahtoosh-gate at the Powells', but Joan had shrugged it off. They told everyone how Mimi had used them as patsies when she struck a deal so she wouldn't be arrested for her own party. It shifted the blame and would have made Mimi temporarily a social leper, but, hey, it was Mimi. Soon the whole matter was dropped.

"The usual suspects," said Wendy, her tone ho-hum.

"It's getting tiresome, isn't it? We need some fresh blood," mused Joan.

"Oh, there's that godawful Tom Fairbanks with Ginny what's-her-name," said Joan.

Wendy felt herself redden as she watched them stop and examine a grandfather clock. They were holding hands.

"I can't believe I ever thought he was right for you. He's so immature, and tacky, tacky, tacky. Those two belong together."

"Yes," murmured Wendy softly. She took a sip of her champagne to hide her quivering lower lip. *That could be me,* she thought.

Billy Crispin walked in and posed with two ladies who were flanking his Zegna sleeves.

"I see the ladies have adopted Billy Crispin as the new walker of choice," said Joan, eager to change the topic.

"Well, it's a natural choice," said Wendy. "They're almost guaranteed to have their picture in *Women's Wear* tomorrow."

Olivia Weston sauntered in, her blue eyes wide as she scanned the foyer. Her two friends—Lila and Rosemary—rushed up and greeted her immediately. She was never one to have to stand alone in a crowd.

"Hmm, Olivia Weston," said Joan.

"She's over," stated Wendy.

"Ugh, and Melanie Korn." Wendy sighed deeply. "She must have nine lives."

"How everyone seemed to have Alzheimer's regarding that *Observer* article is beyond me."

Arthur and Melanie were chatting with a couple in an Oriental rug dealer's booth about where to get the best nursery furniture when Olivia walked up to the bar beside them. At first the sight of her gave Arthur a mini-jolt, but it simmered and died after a millisecond. Yeah, she was a looker, but now that he knew the truth, she didn't do it for him anymore.

Patrick McMullan snapped her smiling coyly as Arthur looked on, but now, instead of watching her with admiration, he studied her at a scientific distance. As she posed like a model for the other shutterbugs who danced around the light of her smile, Arthur realized this species really did exist just in photographs. A party picture, like the girl had said. Funny, Arthur had thought her to be so confident and comfortable in her own skin. Now he looked at her and saw a spoiled, shallow girl who never had to work for anything—all this was handed to her because she was in the lucky sperm club.

Arthur turned to look at his wife and the barely there bump of their growing baby. Seeing her throw back her head in casual laughter made his heart warm. Oh, Melanie, you gotta love her. *With her, what you see is what you get,* thought Arthur. Sure, she'd tried to get in with all those society broads, but she was always, sometimes to her detriment, unabashedly herself. But thank god. All these people around—they were the phonies. Melanie was the real thing. Arthur took his wife's hand in his and gave it a loving squeeze. This whole shindig wasn't just about art and charity: it was a masquerade. And in a packed gilded hall, she was the only one without a mask. And he loved her for it.

Across the crimson-carpeted, cavernous room, Joan and Wendy were yakking away, still installed in their omniscient corner, when they spied Morgan and Cordelia walking in hand in hand.

"Hmph," snorted Joan. "Cordelia's quite lucky that everyone was so sympathetic to her plight that they overlooked that she was a jewel thief! They almost applauded her, thinking it was chic."

"It sure got Morgan's attention," said Wendy, staring at them as Morgan delicately put his hand on the small of his wife's back and brushed a lock of blond hair out of her face. "I thought he was having something on the side, but that must be history—look at them! They're all over each other."

"Even if he did have something on the side, no one would ever know. That man was born under the right stars," said Joan. "He's one lucky bastard."

"Some people just get everything."

"Such is life."

Morgan kissed Cordelia's cheek, and they held hands and marveled at the art around them. Since her arrest and the arrival of Schuyler, Cordelia had felt as if a two-ton weight had been lifted from her shoulders. She felt like she was truthful for the first time in ages. She and Morgan had spent a lot of time over the past few weeks just talking and getting to know each other again, and they actually began to look at their lives together with some perspective.

They had come to the conclusion, with the help of the top therapist at Columbia Presbyterian, that perhaps she had stolen to get the attention she so craved at home. She had been desperately unhappy and yet she had everything, so she was creating problems and putting herself in danger. Now, she no longer felt the need. Morgan had become more than attentive—really a better husband. And little, precious Schuyler had brought back worth and meaning into her life. After all, wasn't that what it was all about? Taking care of another life? She felt as if her family had been given a second chance, and she wasn't going to waste it.

And, strangely, although she would never admit it to anyone other than Morgan, Cordelia sometimes felt a kind of relief not having Jerome around. She would have been horrified to think that previously, but in retrospect, his malicious and constant gossip had depressed her.

When people focus so much on the negative and other people's short-comings, life becomes so petty and irrelevant; but she had needed his love so badly, and he had always given it to her and stood by her side. But now, with her baby's love and her husband's newfound affections, all those compliments about perfect outfits and stunning hair would not have packed the punch they once did. *It's so easy to say something mean,* thought Cordelia. *But it's so exhilarating to think and say something nice. It makes you know you are happy and latching on to what makes life worth living.*

As Morgan kissed his wife's hand, Wendy's spying eyes squinted.

"I heard they were just in Lyford having a second honeymoon," she whispered to her comrade in the gossip trenches.

"I think second honeymoons are kind of tacky," pronounced Joan.

"They are, aren't they?"

"Well, whatever floats your boat, I suppose. I mean, I never thought shoulder pads would come back into style."

"I'm always amazed at how you can get used to things," agreed Wendy.

They glanced around the capacious atrium, their eyes gliding past the Vances, Olivia, old Mrs. Cockpurse, who was wearing a miniskirt with no stockings. Their eyes finally landing on the Korns.

"You know, Arthur and Melanie just sold their apartment at 741," said Wendy, as if the couple had just let go of the Holy Grail. "Can you *believe* that they're moving to the West Side? I heard they just bought a place on Riverside Drive!"

"I haven't been there in years, and I don't plan on going anytime soon," said Joan with a snort, as if they were relocating to Abu Dhabi and would need vaccinations.

"But you know what?" continued Wendy. "We're all going to be lying dead in a Korn casket in forty years, so we might as well live it up while we can."

"Oh, Wendy," squealed Joan, laughing, "you are too much."